A Pirates' Handbook to Magic
©2022, Jordan Hunter

Illustration work by Miranda Claypool.
Editing by Lawrence Silverstein.

ISBN: 978-1-66785-660-5
ISBN eBook: 978-1-66785-661-2

A Pirates' Handbook to Magic

Jordan Hunter

In the dark there was nothing...then one day in the tall dry grass that stretched high in summer's air there was a snap... That snap produced a frost of black smoke, cradling inside a glowing white ball that was the size of a fist. On command the white flicker ripped itself apart and created smaller droplets of itself. Aiding as a glimpse of light to the group of humans. The people on the land, impressed that someone in their group had done this, moved their own fingers out in front of them and mimicked the original snap. Within the hay, the villagers then had their own colorful light shows. Some created something similar to the man's before; others created a small orange glowing sphere, covered with a blanket of red clouds. Other individuals assembled a blue globe enveloped in dancing green smoke.

This is the earliest documented instance of magic.

Prologue

THE roaring of the waves that beat along the wooden surface was just above the howls of the men, blocking dialogues of instructions from their mouths. Vibrating sounds from the sky forcing itself to be heard by all was too powerful against the collective voices that culminated together, synchronizing into one tone of concern towards the odds of survival. A soft sound of a bell beat along with the thrashing of the vigorous ocean below. Soon a robust popping came, loud enough to wake up any mammal underneath the violent water, followed by a clash. Standing on the higher deck amongst the rest of the crew, a man pointed and took one breath before he strained his throat, competing for volume against the heavens. "Pull! Pull!" He shouted, "Pull the topsail!" He pointed with his finger, preparing some men to take care of the lack of control. The wooden surface underneath them had tilted, assaulting some of the men off their feet. These men were on a mission; they were on a search. What was it? Something that was far more valuable than gold. "The storm is too powerful, Ridge!" One of the men cried out.

"Ellington left me in charge," Ridge paused before he continued, "and as your new Captain, I say do not give up!" The waves thrust against the ship once more, pushing the rest of the standing crew onto their knees. The boat stirred while the men pulled the ropes, using all their strength to try to keep the boat balanced. The waves only got more aggressive; the wind whistled harder. The ship creaked loud enough for a handful of men to look down.

Captain Ridge moved along the edge of the boat, holding onto the rail and watching his men, maybe about thirty of them, try their very best to keep the old ship from tipping over. The storm had appeared out of nowhere, and nothing was done to prepare for this. There was another clash from the sky above, soon followed by the sound of a tear. The men that used the sail to steer the ship fell onto their backs once the fabric ripped itself away from the pole. The man in charge looked around; this storm was something he had never seen before.

"Get up! Get up, all you!" He shouted. He held onto the ship's side tightly; he once more looked around the sea; they were indeed miles away from any living soul, forcing this battle to be on their shoulders. A flash of light came down from the sky, hitting the water underneath. The Captain looked around at his crew before another flash of light struck down.

A monstrous amount of the sea had managed to creep up on the main deck, knocking the crew back on the wooden deck once again. The sudden flood of the water muffled the following screams of the men. The boat was pushed once more, and welcomed more water, this captured more of the unfortunate few off the ship. The sky gave another two beats, followed by a sound of a snapping spark. The Captain turned around and ran to his cabin, slamming the door behind him.

Once inside, he moved forward, turned around, and locked the cabin door in one swift move. The tiny ticking of a clock filled the room; it reminded the man of the little time he had to write the letter. He moved around, stumbling everywhere in the tiny room due to the brutal pushing of the boat. The man grabbed a piece of paper and a quill, gripping the two objects in his hand. He placed himself onto the edge of the chair, pulled out the drawer, grabbed ink from inside the desk, and placed it on the table. His hands were shaking while he dipped the feather in the ink and began to write. While he was writing, a loud knock came from the door, followed by the doorknob making an effort to move in circles. He looked up for a brief moment, then continued his writing, transferring the ink against the page faster, ignoring the knocks on the door. Once he was done, he stood up and searched the messy room, picked up a glass bottle, quickly stuffed the letter inside, sealing the top with a cap. He stopped before he had noticed what was wrong; the boat was no longer rocking, the knocking was gone, and his crew was not making a sound. The man in charge silently scanned the room; he could only hear the muffled rain outside. But then a creak came. The door had opened. He dropped the bottle and swallowed. Tick, tick tick.....

CHAPTER 1:

Grandpa's Letter

TICK, tick, tick... The clock that beat along the wall sang a gentle song and brought melody to the room containing only one person. Finally, they woke up from their slumber. She rubbed her eyes to help them readjust to the bright orange light that moved into her room not too long ago. The window was left closed; she had done this last night when she felt nature's bitter atmosphere creep inside. They stretched their arms, guided themselves out of bed, and made their way to that window. She opened the glass to allow freedom between the house and the world. Once this glass wall was removed, she moved her body forward, letting half of herself become detached from the home.

The birds chirped loudly and the running stream, if one listened more carefully, whispered from a distance. The trees that circled around the home gave off a smell of pine. The last time she counted each tree from her bedroom window, there were two hundred and twenty-three trees that tucked away her home's presence from strangers. A distant song of an owl gave one more hoot to those who thrived in the day before going to slumber; this was a cue that it was time to be awake for the residents who lived in the area. She looked down to find the beautiful garden her mother had created a long time ago. If she wanted to smell the flowers, she would have to go down the stairs; a jump would inevitably lead to a severe injury.

She pulled herself away from the window and decided to shut the glass, separating her room from the outside world once again. A sudden thought had told her that now would be the best time to get out of her sleepwear and wear something more appropriate. It seemed that the day would remain this chilly for a while longer; it was the last week of fall after all. Opening the closet, they grabbed a long white shirt with a lace collar for the neck. This followed with black pants; soon after, she buttoned up the red vest with golden buttons that made the shirts' front fluffy lace seem more prudent. She finished the outfit's look by slipping on her long boots. She looked at herself through the reflecting glass that rested in her room; which might have been built for someone shorter than herself. The girl would consider herself tall, or perhaps just a few inches taller than most girls her age.

In the mirror the small golden plack that was pinned on her vest gave a slight wink in the reflection, showing the words 'KEEPIN' in bold. She gave a warm smile; there was nothing more she could do to prepare herself for what the day would bring her.

She walked down the long hallway; every step that was taken there would be portraits of ships surrounded by a frame in dark wooden oak, carried in a variety of sizes. Each ship in the portraits was designed from a different country. Her favorite portrait was that of a giant dark wooden boat that was crafted in Cor'Meum.

They smiled; Cor'Meum, what an honor it was to be born a Cor'Meum citizen, the greatest country in the world. Honestly, she did not want to put down the other countries of the Tetrad Aurum. However, they were no competition to Cor'Meum, the strongest and fastest developing country that any nation had ever seen! Anyone born in Cor'Meum was considered lucky, and those who were not wanted to be a Cor'Meum citizen! Cor'Meum was the best nation.

When reaching the end of the hallway, she stood at the base of the long and wide staircase that led down to the first floor. Behind her was a large portrait of a woman and, in her arms, a tiny pink baby that looked to be very new to the world. The woman in the picture did not look like any other woman that mankind had seen before. The woman had long and silky white color hair which had also matched her pale skin. It wasn't just her hair color that was peculiar, but her eye color was too; they were big and purple. This woman may be deemed a legend to others, but she was their mother.

The portrait of herself and her mother was painted many years ago. Even in the portrait when she was a baby, it was obvious she too would have the unique white hair color. Her mother gave a stone-cold face and from what she had seen in every photo or painting her mother was in, she never smiled.

She read the name that rested underneath the portrait, Marlyn Sanford. Marlyn- a famous woman. She was almost or perhaps just as famous as the legendary Knight and Magician.

The child could recall a handful of memories with her mother until the age of eight. Although she did not nearly have the number of stories about her mother that others around her did, it was interesting to hear what they had to say about her. For example, before she worked with the king and before they were born, she would do things that no other human had done before, like how she took down an entire gang with just a stare. Or how she single-handedly saved hundreds of people from a burning building. Or maybe the time she faced a whole army by herself that tried to take over Cor'Meum; she stopped them with just a single sword, winning the battle before lunch.

It was hard to know which of these stories were based on truth and which ones were exaggerated for good storytelling. She only knew that her mother was loved by all and was a topic of great discussion in every house in Cor'Meum for a while. They moved down the stairs, the sound of her boots giving away a click that would echo miles around the place, but still not loud enough to fill up every room the house had to offer.

In the distance, she noticed the sounds of people chatting, their soft voices barely impacting those who would claim the top of the stairs. She wondered what the people were talking about. The only way to know was to move to the floor under.

Reaching the bottom of the stairs, she moved down the hall to the left. Their stomach, a beast, was clawing away inside, demanding that their needs be filled, roaring in anger. She pressed her hand to calm the creature from its furious demands, forcing her inside the kitchen, her place of desire and where the two voices appeared to come from.

She moved over to the radio that rested in the kitchen; the two people on the channel continued their conversation about the weather and their excitement about how the fall season was coming to an end. The two also talked about how thrilling it was that the last day of the Calamitous War victory, a holiday that was a week long, landed on the first day of winter. Perhaps it might snow! They turned the radio off, not necessarily because she hadn't enjoyed what she heard, but because it was a distraction; she needed to focus on her morning goals, one being food.

In the kitchen, she moved around, finding her way to the pantry to fulfill her morning hunger. She passed a large table, big enough to hold a family of ten, though the truth was there were only two people that lived here. Between those two individuals, they hardly made company with the home in the middle of the woods; air would have more homeownership than the two. She had opened the pantry and grabbed a large piece of bread, essentially what were leftovers from last night. Since it was a rare sighting to see them in this specific kitchen, there hardly was any storage for food. She sat in the room's silence and consumed the leftover bread that had already started to harden. If the two travelers were home more, they might have hired a staff to cook and clean the house. There were more bedrooms than people here, so it would not be too hard to maintain a living space for such people. Though it would be useless, as the travelers rarely came back to the home in the woods, and it was usually only for a week or two, hardly giving them any time to destroy anything. Out of the seventeen years this child had seen this place; she had never once seen it messy, not even a little muddy, making the whole home much like a stranger.

Their eyes moved to the light book she left on the table just the previous night; if there were an individual who saw her frequently from a distance, they would assume that this dirty crimson book was her favorite piece of information to consume. Though the dreadful truth was this was a light book on how to achieve basic magic for high tone seekers. Her eyes had fallen on the pages such a handful of times that she could close her eyes and recite every single word the book carried. She picked it up with dread in her heart; she had to achieve the goals that were laid out. She had to complete all of them before she could advance to the next set. They began to open the book again, but an outside noise grasped her attention. She looked over to her right and noticed that the window was open. That was not supposed to be like that; with her bread out of her hand placed safely on the table along with the book, she traveled towards the open window. Once she had reached her destination, she grabbed the hinges, the smell of pine hitting her immediately in the face before she shut it. Standing in front of the window she began to admire the pretty garden, the one thing that she had loved about this place. The garden was only filled with the prettiest colors of purple, red and blue, similar to the military her mom used to work for. The flowers had always managed to fill them with content. They were indeed a blessing to look at. She turned around to find an animal with gray fur, staring at her; worst of all holding her bread.

"Hey!" She yelled at the animal, only hoping that the animal would respond with an apology deep inside of her. The animal took another bite of the bread. "Stop that! Right now!" She waved her arms at it.

The animal gave a hiss clutching onto the piece of bread, and took another bite in front of them, mocking her for her lack of bread. They furrowed her eyebrows at the creature, challenging it. With one swift move, she grabbed a broom.

"You better drop that now! I am warning you!" She swung the broom up and moved it nicely, almost as if it were a sword, showing off her skills. Unfortunately, it was cut short in mid-spin when she overestimated how much space she had around her, resulting in the shattering of the several glass cups next to her. The animal hissed and dashed off with the bread.

She chased after the animal, hoping if she sprinted fast enough, she could beat it up with her broom; the animal was winning this race down the hall. She chased after him, still holding her broom out; she tried desperately to smack the thing. In the process, the broom only knocked down several of the portraits that had made company with the wall for several years now, only for them to move on to becoming acquaintances with the floor. She took another swing; not only did she miss the woodland creature, but she knocked down the pearl white statue instead. The statue's head rolled on the floor to her feet; the statue's presence wouldn't be missed, the thing had always creeped her out. Even staring at the detached head sent a shiver down her back.

The creature made a sound that had snapped her back into the real problem, her food. The masked creature pushed open a door leading into another room, which had made them stop in her tracks. Grandpa's room. She did not have the heart to wake her grandpa up, and they had seen the sea a lot recently; he needed his sleep. The creature, however, had not cared that her grandpa needed his rest; at this point, it was not about fetching the bread anymore; no, it was about justice. This creature must be punished for not only taking her last piece of bread but for waking her grandpa up.

She pressed her hand on the door and pushed it open; finally, she had cornered the evil creature, his days were over. Only after this moment did she watch the creature stand on the porch of the open window, welcoming all the light inside, give her one last mocking hiss, and jump out with the bread. They stood in the room in silence; the only sound was the pulminting bang of the broom hitting the floor and the birds that continued to chirp away without any care. In front of her were an empty bed, an open drawer that contained no clothes, and an open window.

They stood in the room that had formerly belonged to her grandpa. The room, covered in the smell of the ocean that once made her feel a sense of security, had only made her feel deserted as it was. She and her grandpa had never left each other's side after the day that her mother- she stopped in her tracks. The firepit had looked used; she moved closer to it, scrutinizing the small area. It seemed that he had burned something before he had left. After the investigation was over, she moved to his desk and opened the long drawer that rested under the main wooden land. There she found a ripped envelope with a missing letter inside, she looked back at the fireplace. On the envelope, she kept her eyes on the wax seal; there were two letters on the seal, B and T. While the stained red wax symbol seemed unrecognizable, she felt that she had seen it somewhere before. A distant memory was connected to this unusual envelope; it was too far away for her to trace back.

She paused and allowed her mind to become blank so she could recall where she had seen this envelope. Perhaps.....maybe...It had then clicked in her head; she knew when she had witnessed the envelope before- it had contained a mystery letter that provoked stress from her grandpa the night he had received it. This happened only a few days ago, so why did he decide now was the best time to burn the letter? What was contained inside of it that would make the man burn it? With her new unlocked memory of the envelope, it still had not answered who B and T were. Her eyes finally caught the attention of a letter that was placed on the desk. She picked up the letter and began to read it; there was then a look of immense disappointment.

'Oceana, stay in the house. - Grandpa'

It was not just that her grandfather left her without clarifying why. The letter he left was short, simple, and almost or maybe even colder than the weather outside. In a mix of anger and spite, she ripped the letter up until there was nothing more than paper snowflakes. Then, she hastily left the room back to its rightful state of being uninhabited by any humans.

Oceana remained in place in the middle of the stairs; she decided while she waited for her grandpa to come home, she could go back to her studies. Her eyes skimmed the pages that were for the beginners' book to magic, reading this book now the millionth time in the past ten years.

After what she would call hours of reading the book, though the clock would argue that it had been around fifteen minutes, she began to watch the front door in anticipation. Expecting that somehow her grandpa would come back and realize that excluding her on this mystery was placed on misjudgment. He would also apologize and say he would never do it again and start making her in charge of all their KEEPIN missions from here on out. Alright, getting carried away, but she deserved an apology at least. Oceana and her grandpa covered almost every inch of grass with one another; he wouldn't just suddenly leave. Well, would he? Sitting in the silence of her suffering, boredom would not bring her grandpa back home; if there was something that had pushed him to leave, it must have been important. Though her next question was, what would she do about it?

The solution to her new investigation was immediately answered by an idea that came to her mind. It was evident what she needed to do; she moved diligently down the stairs and made her way to the large front doors. What stopped her from completing her mission was a coat hanger.

The coat rack was accompanied by a coat serving the rack like a blanket to keep the wooden pole from getting cold. The coat itself was incredibly long, with a lighter shade of red than the vest she was wearing. Each of the buttons on the coat was stitched on, much like the words 'KEEPIN' that rested on its back. At the same time, there were areas of the coat that seemed like they had seen better days. The coat could not tell one when it was washed last, but the coat could guarantee that it would serve its primary objective which would be to keep anyone inside warm. Oceana grabbed her grandfather's old coat and threw it on herself. Much like she predicted the coat was long, the ending point was just a bit below their knees. Though, the arms and shoulders of the coat snugged quite nicely, not making it appear as if it was a little red monster that was eating them. They moved their arms around, to test if they wanted to wear their grandfather's coat. When the coat showed only signs of comfort they decided to wear it.

In this coat she felt that she was ready to take on the world, to search what was lost. She knew she could not do this on her own, that she needed the help of someone brave and adventurous. She knew who that person was, a man of many words, and she would describe him as the most incredible guy she knew. A role model, despite him only being just a year or so older. She decided now that she had her coat, handbook, and envelope, the present would be the most acceptable time to advance.

Her blue eyes moved to the giant tin Knight that almost stood proudly next to the front door. "Keep this place safe while I am gone!" She took a look at the statue, a man that she had truly always admired. Before she pressed her hand on the door handle, she paused, her grandpa's words coming from a distance. She stopped and turned around, thinking of the words that her grandpa had always told her when she was young; one should never leave a place without currency. She stumbled through her memory book of how the saying went 'Never be without cash, or you will be last.' That honestly did not sound right, but that wasn't the point. She needed to grab some money before she began her walk in the woods.

She moved to one of the offices, a place she had known her grandpa had kept extra money. Inside the room, her eyes explored more portraits of ships for a brief moment; she had finally snapped back into reality when she found the desk that had stored all the money. A tall desk that was made of a rare dark oak, was what held the money her grandfather owned. She gripped onto the small hooks, she opened the desk, revealing the colorful paper of prelacy, the currency of the country. Her grandpa was always sent prelacies in the mail of this address for his hard work as a

Red division fourth-ranked KEEPIN officer. He never needed to use it, all his items were paid for on the ship, and he never needed anything new. If he did, he would just write the castle a letter, and in return they would send him the new belongings to help with his duties.

She took a moment to look at the prelacies; there were a lot of them, the thin gold and bronze colored cash, all neatly pinned together by a clip. Each ranged from five point five stats of worth to fifteen point ten, epending on which past Cor'Meum King or Queen's face was on it. This was the first time she would take money from this desk. Some part of her felt it was wrong, stealing her grandpa's money. She had never stolen anything before, but she would not need to use the funds stored here if she were lucky. She bit her lip anxiously, feeling the law of the land peer its eye over her shoulders.

Something caught her eye. She walked over to her grandfather's desk, there was a book, a handbook. The book was dark brown, and looked worn up and used. The cover displayed four circles with a star in the middle. One of the four circles was faded. The title was simple, it was written in cursive black ink, 'Handbook to magic'. It told readers exactly what content it carried inside.

Oceana remembered her grandfather would always carry this around, and would always write all his notes in it; however he would never let her read the inside of it. Oceana opened her coat pocket and stared at her own magic book. She placed the book she had been so used to reading on the desk and lifted up the other handbook. She smiled at the book. How should she carry this? She figured she should bring her grandfather's book bag, however she remembered how her grandfather used to carry books in this jacket. She moved her hands inside the coat and began to search for a pocket. She would have missed the pocket if she hadn't seen her grandfather use it before. Inside the jacket under a patch of padded cloth there was a zipper, she opened it. Then she moved the book inside it, which fit perfectly inside. It was almost perfectly designed to hide a book. Well, what he doesn't know won't hurt him.

There was no more time to waste; she moved her hand towards the cash and stuffed her coat pocket. There she was, now ready to take on the world. With her final parting words to the Knight, she closed the front door, leaving the house back to its normal state of quiet and empty.

CHAPTER 2:

The boy in the woods

THE girl traveled along the dirt road, marching along the sea of trees. The trees held leaves of splashing colors such as brown, amber, and gold. Each crisping apart off the wooden branch they had once called home. The tree was to become naked, in preparation for the next season. The sounds of animals surrounded her, each vocalizing their own melody to a song. A bird repeated its chirp from one of the nearby trees, and sang its happy carol.

She reached a long patch of water that guided itself around the wooden area. The water gently made its way along the narrow path, and splashed playfully against the rocks that rested there. Oceana jumped on one of the bigger rocks, creating a small splash when she had landed. She moved her leg out on the rock and rested her foot on the other stone that was comparatively smaller than the one she was on. She moved forward and rested in her new water-free area. Closer to the other side of the shallow river, she felt confident enough to jump to the patch of land in front of her. After a hop, she landed on her feet, causing the ground underneath her to splash the wet dirt upwards, allowing some of the muck to land on her black boots. A small loss, but nevertheless, she trotted forward up the narrow hill by the water, and advanced back to her journey.

A couple of miles down the woods, she finally reached her destination. A small house that rested quite peacefully in the world of these trees. Half of the tiny home was cemented with a white wall, filled with cracks that could count more years than the date it was built. The other half was made up of bricks that were placed nicely, much like a puzzle. However, the reliability of these bricks staying together was a different story. The brick chimney that rested on the far back corner of the home had puffs of gray smoke that escaped its hold, which led them to believe that someone was home.

They made their way to the front door and knocked, hoping they would not break the wooden door that moved dangerously forward with each tap. She heard movements from the inside, along with clashing of what she would guess were pots and pans. The noise created inside had finally presented itself when the front door opened.

A taller boy who had a dark complexion, and hair that was in long tangles, stood in front of her. Whatever he had been doing today, he looked tired, evidence showed from the bags of circles under his eyes. When he laid his eyes on them, the amount of stress he was going through had hit its tipping point.

He looked at her, narrowed his eyebrows, rolled his eyes before he took a step back, and began to close the door on them. He was not ready to continue the day with her existence near him.

"Jamlson!" She shouted out. Attempting to jog his memory that she was not a threat, just a friend! But the shout, for some strange reason, hadn't improved his attitude towards her.

"What?" He sounded sharp; he stopped his process. "What do you want?" He positioned the door to welcome space again, though its acceptance for any company seemed very limited. "Didn't I tell you to write me a letter before you visit? To prepare? It's really inconvenient when you have surprise visits." He said.

"I know and I'm sorry, but this is important!" Oceana racked up their thoughts before they had begun to speak to the boy. "I believe something bad is happening!"

"So?" He raised his eyebrow and crossed his arms in the process, not necessarily seeming like he cared about conflicting dangers.

"So!" She shouted; she paused for a moment, no response came. This was when she believed she should continue. "So I need your help!"

Jamlson rolled his eyes and retreated back into the comfort of his home, Oceana tailed along behind him. She followed him while he made his way down the hall. At some point, her back pressed against the wall, this was due to the tiny space between the hallway and a wooden desk. On top of the wooden desk, Oceana spotted a pile of books that she knew were not Cor'Meum approved. How many of these books had Jamlson read since the last time she had seen him? Oceana wanted to say something about reading such books, but she decided to bite her lip instead.

Once inside the kitchen, that could hold a total of three adults, and if lucky, a small child, he began to go back to work, chopping away the large pile of different types of fruit. "Why?" he asked, keeping his attention on the product in front of him.

"There has been a situation," Oceana stated.

"A situation?"

"Yes!"

"What kind of situation?"

"A bad one!" Oceana ran her fingers through her bangs. She wanted to sound determined, to get to him. "A really, really, bad one." She corrected herself; perhaps adding a second really would get his attention. Of course, one 'really' usually meant it was terrible, but adding double the amount should get him to understand that this was an emergency.

Jamlson moved the chopped berries into a small bag and placed them gently on the desk behind him, among other similar-looking bags. Then, he turned back and began hacking the berries again. "If this situation is so bad, why not ask your grandpa for help?"

"That's the thing!" Oceana shifted herself closer to him, breaking the rules of personal space. "He- he is missing." She felt she said that dramatically, but she needed to get to him.

Jamlson stopped and put the knife down to look at her. He used this opportunity to put a bit of space between them and stepped back.

"How long has he been missing?"

"Errr," She paused, knowing that the information she would tell him would not present itself to be a dire situation. "A day."

"A day? Oceana, how do you even know he is missing? He could have just-" He waved his hand momentarily in the sky, "gone out."

"Impossible."

"Why is that?" Jamlson raised an eyebrow.

It was her turn to take a step back. She ran her fingers once more through her white hair, which had decided from birth that it would remain frosted, almost as if she had already lived a lifetime.

"Well, we have never been apart, at least not like this." She hesitated before she continued to speak. "My grandpa acted weird before he left."

"How?"

She paused and thought about her grandfather's strange behaviors. "We were at this village, and he had gotten this letter." She moved toward her pocket. "It had a strange wax seal, one I had never seen before." She then handed the envelope to Jamlson; he took it carefully and examined it. "He read the letter that came with that."

"Do you have the letter?"

"No. I never got the chance to read it."

"What happened?"

"Um," Oceana stated; she stepped back from Jamlson, to move in circles, trying not to bump her hips against the counter. "He got this letter, and then after reading it, he said it was time to leave the hotel we were at, even though we were in the middle of doing a KEEPIN job there!"

"He said that right away?"

"Yes." She stopped her pacing. "He said that right after he read the letter with that envelope."

"Weird."

"Right! I thought it was strange, too, I mean, he never abandons his post. He is always saying that." She switched her pitch of voice to sound deeper, similarly to how her grandpa sounds. "We gotta stick to KEEPIN guidelines, they are important and-"

"Oceana continue."

"Oh, sorry, right." She moved the medium length hair to the back of her ears. This gave her time to think. "Well, right after I packed my belongings that night and we got on Ol'Sarah."

"Ol'Sarah?"

"The boat!" She corrected herself, "We got on her five weeks earlier than we were supposed to." She folded her arms. "After that, my Grandpa locked himself in the captain's cabin for the rest of the three nights on the deck. He didn't even bother making me do my sword training exercises!" Oceana snapped her fingers, "I never went so long without doing training- or being yelled at to do so." Oceana crossed her arms.

"Did he ever explain why you two were coming home so early?"

"No. He never spoke a word to me." She gave a sigh. "By the time we got to the port, the crew on the boat started it up again, preparing for it to leave without us."

"Has that happened before?"

"No. Never, we are always on Ol'Sarah when she is moving." Oceana waved her hand. "Anyways, we went to the house; my Grandpa said goodnight, the only thing he had said to me after we got off. Well then I went to bed, and when I woke up today, he was gone! Now I am here." She threw her arms up. "I-" She had stopped in her words, she gave her toes a click before she turned herself away from him, "I had no idea who to go to."

Her statement came out crooked. She turned around and looked at the boy's brown eyes. "I am lost."

Jamlson raised his eyebrow and curled his lips, moving his attention to the counter that held the remaining untouched berries. He picked up his knife and resumed his chopping activity. "I wish I could help you, but I have to take care of the family business and continue to make sales here. My mom needs my help." He moved his focus back on the berries.

Though the answer he had given her was quite obviously the one he would pick, she clutched to the plummeting ache of her stomach. The wooden surface underneath her boots creaked when she revolved around him.

"I understand. If I were in your position, I wouldn't want to go either. It's just my Grandpa; he is important, and," she paused, "I didn't know who else to turn to."

"I am sorry." Jamlson said while continuing his activities, "I honestly am."

"No, um. It is okay." She moved back to the table that placed itself comfortably behind the counter that held the envelope. She picked it up before she slipped it back into her coat pocket, fitting itself perfectly. "The help would be nice, but you have to take care of your own family. It would be super fantastic if you could help me, though."

"Oceana."

"Right, okay, fine." She said hurriedly before his mouth could open to start another lecture. "I should be heading off; the longer I stand here, the longer my grandpa is gone." She moved her hand forward. "It was good seeing you again,"

Jamlson looked at her hand; he put the knife down and took their hand with his own, "It was good seeing you too." Then, he said with a slight smile, "Good luck finding him."

Oceana let the boy's hand go, giving a slight chuckle leaning her body forward, stating just above the volume of a mouse, "Jammy."

The comment that could be seen from an outsider as nothing more than a harmless nickname had made Jamlson eyebrows furrow. His eyes gave a wide roll before he pointed towards the door. "Get out!"

Oceana laughed. "I will see you later!"

"Yeah, yeah. Whatever."

Oceana shuffled her way to the hallway that directed itself to the exit of the small home; it was another human that had barracked her path to flee.

A strong woman who wore a dress that was covered in dirt and her hair tied up in a messy bun was what had prevented Oceana from leaving. The woman who had seemed like she spent the afternoon working with the world's muck, brown eyes widened, which was a similar color as the boys.

"Oh my! Are my eyes? Are my eyes tricking me? Or is that the famous Oceana Sanford standing in my kitchen?" The woman shouted.

"Hi Ms. Douglas, uh yeah," Oceana chuckled awkwardly, "it is me." She looked at the woman with a half-smile.

"Well, do not just stand there!" Ms. Douglas wrapped her arms around them, lifting them off their feet in the embrace. Ms. Douglas retreated her arms back, setting her free from her almost death sentence. Oceana had felt her spirits lift, not due to her ability to breathe again; the intensity of the squeeze made her smile. This was a treasured rarity for her that she had decided that she enjoyed the first time Ms. Douglas had done this. Ms. Douglas had the biggest grin when she asked, "How are you, dear?"

"I am good," Oceana said, avoiding eye contact; she felt if she looked at Ms. Douglas, she would spit out every little thing on her mind. That her Grandpa was missing or that there was a weird envelope. She could not remember whether the Knight in her home was named Charles or Charlie. This was a very pressing matter. Maybe not the last one so much, but three worrying things sounded more intense than two.

"Actually." Jamlson had stated loud enough to snap the two back to reality. Oceana had entirely forgotten that he was in the same room. "They were just about to leave." His voice made it sound, as though she were in an immense time crunch to get out. That if she had not left that particular door in that very second, the world around them might just burst.

"What? You were going to leave without saying hello?" Ms. Douglas's tone of voice was sharper than the knife Jamlson was holding. This made Oceana feel slightly guilty for heading off without giving herself an introduction to one of the best mothers she knew.

"Well, mom, they have to go," Jamlson said, moving between the two, probably hoping he could shove her out of the kitchen.

"Yeah, I do." Oceana pitched in.

"Have to?" Ms. Douglas raised an eyebrow.

"Yes, she is very busy, right, Oceana?" Jamlson's voice nudged her, insisting that she should follow along unless she planned to be stuck here.

"Oh, yeah. Very." Oceana moved her head to look over at Jamlson, then to Ms. Douglas.

"Well, I am sure you are not too busy to stay for dinner." She added. She was sly; that woman was, Oceana knew that Ms. Douglas had known that her one weakness was the quality of her cooking. Ms. Douglas was a fantastic cook. Her ability to turn anything into a meal was magic.

"Well, alright," Oceana said with a smile. This had made Ms. Douglas clap her hands in joy. Oceana felt Jamlson's glare from behind just after hearing him slap his front face.

"Great, out you two!" Ms. Douglas moved behind Jamlson frantically. She pushed him towards the hall, and a melody of his complaints followed behind. Oceana moved with Jamlson towards the exit after waving Ms. Douglas goodbye.

Jamlson and Oceana made their way around the range of trees that barricaded them from the city that rested just a couple of miles away from them. Oceana had visited Magna East a handful of times with her Grandpa when they would be home for a week or two. But she honestly had anticipated that they would visit the city this time around due to an event that was now creeping around the corner. A day that would celebrate her life-and the only day in the year that she decided what she and her Grandpa would do. This year would be one in which she would finally be able to sign up for the military!

Instead, the strange behaviors of her Grandpa had not been because of the said event. She thought he had a secret plan, a surprise party! She was wrong. Her grandfather was not planning her eighteenth birthday. The two stealthed their way around the trees' expansion, each reaching a length that would stretch high enough to touch the sky above. The temperature had lowered since the morning; every year when this particular week had begun, the weather would always creep its way down, insisting that the cold must take over.

While they moved, Jamlson kept his bow out, and gripped the tool in his hand, which was wrapped in bandages. Bandages he always carried around with him, to prevent splinters. He was prepared to use it when the time was right. Oceana followed behind the trail of silence he left for her, navigating through the place they called home.

"Do you remember when we played out here when I came home for the week? When we were ten?" Oceana whispered, almost respecting Jamlson's wishes for utter silence. "I think we played hide and seek."

Jamlson kept his eyes around the area, his body must have felt the colder atmosphere too, his hooked nose began to turn a shade of red. However he decided not to break his concentration to the task that he had promised himself that he would fulfill. "Right." He said, "I remember you crying because I was better than you at it." He grinned.

Oceana watched his grin appear and gave a 'hmf' sound when crossing her arms. She scrunched up her face. "I think it was you who was crying!" she said in a mocking and childish voice, but she remembered crying that day after recalling the memory. She believed it was because she had not known the wooded area compared to Jamlson. Still, now looking back on it being significantly older, it made sense Jamlson knew this place better than her. He lives here every day of every year; she only visits the site when her Grandpa needs to rest from the sea for a while. "I remember your mom cooked us something good after we played!" she said. "I can't recall what it was." She snapped her fingers, placing a dish in the empty memory.

"It was a honey turkey pot stew," Jamlson said. "You insisted she make it because you said everyone else was awful at making the dish."

"I still believe that is true," Oceana said almost proudly that her opinions have not changed entirely over the years.

"We had dessert after! That was good! Apple Pie!"

"Apple pie?" Oceana recalled, "I don't think I remember that."

"Apple pie, mom's special dish." Jamlson nudged, "Hide and seek, honey turkey pot stew, and apple pie."

"Yeah, I don't remember that," Oceana said; after that, there was a long pause between the two. Oceana felt maybe if she tried hard enough to remember, she could express her piece of the memory, but nothing came up.

"Right," Jamslon said, now the hidden piece of the puzzle had connected in his head. He had figured out why Oceana struggled to recall the last part of the event. "You left early."

"Oh, yeah," Oceana said, seeing the puzzle pieces aligned with Jamlson. "Grandpa had gotten a letter that his Red division was needed."

"So your grandpa is really still a pirate huh?" Jamlson asked.

"First, you shouldn't call the Red Division pirates. People use that word towards the Red Division as an insult, as if we don't do anything important." She corrected "But yes! Of course, he is, come on," she said. "Don't be silly!"

"Right." Jamlson said, rolling his eyes."Of course."

"What do you mean, of course?" She questioned, her tone dropped.

"I mean, of course, you guys are doing a fine job at.... What is it? Keeping peace in the nation."

"You mean, 'Keeping Everlasting Extravagant Peace In the Nation'? Yes." She said,

"Right." Jamlson said, "That."

"See, I don't know what you are implying here, Jamlson, but Cor'Meum is your country too. Don't forget that we are on your side." She pointed at him.

"Yep, of course." He said. "How could-" His sentence was cut off by a rumbling in a bush nearby. He stopped talking and looked directly at it. He moved one of his arms behind his back to grab an arrow that would be sufficient for the job. He waited in the company of animal sounds that surrounded him. He pulled back the string. It gave a quite long tugging sound but not enough to alarm any unsuspecting prey. He took a breath in and held it until the deer attempted to run, but unfortunately, the guy was no match for Jamlson's skill. When a heavy thud hit the ground of the peaceful land, the birds in the surrounding area halted their songs and flooded the sky with their clan.

The night drifted upon them faster than any of them could count. The already drafty atmosphere of the afternoon decided to dip to a lower temperature for the bright white ball in the sky. All heard the little creatures that play their little song in the coal of time. The wind gently tapped on the window carrying a pack of leaves, which ruffled together in the air. The owl that could not be seen in the abyssal darkness participated in its melody with the tiny critters but only a brief moment. Then, it went silent once again, waiting for the right time to speak again.

Knives and forks clashed in a lurid, off-rhythm beat; each person sitting at the circular table sat satisfied, consuming the meal the eldest one of them had made. Then, finally, Ms. Douglas put her fork and knife down.

"Though I did cook this, you can thank Jamlson for hunting the animal down. He is so talented with that bow and arrow of his." Ms. Douglas hummed.

"Yeah, he is pretty cool, with his little hunting gear," Oceana said. In reply Jamlson only rolled his eyes.

"Oceana, are you still practicing that magic speech?"

Oceana put her fork and knife down. She looked over at Jamlson, who seemed like he was ignoring the two. He had continued to shove food in his mouth. "Uh yeah." she coughed. "You could say I am self-teaching!"

"That sounds really fun! Traveling! Learning magic!"

"Sure, I guess you can call it fun. I mean, my grandpa isn't teaching me magic because he's magicless, but I want to at least try! It's always been my dream to learn magic! Just like The Magician!"

"Right but he's always carrying that book of spells on him." Ms. Douglas pointed at Oceana with her fork. "I have never seen the man without holding onto it."

"When he came over that one time." Jamlson snapped his fingers. "I barely touched it, he got angry at me!"

"He is protective of it." Ms. Douglas said. "I feel bad for any fool that tries to steal it from him." She laughed. Oceana joined in on the small laugh and moved her hand inside her coat pocket, to feel its presence there.

"You know," Oceana said, changing the subject, "Even though Cor'Meum is moving away from magic, some part of me can't help but love magic. It's like" She paused. The thought has crossed her mind more times than she could count. "magic is a part of who I am." She looked up and found the Douglas's staring at her. "I can't explain it! I think if we try hard enough- we can still make magic relevant to society. "

A choking sound came. Oceana had shifted her attention to Jamlson, who had a gray cloth in his mouth. His shoulders slightly shook while he still continued to keep the gray fabric on his lips. He shifted his position then placed the napkin down. "I am sorry, continue."

"No, I want to know what was funny."

Jamlson gave a small laugh, "Sorry for the joke you made. I liked it." He said, his fingers tapped along the table.

"Joke? I wasn't joking."

Jamlson tilted his head. "Oh, but I could have sworn it was a joke, magic, relevant to society, humorous!"

Oceana put both her hands on the table and leaned forward while her eyebrows furrowed. "Who is to say that magic can not serve a purpose in society! Who! Tell me who!"

It was Jamlson's turn to raise his voice. "Are you kidding, Oceana, have you taken a look at the world around you? I mean at all during your travels? There are so many better things than magic!" He crossed his arms

"Sure, like what?" Oceana crossed her arms.

"They just made the lawnmower more efficient. Just hop on and then wow, incredible, your lawn is perfect! No magic!"

"Well, that thing costs money; wanna know what is free? magic!"

"Free, as long as you have the time to practice it constantly, oh and make sure you practice the tone you want; otherwise, no take backs!" Jamlson threw his arms up.

"Well, magic can get things done! Like making clean water!"

"You mean plumbing?" He laughed.

"Come on, there is not an invention for every little thing now,"

"They even have this one mechanical invention I saw that replaces lost limbs." Jamlson snapped his fingers, "Wow, something magic could never do. Who would have thought?"

"Oh, I saw that!" Ms. Douglas tuned in. "You know Mr. Williams, the librarian, they fixed his arm! Almost as if he never lost it!"

"Ms. Douglas!" Oceana complained.

"Oh, you know I support you, Oceana. I always did and always will." She smiled. "But I am a big fan of these new 'gadgets,' I suppose it is what you guys call it. I like it a lot. We are starting to enter a new era. You kids have more technology than I had when I was your age. I never thought we would be traveling by air when I was seventeen!" She looked at Oceana.

"She's too nice to say it but- come on Oceana, magic isn't all that great. We are entering a new age." Oceana sighed. "You sword fight right? Just stick to that, that's an old thing that Cor'Meum will always hold onto. Enter one of their big tournaments that they like to host, to show off their fancy private schools." Jamlson stood up, taking his plate with him in his desperate need to travel to the kitchen, where Oceana had no existence. "Well," he said, "dinner was great. Thank you, mom." He smiled at her and kissed her before he headed towards his journey.

"Yeah, I should start heading out too," Oceana said, keeping her hands on her plate along with the motion.

Ms. Douglas shook her head. "Oh no, Oceana, it is late; why don't you stay the night tonight. Then, Jamlson could walk you back home in the morning." Oceana looked over at Jamlson, who rolled his eyes once more before he had disappeared.

"Oh, I couldn't do that to you." Oceana defended quickly. "Honestly, I don't mind walking back now."

"The guest bedroom is down the hall to the right." Ms. Douglas hummed, picking Oceana's plate along with her's. She then kissed Oceana's forehead before she followed her son into the kitchen, leaving Ocean at the table. Their eyes flickered over to the light, deserted and alone. The candle's job was almost done. The performance of maintaining a visual was impressive for this single light. With no other candles to help or rely on with its days coming to an end, it was time to say goodnight. Oceana leaned forward with a huff; and the candle was out.

The bed used to help them drift off to sleep was in no competition with the bed that she had at home in her room. The covers were thin and scratchy, while the mattress really was just blankets ontop of a wooden surface. After a long while of fidgeting, and having a difficult time deciding which position of this awful bed was truly going to be an aid into dreamland, the door moved open.

"Grandpa!" The little child shouted, seeing the familiar face through the small light that the room carried. "There you are!" She had now forgotten about the discomfort of the bed. "You promised you would tuck me in." She reminded.

"That's what I am here for." He laughed and sat on the side of the bed. "Now tell me, Oceana, how has this month been for you?"

The child gripped the blankets. She moved her eyes away from her Grandpa. She sat up in her bed, letting her back rest against the wall behind her. "I don't know," She said honestly. "I am trying to learn magic just like

The Magician!" She smiled but had remembered how her Grandpa wanted her focus to be on swords, an honorable skill to have in Cor'Meum society. "I also want to do swords like mom too-" She added. Her eyes moved over to the picture of a woman that rested next to her bed; in the photo the woman kept a straight, tired-looking facial expression. Though the photo was in black and white, the woman's hair reflected a white object in the photo. "But when I practice magic, nothing happens- what if I can't do magic like you?" She sucked in and let out a quick "No offense."

"Oceana magic is a hard subject. You will get there soon, I promise." He looked over at the clock that made the ticking sound in the background of their conversation. "We will be docking early in the morning tomorrow. Now, get some sleep."

Oceana began to lay in bed. When completing this process, her Grandpa took her blanket and began tucking it in. He was about to get up, but he was stopped by a tiny hand.

"Will you tell me a story?" Oceana asked,

Her Grandpa ran his fingers through his own white hair that showed hints of what used to be blonde; he smiled and nodded before moving around the edge of the bed to get comfortable. "Alright, young one, be quiet and listen to this old pirate tell you a tale." Oceana giggled, which made her Grandpa give his own chuckle,

"Okay, hush, hush. Once upon a time, magical creatures, such as fairies, mermaids, and dragons lived in harmony with humans." Her Grandpa grinned. "The magical creatures provided humans with magic to help their food grow. The dragons would control the fire and wind to burn last year's crops, then the mermaids would come in and control the earth and water to help the soil, and finally, the fairies would come in to provide just the right amount of light and darkness." He began making big expressions to which the small Oceana giggled. "One day one human decided that because the magical creatures controlled so much, he would take the magic for himself."

"Why did he do that?"

"Well, the creatures began asking for more in exchange for their services. This left the people to starve."

"Oh no!"

"But!" Her Grandpa inclined, "It was okay because the man was able to learn the magic the creatures practiced. He then began to teach everyone in his village magic. Soon the whole world began to know magic! Everyone could choose a tone to practice whether it be from the Fairies, or perhaps the mermaids, or dragons!" He said, opening his arms widely for effect. "Never had humans gotten along, working together with their unique skill to help each other grow."

"What happened to the creatures?" She asked with a yawn.

"They disappeared, never to be seen again."

"Grandpa, is this story real?" Oceana asked tiredly, "Are there really magical creatures out there?"

"Every story is as true as we can make it."

"That didn't answer my question."

"Captain." A voice said. Oceana tiredly looked up to find one of the crew members standing by the door, "We need to go over the coordinates when we meet with the Blue KEEPIN division." He said.

"I will be there shortly." Her Grandpa turned to Oceana and gave one more tuck before standing up. "Goodnight, Oceana."

"Wait, grandpa-."

"Yes, Oceana?"

"Can you sing to me?" Her Grandpa stopped for a moment and thought about what song to sing to the child. He ran his hand through his beard, giving more thought before stopping and smiled down at Oceana.

"When I was a baby, I was taught to be good. I was a child when I found out the world was cruel. Empty stomachs stuffed with fears of tomorrow.

I was an adult when I found out the world won't change for good.

My mother- she swore, that they will give us our fruit, if we played the music to their tune.

Filled our appetite with sugar, bread, and lies. Can't make anything until we die.

We sit on our knees and give thanks to the ones we don't see, but behind closed doors, we know their true worth.

A fire sparks from a circle of charts, and the shadows that keep us up are merely just a show, and the water clean came all from me, this is the fate we get when we place our bets.

The charts, stolen maps from the stars, are where we sit. Oh darling lift this curse from me. We sang through the night.

Oh la la la, Oh la la la,

How lucky we are to eat

Oh la la la, Oh la la la,

This is the cycle that the beasts want to keep.

Oh la la la, Oh la la la, I was a child when I found out the world was cruel. Empty stomachs stuffed with fears of tomorrow."

I was an adult when I found out the world won't change for good.

Break this curse, this cycle this misery, please pass over the magic to me.

After her Grandpa had finished the song, Oceana had already begun to feel herself lose consciousness, her mind entering the world of dreams. The only thing that prevented her from entering the dreamland was the aggressive knocking that came from the door. She opened her eyes, sat up and brought her legs together. When did her Grandpa leave the room? Where was he? Was that him?

"Hello? Grandpa?" There was no response. The knocking on the door repeated, only faster and more demanding. "Who is it?" Oceana asked. The only delivery to her question was more knocking that grew harder. The door was going to break. "Grandpa!" She shouted, now begging him to come save her. She was scared. Who was trying to break in? The knocking kept its pounding beat. The door began to crack. Whoever it was, they were going to break in! Oceana gripped onto the sheets. She couldn't peel her eyes away from the door, then it happened. The door busted open, bright round green eyes peered through, and the only thing Oceana saw next was a knife coming right at her.

Oceana sat up with a gasp, her lungs clutched to any provided air that would be given. Her hands were tight, her head was drenched in her own water. She moved her fists in front of her and allowed her fingers to let go of her palms. It had revealed to her blood, caused by her own nails. She moved her hands down both her sides, smearing away the evidence. She closed her eyes and took in a shaky breath. Her heart felt like it was going to beat out of her chest. In the moment of awakening to such a dream, she had almost forgotten where she was before it came back to her. She pressed both her hands on her cheeks and tapped on them a few times before rubbing her face along with her eyes.

CHAPTER 3:

The Road back to nowhere

THE twig snapped in half after being stepped on by brown leather shoes that were worn by the boy. Jamlson kept pace with Oceana making their way around the familiar wooden area.

"I always forget how far your mansion is from my place," Jamlson said.

"I wouldn't call it a mansion. It's really just a home." Oceana moved along the path finely, careful not to step in any wet patches that might come along.

"No, you see my place, that's a house. Your place can fit twenty of mine inside yours. It's a mansion."

Oceana turned around and looked over at Jamlson; and kept their pace walking backward, they grinned at him before they pointed.

"Why did you bring that?"

"What?"

"Oh, you know, that." She made a hand gesture pointing to her back after she stretched her arms in opposite directions, bending her right elbow.

"My bow?"

Oceana smiled and gave a nod. "Yeah!"

"Just in case I find anything I can use for dinner."

"Okay, Mr. Always has food on his mind. Ask him what he's thinking about, it will be about hunting food! Because that is always on his mind!" Oceana sang.

"Oh yeah, You try walking miles to the nearest food market every day and see how long it will take you to give up and just hunt for your food yourself."

The two continued to keep their pace. Oceana at some point, decided that she was going to walk in a normal direction. She moved along next to Jamlson for the remainder of their journey.

"So I have a question!" Oceana waited for Jamlson's response; his long silence felt like an okay to continue, which she did. "Are you mad at me? It just seems that every time I come back. There is this," she moved her arms back and forth, "Ummm, between us- I just hope I didn't say or do anything that actually hurt you." She moved her eyes to look at him, he was looking away from her. "I mean, whatever I did, I want to say that I-"

"Wait, shush for a moment," Jamlson put his arm out, using it to block her from moving forward.

"Hey what the- I am trying to have a conversation with-"

"Shush!" Jamlson snapped. He stopped and smelled. He moved his head in every direction he

could, not explaining to her what he was thinking. He turned to Oceana and said, "Do you smell that?"

Oceana blinked at him, though her first thought was to yell at him; but now that he had mentioned it, she had smelled something. The pleasant smell of pine that had previously surrounded the area was now covered with this new scent. Unfortunately, it took Oceana another second before she could place an identifier to the scent.

"That smells like smoke!" The two looked at each other, then looked up, past, and beyond the trees, there was a dark cloud that had covered what would have been a blue sky. Oceana and Jamlson in that moment had the same thought, which led the two to run towards the location of where the black fog was coming from. It couldn't be, was it? Oceana felt her heart beat out of her chest, and moved her legs at speeds she never knew she was capable of. The smell of smoke grew stronger past the river and past the pile of leaves.

The two stopped once they hit the end of the surrounding trees, entering the open grassland that accompanied the home formerly belonging to Oceana's mom. The state of the home was vastly different from the last time Oceana had seen it in the day of light. The home held inside the remaining flames that had survived the night when the damage was first done. Oceana allowed her feet to move closer to the home, not peeling her eyes away from the grisly sight. She looked around at it, the garden below her bedroom window was reduced to nothing but a black smudge. The home's beautiful golden brown walls were nothing but reminiscent of the events that occurred in the night.

Jamlson looked around and pointed to the windows on the bottom floor. "This was no accident."

Oceana had no idea what he was talking about until she decided to have a closer look at the windows. Each window had some wooden paddle nailed into it. She walked over to the burnt front door and noticed that the door had matched the window's taste in fashion, holding a wooden paddle nailed in front of it. When she had left to go to Jamlson's home, none of these wooden barriers were there.

"Someone did this, and their intentions.." Jamlson stopped and looked at Oceana, "Do you know anyone who would do this?" He asked immediately, "Anyone that you and your grandpa may have run into?"

Oceana shook her head in response. She took one breath in, holding back any possibility of tears. But instead, she felt a fire of her own built up inside her. How could this happen? Who wanted to- well let the existence of her and her grandpa escape this world? Why? Her stomach turned into knots. That's when she took her hand and ran it through her hair; at that moment, she turned in the opposite direction and began marching away from home.

"Well, okay, okay. How about you stay at my place until your grandpa comes back, and we can figure this whole thing out!" He turned around to look back at Oceana, who was already a mile away. "Hey! Oceana!" Jamlson yelled, letting himself chase after her. "Where are you going?" He asked when he had finally caught up to her.

"I am going to find my grandpa."

"What? Oceana I- I don't know if you saw what I just saw! But there is someone out there who wants you and your grandpa gone!" He emphasized. "And when I say gone, I mean-" He stopped. "This is really bad."

"Which is why I need to find him."

"Oceana, can you think about this for a moment?"

"I don't have time for that." She continued to walk forward and passed Jamlson. Jamlson stood there and blinked, then turned around and continued to follow her.

"You are putting yourself in danger! You can't do this alone!"

"I am going to find my grandpa Jamlson, don't even try to stop me. It won't work." She said with a huff.

"No, No." He spoke loud enough to hook her attention in, "I'm coming with you."Oceana stopped walking and turned to look at him. She raised an eyebrow at him.

"What?"

"This is dangerous, you can't do this alone, so I'm coming with you."

"No, No, you can't do that!"

"Yes, I can."

"No, you can't."

"I actually can, and I will." Jamlson said, looking at her, "Plus, if you died, and I hadn't come, I would never live with myself."

Oceana looked at him and grinned. "Okay, fine, I wouldn't want you to not live with yourself. That wouldn't be good."

Jamlson rolled his eyes. "Whatever, poor choice of words, you got my point." Oceana laughed before throwing a smile at him.

"Alright!" They pressed their hand inside their coat pocket and pulled out the envelope. "I think we need to find out who B and T are; I believe this might be the first step to finding my grandpa." Jamlson kept his attention on the envelope and scratched his chin before he gave a grin.

"I think I know a place where we can find out."

CHAPTER 4:

A Hero's Journey

THE bustling sound of construction, loud enough to disturb the calmness of the woodland neighbors who resonated just a couple miles away, made a loud and obnoxious sound. These sounds were a constant reminder that technology was developing. A prolonged honking of a very long vehicle that could carry thousands announced its arrival at its destination. Hundreds of people came out smiling, carrying on conversations that had birthed from the ride to the city.

The people who came out wore vastly different outfits from the wardrobe that Oceana advertised on herself. Most young women held tightly fitting top garments, with bottom apparel being either loosely fitted or much similar to the top, being compact. The heavier skirts share a similar color as their tops, with lengths ranging from either touching the ground or resting above their knees.

Each of the young ladies was giving off an omen of confidence, in one way or another. The women who leaned on the older age seemed to mostly wear skirts that reached the floor below them, giving a sense of old traditions. The men's outfits were mostly long coats, and fancy ties, with a vest. It wasn't as extravagant looking as the woman's but it was still aesthetically nice to look at.

Most people in the town wore the words 'KEEPIN' on themselves. Whether it was through a pin like Oceana, or words that were stitched on their clothing. Those who wore the words wore it with pride. It was almost embarrassing if a person didn't have the words "KEEPIN." somewhere on them.

Oceana looked over at Jamlson who wore a burgundy sweater, along with his long dark coat complemented by his purple scarf. Jamlson probably didn't feel excluded in the pride.

"Oh how marvelous!" A woman said, holding onto the arm of one of the men. "Do you think we will be able to visit the skyships?" She questioned.

The man chuckled, "Of course, why? Would we check out waterbound ships? What are we, savages? This is Magna East." He laughed; The two moved along the pack, blending into the rest of the people. Oceana looked up at the skyships that floated so innocently in the sky. She had then watched small golden-like boxes fly off the ship; wings that rested on the top of these vehicles propelled them to soar, almost if they were all light as a feather. Sky Cruisers. Oceana read about them before. They really only carried them on Purple division skyships. They must be scouting for something if they are releasing them like this. Oceana decided that she couldn't spend the rest of her day staring at the tin machines in the sky, and quickly began her journey forward.

Each building brought a unique presence, ranging from a couple stories high to just one level below the ground. One of the buildings had a spinning golden circle attached to it. The moving helped the clock keep track of time. Despite the diversity in building structure, they all made sure to follow the same color scheme of gold, blue, and amber. People everywhere around them; much like the two of them had a destination that they were headed towards. Outside a shop Oceana watched a man hold a silver square remote that she assumed was connected to the golden dragonfly that spun around him in a decorative arrangement.

"Come get the state of the art toys! Only here! Better than magic!" he shouted, still keeping his concentration on the gadget. The dragonfly buzzed around in the air, displaying its beautiful design to the public.

Crossing the paved concrete was almost impossible, the bustling city had a variety of different vehicles that sped outside of the designated field for those who chose to use their feet to get by. A man in a large cycle honked his horn and proceeded to yell obscenities..

"You gotta be careful, make sure to stay on the sidewalk." Jamlson informed. "Don't want to get hit, right?" He grinned. Jamlson found it amusing that she was having a difficult time navigating herself with so many people around her. She was still determined to show him that she was more than a child who mostly traveled by boat. She took a breath in and puffed out her chest, staring directly at him, hoping to invoke a bit of fear into him, or rather confidence she could go a second without being hit by a bike.

"I know where I am going!"

Jamlson laughed, "Alright."

When continuing their path, a loud sound of vibrations interrupted the two. They both looked up to get a view of the object who contrived such a loud clamor. A large boat, one that presented similar to those that would be seen crossing the sea; except instead of having a topsail, it held a large balloon. Underneath the boat were giant fans that helped propel the boat to fly up. After the boat's introduction with the large amounts of turbulence, it moved on further into the city.

Oceana couldn't help but compare these ships to the water bound ones that her and her grandpa use. These inventions were cool, but Ol'Sarah was incredible, considering how well equipped it was when it came to facing storms or any sort of weather, which the flying boats couldn't do quite yet. Putting the flying boat in a storm right now would put people on board at risk- which is why the Purple division were the only ones that held ownership to all of them currently. Though from what Oceana had heard, within the next five years all the KEEPIN divisions will have some sort of upgrade. Perhaps flying boats for the Red division, the only division that spread outside the land of Cor'Meum, would be safe enough to fly over sea with. It was a long and tedious process creating flying boats that held that amount of mass, but Cor'Meum did it! No other country was skilled like Cor'Meum!

Jamlson raised an eyebrow, then moved on towards their walk down the chalked pavement that was colored in crimson and gold. Children sat together on the walkway. One of the kids showed off a golden circular object with four legs. He took the key on top of it, spun the key counter-clockwise, placed it on the ground, and watched it run around with the other children. A golden tower struck and echoed its jingle much like a lion pronouncing its roar, informing the people that a new hour had come.

On their journey, Oceana noticed a small girl through the window in a coffee shop. She seemed to be lost in the world of the pages in her possession. An older woman dressed quite identical to the girl came from the corner and sat next to her. Her lips moved, beginning to engage in a conversation with the small child. She had not realized that she had stopped for so long until Jamlson grabbed her arm, eager to get them to their destination.

Moving through the bustling street filled with conversations that never had an end, talking about various topics, Oceana stopped and looked at the vending newspaper dispenser. Inside, Oceana saw a magazine pile all from the company, Cor'MeGOLD. A well-established fashion magazine company that listed top people, usually celebrities, in various settings. It looked like Princess Aster Roseario was on the cover. She had her eyes locked on the camera. Her hair, which had usually bounced up from her strong curls, was tied down in many braids in this photo. The photo's title read 'Princess Aster nominated as Cor'Meum's most beautiful woman for 1925.' She did look beautiful. The lighting in the photo reflected off of her dark skin, and made her eyes pop gold. The photo even caught the mole under her right eye. When the two were little, Oceana could strongly recall Aster's ambitions to become the best at everything. Oceana felt her face go red. Perhaps she shouldn't stare at Aster's photo for too long.

Cor'MeGold always handpicked the most gorgeous women and men to be in their issues. To be on the magazine's cover was a huge honor, and one had to reach impossible levels of beauty to accomplish that. Oceana knew that her mother held the record of being on the cover of Cor'MeGold for the most consecutive years. She believed she was nominated at least three years in a row. Her mother was beautiful, intelligent, and extremely powerful; all of this had made her disappearance strange. Oceana shook her head; this was not the time she needed to focus.

While traveling along the path, Oceana watched a KEEPIN soldier wearing a blue uniform hand a small girl a flower; she flashed him a wide grin. Oceana had no idea what Jamlson went on about yesterday, KEEPIN soldiers were incredible. They protected the people of Cor'Meum, made sure that each citizen felt safe, which they always had excellently done. The Blue division soldier was snapped out of his conversation with the small girl, when flashes of light appeared in the sky despite the day being so young. He sat up and immediately was able to identify the criminals creating such a ruckus, a couple of teenagers.

"Hey!" He yelled.

"Run!" The leader shouted. The tiny fugitives began to run, leaving a trail of laughter.

The Blue division officer grabbed his whistle and blew it, before he engaged in chasing after the kids.

Oceana laughed after the comedic events that occurred before her; watching the bright, happy people of this city was what made Oceana's experience memorable every time she visited. Jamlson rolled his eyes and continued their walk down the big city of East Magna. Eventually, the two made it to their destination, or what Oceana would assume it to be, once Jamlson had stopped moving forward, putting their exploring to an end.

They were in front of a large glass door attached to a long gold building that placed itself nicely between two blue buildings. The building must have decided at one point that it wanted to be conspicuous to any traveling passenger. Oceana placed their hand on the doorknob, opened the glassdoor and moved inside. The city sounds almost didn't exist when the door behind her closed. The muffled excitement outside sealed itself away, granting the building permit to have a quiet atmosphere.

Oceana admittedly never found herself in the presence of a library often. It was hard for her to tell if this library was insane or a textbook definition of what a library should be. She had never seen so many books collected together before while also displayed engagingly. To the right of her, there was a long pole that held the building up, yet was also used to display books. There was another bookshelf that she could see to her left that was shaped like a tree, with the title on the top called "Agriculture." She looked over at Jamlson, who gave a quick nod before he moved down the hallway, Oceana dragged on with him.

Guiding down the quiet place, Oceana noticed that the sound of a clock ticking with each second caught her attention. She stopped moving down the hall to stare at the clock. She kept her eyes on the flickering handle; each tick of a sound marked the end of another second. The clock was above the section of books called "History and Today." To which had lights that were nicely decorated on the shelf. Out of synchronization with the clock, they blinked every other five seconds, giving off another color with a sound of a buzz. Though if Oceana could put in a recommendation, it would be to replace the two missing bulbs in the middle with new ones, which made the decoration quite awkward to look at. Oceana felt Jamlson's hand grab her arm, forcing her attention once more to the journey ahead.

While making their way down the library hallway, Oceana tripped forward for a brief moment. When she looked down to find what had made her fall, she had not expected what was presented in front of her. In front of her was a tiny android; it was at least six inches. Its little body was a square, and it was carrying a book, or at least was before Oceana tripped over the small guy. The little box moved around; it had fallen on its back and had the most difficult time getting back up again. Jamlson grabbed him, and propped the square guy onto its feet. It immediately picked up the book and moved forward to its destination when achieving the ability to walk again.

Oceana looked around the room and noticed that the robot was not the only one that made a living in this room; from all over the place in the library, Oceana found many of them everywhere. Each of the tiny little robots was either holding a book or organizing the books. Their only purpose was to make sure that everything was in proper order in the library. Oceana and Jamlson looked at each other before determining that the present was the best time to move forward.

One of these tiny robots must have not noticed Oceana, and tripped over her shoe. It had fallen down along with the book it was carrying. The robot then stood up and shuffled away quickly, leaving the book behind. Oceana picked up the book and turned the pages to find the context of the book; she shortly discovered it was a history book.

World history from yesterday to today: 1925!

This book will tell readers all the details about the establishment of 1888 of Tetrad Aurum. The goal is to give readers an understanding of Cor'Meum's relationship between the other countries of Tetrad Aurum; Fortis Tacet, Aurum, and Vibrius (a country we are still leading towards peace today!)

The Content and Materials in this text are State approved.

Oceana moved the book to the library's history section, hoping she placed the book in its rightful place. She couldn't help but smile, Cor'Meum sure was great! It was wonderful that Cor'Meum had KEEPIN officers in Vibrius to help guide them to the direction of peace!

At the end of the hallway there was a wooden desk that was not permitted to be used by the public. There was a man whose back was facing the two. He kept muttering to himself. Oceana could not tell whether or not these words were the most appropriate to be used in a communal setting. The man was clearly frustrated. She looked over at Jamlson, who gave her the most helpful response, a shrug. She shook her head, turned to the librarian, and coughed. He must have not noticed; his whispering nonsense continued. He was stuck in his own world. Finally, he stopped muttering and grabbed a book and went around the wooden desk. Once he stepped out of it he moved past the two and made his way down the hallway. He kept his pointy nose stuck in the book he possessed. Oceana looked over at the desk and noticed behind it there was a door; the door had a proud sign on the front of it that stated 'Restricted access. Do not enter. Employees only.'

Oceana jumped over the wooden desk, ignoring the tiny patch she could have conveniently used instead. She turned around and looked at Jamlson. He looked around before acting like a normal trespasser by going around the desk.

"What are you doing?" He whispered.

"I am just gonna check something out." She placed her hand on the doorknob, she looked behind her to make sure that no unwanted eyes were watching or spectating the activities that pushed beyond moral boundaries. She twisted the silver handle, which in response gave a modest squeak, as she pushed the door slightly open. She looked back at Jamlson, who kept moving his eyes back and forth, scanning the perimeter; he looked over at Oceana, who nodded her head before going inside.

The room was a lot larger than what Oceana had expected. Each wall in the pentagon-shaped room had a long wooden shelf, filled with books, and above the shelves were paintings of water-bound ships. Each water-bound ship looked different from the other. Oceana could hear little buzzing sounds that filled the room with noise. She looked up and found miniature flying boats. Each tiny boat had their own design. Each ship fluttered around the room in its own direction and pace. Perhaps about ten of them fluttered around the room, making little humming sounds where they went. Oceana looked back down at the large room. She walked around the room and examined the hardback book titles that held names such as "How to create the impossible!" or "Human or Mechanical? You tell me." and "Will this explode if I press the button?" There was a pattern on this shelf on the variety of ways one could become the perfect inventor.

Oceana turned to look over at Jamlson, who had begun reading the covers of the books too. Oceana, in her examination, looked down at the bookshelf and noticed that there was a drawer attached to it. She pulled it open. Inside the cabin there was nothing out of the ordinary, the drawer carried broken gadgets, some tools, and a couple of broken tiny boats.

Oceana turned around and noticed that there was a desk in the middle of the room. She walked over to the red table, curious as to what content it had. When she approached it, the first thing she immediately noticed was an officer badge on the desk. She looked over at the corner of the desk and found a picture of Mr. Williams, or what she would assume was him. The man in the picture looked just like the man she saw earlier, however he looked younger. In the picture of younger Mr. Williams he was wearing a Red division KEEPIN uniform. Oceana could tell it was a Red division uniform despite it being in black and white. In the background of the photo, there was a ship. It looked familiar, almost like Ol'Sarah. Was it Ol'Sarah? She squinted at the photo, and leaned on the desk to stare at the picture a bit longer, until her hand slipped forward. She moved her hand and underneath her fingers was a sealed letter. The letter had the name Ellington on it. Ellington? Why was his name written here? They had then lifted it up in a better light to ensure she had read the name that it held correctly.

"Hey!" A shout came.

Oceana turned around to find the source of the noise. They stiffened immediately when their eyes met, not what they hoped would be Jamlson's. Instead she found a pair of green eyes behind square glasses that stared at her. An angry-looking boy stood by the front door. His choice in fashion was much more upper-class than the pirate and hunter that stood in front of him. He had a clean brown jacket. He wore a white collar shirt with a purple vest and tie. On the right corner of his vest, written in cursive, said the words 'KEEPIN.'

While the kid in front of the two was much smaller, Oceana could not help but fear him. He was scary.

"Sorry," Jamlson was the first to speak. "We wanted to talk to Mr. Williams."

"He isn't here."

"Right, I see that now, thank you," Jamlson said nervously.

"Sorry, we didn't mean to intrude. We honestly just wanted to ask Mr. Williams something."

"He is busy." The boy repeated, "You two need to leave." He pointed towards the exit, reminding them where the general direction to leave was. "Now."

"Honestly, uhhh." Oceana squinted at the boy's vest to see if any form of name tag was attached to it.

"Headworth."

"Headworth! That is a wonderful name!" Oceana brightened, Jamlson nodded. "Headworth we can not stress how important it is to speak to Mr. Williams now."

"I told you he is busy and that you need to leave." He began to sound irritated that the two trespassers in front of him seemed to miss the words he had spoken.

"Headworth! What is going on?" The man from before came in. At that moment, despite his long-tailed suit and collar shirt, Oceana had noticed his golden arm. The man used this arm to push his spectacles back on the bridge of his pointy nose. One of the lenses on these glasses had three smaller lenses inside. He used his left hand to spin the smaller lens to get a better look at the two strangers.

"Dad, I found these two in your office," Headworth stated. The man ignored his son and moved closer to Oceana. "Oh, wow!" Before moving in circles around Oceana, he stated loudly, "The hair-color! The red jacket! You must be Marlyn's kid! What an honor it is to meet you!"

Oceana looked at him "Are you Mr. Williams?"

"In the flesh!" he shouted, and took a step back, taking his top hat off, exhibiting his distinct hair on the top of his head. He moved back up and noticed Jamlson, "Ah! Jamlson! I haven't seen you since you were just a baby!" He grinned. "You have grown up! Incredible! Life does that! Doesn't it." He chuckled.

Jamlson rolled his eyes, got behind Oceana, and pushed her forward "Mr. Williams, Oceana has a question for you."

"Oh, what would the famous Sanford want from me?" He grinned. "I would be honored to help!" Oceana felt her cheeks turn red, before she continued.

"Mr. Williams, we were hoping since you have access to information about signatures and labels. Well- um- and knowing who they belong to, you would know who B and T is." Oceana grabbed the envelope from inside her pocket and handed it to the man.

Mr. Williams twisted his lense once more before he gave a good look at the envelope, he examined the wax seal in front of him.

Jamlson moved forward "Mr. Williams," He started looking at the man in the eyes. "This is important you see, their grandpa, he is-"

"Fine!" Oceana stated loudly. "My grandpa is fine! Everything is good, Jamlson here is just worried because my grandpa," Oceana paused, looking through the excuses folder in her brain, "he is a bit under the weather." She smiled.

Jamlson gave her a strange look and then nodded at Mr. Williams. "Uh yeah." He said sheepishly.

"Yes! The envelope was attached to a letter that is now missing. So we need to know who sent that letter to my grandpa; he would be here himself, but he is sick, and yeah." Oceana gave another smile

Mr. Williams looked at the two, smiling; he shook his head and handed the envelope back to Oceana. "Unless your grandpa comes here to ask me personally, I would be happy to, but until then." Mr. Williams gave a half-smile, "Wish I could help you."

"It's fine." Oceana grinned.

"If you can, tell that pirate that his old pal says hi! Also emphasize that I say pirate as a term of endearment, not an insult to the Red Division!" Mr. Williams smiled. Oceana gave half a smile.

"I will. Let's go Jamlson." The two moved towards the door exiting the room, leaving the two owners alone.

CHAPTER 5:

Headworth's deal

J AMLSON and Oceana stood outside the shop, watching the vehicles and people pass by without any burden of life-threatening stress.
She wondered if anyone in this entire city has ever faced this amount
of confusion and loss all at once. There was some part of her that felt that if
she went back in there and told Mr. Williams the truth about her grandpa
being missing he would be more inclined to help them. Well, actually she
had no idea if she could trust him with that information. Who would he
tell anyway? She gave a small sigh; it felt that this moment had just become
a big defeat.

"Do you think there are other record places that are connected with
libraries?" Oceana asked Jamlson, who seemed to be in his own world of
thoughts. Jamlson gave a shrug.

"Not that I am aware of, I've never gone beyond the city borders."

Oceana sighed. She took out the envelope to stare at the wax seal again, wondering if maybe the crew on Ol'Sarah knew who this person was. Now that she was thinking about it, did the crew know what was wrong with her grandpa, or were they just as confused as she was? What was her grandpa hiding from her that made him leave so suddenly? Her cycle of thoughts was cut with a cough. Both she and Jamlson looked behind themselves to see the kid with the curly dark reddish-blonde hair from before.

"Headworth?" Oceana asked with a raised eyebrow, "What are you doing here?"

"Oceana and Jamlson, I presume, right?" He asked while he pushed his square glasses back up to his much similar pointy nose, like his dad's.

The two looked at each other and nodded.

"Right, well, it seems that you two are desperate to find out who's behind the wax seal of yours."

"Do you know any places that might help us?" Oceana asked curiously, wondering why he was bringing this up.

"I can do you one better." He gave a coil grin, which revealed the small gap between his front teeth. "I actually know who you are looking for!" He pronounced with pride, "Not only that, but I know the location of where this human is." He held a folded piece of paper out in front of him.

"Really?" Oceana jumped up excitedly. Jamlson, at that moment, also stood up with suspicion, his eyebrow raised along with his arms crossing, completing the fashion of misbelief. Headworth stopped Oceana from reaching the note,

"Before I give this to you, I would like to ensure that the payment would be in the line of accompanying you on this journey," Headworth said.

"Alright!" Oceana stated, "You can come!"

"Wait hold on Oceana!" Jamlson said before he moved in front of them; almost as if physically getting between her and Headworth would prevent her from rushing into this notion. Jamlson had to know by now that Oceana was not the most logical person when it came to thinking through an action. All her reactions since he had begun traveling with her were in the moment. Jamlson, at this moment, decided to ask the question that would determine what this kid's intentions were.

"What's in it for you?" Jamlson asked with his eyebrow raised up, "Why would you want to help out two people you don't know? I highly doubt it's for good reasons." Jamlson crossed his arms. He was already on the mechanic's shoulders about this.

"Well, I don't have the means to travel by myself. My father revoked my allowance after I blew up the basement; he said perhaps along the lines of having 'reckless behavior'?" He said, while he waved his hand back. Oceana honestly could not tell if Headworth was actually confused with what he did wrong. Perhaps Headworth just had an extraordinary sense of humor that Oceana would never get.

"Oh well, I can pay for your ride," Oceana said. She packed enough prelacies to pay for all means of traveling. Maybe she could buy them all horses, and they could travel together on those. That would be a dream come true. Horses and finding out the mystery behind why her grandpa disappeared, just like the Magician and the Knight. In the stories she read about them, they had to solve mysteries on their feet before getting to their final destination, working together on their big adventure. They would all become just like them, having an adventure, perhaps becoming legendary. This was something she had always dreamed about. Things just got a bit more exciting in her head.

"There is also another condition." Headaworth's voice snapped her back to reality

"Yeah?" Oceana asked.

"We stop at Fovero before we reach the destination."

"Fovero?" Jamlson's voice boomed. "That trash town? Why would you want to go there?" Jamlson asked with his eyebrow still raised. He looked up and down at Headworth, almost in a judging way. Oceana understood where Jamlson was coming from on this one, Headworth hadn't seemed like the type of person that would want to associate himself with the town of Fovero; he would be the type of person to believe the town was beneath him.

"That does not concern you," Headworth said scrunching up his face; which only made the thousands of freckles on his face pop out more.

"It's fine, Jamlson." Oceana said while they turned to Jamlson, "A quick stop won't hurt us." Jamlson leaned in to whisper to Oceana,

"I don't know. He seems more trouble than what he's worth."

"It will be fine, Jamlson. I got this." They winked at him, only for Jamlson to roll his eyes at them. She then beamed at Headworth. "Thank you, Headworth!" She said, "We will stop at Fovero, in exchange for helping us on this quest."

Oceana made her way down the pavement putting in the small effort to open the note that had rested in her hands. Headworth and Jamlson followed behind. Once she had finished opening the paper, she read the written words inside. She stopped and turned around. She looked at Headworth, and shook her head. "This is real? This isn't a joke?" She said holding the paper high.

Headworth scoffed, "If I made a joke, you wouldn't get it." he looked at the two and paused before pushing his glasses up "No."

Oceana grinned and jumped up and down before she pressed her hand to her face to muffle her scream. "Of course! Of course! Oh my- I- How could this fly over my head!" she yelled; she laughed and held the note to her again, she tapped both her feet on the ground.

"What is it?" Jamlson asked, obviously worried for the sanity of his friend.

"Jamlson! The note! Or the letter or whatever! It came from Bellus! The Bellus!" Oceana ran her fingers through her hair. "Oh my-! Seriously! This is amazing!"

"Bellus Timidus?" Jamlson asked.

Headworth gave Jamlson a glare. "Are you serious? Don't you know basic history?" Headworth looked up and down at Jamlson once more and shook his head. "Never mind, don't answer that question."

"Bellus Timidus is a hero! The hero! You know, The Kight, the one that killed Sage Magnus!"

"Of course, I know who you are talking about," Jamlson said, rolling his eyes, then pressed his hand to his face. "I was asking for confirmation."

"Yes! It is him! He! Bellus! The guy that killed the evil king! He ended the Calamitous War! Wow my heart! Headworth, how are you not freaking out?" Oceana asked with a grin, "I mean, he killed the Sage Magnus. He stopped the Calamitous War! Single-handedly! Well, him and the Magician."

"Technically, the Calamitous War went on for another year after that. In addition, approximately four hundred KEEPIN soldiers, originally called the Mid Knights crew, died. But it was then once we conquered Vibrius, which was easy due to them having no real leader when Sage Magnus was defeated, the war was marked to be over." Headworth said, reciting the historical information he had memorized. He looked over at Oceana, who was giving the brightest smile. "But I suppose yes, he did contribute to the ending of it."

"How are we going to find him?" Jamlson asked.

"According to Headworth he lives in Westside Mountains," Oceana looked at the paper once again, grinning like a fool.

Jamlson crossed his arms. "Isn't that miles from here?" He asked.

"Yes, but we can get there fairly quickly," Headworth looked behind him. The long vehicle, almost on cue, had just started making its way to its destination. It gave a long, loud hoot, announcing its arrival, warning travelers to clear the way; once the vehicle arrived.

"Trains?" Oceana raised an eyebrow. She scoffed at the idea.

"Yes, we won't make it to our destination without them." Headworth stated, "Unless you were actually thinking of riding a horse." He laughed.

Jamlson looked over at Oceana, who sucked in her lip and shook her head. "Of course, I wasn't thinking that! That would be silly!" she waved her hand momentarily in the sky.

Jamlson crossed his arms. "It seems like the longer we stand here, the more time we waste."

"Oh- Well yeah, you're right! Let's get on this, uh, train, I guess." Oceana marched forward with the two following behind.

CHAPTER 6:

Now a special word from our sponsors

T H E three of them picked an area on the train that would allow a conversation to flow naturally without the disturbance of others. Oceana placed herself in front of Jamlson and Headworth, who quietly agreed to sit next to each other. With Jamlson getting the window seat, he could look outside to the city that he lived near.

Oceana looked at the note once more, reading over the name stained in black ink in front of her. She had grown up reading books and listening to stories of Bellus Timidus, how he and the Magician worked together to take down one of the most hated men in history. If he were communicating with her grandpa, that would mean that her grandpa might know the identity of the Magician, right? It was strange that her grandpa had never told her he knew Bellus Timidus personally. This wasn't the kind of information one could happen to forget to tell someone, like washing the dishes. Or to buy eggs at the market. Her grandpa had purposefully kept this information away from her. Now she had to think, was it because he had not trusted her? He hadn't trusted her enough to take her on this journey with him.

The train hooted once more before the force of the train's movement pushed Oceana forward. She watched the outside of the compartment, all the trees blending into one green smug; the city close to home became nothing but a tiny spec. Oceana looked over at Jamlson who couldn't peel his eyes off the town. The place that he had grown so close to now became so distant. He truly never counted miles farther than where he was right now. Yet, Oceana from her side could still see the city's lights in the daylight and the small flying specs that would be the flying ships that docked around the area.

Headworth stood up and stretched before yawning, "I am going to find a bathroom," He moved away from the two, walked down the long narrow hall that was the train. Once he had left, Oceana leaned forward.

"Jamlson, I found something in Mr. Williams' office." She said in what she would call a whisper, but it was quite above room volume to anyone else.

"What, what did you find?" He raised an eyebrow.

Oceana reached into her coat pocket and pulled out a sealed envelope with the name Ellington on it, "That's my grandpa's name. Wilic Ellington."

"What was he doing writing to your grandpa?"

"I don't know." She looked at the envelope.

"Aren't you going to read it?" "Uh- yeah, I just don't want Headworth finding out I took something from his dad." She said, looking back at the letter.

Jamlson shrugged. "Oceana, I honestly don't think he would care,"

"Care about what?" Headworth asked. "Who would care?"

Oceana managed to tuck away the envelope, "Uh, Bellus, I don't think he would care that I practice magic." She said, her eyes kept on Jamlson, who only shook his head before he placed his hands to his face. "Well, at least attempting to." She said,

"You practice magic?" Headworth raised an eyebrow.

"Right," Jamlson agreed, his face reappearing once again. "They're completely ridiculous." He smirked and looked at them, to which Oceana crossed their arms in response. She moved her posture up and narrowed her eyes at the two boys, who now began to taunt her at a hobby that she loved dearly.

"Yeah, magic is only used by the depressed."

"To which means?" Oceana snapped back.

"That only people who use such an outdated resource are the same ones who cling onto the past."

"Oh, that is not true!" Oceana said, still crossing her arms.

"Then why do you use magic?" Headworth said, reaching for his bag.

"Because it is tradition!" Oceana threw her hands up.

"See, the past." He had then pulled out a book and began to indulge in the content inside. He felt reading the book was a better use of his time than carrying the rest of the conversation. Oceana raised her eyebrow, looked back out the window, and Jamlson moved up.

"Oceana,"

She looked up at him.

"Uh- I am going to find a paper and ink to send my mom a letter explaining why I won't be coming home for a while." He said, "I will be back shortly." He guided himself past Headworth, who only lifted his knees to his chest to give the other boy room to leave his seat.

Oceana tapped her fingers on the small bridge between the train window and seat that maintained a permanent position there. She looked over at Headworth, who kept the same blank face, his eyes moving in a rhythmic beat along the pages.

Oceana looked around the cars and noticed that everyone else had seemed to prepare for this long trip by indulging themselves with content from the books they held. For instance, the man in the compartment next to them was flipping through today's article that had the title. "Princess Aster won her one-hundredth gold medal in Cor'Meum's Art of Swords tournament! Has another one coming up this week!"

This moment felt like it would take almost forever, much similar to watching mules trot on dry land. With every second that passed by, she suddenly remembered the handbook- she couldn't believe she had taken it. Should she read it? She felt nervous doing so- then again she did take it. She also saved it from being destroyed in the fire. Perhaps she should reward herself for being a hero and read the mystery content that the book held inside. She opened the book and began to read the first chapter,

"This book contains an in depth detailed analysis of the many concepts of magic. For example this book will explain to readers the symbols within magic. The compositions of material of what each magical element is made up of. It will also explain where magic originated from. Why humans are capable of magic, and why we can not produce magic at the speeds we wish."

This handbook was somehow worse than the last one. It was hard to read this without wanting to fall asleep. Oceana was amazed how someone could make magic so boring. She sighed, which moved her bangs up slightly, this distracted her for a moment, but she had to read on. She sighed again which invoked the same action, and it made her chuckle this time. With that, she pursed her lips and tried to blow her bangs up again, taking a breath in and pushing her breath out as hard as she could, mastering the same trick as before.

A book slammed, and Headwoth's eye twitched. "Do you have to be doing that?" He emphasized with a tone of disgust.

Before Oceana could answer, the lights on the train dimmed. This guided everyone's attention to a woman on board, who wore a uniform blended in purple, blue, and red, the colors of the Cor'Meum flag. She was also wearing the Cor'Meum flag pin on her right shoulder. Oceana could tell it was the Cor'Meum flag from where she was sitting because of the bright blue eye that rested in the middle of the flag, how it looked almost if it were encrusted with diamonds. She wondered if that was the regular uniform for her or if she was wearing it due to the week-long holiday celebration of Cor'Meum's victory. She gave a wide bright smile that was easily distinguishable through her blue lipstick.

"I hope you are all enjoying your ride here through Cor'Meum's finest railroad company, Tracks! Tracks, we will keep you on track to your destination!" She winked at the crowd, who gave a small laugh. "Now, if you would direct your attention here!" The woman pointed at the white sheet that made its way down the ceiling. A clicking sound went off, a light not too far from the sheet of paper began projecting images. All while the paper gently swayed from its place. "You will find we have some entertainment to present to you for our ride. Now here is a wonderful movie that represents the bravery of Cor'Meum and how we won the Calamitous War against the country Vibrius, forty years ago. Our King also approved this film! King Erebus!" She smiled and moved away from the image to give the passengers a better view of the screen.

Oceana directed her attention to the screen, which had a standstill image of King Erebus. He gave a thumbs up and a smile, with text on the side that stated, 'This Film was approved by King Erebus and the state of Cor'Meum.' The next set of images flashed, showing another stand-still photo of a mountain with a castle attached to it from a far distance. In the background played menacing music, or what she would call menacing with the piano's rapid sounds. The scene cut to a man in long robes. Though Oceana could not see the colors of the robes that this man was wearing, she assumed it to be Vibrius colors of green and brown. The man had exaggerated eyebrows and dark eye shadow around his eyes. The actor also had a fake crow attached to his shoulder. He began to talk, which inevitably transitioned to the next scene, a text box of what the man had said.

"I, the evil Sage Magnus, king of Vibrius will take over the country Cor'Meum and claim it as my own- muahahaha!"

The next scene cut back to the man playing the role of Sage Magnus laughing with his face zoomed in. He stopped laughing and looked off-screen; that was when the camera had cut to a doorway, where two very handsome young men walked in, one carrying a sword, which was obviously fake, the other a handful of glitter, that leaked from his hands. The lips of the actor who carried the sword began to move, indicating he was talking.

Oceana squinted at the screen and tried to clarify what he was saying, but she gave up figuring it out and waited patiently for his lines to pop up on the screen.

"Found you evil king! You won't take over Cor'Meum today! Or ever! The Magician and I will stop you!"

The passengers on the train began to clap at the dialogue, some had even gone far enough to cheer at this exciting retelling.

The music shifted to a less serious tone after the box that carried the dialogue went away, leaving the viewers with the scene of all three actors engaging in a fighting sequence. The actor that had played Sage Magnus reached in his hood sleeve and began to throw balls of paper at the two actors.

Both of the heroes in the film dodged the balls of paper and moved to prepare their own set of attacks, the actor that was playing the role of the Knight threw in some swings, while the actor who was supposed to represent the Magician grabbed his own paper balls and threw it at the actor playing Sage Magnus. Sage Magnus, in the film, began moving his lips while falling to the floor.

"No! Not my ugly face!" When the audience had read the new dialogue, they all broke into laughter. Oceana could not help but laugh along with everyone else, the retelling of this critical part of Cor'Meum's history was not necessarily comical, but knowing that the heroes defeated him together gave her a sense of pride for Cor'Meum. She smiled and felt her spirits lift when she began to acknowledge how wonderful it was to be part of such a great country. This also gave her excitement that she was on her way to meet the real hero that the film was representing. She turned her attention back to the moving pictures. They watched the protagonists high-five each other on the screen while Sage Magnus remained on the ground. Then, the Magician began talking to the Knight.

"Now that Cor'Meum has won the Calamitous War; we can peacefully guide Vibrius in a good direction!" The text said. The film switched back to the two heroes who looked at the camera and gave a thumbs up with wide grins. The lights began to dim back up again, but not entirely to the point to which it would brighten the compartment all the way. But it was enough to notice the sudden change in setting The woman from before presented herself to the audience.

"And today, we are still guiding peace to their country." The woman smiled, which allowed the rest of the compartment to clap for the brave soldiers that were guiding peace across the country of Vibrius. Oceana felt proud that her grandpa was part of such a great nation as Cor'Meum. They truly were incredible at directing a luxurious lifestyle for the people of Vibrius.

"Up next! A romantic comedy!" The woman said. Oceana had no intention of wanting to see a film that wholly involved romance; she could already feel the heavy flatness of the film bring her mood down. She supposed that now would be an excellent time to see what was going on in the other compartment.

When Oceana stood up, she could feel some of the heavy boredom lift itself off of her in the process. A new action was being made besides sitting. Oceana never thought she would gain so much entertainment from moving. She had decided she wanted to keep this form of entertainment before she had to remain back in her seat. She put the book back in her jacket coat. "I am going to use the bathroom." She said with a laugh; Headworth had ignored her, his eyes continued to scan the book in front of him.

Oceana moved down the compartment, and was thoroughly interested by the lavish outfits the passengers wore on board. At that moment, the corner of her eyes caught her attention. She looked up and glanced through the window of the other compartment ata crowd of people. She opened the door to begin her investigation into what could cause so much commotion on such a boring train ride.

Upon entering the new compartment, which looked similar to her own, she moved along the crowd that began shouting and cheering in mixed patches of excitement and frustration. Her curiosity had taken the best of her, and she wanted to know what had brought so much excitement. The group blasted another cheer before Oceana, slithered her way between the bodies, so maybe she too could reach that level of capacity of entertainment. Her bright smile moved open when her eyes unfolded the scene in front of her.

Jamlson was holding a large card deck; he had a sly smile on his face; the man in front of him was drenched in sweat. He hesitantly put a card down in front of him, to which Jamlson grinned and put a card from his hand down on the table. He flipped it over to reveal the card to the other passenger. This had marked his victory, or at least what Oceana assumed to be, due to the other man's body reaction. He hit both his hands on his head and leaned back in shame or embarrassment, or perhaps in distress; Oceana could not tell. Jamlson leaned forward and grabbed the brown pouch in front of him. In his victory, Jamlson began to drink from the dark bottle that was placed in front of him that read 'Lemon Fuzz.'

"This is almost too easy." Jamlson stated, taking a casual sip from his drink, "Come on, anyone else want to challenge me?" He asked amongst the crowd. Oceana soon noticed- it looked as though Jamlsons jacket was stuffed with brown bags. It seemed like he was on a winning streak.

"Jamlson." Oceana coughed.

Jamlson laughed, but when his eyes met with Oceana's he frowned "Oh," He said before he coughed "What are you doing here?" He asked before he took another small sip from the drink in his hand.

"I was wondering the same thing, I thought you were writing a letter to your mother?"

"I was, but I saw some gentlemen were playing my favorite card game, and I wanted to join. Add onto the friendly wager, if you will." He grinned and moved his hand in the air momentarily. "Having fun isn't a crime, is it?" He asked.

Oceana puffed her cheeks and crossed her arms, "No!" "Then relax. It's not like going to Westside Mountains will take longer; if we are having fun." He said with a slight grin.

"If you are done talking to your girlfriend, I would like to challenge you." A large man announced, which made Jamlson lose his attention on Oceana, to face the man who wanted to prove his greatness to him.

"He is not my boyfriend!" Oceana said loudly. "Just to be clear." She looked around. It seemed no one was paying much attention to her. She crossed her arms in response.

"What are you betting?" Jamlson asked.

The man placed a large sack of gold down. The heaviness of this sack was more enormous than four of the small bags that Jamlson held in his jacket. Nevertheless, the man who looked almost as though he could carry the entirety of the compartment, grinned.

Jamlson moved his hands to his coat pocket, gripped on all the pouches of gold that he had carried, then placed them on the table in front of the man, and threw a grin back at him.

"Not so fast, pretty boy." The man stated with a hand up. "My bag is worth more than yours, this seems a bit unfair, doesn't it?"

Jamlson looked at him. The silence between them lasted not too long when Jamlson shrugged, "Suppose you are right." Jamlson moved forward and began to take his bow off of him, along with unbuckling the strap to his arrow, to place neatly on the table along with the bow. "The believers of the non-magics designed this weapon. They crafted this so people of any class can go another day with food in their stomachs. This design is almost a century old and is the first of its kind. You could say it's a rare collectible." Jamlson paused, then moved his hand in his pocket and placed a white wrap on the table, "Also this for the box, you can get sore hands quickly if you use it all the time. But still better than getting sore hands from using too much magic." He chimed. The man picked up the arrow, srcunizting the structure and design of it. Oceana had also started to pay closer attention to the bow, carrying around a golden paint with a silver coat while also not taking the attention away from the brown oak it was made of. She had never once seen Jamlson without the thing, she could not believe that he would place such a valuable item for a sack of coins.

"Jamlson, what are you doing?" She hissed, "You love that bow, don't be stupid, you'd really give it up over what? Money? Come On! Also, you need it for you and your mother!"

Jamlson ignored her protest and pulled out five cards from the deck, along with the man in front of him. Oceana had no idea how this game worked, she would remember that the other crew members along her travels would play this game together, but she had never gotten the chance to join them with her grandpa constantly reminding her of her training. She just knew that when the crowd cheered, something good was possibly happening. She listened around the crowd she was in, it seemed as though Jamlson and the man were not the only participants who were betting on the results of the game. Oceana shook her head; the culture of this made it hard for her to wrap her head around the idea of these men placing bets on such an insignificant game.

They moved their heads up to watch Jamlson sit in silence, his eyes on his cards. He placed two cards down and picked three up in exchange. The man did the same thing. When the time felt like it was running a long marathon, the finish line didn't seem too far ahead when the man and Jamlson were down to their last card.

Oceana bit her nails nervously, she looked over at the man who seemed confident in his play. He took his card and placed it on the desk before him, this revealed a powerful card. At least what Oceana assumed to be, due to the moment the card's face was announced, the entirety of the crowd screamed with excitement, ultimately being displeasing to her eardrums. Jamslson chuckled, which silenced the crowd. He carefully flipped his card over, which must have been another good card, to Oceana's guess. The man's face dropped, and waves of silence passed over the crowd, before another loud cheer washed over them.

Jamlson leaned forward and took his arrow and bow back, clipping them on his satchel, reuniting them to the place where they belong. He moved and grabbed the giant pile of money, he hugged it tightly with a grin. "Sorry, chief, better luck next time." He stood up, lifting the heavy pile of money along with him. The man did not give Jamlson the congrats back to him.

"Are you done now?" Oceana asked, waiting for Jamlson to stand up with all his new money.

"Yeah, yeah. I can keep you company now." He laughed, gripping tightly on the bag of coins, moving with Oceana to go back to their temporary home of comfort.

They weren't in their compartment for a full minute until the presence of someone stopped them from moving to their table.

"Hey." The man who was the nominated loser of the card game said. "I want my money back."

"Hey," Jamlson repeated after him, "you can't be a sore loser." Jamlson said with a sly smirk, "If you want it back, maybe we can try another game sometime." "Yeah, I don't play with card shufflers." He said, crossing his arms. Two more large men appeared behind them, both of them held a face of anger.

"Jamlson, what is he talking about?" Oceana whispered to him.

"Card shuffler? I don't card shuffle." Jamlson crossed his arms.

"Don't play me kid, I know all the tricks in the book."

"I have no idea- ah!" Jamlson's sentence was cut off quickly when the man moved forward, sending his arm to launch to the back of Jamlson. He gripped his jacket from behind was able to lift his jacket in the air along with Jamlson. The stapes to his bow had stopped the jacket from ultimately coming off of him. Despite this barrier, the man was able to complete what he had fully intended to do, which was to expose him. Cards began to fall on the floor, creating a small pile around Jamlson. The man looked angry, and in reply Jamlson handed him a grin and gave a shrug.

"Oh what- those? How, how did those get there?" Jamlson knew he was not convincing. The reply Jamlson received was him being put down by the much larger man. He cracked his fingers, playing a boney melody that could entail violence. Whispers throughout the entire compartment filled the room, peering eyes from the other passengers specktaded, wondering what would happen next.

Oceana got in front of Jamlson, holding her fists out, with narrowed eyes. "If you want to get him, you will have to get through me. I must warn you. I am a Magician in training! So this fight won't be fair for you!" It seemed that just for a moment that there would be a fight, she had her fingers hovering over next to each other. She was fully prepared to attack them, hoping that the magic in this situation would trigger. But, in that same minute, she was interrupted by the woman who had played the previous movies.

"Attention, everyone!" She coughed. "We were just radioed by the five am train that there had been a breach in the train tracks." Once she spoke, everyone began whispering to one another, Oceana was confused about what she had meant.

"What breach?" Someone from the audience questioned

"Well um," She pulled her shirt collar, "There was an explosion and it was unfortunately made by Vibrius people." she said. Immediately everyone started shouting their own questions, demanding instant answers from the woman. She tried to talk, but no one listened to her. Everyone carried on their questions and shouted, filling the compartment with loud noise.

"Enough!" A man who had entered the compartment had shouted. Silence immediately rushed over everyone, awaiting what the man had to say. Much like the woman, he was also wearing the colors of the Cor'Meum flags. He was in a similarly styled uniform as her. He looked around, waiting to see if anyone would have the courage to try to speak when it was his turn to deliver the current news. "Yes there was an explosion, which means all trains heading west are no longer in service for the time being. Our next and final stop is at Ferndale, if Ferndale was not your original destination, you could go to the post box outside the station and see if they will give you a refund." He silently stared at everyone, "That is all." He said before he moved on to the next compartment, to probably give the same recorded speech.

When the door had closed behind him, no one hesitated to begin complaining loudly to the conductor there; Oceana had looked around and noticed that the men were distracted briefly, she grabbed Jamlson's arm and pulled him into the crowd.

"Hey, my earnings," Jamlson complained, making their way farther from them.

"Oh, they aren't really yours." Oceana hissed at him. They had finally made their way to their seats, the place where they should have never migrated away from.

"I can't believe we have to stop because of an explosion. I mean, why did they do that?" Oceana questioned, "We are always so nice to them, even though they lost a war that they may, I remind, started!" She huffed. "Now they are going around blowing things up? Crazy!"

"I see where they are coming from." Jamlson said, "I know that they have also attempted many times to peacefully plead to Cor'Meum over the terms and conditions we provide for them. But, unfortunately, they haven't been the happiest in the past forty years." He sighed. "I guess they feel like they are out of options. Makes sense. We really aren't the nicest to them."

"Yeah, we are! We have KEEPIN soldiers all over their country, helping them keep the peace! We are nothing but charitable to them!" Oceana said, Jamlson only rolled his eyes in response. It seemed that he did not want to carry on the debate, he leaned over his seat and waved his hand for a brief moment,

"Can we get another glass of lemon fuzz? Thanks." He said before looking back at Oceana, who rolled her eyes in response. She decided that if she wanted to make it through the rest of the train ride, she would follow Headworths lead by sitting in silence. Oceana lived with KEEPIN soldiers, and never had she heard any of them mention any sort of unfairness, Jamlson must have been reading unapproved books from the castle. The same books Oceana always vocally disapproved of whenever she would see Jamlson read them. The three of them had all mutually decided not to speak a word to one another until the train reached its destination.

CHAPTER 7:

Child of a Hero

W HEN the train had rolled to a complete stop, Oceana could not have been happier to finally escape the dreadful ride. Though her departure from the train was much faster than it had originally intended it to be, it was nice to be separated from it. Leaving the train and smelling the air had never felt more refreshing. Finally, she was out in the open. She closed her eyes and decided to take one long breath in, which she immediately started bursting out into a coughing fit afterward.

"Yeah I wouldn't breathe the air here too much," Jamlson commented. Oceana opened her eyes and looked around at her surroundings, Ferndale was littered with buildings, though much smaller and less colorful than what East Magna looked like. The town, unlike East Magna, had fully embraced the idea of machinery. When Oceana stepped forward away from the crowd in the train station, from where she stood she saw a birds-eye view of the whole metropolis. She pressed her face on the glass window of the train station to get a better view of the place. She could never recall when the train tracks had left the ground, but she could see where they had rested from above the ground above the building. In the distance, she found a giant robot, or at least half a robot's body on top of a building waving at the people from below.

"Woah," Oceana said.

"Ferndale is the first of its kind. Experts say that ten years from now more than half of Cor'Meum's towns will be as innovative as Ferndale." Headworth commented next to Oceana. Oceana kept her face on the glass and watched mechanicals moving levers in circles, making confetti pop out from above a building. This evoked a lot of the pedestrians to clap in amusement.

"Where's Jamlson?" Oceana asked,

"Getting a refund on our tickets."

"Great! It looks like it's getting late! We should probably find a place to tuck in." She said, looking back out the window. "Do you think Ferndale has any places where we can sleep?"

"With the capacity of around ten million people that visit every year to get a glimpse of what could possibly be a new formatted design that many towns will adopt? Yes." Headworth said.

"Then we should probably find a place before it gets full." Oceana smiled at him.

"Hm, yes, that would be ideal."

When it seemed like the two would be trapped at the station forever, Jamlson returned, saving both Headworth and Oceana from the long-lasting dullness of doing nothing but stand. He moved up to the two and held out his hand full of coins giving Oceana her money back.

"I suppose we could always hitchhike our way to the next town over." Jamlson said, looking out the window, viewing the incredible amount of cars that made their way down the street. Oceana looked out the window and grabbed both Jamlson and Headworths sleeves to get their attention. "Guys, look! A parade!" She shouted The shout brought upon the most displeasure to the two's eardrums. "We have to check it out!" She insisted. Both Jamlson and Headworth looked at each other and exchanged looks, knowing that there was no way to get out of this situation.

"Sure, why not," Jamlson said with a shrug. Oceana grinned, clapped her hands, and headed towards the exit, leaving the train station and hours of stale flatness behind her.

After exiting the tunnel, Oceana was presented with long, wide stairs that headed down; from where she stood, she was now getting a better glimpse at the parade happening below. The streets were filled with auto vehicles. Some parts of the road were covered in small aircraft. They all hovered close to the ground.

People were marching with the vehicles on the street, giving the audience the joy of loud music. While some marched along the streets, others danced, and very few sang, all of these people had something in common: they were all wearing the colors of the Cor'Meum flag. This came to be obvious; it was a celebration for Cor'Meum as Oceana watched some of the participants wave the Cor'Meum flag proudly in the air. Not only were there Cor'Meum Flags, but KEEPIN flags also made their debut, a flag that also employed an eye that looked like it would be covered in diamonds. Oceana decided she wanted a better look and headed down the stairs, hearing the two boys behind her catching up with her.

"Celebrating Cor'Meum's finest! KEEPIN! Celebrating the fortieth anniversary of the ending of the Calamitous War!" A man who stood on the roof of one of the vehicles had shouted. "Keeping everlasting extravagant peace in the Nation!" The crowd clapped and shouted with excitement in response. The music that played was that of the Cor'Meum anthem, an upbeat song expressing joy for Cor'Meum. The air had a smell of a mix of popcorn and caramel. Children blew bubbles from the sidelines feeling pride in their bit of contribution.

Oceana began to clap along to the music. She watched Headworth keep a bored expression on his face while he joined in on the clapping. Jamlson, however, had kept his arms crossed. Oceana looked at him and nudged him with her elbow, to which he rolled his eyes and began clapping, his beat significantly slower from those around him.

"Now tell me folks, who's the best country in the world?" A man who wielded the power of the megaphone shouted.

"Cor'Meum!" The crowd shouted in unison. Before going back to clapping and cheering for the parade floats, and the balloons that danced in the air for the adventitious celebration of Cor'Meum's victory. Oceana looked over behind one of the cars as a row of Blue division KEEPIN soldiers marched in unison down the busy street. They all waved and smiled at the pack of people, who threw flowers in their direction. A variety of balloons colored in different patterns marched with the citizens; their attendance outmatched the people. Some balloons took on the shape of people. One even looked like King Erebus; at least that is what Oceana assumed. It was a balloon of a man with a crown, who had shoulder-length blonde hair and that twirled mustache he was known to have. She also assumed the other two balloons of the people were the rest of the living Roseario's; his children Aster and Crocus. While the parade was staged to be a celebration for all the KEEPIN soldiers; Oceana had only spotted blue ones throughout its entirety. Red division soldiers were always so scarce, while Purple division soldiers remained around the castle or were spotted if they were investigating high-end crimes. The blue soldiers continued to smile and wave at the people, reassuring them that they would be safe in their care.

Shortly after the wave of first ranked Blue division soldiers walked by, behind them followed a section of fourth-ranked Blue division officers, the crowd in unison stopped clapping when they passed by and gave them a quick Cor'Meum salute. Oceana followed the crowd, placed her right fist on her heart, and placed her left hand on her forehead, only using her index and middle fingers. She watched Headworth, who gave a salute, and Jamlson, who kept his arms crossed; Oceana decided that she wouldn't argue with him about it. Once they were out of sight, Oceana and the rest of the crowd went back to their clapping.

"Hey, the sun is starting to set. We should find a place to stay," Jamlson said to Oceana. Oceana looked over at Jamlson. Though her heart desired to be in the company of this celebration for a while longer, he was right. They should find a place to stay before rooms start getting booked. She gave one last glimpse at the parade before she moved away from it with Jamlson, who grabbed Headworth's arm and made their way away from the place.

"Headworth what did you think of the parade?" Oceana asked him. To which he tapped his finger on his chin to think about it.

"Hm, I would say that it exceeded the normal standards of parades. But could have used its resources to create a more collaborative experience." Oceana smiled and raised an eyebrow,

"Yeah?" She questioned. "I thought it was great. I will not even ask you, Jamlson, how it was because you'll only roll your eyes at my question." She crossed her arms. Jamlson looked at her and rolled his eyes, and continued walking. Oceana pointed at him and screamed, "Ha! Called it!"

The three of them were far enough from the ongoing parade where the sound that came from it became nothing more but just blurred-out noise. Headworth had read about Ferndale once just not too long ago, which allowed him to locate a good hotel along with a good price for their visitation.

When they entered the hotel, a man stood by the counter, waiting for visitors to check themselves into the hotel. The hotel lobby was large. Filled with people either sitting by the bar or lounge room engaging in peaceful conversations. Sometimes the hotel had visitors running down the hall not paying too much attention to the items that leaked from their suitcases. The hotel certainly kept a high number of people.

Oceana looked up at the ceiling, and was faced off with a golden chandelier. However this chandelier was built to look identical to the castle that King Erebus lived in. Even though Oceana was little when she had lived in the castle, she could never forget the strange and unusual details the appearance of the castel carried.

Oceana moved her eyes around and there were portraits of King Erebus and his children, Crocus and Aster. She wondered how many hotels in the country had original paintings of the family. It surely had to cost more than the golden floor she stood on.

Jamlson decided he would be the one that would walk up to him. He tapped on the bell and looked at the man behind the counter.

"One room for three." Jamlson said.

"Yes, of course." The man said and began writing down something on a piece of paper. "How many nights would you be staying?"

"Just one," Jamlson said.

"Right." The man said and looked up at Jamlson. "That would be," The naming of the price was never known because at that moment, when his eyes fell on Oceana's, his words were gone. Oceana looked around before she handed him a small wave. The man looked at her in complete silence. Fortunately he did break that silence by moving around the counter, marching right up to her.

"Are you Marlyn's kid?" He asked her. Oceana nodded in response, triggering the man to jump up with joy. "Marlyn was my hero! What a lucky kid to have such a cool parent!" The man said, then snapped his fingers, "You don't mind if I get a photo?" He asked.

"Oh no, not at all!" Oceana waved her hand, managing to keep her smile on her face. "Go ahead." She said, The man made a break for the door that was behind the counter and pulled out a camera that was attached to a stand. He traveled around the counter with the heavy thing in his arms making his way back to Oceana with the fattest smile.

"Stand right there!" He pointed to a random place in the hallway, one where the travelers wouldn't ram into them. Oceana moved in the direction to where his finger had pointed. He prompted the camera on the floor, pulled out the sheet, and got underneath it. "Alright, Sanford, I want you to give me your best smile." Oceana looked over at Jamlson and Headworth, who were only staring in silence. Oceana looked back at the camera and gave a thumbs up smile. The camera flashed, and Oceana began to blink, rubbing her eyes from the sudden burst of light. The man got out from under the sheet, moved to Oceana, and shook her hand. "Wow, it's been such a pleasure to meet you." He said. "You can have room five on the house. For all the services that your family has done." He said, handing her the key.

"Oh! Are you sure? I really don't deserve it. I can honestly pay for it." Oceana said, feeling her face blush a bit.

"Your mother is a legend, just like the Magician and Knight." He said. "If I could do anything to repay the work she has done, this would be it." He said.

"Well, uh, thank you," Oceana said awkwardly, taking the key from his hand. After her exchange with the man she walked back to Headworth and Jamlson who had been waiting patiently for her return. While they made their way up the escalators that moved them to the floor where they needed to go, Oceana moved her hand behind her head, "I honestly didn't expect to get recognized for being my mother's child." she said.

"Yeah! Because there are so many people in this world with bright white hair." Jamlson said. He reached over to her and flicked the ends of her hair.

"Okay, okay." Oceana waved her hand in front of him.

After inserting the key to the room, granting the door to open, Oceana's jaw dropped, this happened along with Headworth's and Jamlson's too. The room was wide and had three beds, a large window that accessed a very nice view of Ferndale, and it had portraits of KEEPIN soldiers all over it.

"Oh hey, look! A talk box!" Oceana pointed at and moved up to it. She turned the dial and flipped a switch. After she had done this, the large box began to play upbeat music from a variety of instruments harmonizing into a rhythmic beat. She moved around the room and began to follow the music direction of appropriate body gestures. Oceana gave a twirl and a skip, not really amusing anyone but herself.

"How did we acquire this place for free?" Headworth asked, looking around the room.

"Oh, my mom is Marlyn Sanford!" Oceana said though it felt almost strange to say those words

in that order. It had been so long since she had last seen her mother yet heard about her almost all the time. Almost ten years. The connection she had with her mother was similar to the characters she read in her books during her travels.

"Who?" Headworth asked.

"What?" Jamlson said, moving his eyes away from the KEEPIN portrait, losing the glaring contest he had picked up with it. "You are telling me you have all these things memorized; maps and facts and such, but you don't know who Marlyn Sanford is?" Jamlson questioned.

"I don't necessarily pay attention to celebrities." Headworth pushed his glasses up, "I am far too busy for that."

"Marlyn Sanford- or rather my mom." Oceana corrected it. "She was a national celebrity. She was really skilled at sword fighting- so she was a national treasure- She caught a lot of bad guys, and she was known for having white hair like me. King Erebus was the one that promoted her to a fourth ranked Purple division officer after she worked for his father up until he died- in nineteen-o-seven- I believe?" Oceana said.

"Fourth-ranked is incredibly impressive, especially with the Purple division. One and a million get to achieve that," Headworth said. "I see now why the man has granted you a free room."

"Yeah, but I already got my fair share of free stuff. Mom and I lived in the King's castle for a year!" Oceana flopped on one of the beds, tired of dancing alone while claiming the bed to be hers. "This was all before she decided to quit, and after that, we went back to the house, and that's when-" She stopped in her tracks, yeah, the last night she had seen her mom was when they had left the castle after her self termination. Her mother was frantic that day. She couldn't remember why. It was almost like she was constantly looking over her shoulder. She immediately sat up from the bed and stretched. "Wow, it's getting late isn't it?" She said, "The sun has already set and everything!" She pointed. "I think we should call this one a night!"

"If we want to catch the official taxi services, which opens at ten. I would best suggest that to be, well, a good call." Headworth commented, already diving into the world of mattresses. "Right, well, goodnight," Jamlson said before he made home with his own bed.

"Goodnight," Oceana whispered before she closed her eyes and went to sleep.

The sun decided that it was time to shine once again. Much like most people, the sun had a hard time working its way to wake up. For now the ball rested on the mountains above, not giving the world the blue that they had come to recognize but a shower of gold that would only remain for a few moments. Oceana stared at the sunrise through the window, watching how along with the sky, the clouds that remained dangling near the sun carried the tranquility of light that shared the golden present; what would be their fluffy white state much like the sky that they lived on was a honey color. Oceana moved her hand in her pocket, before long, she had held the letter in front of her once again. It felt that now was the perfect time to read the contained information inside, with nothing to disturb her from consuming it.

She looked behind her; she watched the boys linger in the world of dreams. Finally, Oceana moved her attention back to the letter. She began to rip the envelope, setting the following pieces of paper-free. She held the letter in her hands; she moved it to her chest and closed her eyes for a moment, knowing she was about to read something that she was not meant to acquire. Oceana moved the message back in front of her, permitting her eyes to read along the lines.

'Dear Wilic; I have completed the task you needed, or at least partially. I was able to locate them. They are real. I really hope by the time you have received this it isn't too late. I am afraid to mail this to you. Scared unwanted eyes will read this. You were right though they are real, after many years I believed them to only be a fabel. They are real and they are hiding in the shadows, The Legend of Icarus, it's real... Wilic I must also ask if you know anything about the whispering going on? There are people who suggest that Sage Magnus truly isn't dead. I know you are in close contact with the Knight and the Magician. Please confirm this to be false. I fear that Cor'Meum's golden days are coming to an end.

- Mr. Williams

Oceana put the letter down, her heart beating, her mind going thousands of places at once. What was going on? Why was the world so blurry? Why did she feel less powerful? Was this true? Was this real? She felt so weak she gripped the note in her hand. Was Sage Magnus back? What were the whispers? Also, what is real? The legend of Icarus? What was Mr. Williams talking about? She needed to find out this information quickly. She needed more answers. She felt herself move, she got up on her feet and looked over at the sleeping boys that rested in front of her, "Men!" she yelled "Men! Wake up!" she shouted again, to Jamlsons and Headworth who did not appear so happy being woken up the way they did. "You know when my father wakes me up, he always presents me with fresh pancakes with a smile and good morning," He reached for his glasses. "Not 'men wake up'."

Jamlson looked over at Oceana. "What's going on?" He asked.

"Jamlson, this is bad. We have to find Bellus soon! Or like now! Like now, now." She ran her fingers through her hair. She had felt her stomach turn when she reflected back on the words that were engraved in the envelope. "I- can't believe that-"

"Oceana, you need to tell me what is going on." Jamlson said calmly, "You need to breathe."

"Jamlson, I just read Mr.Williams' letter to my grandpa." She began to move in circles. "Sorry I went through your dad's stuff, Headworth." She said to him, to which he only responded with a shrug. "Mr. Williams said something about something not being real, well being real." She said, "He also said something about hearing rumors, and I mean I personally would never listen to rumors. I actually don't know where these rumors came from-"

"Oceana focus." Jamlson said.

"Right, well the rumors said that, well," She paused and looked at the two. "Well, that Sage Magnus is back!" They almost burst.

"Sage Magnus, as in the guy that's been dead for around forty years?" Headworth questioned. "Ok." Jamlson looked over at Headworth and raised his eyebrow before he looked at Oceana.

"As much as I hate to agree with Headworth, but, yeah? Sage Magnus has been dead for quite a while. So what makes you think he is alive?"

"I don't know if it just makes sense to me, sort of," Oceana said. She moved to the window and looked outside of it. Were she and Mr. Williams being paranoid? Or was this Sage Magnus' new comeback? The rise of violence amongst the Vibrius people has been high lately, was this due to Sage Magnus? Also, what was the part about them being real? She couldn't understand any of that letter. She could feel her mind spinning rapidly in circles. She revisited each word that her eyes had laid upon that letter, what she had originally thought about the letter answering questions that she had, only to lead her to more.

"Hey." She turned around to see Jamlson concerned. "Look, I don't know what this letter means also, but I know it doesn't help to ponder over heavy things with an empty stomach. Let's go out and revisit the letter later." "I second that!" Headworth chipped in. Oceana looked at Jamlson and sighed. Right, perhaps she was a bit on edge. There wasn't solid evidence that this was happening. Maybe she was being a bit paranoid, a thing that could be fixed with a stomach full of food.

"You're right. Let's get food. This place is pretty big. I am sure that there is some good food around here somewhere." She noted.

"Yeah, let's do it," Jamlson said. Oceana nodded, moved forward, picked her jacket up from her bed, and threw it on herself. She turned around and looked at the guys standing in front of her, smiled, turned around before she opened the door to head off back into the town of Ferndale.

In the town of Ferndale, now under the light of the sunrise. It was easy to see why people had commented on what made this town so different. Oceana had always believed that her home East Magna had already joined the innovative bandwagon, but it seemed that Ferndale was already way ahead of them on that note. She found tall and bulky machines lined up in front of shops sweeping the ground with the broom they held everywhere she had turned. One of these big bulky machines tried to move forward, but the cord on its back did not extend to the length that it wanted to reach to sweep, causing this machinery to fall over on its front. All the lights had turned off before it had hit the ground. A man ran out from the shop and began panicking while the other machine continued to do its sweeping. Oceana looked up at the sky and found children riding sweeper bikes; the wings on the children's bikes allowed them to move in the air. Oceana tapped on Headworth and pointed at the children who were now down the street flying in these bikes, "Reminds me of your dad's inventions in his office." Oceana said with a smile in response, Headworth raised an eyebrow.

"My father's inventions? Those are my inventions." He said.

"What? You know how to make flying little stuff?" Oceana questioned.

"Um, does a croak frog sing at a five loop interval?" He asked, pushing his glasses up.

"Uh?"

"Yes." Headworth sighed. "It's actually quite easy when you know how each of the wiring works. Especially when you can figure out how to hand build your own motor. So it doesn't weigh over six pounds, increasing the flexibility of the take-off range."

"Oh, so did you also build those tiny robots that we saw in your dad's library?"

"Designed them from scratch."

"Incredible!" Oceana said, "You're brilliant!"

"Yep." Headworth responded. Oceana continued to admire the way Ferndale was structured secretly, it was incredible. At some point, the three of them had to use a crosswalk. Due to how many vehicles there were, it was impossible to cross the street without the crosswalk. Otherwise one would become a pancake in the middle of the walk. These cars were ridiculously fast, and it seemed that everyone just seemed that they had somewhere to be constantly.

The food options were extraordinary; there were so many options to choose from, all of them looked too good not to pass up. Each building seemed incredibly rich and clean, similar to the one before it. They all had great food deals for something that looked to belong in a five-star restaurant. It was also quite the adventure for Oceana to walk up and down stairs to look at restaurants to see where they had wanted to designate their official eating spot. Oceana had also noticed the higher the restaurant rested, the fancier it was. This also applied to the fashion strips that were around. While walking along the balcony of the third level of Ferndale, the three of them passed a couple that wore outfits similar to Headworths, clean-cut and very modern.

"Is that a sea pirate? Don't they know that kind belongs in that gross little dinnery below the first floor."

"Hey Pirate! Bovarks Basement is that way!" The man shouted, which made the woman only laugh in response. Jamlson looked at Oceana, and got in front of her.

"Hey, ignore them. Let's check out some more places. I think I am settled for that one." Jamlson pointed at one of the bright, flashy restaurants. Oceana looked at him and gave a smile.

"Actually, I don't want to ignore them. I wanna see what this ground thing is!"

CHAPTER 8:

Bovark's Basement

I T almost took an hour of their time. But they had found the grounded diner that the couple had talked about. In front of them was a small building that looked to be run down. The building had stairs that led down to the place's front door. This building was an introvert, it wanted no participation in the culture the other buildings had surrounded itself in. There was nothing fancy about the building. There were no light shows or demonstrations of anything that could indicate anything new. There was only one sign posted at the front that said 'Bovark's Basement.' Oceana looked around too. They were also in a part of town that didn't attract many pedestrians, which honestly made this place very unique.

"Let's go!" Oceana said.

"I have questions about where you choose to digest your food," Headworth said.

"What do you mean Headworth?" Oceana hummed.

"Oceana, this place is a dump!" Jamlson pointed out. Once he had done so, the only sign that the place possessed had a chain break. This made the sign fall flat on the ground. Jamlson looked at Oceana and motioned his arms to the building once again. As an attempt to convince her to turn away from any potentially good qualities this building might possess.

"Come on, guys, I am sure it isn't bad! Gotta keep your minds open!" Oceana was the first to run to the stairs of the building, eager to find what was inside this diner.

Once inside, the dreadful stench of alcohol and sweat hit her face. Oceana wrinkled her nose in response. The room was full of people chatting, playing games, and overall it appeared they were having a good time. Oceana never thought so many people would be at a bar so early in the morning. One would believe that there was some celebration happening. She moved down the bar and sat on a stool. Her eyes scanned the room; this place almost felt like a dream or a memory.

"So, is this where we are really eating?" Headworth asked, leaning forward to talk to Oceana, while Jamlson still remained on the bar stool that stood between the two.

"Yeah!"

"I suppose living for fourteen years was good while it lasted," Headworth muttered. Oceana ignored him and continued to look around the area, something about this really stuck out to her, but she could not recall where.

"You recognize this place?" Jamlson asked, taking note of Oceana's gaze.

Oceana nodded. "Yeah, something about this, it seems familiar. I have a feeling that I have been here before." She looked around the bar area. The top of the bar held up flags, each representing a tone of magic. One high tone, which was a green shadow of a dragon. The design appeared to be framed on stained glass. Another design was a teal color of a fishtail. This must-have represented to be middle tone magic. The last one, much like the others, was designed as if it were stained glass. The design had black wings; this was low-tone magic. Oceana could not recall when she found the magic tones of the flag being waved so proudly in a public place, especially in a city like this in Cor'Meum. They probably wouldn't have believed that they were still in Cor'Meum if it weren't for the people in the bar wearing their "KEEPIN" pins. Though aside from the flags, the business did not put extra effort into decoration.

"If we are eating here, I am putting my bag down." Headworth let go of his large bag. It hit the floor with a heavy thud.

"What can I get you?" A man behind the counter asked. Oceana lifted the menu, which was a bit dirty. There was a warning label on the side of the menu, disclaiming any responsibility if one were to get sick from the food. Oceana went through each item on the menu, trying to figure out which one had seemed like it was the best for her.

"Three breakfast specials, please," Oceana said.

"Yes- and while you're at it, make sure she pays for not just the bill but my hospital one as well." Headworth waved.

The man nodded formally, then made his way back into the backroom. What was this place? Why are they so pro-magic in such a technological place like Ferndale? Perhaps that was the business strategy, to be very different. Well, she liked it, and this place seemed busy enough to remain open, so other people must had liked it too. She never knew that others like her enjoyed the arts of magic more than the revelation of technology. She wondered how many people were training here to become a Magician. Maybe some of these people are Magicians hiding here because society has claimed magic to be a terrible waste of time. Whispers had cut her off from her active thinking. She moved her head up and saw their previous waiter talking to a skinny old man dressed in traditional Magician attire. Despite it being currently scrunched up in anger, his face had an intimate place in her head. After a small debate about whether it would be a good idea to introduce herself to the man based on her gut feeling, she was determined to take that course of action. She jumped off the stool, placing her feet rightfully on the ground.

"Oceana, what are you doing?" Jamlson asked but was only ignored by her.

"I am sorry," The waiter said. "It won't happen again.'" He moved his face to look at the ground, clearly embarrassed for what he had done.

"Do you realize how expensive these plates are?" The old man held half of an abused plate.

"Yes, I promise it won't happen again. You can take it out of my paycheck!" The waiter pleaded, not wanting to lose the job that he had.

"It's not just how expensive they are. I also have to get ready to go to the market, then actually go there and find the plates that are just like these. It is a complete waste of an afternoon." He jumped, "Then I have to talk to that same owner, who doesn't know how to end a conversation." He groomed his chin. "It just gets awkward."

"Sorry, sir, it won't happen again."

"You bet it won't!" The old man explained.

Oceana had managed to creep into the conversation about the pediments of awkward social interactions at essential places. "Excuse me," They said without thinking,

The old man raised his eyebrow. "Yes?" He questioned.

Oceana now realized she had not thought through what she had planned on telling the man. What? 'Hello, I had a feeling I have seen you before.' Ridiculous. She had to say something, though, she interrupted their conversation, and she could not stand there in this dry silence forever.

"Wait." The old man had said, "I know you."

Oceana had not realized that she was holding her breath in when she had let her breath out and felt her lungs rejoice in the celebration of the follow of oxygen again.

"I remember you! You are Marlyn's kid! How tall you have grown! You are about the same height as my great-nephew, Abner!"

"Yes, sir, I am-" Oceana said nervously.

"You don't have to call me that! I am Bovark Barkinvie, but you could call me Bo." He smiled before he gave a wink.

Oceana shot him back a smile, "Oceana Sanford." she stated. "But you already knew that." She threw in.

"If you are wondering when we met, I believe it was the week your grandfather took you in. So you were about umm."

"Eight," Oceana said.

"That young? It was before you two had set off with your grandpa's crew. He came here with you." Knowing why this place had seemed so familiar, she racked her brain for the memories, a glimpse waved by, but it was not anything she could necessarily hold onto. Nevertheless, the contents of this place had reconciled with her as a place of memories.

"I have been waiting for you for a long time, Oceana Sanford." Bovark stated.

"You have?" Oceana asked,

Bovark nodded, "Come with me. I have something that belongs to you." He began to make his way to the door that led beyond the bounds of the bar area.

Jamlson, at that moment, caught up with the two. "Oceana, where are you going?"

"I am going to follow Bovark. I'll be back!"

"What?" Jamlson raised an eyebrow and looked over at Bovark

"Your friend can come too," Bovark said, passingly opening the door.

Oceana and Jamlson looked at each other before moving along to follow Bovark beyond the door. They both moved into the kitchen. They all traveled towards the end of the kitchen to stand in front of a strange-looking door. Once he opened the door, Oceana only saw stairs that led down to a dark abyss. Bovark took his first steps to begin walking down, instructing that Jamlson and Oceana should follow his lead.

Oceana moved forward and pressed her hands against the rocky wall that the stairs comfortably rested next to. Which helped guide her journey down. It seemed that Bovark had no problem moving down the stairs with the guide of the rocks. It was scary and impressive to Oceana. Before the door shut behind the three of them, she was happy to see that she was not the only one struggling to move down the stairs. She watched Jamlson clutch onto the rock wall, almost as if his life depended on it.

"Oceana, you are aware of magic culture, yes?" Bovark asked simply

"Yes! There are three types of magic! High, middle, and low."

"And?"

"High magic connects with fire and air. Middle magic connects with water and earth. Low magic is light and darkness."

"And?"

Oceana racked her brain. She tried to explore what more she could say. She paused, then snapped her fingers together. But, of course, she was missing the last step. "And you can only choose one!" she stated proudly.

"And?" Bovark replied once again, obviously not impressed with her last answer. Oceana couldn't think of what more he wanted. She had no clue what he could possibly want to know more of. What was she missing? What would satisfy his answer?

"What about you? Jamlson, is it?"

Jamlson coughed, "I don't know, and I don't mean to disrespect." Then, Jamlson paused, "I just don't see how magic is useful, well..... anymore."

"I believe you are blind-sighted to what magic actually is Jamlson. Let me shed some light."

Bovark snapped his fingers, creating a spark, followed by a small cloud of dark smoke that spun around momentarily before a small ball of white light appeared. Bovark had both his hands out, protecting the spinning smoke. Oceana felt the breeze run through her hair as Bovark held the magic. He moved his hands up in the air and the clouds of smoke dissolved into the white light. The light then expanded into the room, giving each light bulb a hug before the bulb lit up.

Oceana was now able to see the stairs in front of her, and she was two steps away from reaching the floor. She moved down and walked into the small open room. It was surrounded by ground, which ate up the walls and floor beneath them. It only had one item in the whole room: a tall wardrobe. "Tell me Jamlson. What do you know about magic?"

"It's a thing people used to use all the time? Mostly used for agriculture purposes I guess." He shrugged.

"Hmm. I suppose that's not a bad response." Bovark took a breath in "Well," He moved over to the middle of the room, "What you two don't know about magic, is that it is interconnective. Each one relies on the other for guidance. magic is a tool utilized to bring peace and allyship amongst people. Each tone of magic is used to bring people together to survive on the natural resources we are given. High magic needs middle magic to bring life to the crops. Low magic darkness needs high magic fire for hunting."

Oceana watched Bovark stand in the middle of the room. "We each have to find the balance in ourselves, Darkness can be blinding. But too much light" He snapped his fingers again, the small sphere that Oceana could hold in one hand if she could. The light was also covered with the dark clouds once more. Bovark opened his hand under the magic smoke. This made the room suddenly very bright. Oceana and Jamlson both closed their eyes right away. "Can also be blinding." He closed his hand. This made it easy to see the room once again. . "Do not fall for what you don't see." He said. "That's something to always remember about low tone magic. It's an important lesson to understand when performing this magic, but all tones have their own little lessons in them though- it's good to have them memorized, especially if that's the magic you strive to go after."

Oceana felt her eyes creeping up with a burning feeling. She rubbed her eyes right away, trying to make the uncomfortable sensation disappear. She looked over at Bovark.

"Right, I do believe Grandpa did teach me this. Each element of magic connects to another. This is how our ancestors survived."

"We must become friends with our magic and understand them to work with them."

"We can only choose one, though." Jamlson jumped in. "Because you are using low tone magic or whatever, you could never use the other tones."

"That is where you are wrong." Bovark hummed, "We do not choose magic; magic chooses us." Oceana was impressed, but she could see Jamlson roll his own from the corner of her eye. "Understand that magic is what brings out what our true characters are." He said, "magic is a reflection of our values, what drives us as people. A man who does not want to see the world beyond himself could never perform low magic, for low magic only brings out the light to our dark thoughts and sheds truth into our light." Bovark made his way to the wardrobe. Jamlson gave Oceana a concerning eyebrow raise.

"What does that exactly mean?" Jamlson asked.

"It means." Bovark hummed, "magic is us, and we are magic." He paused, "To put it simply, high tone users are guided by their emotions. In most or not all situations, high-tone seekers will let their emotions take over. While middle tone users are guided by their, how do you put it? Gut feeling? Perhaps instinct? Low-tone users are guided by what is more logical, regardless of emotions or instincts. We low tone users thrive for the most accurate results." He stopped. "That is what I mean when I say magic reflects our character."

"I want to learn as much as I can about this! I have been trying so hard, but I just can't do it! Is there a possibility I am magicless?" Oceana asked. "Or maybe I am trying the wrong set of magic?"

Bovark shook his head. "There is no such thing as a magicless person. We all have magic inside of us." Oceana opened her coat and looked inside of it, there inside the pocket was her grandfather's handbook to magic.

"Not my grandpa." She moved to close her jacket. "He's magicless. What if I'm not talented? I just inherited no magic from my grandpa! Did my mom even do magic? I don't think she ever had!" They shook their head "I really am trying to learn! That's all I wanna do! What if I am magicless like them?"

"Oceana," Bovark coughed, "if you allow yourself time, you will be able to utilize magic." He said, "You can't force magic out of you."

"But I don't have time, though!" Oceana began to pace. "My grandpa is missing! I need to know magic! Like you said before, magic protects you from nature! I have nothing but these!" She held out her fists. "I need protecting, now!"

Bovark turned around. He stopped his action from opening the wardrobe. "Oceana, you must learn to be patient with magic. Do not force it out of you. I see you and see that you have a great ability inside you, but if you do not become patient with magic then magic will not be patient with you." He turned around. "Oceana, I have something to protect you from whatever may come your way. But you must be careful with this. I know one of the many things Wilic had taught you was to utilize the art of swordsmanship. A skill developed by the people who had no intentions of using magic. An honorable skill to learn in Cor'Meum." He opened the wardrobe, and there rested a sword covered in a silver coat, with writing that filed the scabbard. The scabbard was colored in rings that each represented a tone of magic in order.

"That sword! I have seen it before!" Oceana snapped.

"This sword was used by your mother. It is engraved with all three animals on the blade in order, the dragon for high magic. The fairy for middle tone magic. Then the mermaids for low-tone magic. This sword was created to bring harmony between magic users and non magic users. Now it is your turn to use the sword to guide you on your own journey." Bovark handed Oceana the sword. She took it carefully and clipped the scabbard to her belt.

"I won't let you down." Oceana promoted confidently. She then looked down; her lip had tucked in. She breathed in through her nose sharply. She looked up at Bovark, who seemed confused by her sudden behavior change. "There is something you should know. I stumbled upon a letter, and well." This was hard for her to say. She did not want Bovark to think that somehow she conveyed this conspiracy to be true in her head. She knew it sounded berzerk, but if Bovark does not obtain this information, what if something happens? Or maybe does he already know? She had to reveal the truth. "The letter said Sage Magnus was back or rather that there is a chance of him being alive." She blustered.

Bovark looked shocked and stood there in silence for a moment. It seemed he had no idea what to say or how to respond. Oceana felt her stomach turn; the silence was too long. Maybe she should not have said anything.

She looked over at Jamlson, who was still silent too. Jamlson looked away from her in response, which to Oceana's guess, he had no intentions of interjecting. He was still embarrassed from being called out earlier by Borak.

"Oceana." Bovark finally said. "Sage Magnus is dead. There is no question about it. So don't believe those rumors." Oceana felt her cheeks burn; perhaps he was right, and she was being paranoid.

"Alright.." There's no such thing as people coming back from the dead. That just didn't happen. She had to be overthinking. She knew she had to be, so she shook her head and waved her hand. "Right, I am silly." Oceana laughed, "I guess I just got really paranoid over this letter that was intended for my grandpa. I think the man who wrote it is a bit on the nutty side." She smiled. "I mean there was even this weird part of the letter that said, that the Legend of Icarus is real?" She threw in another laugh, "I mean what is that?" Bovark's facial expression changed into something that leaned to a more anxious look, he took a deep breath, it seemed that his next choice of words weighed heavily onto him.

"Oceana." He expressed firmly. "You must know that, the Legend of Icarus, well." he paused. "It is real."

"Um, what is the Legend of Icarus?" Jamlson interrupted. Bovark looked at Jamlson and Oceana, and he turned around. He started to rub his hands together, and a deep sigh filled the room.

"The legend of Icarus is a story about a man, who lived hundreds of years ago, sick of the way magical creatures were treating humans, he decided that he would trick the-"

"Animal creatures into teaching him magic." Oceana interjected what Bovark was going to finish. "My grandpa would tell me this story all the time when I was a kid." She threw in the last part in a quick sentence. She felt terrible for interrupting him. "But that's just a children's story."

"Every story is based on truth. However, there's one thing different about the children's story from the Legend of Icarus." Bovark turned to look at the two. "There was one more tone of magic." Bovark said.

"What?" Oceana stated, "There's only three. It's always been that way."

"Yes, there are three that humans can use. But there is a fourth one. Destiny and Karma. This was magic that was only owned by the unicorns. In the Legend of Icarus, because the unicorns had not taught him magic he murdered all of them. Something the children's tale had left out. Because of the actions of Icarus, humans and magical creatures will no longer be allies."

"Wait-wait!" Oceana moved her hands around. "Are you saying that magical creatures were real? Yet you said my theory about Sage Magnus being alive is fake?"

"Yeah." Jamlson intervened, "magical creatures are made up to help kids fall asleep. They aren't real."

"Don't you ever grow tired of being closed-minded Jamlson?" Bovark said, in which Jamlson just crossed his arms.

"There is another thing that might make your theory make sense. There is this golden apple, The golden apple it is-" Though in that instant, the door from upstairs slammed open before he could continue.

"Bo! There are intruders!" Oceana looked over at him. He instantly guided himself back to the top of the stairs to investigate the statement. When uncovering the scene in front of him, along with Oceana and Jamlson, the bar was full of five men in all black suits with black gas masks. The eyes of the masks were bright green.

"We aren't asking for much! We just want Bovark!" One of them shouted at the crowd. He held his gun up in the air. Everyone in the crowd gasped and held their hands up; no one was brave enough to fight these masked men. Despite it being a bar open to people of all magical usage, Oceana could not tell how many people actually practiced the art of magic, or if they knew how to use it in combat. Though it was highly discouraged to use magic for violence in the true magic community, how many people actually listened to that statement? One of the masked men approached a tall skinny guy, gripped him by his hair, and pulled the man close to himself. The masked individual pointed the gun he possessed at the head of the man, who began to sweat bullets. He tried to struggle against the masked man's grip, but the masked individual was stronger. Finally, the masked man moved his thumb to the top of the gun, clicking it back.

"With every second we don't see him....well, let's just say the more we wait, the more lives we will take!" The masked man said, moving the gun from the man's head to the bottom of his chin. They walked around the room, hoping to find him hiding in the crowd somewhere. Everyone stood in silence as the masked strangers appeared serious about their tactics. No one wanted to step in. "Fine, I will count to three-" He shouted, "One!" The man who was held hostage screamed. "Two!" Nothing, there still wasn't a sign of Bovark anywhere. The man sighed and moved the gun to the side of the man's head again. "The blood is on your hands Bovark!" he screamed, "Thre-"

"He's right here!" Bovark yelled, catching the men's attention immediately. Oceana watched Bovark turn himself in to the masked men from behind the door with Jamlson. The masked man dropped his hostage, who immediately crawled away from him. Jamlson and Oceana watched him gradually approach Bovark.

All five masked people turned their attention to him, immediately raising their guns. A chuckle came from one of the men in the suit gang. He moved up, separating himself from his group of identically dressed allies.

"Incredible. When The Boss said to catch Bovark I hadn't expected him to be a frail old man." He moved closer to him and pointed the gun at his head. "Comeon now let's make this easy." Bovark snapped his finger, a white sphere appeared in front of him. He pointed at the white ring and moved his finger in a circular motion behind it. The dark cloud reacted to this movement. The cloud expanded and surrounded the man's eyes. His attention was no longer directed at Bovark but at the sudden lack of vision in his eyes.s. He moved one of his hands under his mask while the other hand kept a firm grasp on the weapon he wanted to use against Bovark previously.

Oceana stepped forward in front of Bovark, who already had a barrel pointed at him from another person in the group. They moved their sword up. The sound of the blade being released from the scabbard let Oceana know that the sword was just recently sharpened. Before the masked man could consider moving his gun to shoot at the girl, he ended up using it to defend her attacks towards her.

Jamlson moved backward and kept his eyes on the one who was blinded temporarily, he was still tending to his aching eyes. Jamlson kept an eye on the long gun that he held out, too distracted with his pain to notice anything. He slung back his arrow, directed it at the weapon itself. He fired his shot, which hit the gun's neck. This took it away from the man's grip to become a new wall decoration along with the arrow.

Oceana fought the man in front of her. He swung his gun, using it as a weapon for direct combat. His swings were sloppy and had no real direction in how he moved the gun in front of him. This is what made Oceana confident in her victory. Her first real battle against someone, and they stood on two very different skills. This was a guaranteed win.

She took another swing, moving her hands high yet using arms to defend her exposed body. The man only used his gun again to defend himself from her attack. While he kept an eye on her sword attacks, she moved her leg up and kicked him in the torso which threw him on the floor. Then, she pointed her sword at him, threatening him not to move from where he had laid.

When Oceana looked up, only two other people had joined the fight and were swinging fists at the other men in the gas masks, the ones without a gun. Perhaps they were going to take down these masked individuals after all; after they take them down, she could call KEEPIN to have them arrested. She was just happy that it wasn't just her, Jamlson, and Bovark. Others wanted to take down these untrained thugs. It would be a victory that she and the rest of the barmen would share. The two men fighting the masked individuals landed incredible punches on them. It was impressive.

Perhaps these two masked men should have also come to the fight with some sort of weapon. Instead of letting themselves be exposed to the fists of the men that occupied the area. Another swing! Oceana could feel herself almost jump, happy for the civilians who stepped in.

The men in the gas masks looked at one another after the next punch was thrown. They both nodded and then snapped their fingers. Under their hands was a ball of blue light, surrounded by a green smoke. They both took their pointer finger and began moving it in a circular motion in front of the green smoke. The smoke began to spin, twitching, as sparks of green electricity escaped its hold. The men looked at one another and dropped their own green smoke on the ground, the blue sphere inside disappeared.

Within that second the green smoke moved up into the air, as the smoke expanded up, it hardened behind it. Anything left of the smoke turned into rock, which had taken the form of a spike that was the size of Headworth. Shooting up from the floor and not wanting to become suddenly impaled by the spike, the attendees jumped out of the way, barely dodging the magic.

Wait- magic!

The force of the magic pushed Oceana and those who were also inspecting the fight off their feet. Tables and chairs flew up too in the process. Oceana felt her back hit the floor. They could feel the pain course through them. They moved up immediately, their eyes and head not fully comprehending what they had just witnessed. Oceana had never seen the use of middle tone magic so close before. So what were Cor'Meum citizens doing with magic? Wait, were these people Cor'Meum citizens? Almost every Cor'Meum citizen Oceana had known believed that magic was a waste, magic was cheap tricks and technology was just more efficient.

Oceana moved back on her feet, though not before she watched more of the bar's regulars try to utilize their teamwork to defend their beloved bar owner, only to be attacked by more spikes. Another one of the masked men snapped his fingers. This time an orange sphere appeared, surrounded by a red cloud. He expanded his hands and the ball twitched. The orange glow popped, making the red clouds disappear, however it came with a sudden wind

that knocked the remaining standing crew onto the floor. What was going on? Oceana looked around for Bovark! If these guys knew magic then Bovark had to get out of here! There was no way he could win this fight- two magic users against one? Bovark was going to be outmatched!

"Well, it is about time you are here!" A hiss came from out of nowhere. Oceana's thoughts were interrupted, and she looked around for the source of the noise. She could have sworn it was directed at her. "Down here." The hiss came again. Oceana moved under the table to find Headworth hiding.

"What are you doing there?" Oceana asked while she bent down to talk to the cowering Headworth.

"What does it look like? Trying not to get shot at."

"Why don't you move outside?"

"And get caught in the crossfire? Uh, I think I like my chances here." Then almost on the beat, a man flew between them, landing on the table smashing it in half. Headworth's screams blended in the background of Oceana's head when she looked over at Bovark, who had kept his eye on the man that fell on the table. She watched him move right away, getting ready to avoid another attack from the enemy. Oceana moved around the table, governing herself to Borak, to help him take on the next guy ready to attack. She may not know any magic right now, but she had to protect him- make sure that these people didn't get him! At that moment, she noticed something. This had also caught the attention of Borak too. The masked man put his gun down.

"Oceana!" Headworth yelled, "Cover your face!" He shouted.

The man lying on the table had stood up enough to see that he had a black square in his hand. What was it? The man dropped it. The moment that it touched the ground, green smoke sizzled up, polluting the area, eating the room of any clean air. Almost immediately, everyone burst into a coughing fit.

Oceana covered herself with her jacket, trying to muffle her breathing, hoping to catch any air that the green gas had not overthrown. Oceana felt an arm around her. The arm guided her towards the exit of the building, directing her to a place where the air was real.

When she could finally breathe again, she turned to see Jamlson, who also managed to find Headworth in the green mix. He was in a coughing fit on the other side of Jamlson.

"Where's Bovark?" Oceana asked almost immediately, looking around the area. The start of a vehicle caught her attention. She watched an unconscious Bovark be shoved into the backseat of the vehicle. She moved to run after them, but at that moment, they hit it. The automobile gave a loud screech before it sped forward, throwing a dirt cloud at Oceana before disappearing.

"Great," Jamlson said, catching up to Oceana.

Being shoved in the back of a moving vehicle was now on the list of Bovark's least favorite activities to be involved in. His hands were tied back in knots, so he couldn't move his fingers unless he decided to break them, which would obviously be pointless. The masked people pierced their own glances at him underneath their green goggles.

"Do you realize how messy you made my shop? How much money and time I am going to have to spend to make it look neat again?" He shouted.

"Shut up." One of the masked individuals said.

"What do you want?" Bovark snapped.

"You have information that The Boss wants." The masked man said, "Information about the Magnus family."

"What? Why would you want to know about that?" Bovark said. "They are all dead! There are no living members left of the Magnus family! It doesn't matter!" He said, keeping his eyes on all the masked men. He could feel their green goggles peering through his soul. They all knew Bovark was lying. He knew the truth, and now so do they. No, not all of them were dead. The family was very alive. He stopped speaking and looked away from all of them. How did they find out? Unless...

"Rumor has it," The man snapped Bovark into reality, "that after spending a decade with fairies, they start to tell you things. Things like an apple?"

"What- No! No one should be searching for that apple!" Bovark yelled. "You would be a fool if you took a bite out of it! It can-"

"We know what it does. That's why our boss wants it. But first, we want to know what you know about the Magnus family secret, or" The man pointed his gun at Bovark's stomach. "I will spill your guts for you."

CHAPTER 9:

Fovero

THE sun would fade away soon, much like it had done the day prior, and how it would do again tomorrow. Usually, Oceana would enjoy this time in the afternoon, but today she could not help but wrap her mind around what had just happened. She watched the people in the small town walk by the three of them, having the same conversation about this morning's events. Bovark wanted to say something to her. What was it? Was it him indicating to her that she was nuts for saying something so bewildering? Or maybe it was about her grandpa? How did her grandpa know this man? Why did her grandpa take her here when she was little? She had never heard her grandpa mention Bovark before, yet this man had her mother's most prized possession. She took a deep breath; what was going on? It just seemed like the closer she got to the truth, the crazier things got, and the less she understood.

"Well, it doesn't seem like there'll be any taxi rides for the next few days," Jamlson said, coming out of the building behind Oceana and Headworth. "We might be stuck here for a bit longer than planned."

"Hmm." Oceana responded.

"What's on your mind?" Jamlson asked.

"Bovark, he knew my grandpa. He also had my mother's sword. But why haven't I heard about this man? I didn't know who he was until today." She wished she understood.

"I can't tell you Oceana, but I am sure we will uncover the truth soon."

"How?" Headworth interrupted, "How are we finding the truth or finding anything? No taxis are coming! The train is closed! We are actually trapped here!"

"Are you kids looking for a ride?" A guy asked.

"Uh-" Headworth stated, but Oceana instead got in front of him before he could say anything negative.

"Yes, we are!" Oceana explained.

"Well, you are in luck!" The man said. "I happen to be heading to the next town over, Fovero. If you guys need a ride, I don't mind providing one," he stated.

"That would be so nice. Thank you so much!" Oceana said in a cheery tone of voice.

"Yeah, it's no problem. Y'all don't mind being carried in a horse-pulled carriage, right?"

Oceana looked over at the ride that the man stated was his own. The carriage was small and consisted of only a single horse that stood dully next to a small wooden wagon. Oceana watched Jamlson facepalm, a sound of disgust leaving his mouth.

The three kids sat on the edge of the back of the wagon. The sun was starting to set, returning to its comfortable bed between the mountains Headworth sat in the middle of Oceana and Jamlson. He was jotting down notes in a notebook that he had in his backpack,

"Since going to Fovero was always a plan of mine. It worked out well for me." He said, "There should be a hotel for us that is available, due to this town not being the most attractive to tourists." He said. "With its long history of crimes and usage of illegal gifts."

"Shouldn't be a problem if we don't go around poking our noses in the wrong places!" Oceana smiled.

"Oh right, because we never do that," Jamlson responded.

"Factually whether or not if we 'stick our noses in the wrong places' would not necessarily save us from being attacked due to the overwhelming amount of criminal habituation, it is a probability just walking to a store there is a thirty-five percent increase of getting mugged then your average city here in Cor'Meum than any other place."

Oceana and Jamlson fell silent after that. Headworth had not noticed the death of their conversation due to him being preoccupied with scribbling in his notebook. Oceana kept the thoughts to her mind. She had so many questions. Who was The Boss that those men were talking about? She wondered if they were really Vibrius citizens, with their abilities to do magic so well. She could not think of any Cor'Meum citizen that would dedicate so much time to magic like that. The people here were just not that into it, which was crazy. magic is so amazing. Oceana brushed her hair behind her ear and let out a sigh. This was confusing; she did not know if the letter was correct, was Sage Magnus was back?

The ride to Fovero ended when the generous man who provided them the ride halted the horse. He plopped off, made his way to the back, and tipped his hat with a smile.

"Here you go, kids."

"Thank you so much for the ride," Oceana handed him a few prelacies, which made the man smile. He had probably not expected her to pay him, especially so generously. He handed her a nod, made his way back to his cart, taking off into the night.

"Alright, let's find a place to stay for the night to find another way to move closer to the Westside Mountains," Oceana said, scanning her eyes around the city. Similar to the last town they were in, this town had not stretched itself far. It was small yet full of taller buildings whose lights ate up the night sky. A couple of the locals were scattered around the night, going forward in their evening strolls. Oceana pointed at a building that held a sign with the word 'Inn' on it, which stood brighter than its neighboring building that carried no burden of providing a visual for any visitors. She made her way to the building, with Jamlson and Headworth following her trail.

When she reached inside, she noticed how empty the place was compared to the number of people walking outside. This place must have trouble gearing in customers with the town's notorious reputation. Oceana watched a man sitting by a desk next to the stairs leading up to the next story. He had a big chat box in front of him; he rested there with a bored expression on his face while the box continued projecting its chatter.

"You are right, Ellvanora, It seems as though Pséftis has lost his touch!" The voice on the box yelled.

"Well," The other voice, which could be assumed to be Ellvanora, said, "It looks like with the movement of films getting more popular, many talkbox stars are gone out of business." But, then, Ellvanora said. "Anyway, this segment was sponsored by our military KEEPIN, Keeping Everlasting Extravagant Peace In the Nation!"

Oceana decided that it was now time to try to arrange a room, now that the talkbox was only informing the listeners about their latest ads, figuring she had not interrupted anything vitally important. So they moved up to the man in uniform, who listened to the thin grasp of entertainment he could receive that night.

"Hi!" She said with a smile.

The doorman looked up at her. He must not have registered that they were there. At that moment, he immediately sat up straight, moving his arm in a swift motion to turn off the talkbox that rested in front of him. He then stood up and gave a big smile; despite having only fear behind it. Oceana figured that he was most likely not allowed to listen to the talkbox on the job. The moment she set her eyes on it, he grabbed it and shoved it under the desk "Hello, valuable customer! How may I help you this evening?" He kept his smile.

"We would like one room!" Oceana said loudly. She paused, clapped her hands together, rubbing her thumbs swiftly, and smiled, "please." she concluded.

The doorman sat down on his chair and looked through the clipboard that rested in front of him. He wrote some quick notes, then put the board down. "The room will be thirty point fifteen prelacies." He said.

They handed him the cash. In return, she received a key; she flashed him one more grin before she made her way back to Jamlson and Headworth. But, of course, Jamlson and Headworth had nothing to say about the bumbling conversation that appeared in front of them. Despite how weird the exchange was, Oceana would have still done a better job than the two boys in front of her, who carried one normal set of social skills between them.

"Alright, according to this key, we are staying in room fourteen."

Once they all found room fourteen, located in the middle of the hallway to the entrance, they discovered why the hotel was not incredibly popular. There were only two beds, both small. Neither of them had been made up in anticipation of their arrival. One of the beds had food crumpled all over the sheets.

Headworth yawned and threw his bag down, making his way to the bed. "Oh boy, I sure am tired. Why don't we all sleep." Headworth said, looking at the two.

"We just got here. Shouldn't we settle down before we call lights out?" Jamlson asked, placing his arrows and bow somewhere safe in the corner of the room. "Also, wasn't there something you needed to do here?"

Oceana yawned. "Eh, relax Jamlson. I think it's a good idea to call lights out now. I mean, we all had a pretty long day." She flashed a tired smile.

Headworth had nodded along with what Oceana had said, "Yeah, sleep then eat." Headworth stated. Without a second thought about the state of the bed, Headworth crawled into it and threw the blankets over himself, "Goodnight."

Jamlson grabbed some blankets that had demonstrated their exis-tence by spreading themselves all over the floor. "Well, I will refill my gas next to my arrows," Jamlson said. Oceana raised her eyebrow. "Uh, a meta-phor I once heard," Jamlson explained.

"You aren't going to sleep in a bed?" Oceana asked.

"The beds are too small for both of us," He said, taking a quick look at Headworth, who seemed to be in his own dreamland. "You should get the other bed. You were the one who paid for this place." Jamlson began laying the blanket on the floor.

"Alright," Oceana said before she crawled into the empty bed, "Just don't breathe in too much. You just might inhale the dust." She smiled.

Jamlson chuckled, "I will try not to."

"Jamlson,"

"Yeah?"

Oceana paused, and before she continued to speak, she still had a sinking feeling about the events. "Do you think Sage Magnus is back?" Jamlson remained silent. It almost took him a while to respond; Oceana's stomach tightened with the prolonged silence.

"I don't know." He answered, "Honestly, but I say we shouldn't rush to conclusions. We don't have all the evidence. So for now, it's only a theory."

"Maybe you are right."

"Get some sleep, Oceana."

"Alright, Goodnight Jamlson."

"Goodnight."

Oceana pulled the blanket over themself before she closed her eyes. Her mind played back the events that happened today. The men in the masks, Bovark being taken, the magic. She wondered if this all had to do with Sage Magnus coming back from the dead, or rather not being genuinely dead. There were too many questions. It felt that none made sense. It hadn't taken her too long before her mind grew tired from the rapid thoughts; she eventually drifted off into the land of dreams.

Perhaps it had only been an hour, maybe it was less, but Oceana sat up from her bed. She couldn't sleep. Her mind kept thinking about Bovark and the people with the gas masks. What did they want? Why did they take him? How did her grandpa know Bovark?

Oceana moved the blankets off of her and crawled over to her jacket and opened the inside pocket, where she pulled out her grandfather's handbook to magic. She held onto it and moved to the small space in between the wall and the bed, where she decided to sit. Mostly because she left the light on, and sitting under it could help her see the pages better. She turned to open the book. Alright- she was going to try to learn magic from here, her grandfather's secret notes. Except, she stopped; there was a name in there that was foriegn to her, and next to that name was a sketch of some sort of bird. She couldn't tell what it was. But the name read ....

Sanford Ellington.

That was strange. Someone had the last name of both her and her grandfather. It hadn't taken her many pages to find that this was the original author. So this book on magic was a combined effort between her grandfather and this mysterious person? Perhaps her grandfather needed help learning magic. Her grandfather has told her there are many scholars who study magic without actively practicing it themselves. Was Sanford the person he was talking about? She wanted to know more about this Sanford guy and why he and her grandfather wrote this book.

All the chapters were highlighted in purple ink, and it was no surprise the opening of the book explained what magic was. However, the explanation was in more depth than any Cor'Meum approved book that Oceana had ever read on magic.

'Magic; it's broken down into two forms when born from the snap of a human. The smoke and the sphere. Much like how humans can only use one set of magic; High, middle, and low, when performing within the tone sets, human's can either choose to pull the magic from the sphere

or the 'smoke.'

Both the ball and smoke are materializing the components of the elements in the atmosphere the moment they are born. This perhaps makes magic more grounded in the elements of science, more than we think.

The orange ball for high tone magic is filled with air. The blue ball in the middle tone is filled with water. The white ball in low tone is filled with light. While the red smoke in high tone is fire. The green smoke in middle tone is filled with what will be the formation of rocks. The black smoke in low tone is filled with darkness.

It is not surprising that the initial intent for magic was for agricultural purposes.'

Oceana moved to the next few pages and landed on the chapter that had focused on hightone magic. Which was written in highlight as 'Dragon Magic,' She felt a strange shiver run down her spine. The book told her to take a deep breath, to feel the fire inside her, to allow air flow to run through her. Oceana closed her eyes. She took a breath in and then took one out. She felt herself relax and let the wind sway her. She moved her hand up to her face, and continued to take deep breaths. She then snapped her fingers. She opened her eyes- and- nothing.

Oceana decided to move onto the next few pages of the book. What other information had this book held? As she read the book, she reached the next chapter, which said "Unicorn's Curse." A Unicorn's curse? As in real unicorns? Bovark told her that they were real, a long time ago. Though weren't they all killed? What was this unicorn's curse? She should continue. However something stopped her, she heard shuffling. Oceana closed her book and held her breath.

After a long silence, she watched Headworth quickly leave the room, and shut the door behind him. Where was he going? It must have been important because when he left, he must have not realized that the door had slammed, which woke Jamlson up.

"Huh? What happened?" Jamlson said in a rush.

"Headworth just left." Oceana replied.

"What? Let's follow him!" Jamlson got up.

The two made their way into the night. The critters chimed in their tunes once again when the moon made an appearance in the sky. The atmosphere was quiet, for everyone had decided it was time to slumber away in the dark. She felt the gloom of the atmosphere make its way behind her neck, which reacted with a shiver. She pressed both her hands on each of her arms in hopes that would make a difference. Oceana could recall her nights on Ol'Sarah, when temperatures would reach this capacity of bleak. Sometimes even crispier. How she could never get used to it. Nights were spent shivering under the covers in the cabin of her room. The smooth rocking of the boat against the ocean was the only thing that cradled her to sleep.

The cold was slightly bothersome; already, she could feel her toes begin to numb inside her boots. Aside from the small rapid melody of the wind, a motor vehicle drove past the two of them, creating some of the street lights to flicker on, giving a better glimpse of their surroundings. Jamlson pointed,

"There," he pointed at the young freckled kid they had known. He grabbed Oceana and moved behind a building, preventing them from being seen by anyone who might pass by.

"Jamlson, what are you doing?" Oceana asked, yet cooperated with remaining hidden behind the structure.

Jamlson looked over at Headworth from behind the building. "I think he is up to something that isn't good." Jamlson said, "I don't trust him."

Oceana would have normally protested at Jamlson's lack of trust in people, but she could not find a reason to defend why Headworth was acting so strangely behind their backs. So instead, she moved next to Jamlson to spy on what Headworth was up to.

Headworth looked around his surroundings. Another vehicle passed; he remained still until that vehicle moved out of sight. Now that he believed to be completely alone, he moved to the door and knocked on it. He took a step back, waiting patiently for the door to open on command.

On beat when the door had welcomed itself to any outsiders, there was a woman on the other end; Oceana squinted, trying to get a better look at her, which was not an easy task with the woman's hood being up. When Headworth handed her the bag he carried, she snatched the item in one swift move. She opened the pouch on the top, took a peek inside, closed it then held her hand out. Headworth looked confused, which made the woman step back inside and slam the door.

Oceana looked over at Jamlson, who still kept his eyes on the scene that had just unfolded. Oceana still felt the creep of the night touch her, sending cold knives inside her skin. It had been hard to pay attention with the dark surrounding them with the unpleasant atmosphere.

Headworth knocked on the door once more, hoping Oceana guessed that the woman on the other end would open it. When no such response had been given to him, Headworth pressed both his hands on his arms and shivered. Then, he walked down the narrow stairs, which allowed him to separate himself from the property.

Oceana looked over at Jamlson and brushed her fingers against her chin, "Well, that was weird." she whispered, "Glad it is finally over." She said with a heavy sigh.

"I am going to confront him," Jamlson said.

"Wait, no, let's not do that!" Oceana insisted, "Nothing happened. We don't need to create trouble!" She whispered.

Jamlson ignored her protests and made his way in the direction Headworth was walking, blocking him from continuing his path. "What the- what was that?" Jamlson pointed to the house that rested a block away from them. He said this making his way toward the boy.

Oceana shook her head. The jig was up; there was no point hiding behind the building anymore. She moved down the route Jamlson had taken, paying attention to the unfolding scene before her.

"Did you follow me?" Headworth asked, "Why?"

"Why were you leaving in the middle of the night without telling us?" Jamlson asked. He stopped in his tracks, a foot away from where Headworth stood. He had his arms crossed and back straightened. Though he was much taller than the boy in front of him, he tried to appear taller.

"I told you." Headworth pushed his glasses up. "That as long as I help guide you two to Westside Mountains, it shouldn't concern you what I do."

"Yeah, that is not going to slide anymore," Jamlson said with a huff. "There is too much at stake to keep secrets here; Oceana's house was burnt down, we were attacked in broad daylight, whatever you are doing if it is putting our lives at risk," Jamlson pointed at Headworth. "Then we want nothing to do with it." He said, "We already have enough trouble to worry about as it is."

Oceana watched Jamlson intensely stare at Headworth. She could not recall a time Jamlson was this annoyed at someone aside from herself. It admittedly felt good to not be on the other side of his acrimony for once. While she did not believe that Headworth needed to be treated this way, it was suspicious that he was sneaking off in the night and meeting with strangers in mysterious locations.

Jamlson continued to stare at Headworth. The only thing that disturbed the silence was the noise of the critters that made jingles in the blanket of the night. Headworth was determined not to say anything. Finally, Oceana moved past Jamlson and walked up to Headworth. She looked down at him with a small sigh and then a slight smile.

"Headworth," She said, "I know you had this code to not tell us what is going on," she put her hand on his shoulder. "But you can trust us that we won't judge you for whatever you are doing." she paused and waited for him to look at her before continuing. When he had, she finished off the rest of her statement, "We just got to know so we can prepare for whatever it is to come." She smiled.

Headworth looked over at Jamlson, who kept his arms in place, then Oceana. He sighed, "Fine," he said in defeat, "Fine, I will tell you what I am hiding." Headworth ran his fingers through his hair and moved his eyes away from the two. He tapped his foot and looked down "I am," He clicked his tongue, "I am building a mechanical." He finally said.

Jamlson unfolded his arms and scrunched up his face. "What?" He said, "A mechanical?" He asked to clarify what Headworth had said.

"Yes, mechanical," Headworth repeated.

"So you are building those cool little spinny things I have seen lately!" Oceana snapped her fingers. "The ones that have this little box, you know, and you can use that box to control this, uhh, this mechanical thing!" She smiled. "That's incredible!"

Headworth facepalmed, then proceeded to rub his eyes underneath his glasses. "No," He said with a sigh, "No, not that." he looked at the two. "Those are called mechanical knocks. I am not subjecting myself to that low-class invention. Give a monkey a wrench, and he could even build something that easy!"

Jamlson and Oceana looked at him, carrying the same expression of confusion. Headworth put his hands up in defense.

"A joke." He wanted to clarify to the two of them.

"So, what is this mechanical you are building?" Jamlson asked, moving past Oceana to look at him.

"It's this project I had been working on for a while" Headworth pushed his glasses up. "But, uh, I haven't been doing this project by the book, one would say."

"What?" Oceana asked, "What do you mean by that?"

Headworth scratched the back of his head and looked away, "I have-uh" He said, tripping over his words for the first time, "This is why I wanted it to be a secret." He mumbled.

"Headworth, the longer you don't tell us what it is, the harder it'll be for you," Jamlson said sternly.

"I have been trading in library documents in order to send shipments to this specific location. I send the people information they would like access to, and they hold my mechanical for me." He said.

Jamlson looked at him "Headworth!" He said with a snap, "You can't just throw people's information like that!" Jamlson said with his eyes narrowed.

"Then what would you call this?" Headworth asked, narrowing his eyes back at Jamlson. "The only reason I am here with you two on this trip was that I gave you someone's personal information."

"That's different!" Jamlson said.

"How?"

"Well-"

"No, stop. He's right." Oceana said, "We did take someone's personal address without their permission. We have not been doing things by the books either." She sighed. "We can justify it all we want, but we are just the same as that woman with a hood," Oceana said, shaking her head.

Silence fell upon them once more. None of them knew what to say.

Headworth coughed slightly, "Oceana." he said below the whisper of a mouse, "I have a confession to make."

Oceana looked at him. "What is it?"

Headworth took another deep sigh in, "I am so sorry about your home. I had not considered the damage that this would cause to other people."

"What are you talking about?" Oceana asked though she had already known where this was heading.

"The last document I had sent to them was under the name Oceana Liesbeth Sanford."

Oceana had no idea how to react to this news. She could feel herself clenching onto her stomach. She felt her heart race at speeds that were faster than any motor vehicle around. Darkness crept its way to the corner of her vision. It was almost as if every feeling she felt about her home being destroyed came to her all at once. The world around her that she had once perceived fell into an abyss.

She had not realized how long she was silent or how hard she was clutching onto her stomach until she felt Jamlson press his hand onto her shoulder. This simple touch had managed to snap her back into the physical world she had known. Oceana looked over at Headworth, who still looked scared and guilty. It seemed he was ready for an extreme reaction, for Oceana would usually give, she had been reacting to everything placed in front of her by the guidance of her emotions, but instead, she took in a deep sigh.

"Okay." She said, "Thank you for your honesty." But, then, she felt that she had to throw the words up. Everything she had ever loved and hated about her home was gone. Nothing she could say or do to Headworth would undo what had been lost.

"Thank you," Headworth said, pausing before he looked away. "I know I am in no position to be asking for services, but there is a pressing matter we must confront."

Jamlson raised an eyebrow, "What?" he asked with a snap.

"I need your guys' help in getting my mechanical. They have it in there." He pointed back to the house.

"Are you kidding me?" Jamlson asked, "After what you told us, why would we help you?"

Oceana thought to weigh the options in front of her for a moment. Yes, it was true that what Headworth had done led to the destruction of her own home. Or perhaps it could be the reason. Still, whatever Headworth was building probably did not belong in their hands. This was a difficult choice, but she knew she had to do what was right.

"Okay." She said

"What, Oceana, you can not be serious. You understand what this thing has done to you ." Jamlson could very well be referring to the mechanical inside or Headworth.

"Yes, I know." Oceana sighed. "But do we really want, whatever it is," she moved her hand in circles, "with people who are clearly not right in the head." She pointed to the house,

Jamlson shook his head. "Could be dangerous."

"But we have to do it." Oceana stated, "Headworth, do you know where your mechanical is?" Headworth nodded, lifted his arm up, and pointed towards the bottom of the home, where it had a single window. "In the basement. When I received a letter about the update of my mechanical, they said they kept it safe there."

Oceana nodded. "Alright." She said, "Let's go." She moved towards the cottage home.

CHAPTER 10:

TOAD

THE three of them stood next to the house, underneath the still bright window, declaring the activity of others inside. They all sat near the bottom window of the home, which innocently rested next to the grass outside.

Jamlson stood up for a moment and took a peek inside the window that was above them. He moved back down and looked back at the other two. "There's only three people inside. Headworth, you sneak in with Oceana. Then grab your mechanical. I will stay here and keep guard and wait to help you two pull it here."

Oceana nodded, "Yeah, Sounds good." She placed her hand on the small window and wrapped her fingers around the hinges. She hoped that the window wouldn't be locked. When she found that she could lift the window up, she smiled. Oceana looked inside then began crawling into the basement of the home until she was stopped by the handles of her sword.

Jamlson facepalmed, "Oceana you-"

"Yeah, I know," She stopped attempting to crawl in the window, to move her hands to unbuckle the sword from her hip. "I won't need it. We are only retrieving the mechanical." She resumed making her way back in, feet first, this time without any distractions.

When she was inside the basement, her fingers held onto the outside, she looked down and found a bench she could fall on without creating too much noise. She dropped onto the small wooden plank. Then immediately stepped off of it, granting space for Headworth to sneak in along with her.

Headworth had a difficult time sneaking in the basement window. His argument was that he was smaller than Oceana, so her ability was impossible for him. This reason, in his argument, was only due to the height difference and nothing else.

She looked around the basement; it was hard to see anything in the dead of night. The only light that granted them the ability to distinguish one object from the other was the street light that came from outside, which hardly acknowledged the cellar.

Headworth moved forward and looked around the room, "It should be in here somewhere." He clicked his tongue and shuffled around the small space around them.

Oceana nodded and conducted her own little search herself. She walked around the dark margin. She did so at a slow pace, not wanting to step on anything that would indicate to the people upstairs that intruders were inside the home.

"What was this mechanical built for?" Oceana asked while searching the place.

"To hold your laundry."

In the small shaded basement, piles of boxes made the room smaller than it was. Upon boxes, there were more boxes. It seemed that there could be an endless number of boxes that would only last for eternity.

Oceana found a promising corner in a place where she could perhaps start going through the variety of mysterious crates displayed in the most unfashionable way in front of her. She decided to open one and what she found was a little toy mechanical soldier, he moved his arms up and down, his eyes glowed a bright yellow when he did so, after a minute he stopped and shut off.

"How would I know which is your mechanic?" Oceana asked after she placed the toy soldier back in the box.

"Trust me." Headworth said below a whisper, "When you see it, you will know." He continued his own search away from Oceana.

Oceana moved around the darkroom to find a cluttering mess that was scattered about. However, she did discover that not only were boxes a consistent theme of this weird underground basement, but the dust was too. After some coughs, she heard something thud shut.

"Found it!" Headworth said.

Oceana moved in the dark with her hands out, and moved at a pace that she believed would prevent her the most from tripping over and breaking an arm.

"Here." She heard Headworth once more.

She moved over to him and found that he was sitting in front of a long golden crate, each side had a handle made up of rope. The front of this box had a buckle that allowed anyone to open it from the outside. Only to trap anything that would be placed inside.

"Okay." Oceana said in a hushed voice, "Let's get out of here." She grabbed one of the rope handles, as Headworth held the other one. When they lifted the large crate, Oceana had not expected how heavy it would be. But she continued to move back towards the window from where they came.

When the two reached the window, Oceana stepped back on the wooden bench that was left there, bringing the box up in the process, with Headworth still holding on to the bottom part of it.

"Jamlson." Oceana whispered.

"Yeah?"

"I'm going to lift this box and move it to you."

"Sounds good."

Oceana kept one hand on the rope of the box and used her bottom hand to push the box up. She placed the box to the window; she felt its weight lift when she could feel Jamlson grab the rope part.

"Uh," Jamlson said.

"Yeah?" Oceana asked.

"It won't go through."

Oceana felt the box's heaviness once more, "What?"

Jamlson had let the handle go and replaced Oceana's vision of the outside with his own face. "I said, the box, it's too big."

Oceana looked over at the box that she was holding. She had a feeling that the box would not be able to fit through the window after she had her own struggles with it. "Frogs on a stick," Oceana whispered

"What is going on?" Headworth asked, his feet wobbling from the weight of the box.

"Uh, hold on," Oceana said with a hast breath. "What now, plan guy?" She asked.

Jamlson pressed his hand against his chin and gave a quick thought. He snapped his fingers and looked back at Oceana. "Okay, this is the only plan I have. I can distract the people, you two can go to the second story, and we could figure out a way we could bring you two and the mechanical down then. But find the stairs and don't get caught."

"Alright," She said. She paused. "Don't get hurt." This was more or less a demand rather than a tone of concern. Jamlson nodded, stood up, and made his way to the front door.

Oceana moved off the bench and turned to Headworth, who looked like he was going to collapse from exhaustion. "New plan." Oceana said, "We are heading upstairs."

Headworth had not protested the new idea Oceana explained to him. It seemed that he was willing to be on board with any ridiculous plan if it meant that he no longer had to carry the heavy box.

The two made their way towards the stairs, tucked far away in the corner of the room. Oceana moved her feet behind her, making her way up the stairs, her back facing the light that rested on the top.

Headworth moved the box along with her. He was able to control his grounding more than her, considering he was not the one walking backwards up the stairs. Despite his access to the stairs being more accessible than Oceana's, he kept heaving the box up every now and then, which Oceana assumed was his fingers were already tired of carrying the heavy thing.

Oceana looked over her shoulder and saw she was near the top. Oceana placed the box on the top of the stairs. A foot of wall covered the end of the stairs. Which granted both Oceana's and Headworth's fingers a break.

In the open room of the home, three grown adults were sitting at a table; two of the adults were men and the other a woman. The three of them were gathered by a talkbox who continued to speak about the latest announcements; despite how far in the night it was. It seemed that the twenty-four hour news on talk boxes gained popularity after last year when Pséftis pulled off a one-man show, which lasted twenty-four hours.

"In recent news!" The woman on the talkbox said, "KEEPIN! Is looking for new Blue division recruits! Do you have what it takes to be part of KEEPIN? KEEPIN! Keeping Everlasting Extravagant Peace in the Nation!"

"Shut up!" One of the men yelled. He threw his teacup at the talk box. "What do you know about Peace?" He said, adding a disgusted tone to his voice.

"Sir!" The woman hushed him. "Are you trying to expose us? Keep talking loudly like that, and we will have KEEPIN soldiers at our door! Now, is that what you want?" She moved to the now broken teacup picking up the broken shards scattered around the room.

"Sorry." The man responded. "It's been frustrating-" The man said. "How are we supposed to tell The Boss when we went to the address- that the brat sent us-" He paused. "Ugh."

"I know-" The woman said. "We still have the robot at least, that will help us."

"What's the use of the robot if we don't have the book?" The man growled. "We need that pirate's handbook." He hissed under his breath.

"There's a good chance it's out there somewhere- Sanford might have other copies."

"Pakimet." The other man interrupted. He looked as if he was older than the two combined. This triggered the woman, Pakimet, to look at him.

"Yeah?" She responded

"I heard that KEEPIN soldiers will be identifying people by badges soon. I overheard some guys in the Red division speak about it. Might even identify people to ride trains." He drank his cup and put down the book he had been reading. From where Oceana stood, it was a book that was not given a seal of approval by the castle.

"Why haven't you brought this up till now?" The younger man yelled, slamming his hands onto the table in anger.

"Slipped my mind." He said.

"Yeah, right, something like that slips your mind!" The other guy yelled at the older man.

"Shhh again!" Pakimet said, pressing her finger to her lips, "I some-times wonder if you are deliberately trying to get us caught." Pakimet, from

Oceana's perspective, looked stressed. Pakimet moved in circles, her boots clicking with each step she took. "Oh." She waved her hand. "We will find fraudulent identification badges tomorrow. It doesn't have to be perfect. It just has to work," she said casually. The two men looked at one another and gave each other a nod, seeming simple enough.

"When will The Boss pick up the mechanical equipment that we have?" the younger guy asked. "It's been months since we have been stationed here. Starting to feel as though The Boss forgot about us."

"The Boss did not forget about us." The woman hissed, "Or rather wouldn't forget about me." She mumbled, and placed her hand on her heart.

"So what's the plan, sub-boss?" The young man asked.

Pakimet clicked her tongue and thought for a moment. "I know an underground market that's not too far from here. We can get fake badges there."

"You aren't talking about the one underneath the abandoned oil factory, are you?" The old man spoke, taking another sip of his drink.

"Yeah, I am," Pakimet responded.

"That place is too dangerous. Many sketchy people roam there."

"What does that make us?" She snapped, "If those people are sketchy?"

The old man looked away and continued to drink the rest of the liquid inside his cup in silence. Clearly hee believed he could have worded that better.

"Cor'Meum is a country based on a lie," She hissed. "It's the people here who are sketchy. Celebrating a week-long holiday while the people of Vibrius are starving! Makes me sick!" She stopped and looked out the window, "We will expose this place for their real colors soon enough." Pakimet said sternly.

"I agree. Screw this place." The young man said. "Cor'Meum will be nothing in the next couple of days! Years of suffering will soon end. The future for us and anyone with Vibrius blood running through their veins will have a safe future!" He raised his glass up. "All thanks to our work! We are witnessing the waking of the dead! Lucky to us that we get to be involved in such an event!" He grinned at Pakimet. "To The Boss," he said, his words came out in a slitter. Pakimet looked at him and grabbed her own cup.

"To The Boss." She said with a straight face.

Oceana watched while the two adults drank what she could assume to be tea in celebration. What were these people talking about? The end of Cor'Meum? If her grandpa were here, he could merely arrest them for speaking such things. It would be his job being a fourth Red division officer. These people were evil, and it seemed that they had full intentions to use Headworth's mechanical against the country they stood on.

Oceana heard a clicking sound. They turned around and watched Headworth roam around inside the cargo.

"What are you doing?" She hissed at him,

"I want to check something out." He responded,

Apparently, Oceana was not the only one who had heard Headworth click open the box. The three people did too. Their conversation dropped immediately.

"You heard that too, right?" The young man said. He looked over at Pakimet, who gave him a confirming nod.

"Check it out, will you?" She asked him.

He gave a heavy sigh and pushed himself up in the process. He then made his way towards the wall that was behind the door. Before he made it to the wall, a knock from the door was heard. He stopped in his tracks to look over at the door.

"Who could that be?" He asked, "And at this time at night?"

"Open it." Pakimet insisted.

The young man went to the door. Another knock came, he grunted in response before turning the handle to reveal who it was.

Oceana peeked their head out to watch the scene that was about to unfold before them.

They watched Jamlson giving probably the biggest smile they had ever seen. To them, he already seemed nervous, but maybe that was because they knew him personally. They also noticed that Jamlson took off his bow and arrows, making him defenseless, probably not wanting to appear a threat.

"Hello!" Jamlson said with a wide grin, "My name is Sir, Pséftis!" He announced loudly.

The old man who remained in his seat gave a chuckle. "Like the celebrity?"

"Yes!" Jamlson responded. "I have exciting news!" It seemed like he was forcing himself to shout.

"We don't want to hear it." The young man said, who was about to slam the door in his face.

"Wait! But you do!" He yelled, waving his arms. "This is very exciting! Yes, yes, really exciting!"

Jamlson had now caught the attention of Pakimet, who looked at him before moving next to her friend, who still maintained his concentration on Jamlson. "This is an event you should participate in!"

The young guy crossed his arms, moved his eyebrow up, then gave his eyes a narrow. "Yeah?" He said, "Why?"

Jamlson then pulled out a flier from his pocket and held it up. The poster was obviously stolen from a nearby tree. "Let me explain to you modern music!" He smiled. "Why should you join this concert?"

Oceana watched Jamlson talk. He managed to catch the attention of the three people in the room to buy Headworth and her more time. Oceana looked over at Headworth, who seemed he was still rummaging around inside the box.

"Headworth." Oceana whispered. "What are you doing? We gotta move this thing."

"Just give me a minute," Headworth said, keeping his attention inside the box.

"I don't know if Jamlson has that much time. He can't speak forever." Oceana looked over at the door to see all their backs turned from the two still. "This is the only chance we got. Come on."

"Just a minute," Headworth repeated.

Oceana threw her hands on her face, she felt like screaming in them, but before she had, she removed her hands and looked over at Jamlson, who had still managed to buy them time. Next, she looked over at Headworth, still rummaging inside the box. "Are you done yet?" Oceana asked.

"I will be soon," Headworth replied.

She could feel her back tighten from his reply with its lack of motivation to stick to Jamlson's plan. She could not fault Headworth for being an agent of chaos, but there are times to play the wild card. She was impressed that Jamlson was talking to them. Still, he probably felt frustrated with their lack of moving too. Jamlson really could not speak forever, but Headworth was sure acting as though Jamlson had that capability.

"Come on Headworth." Oceana said, "We gotta lift the box." She insisted.

"Alright, fine." Headworth closed the box and grabbed the other handle along with Oceana, and pulled the box in the air; they were finally moving forward. Headed towards the second story, they could figure out a plan to get this down, and then she could go back to the hotel and curl up in a warm blanket. Something warm seemed to be the driving motivation for Oceana to get out of here. She had no plans of being awake at this passing of the night. Anyone who willingly stayed up this late would forever constitute a crazy person in her book.

The two had moved away from their hiding place on the floorboard of the stairs, lifting the heavy box, trying to remain the quietest they could be. With the room only filled with Jamlson's dialogue, it posed a challenge to mask the most minor creeks they encountered. But, they were doing it, they were following the plan, and they had now guided themselves to the base of the second set of stairs in the room.

"Ok!" The young man shouted, "This is ridiculous. Why am I bothering to even listen to this nonsense?" He called, "Thank you, sir," The young man spat. "But we want to go to bed now, Goodnight."

"Oh, but wait!" Jamlson shouted, but it was too late; the young man turned around and found Oceana and Headworth carrying the box by the second set of stairs.

"Oh what the-" The young man shouted. He moved his long coat back and pulled out a gun. He immediately pointed it at the two. "Drop the box."

When the gun was pointed at them, they both put their hands up, showing the man they were unarmed and posed no physical threat.

"That's Headworth." Pakimet whispered to the young man.

"Yeah, I know," He said, not keeping his eyes off the two, "The boy who sent us all that nice information from his daddy's day job." He grinned. "Thank you, kid, you saved us so much time these past months." He laughed, "Which means what I am about to do will make this hard." The sarcasm in his voice said otherwise.

"Wait." Pakimet put her hand up in front of the gun. "I recognize the kid." She looked up and down at Oceana "Oh-" She stopped and blinked a couple of times before she moved her face next to the young man's ear. Pakimet whispered something to him, but whatever she had whispered gave the young guy a jump.

"What? No!" He pulled away from her and looked at her, his face full of shock, "You are not saying?" He said, "They can't be-"

"Pay attention!" The old man spoke up before he fell into a fit of coughing.

When the two looked back at Oceana and Headworth the box was open, they had both ducked behind it.

"Oh you little-" Before he could even think about finishing the rest of his words, a loud smack echoed throughout the home. Immediately after the sound, the man paused before falling onto his knees and then onto the floor. When his body was removed from the scene, Jamlson held a broken tea cup from behind him. To Oceana's guess, he had taken it when it seemed that everyone's attention was on her and Headworth.

Pakimet turned around and watched Jamlson. She looked at him while he looked at her. They must have shared a brain at that moment, for they both ducked down and reached for the gun that was still in the knocked-out, younger man's hand.

Jamlson knew he wouldn't be able to duck for it faster than Pakimet would, which resulted in him kicking the gun, which slid over to the other side of the room. Jamlson moved like a light next to Oceana and Headworth. Pakimet made her way to the old man on the other side of the room.

"Enough games." The old man stood up for the first time on his wooden chair. He grabbed a gun that was locked on his own hip. He pointed it at the three of them, "Put the box back." He said with a stern tone of voice. "Then we can figure out what to do with you three."

All being unarmed again, the three of them kept their hands in the air. Headworth looked down at the box, then flashed a grin at Oceana.

"Oceana," He whispered to her.

"Whatever it is, Headworth, you need to wait until we are out of this mess." She spoke in one breath.

"Look." He said he moved his eyes down to look inside the box.

Oceana's eyes had followed Headworths, and she looked inside the box. It appeared it was glowing a variety of purple, green, and red. She could not tell what was happening to the mechanical that remained inside the box, but she could guarantee that the box had not been glowing before.

In one action, before anyone could process what was happening, the mechanical that used to remain motionless jumped out of the box, pointed one of its claws in the air, extended each of the hooks attached to it, and opened it.

It seemed everyone in the room had been penetrated with an arrow of silence. No one in the room could tell the others what they had seen. A mechanical, just as tall as a very tall person, was standing right in front of them.

Oceana saw that the mechanical had a see-through chest, where the gears inside moved. They were bronze much like the mechanical itself. There were three tubes on the mechanical lower back, each carrying some liquid inside. They were all bright colors of purple, green, and red. The color tubes differed from the mechanical's own color. The mechanical, Oceana had noticed,was carrying Headwoth's backpack. Some wires sticking out of the backpack remained attached to the mechanical. On top of the meachanical's square head,, which had a skinny neck connected to its square body and bendy limbs, had an antenna that bounced with its movements.

Pakimet was the one who had the courage to speak. Everyone remained shocked. She lifted her voice to break the silence that washed over the room. "Oceana! I know-"

At that moment, much like how Bovark was interrupted, the mechanical shot up tiny bullets in the air. They had not gone too far up due to the ceiling barrier preventing them from extending any higher.

This motion created a rumbling of the ceiling and decorated new cracks in the walls around them. White powder fell much like snow all over them. Loud noises of snapping and cracking filled the room before the weight of the broken ceiling decided that it was too weak to hold the floor above it, which gave out and piled itself all over the floor, creating a new wall made up of ceiling between the two parties.

Jamlson grabbed Oceana's and Headworth's hands and made it towards the open area where the wall had been destroyed, climbing between the cracks to separate them from the people inside. Oceana noticed how Headworth had held onto the wrist of the mechanical that created the damage.

Once they were all out of sight from the newly destroyed home, Oceana jumped back and pointed at the mechanical that had started it all and had followed them out on the field. "I can't believe you let that thing come with us after what it did!" Oceana said. "Are you trying to kill us?" She whispered under her breath.

"Relax TOAD is harmless." Jamlson scrunched his face up and looked at the mechanical. "TOAD?" He questioned.

"The Oculus Addition to the Division." Headworth recited smoothly.

"I am sorry, what?" Oceana asked, still feeling like her heart might explode if she stood next to that thing any longer than she had to.

"The Oculus Addition to the Division," Headworth repeated. "TOAD."

"Yeah we got it." Jamlson waved his hand. "I think she is more concerned about the damage this thing can create."

"This thing," Headworth hissed, "Like I said, is harmless. He shot up all the bullets that he had." Headworth shrugged. "I think."

"Remind me what that thing's original purpose is!" Oceana pointed.

"TOAD is harmless- " Headworth reiterated "the original purpose was to make the perfect toast."

Oceana could feel herself slightly less panicked. She couldn't tell whether it was due to her taking comfort that the thing in front of her had no more bullets or that she just might go into shock. There was no telling which one was going to come first. She looked around the mechanical, which remained still in its place. When Oceana moved around in a circle to better look at the mechanical, it moved its head in reaction. Oceana jumped back and screamed before she realized that the thing was not going to attack her.

"I promise TOAD is harmless." Headworth repeated, "He has the brain capacity of a five-year-old child."

"I am sorry, but you built this by yourself?" Jamlson asked while he moved to the nearby bush that held the prized possessions of his arrow and bows.

"Yeah."

"Can you remind me how old you are again," Jamlson asked, walking up to Headworth and getting a better view of TOAD.

"I am fourteen," Headworth said, pushing his glasses up.

"Wow," Jamlson replied. He seemed not as frightened by the mechanical to the extent that Oceana was.

"Yeah, TOAD is very fragile right now," Headworth said before pointing at his backpack that rested on TOAD. "That backpack carries all his information and is the sole reason he can move and such," he said. "You could call this backpack his heart. It will have to remain there till I can build him a proper grip to place it." So he said, walking around TOAD himself.

"Headworth, why?" Oceana asked, taking a step back away from TOAD. "Why did you build this?"

"Why do you do anything?" Headworth smiled. "For the sake of the future! Every household needs a TOAD! A robot whose sole purpose is to hold your grocery list while you shop!" Can you imagine?"

Both Jamlson and Oceana shook their heads, to which Headworth gave a gloomy look back at them with a small sigh.

"I mean," Jamlson said, focusing his attention on TOAD. "This mechanical is pretty cool."

"Uh yeah," Oceana said nervously. "I guess it is." Oceana hesitantly put her hand on TOAD, which made him look at her. She yelped and jumped back in response to his movements. From the moment he was introduced, TOAD gave her nothing but high anxiety. But much like what Headworth had stated, having the mentality of a five-year-old, he shouldn't be too much of a hazard. Oceana decided to try her best to be less horrified by TOAD.

The four of them made their way back to the hotel where they were supposed to sleep, all of them failing at this effortless task that had not required much skill. When Oceana opened the door to the dark hotel room, TOAD stepped in, his bright yellow eyes illuminating the dark. Oceana immediately went to her one true love, sleep. Once she successfully reached the bed she claimed, she rested her head on her pillow and instantly brought the covers up around her to wash away the cold of the night. When she began to feel her toes once more, and her body had forgotten how the darkness felt, she decided to close her eyes, counting backward from ten. That was when she passed out, only making it to eight.

CHAPTER 11:

KEEPIN

O CEANA woke up to the song of the happy birds that rested outside the hotel window. When she heard the familiar song, she almost expected to wake up in her room in the woods. But instead, it took her a handful of seconds to fully realize where she was and why she was there. The birds continued to chirp, and the dark hotel room brimmed with light that revealed the unseemly yellow wallpaper that hid in the shadows of the night. If only the night could come back to cover the space with darkness again.

Oceana looked around and noticed that Jamlson, Headworth, and TOAD were all gone. She wondered why that was. She moved out of bed despite the heaviness of her body and the want to go back to sleep, forced herself to grab her sword, which she clipped back on her belt, and her way to leave the ugly room.

They moved down the hallway towards the stairs to the bottom floor, back where they had checked in the previous night. There was no sight of her friends anywhere, though once she looked around the room, she was hit with the smell of freshly cooked food. This, to their guess, was probably where the boys were. Allowing their nose to guide them, they found themselves moving down the vast hall of the bottom floor. She moved to the left to find a dining room full of tables and chairs, with only two people and a mechanical, that occupied the space of the eating area.

She lifted her heavy feet to the table and sat next to Headworth, who was enjoying bread and eggs. Oceana could feel her own stomach growl at the beautiful dish that rested in front of Headworth, making fun of her for her lack of delicious breakfast foods. Yet, in that very same minute, something incredible had happened. One would call it a miracle; others may say a gift from heaven. Oceana had not noticed, but Jamlson had placed a plate of eggs and bread in front of her; it was unimaginable: this gift would be cherished forever or until she consumed it all. Oceana wasted no more time and began eating the delicious food placed in front of her, making her stomach very happy that there were no evil woodland creatures this time to steal her bread. She was at peace.

"What were you saying about TOAD?" Jamlson asked Headworth, picking up the conversation and the drink, which Oceana assumed was more lemon fuzz, thathe and Headworth were having before Oceana's awakening.

"TOAD, can playback sounds that he's heard!"

"So wait," Jamlson took a sip from his drink, trying to understand what Headworth was explaining to him. "He listens to sounds, then he keeps it?" Headworth nodded,

"Yeah, he can playback anything you want." He said.

"Incredible," Jamlson said while keeping his eyes on the mechanical.

"Yeah, this feature of his was made by accident, though." Headworth shrugged. "I figured out how to play back the sound while building him. I could have taken it out, but I thought it was pretty funny that a big mechanical like him had that. I kept it." Headworth began drinking from his water cup. "But since I have the papers on how I did that, I will use that playback idea on another mechanical device; I want TOAD to serve a different purpose than playbacks. I want to stick to his original purpose."

"Remind me, what was that?" Jamlson raised an eyebrow at Headworth, who flashed him a grin, which revealed more freckles that were hidden on his face.

"Why, of course, to clean!" Headworth jumped up. He had then clapped his hands together "TOAD." He said, attempting to make his voice sound more profound than it actually was, "Clean this mess." He waved his arm over the table.

TOAD sat up straight, got out of his own chair, and began picking up Headworths dishes. He made his way to pick up Jamlsons after. TOAD moved over and picked up Oceana's plate, which she had not entirely finished yet.

"Hey! Wait! I didn't get to eat my bread!" They shouted.

TOAD held the plates high in the air before he moved his arms forward and launched them against the wall, breaking them into tiny pieces.

"My bread!" Oceana cried.

"Hm." Headworth said, "Probably need to work on some rewiring later." He shrugged. He moved over to TOAD and patted his back. "Good job TOAD! You were almost at it! Maybe next time." He smiled.

Jamlson and Oceana looked at one another, and both raised an eyebrow at Headworth's human affection for the mechanical.

"How did you find time to build this thing?" Oceana asked in curiosity.

"Well, I suppose when you graduate from school a couple of years early, you try to occupy yourself with anything to keep you from being bored." He said. "Since I was around seven, I had always found a love for machinery." He pushed his glasses up.

"Do your parents support it?" Oceana asked.

"My father, yes," Headworth said. "My mother; well, I don't believe I will ever know." He said. Oceana felt her heart drop. She understood the absence of parents. She hadn't spoken to her mother in almost a decade, and her father? She had no idea who he was, whether he was even alive. Oceana always liked to pretend that her father was some farmer that no one had ever heard about, that he lived a quiet life somewhere in the woods. Though it is unclear what happened to Headworth's mother, Oceana did not want to pry him of any more personal information.

The warm breakfast peace had come to a halt when they heard a wave of shouts from outside the hotel. They all exchanged looks at one another. They each decided to explore what was going on. Each of them stood up from the table and left the dining room alone.

When they left the hotel, they could put a pin in where the loud noise had come from. A large group of people shouted angry profanities at the action placed in front of them. KEEPIN soldiers in uniforms of blue were escorting some of the citizens in handcuffs, bringing them to motor vehicles labeled, "KEEPIN property." While some soldiers moved people to the motor vehicle, a large group of these soldiers were scattered around the crowd, keeping others from moving into the scene.

"You can't just come here and arrest people without a cause!" A woman shouted.

"Cor'Meum is a lie!" One man said.

"Where are you taking my husband?" a woman cried in the crowd. "We are Cor'Meum citizens! You can't do this!"

"We demand answers!" Another person shouted.

The soldiers did not respond to the crying demands of the crowd. The crowd attempted to push their way to stop the arrests, but there were too many armed soldiers.

One of the soldiers who stood on one of the car's roofs held a megaphone and started to speak into it. "Attention, citizens of Fovero!" The man's voice pierced through the angry shouts of the people. "We are only here to arrest non-Cor'Meum citizens. If you are Cor'Meum blood, there is nothing to worry about. Go back home." He shouted into the speaker.

"Oh yeah, right!" Someone could be heard yelling into the crowd.

"King Erebus is the devil!" One woman cried.

"You aren't Keeping the Peace! You are all monsters!"

Oceana moved around in the crowd to better look at the arrests that were happening. She got on her toes and watched the scene unfold right in front of her eyes. She watched the Blue division soldiers treat the people in cuffs roughly, shoving them inside the vehicles. She was almost in utter shock when the busboy from last night was handcuffed by one of the Blue division soldiers. She watched him be practically thrown into the motor vehicle amongst the rest of the people that were being arrested. She found the two men from last night in cuffs by a Blue division soldier. She looked around to see if she could find the woman who was with them, but she couldn't.

Oceana watched another man in cuffs being escorted by KEEPIN soldiers, on his way to confinement, when he suddenly snapped his fingers, and then there was a glowing teal circle on the ground. It moved around in a circle and pushed up water. It was harmless; however, a KEEPIN officer was now drenched.

"Hey! He used magic! He can't do that!" One of the KEEPIN soldiers shouted as the rest of them surrounded him before he could use more magic against them. Then the man attempted to run for it, but the soldiers grabbed him, and the circle disappeared.

Oceana slipped away from the crowd and returned to Jamlson, Headworth, and TOAD. None had any desire to get a closer look at the arrest.

"Geez," Jamlson said, "Looks like they are serious about not wanting Vibrius citizens in certain parts of Cor'Meum." He said. He raised an eyebrow directed at the soldiers who were having a difficult time attempting to settle down the crowd.

"I don't understand why Vibrius people keep wanting to come here?" Oceana said, "They have a home in Vibrius, and we give them almost everything they need."

"You know, I thought you would understand how wrong that sounds since you travel all the time."

"What do you mean?"

"I mean don't you see this all the time? The violence that is placed on Vibrius people?" Jamlson asked with a raised eyebrow.

"Violence? No! We spread peace! When I was with my grandpa and his crew, we talked about magic! We talked about how powerful it is and yet wonderful!"

"Did you talk to them about magic directly, to someone who was a Vibrius citizen? Or just other KEEPIN officers?" Jamlson asked.

"I- I mean, our division never needed to interact with Vibrius people. We were there to deliver goods and educate the officers stationed there about magic. But KEEPIN officers aren't violent! They provide nothing but peace!" Oceana insisted. Now that she thought about it, she never interacted with anyone that wasn't a KEEPIN officer on those trips. Unless going to a market and talking to one of the employees to ask for directions. Or perhaps telling a waiter at a restaurant what she wanted; on the few occasions that she and her grandpa would go out to eat, she was usually surrounded by other Red division KEEPIN officers from different locations. Had she really ever left that boat? This was something she needed to think about; she was Oceana Sanford, the pirate that traveled around the world! Right? Why was it so hard for them to wrap their head around this?

"Then what do you call that?" Jamlson asked, looking back at the crowd, where the sounds of a man growling in pain were noted from a distance. Oceana looked through the cracks of the bodies that circulated around the scene, and her eyes did not believe what she was processing. Two KEEPIN officers were on top of the man who performed magic just not too long ago, giving him a continuous beating. KEEPIN officers were supposed to be good, not bad. So why were they hurting this man unprompted? She couldn't watch the beating anymore and looked away from the crowd. She felt her face squish up in disgust at the cruel actions that they were taking.

No, Cor'Meum soldiers were good, her mom was one once, and her grandpa is one. Her family aren't bad people! But what did she know? Was her mom a good person? She spent so much time seeing her from the same perspective as the rest of the world. What did her own mother mean to her? Now she had to come to think of it, did her mother represent the beautiful garden she had left for her when she was small? Or was she...; Oceana did not allow herself to finish such thinking. This was not how Cor'Meum citizens were supposed to think. They were supposed to love their military. She had to stop thinking such bad things.

Before another contradicting thought took form in her head, she was interrupted by a scrubby man who had just walked up to them. His presence made all of them fall silent. The man looked to be the same age as Oceana's grandpa. He had a white beard and a face that had more folds than one would ever want in their life. Or at least half the folds. The right of his face was covered in metal, his eye, seen through the metal plate, was blue. The man's right arm and leg were also metal. This must have been the reason he had a cane. He was wearing a three-star Blue division uniform, two stars higher than most soldiers there. He kept a frown on his face when his human eye was placed on her.

"Oceana Liesbeth Sanford." He said in a flat tone of voice. "When I was called to Fovero, due to how messy it was." He paused and took a breath before he tapped the ground a couple of times with his cane. "I should have figured that a pirate-like yourself was here."

"I am sorry, what?" Oceana almost yelled, "I did not cause any trouble!"

"Oh." He said, almost forcing a smile. "So you weren't involved with the collapsing of a house last night?" He asked.

Oceana opened her mouth, only to close it, falling silent.

"That is what I thought." He said.

Another Blue division KEEPIN soldier ran up behind the man and gave a salute before he began to speak to him. "Sir Hildith!" he shouted. "Fourth-ranked commander is on the phone! He wants your attention immediately." He said.

"Tell him I will be there soon." Hildith threw his human hand in the air, shooing the soldier away.

"Third-ranked still?" Oceana questioned, "Face it, you will never be fourth-ranked, like my grandpa and mom." She gave him a smile.

"Proud of your family? Full of people who just disappear." Hildith hissed, "Proud of a mother who failed her duty as Purple division officer, abandoning her country, for her to only fail as a mother, abandoning her only child." He grinned.

Oceana narrowed her eyes, she stepped forward, but she felt Jaml-son grab the back of her jacket, indicating that the fight was not worth it.

"At least you have your grandpa to be proud of- oh no." He said, his smile revealing his broken teeth. "You can't be proud of him after what he did- you know." Hildith groomed his bread.

"What?" Oceana raised an eyebrow. "What are you talking about?" She asked.

"You don't know?" Hildith asked, "Oh well, it would be a pleasure delivering this news to you."

"What news?" Oceana asked though she knew deep inside that whatever Hildith had planned on telling her, it would not be good news.

"Your grandpa, Wilic Ellington, is a traitor to Cor'Meum." He grinned.

At that very moment, Oceana could feel her whole world turn around. Something about the news could not sit properly with her. A traitor? To Cor'Meum? Their country? How? Her grandpa would never betray this country. No, that would not happen. But would it? These past few days, it had felt like everything she had known about her grandpa was some sort of lie. She could not tell what was real or fake with him anymore. Was that why he left her alone in the house? Because he had betrayed Cor'Meum, and now he was a wanted man on the run? No. Maybe? This was too much for her to handle. She needed to think about this later. She did not want Hildith to know that he had attacked her weak spot. She closed her eyes and looked up at the man who remained in place.

"I see." Oceana coughed.

"That is right." Hildith moved his mechanical arm to straighten his front collar, "My troops and I are currently looking for him. This has become the top priority for us to find him and take him alive."

"That would be ideal," Oceana said, containing her mixed emotions about the situation. Alive, well, at least they don't plan on killing him. This was a significant relief for herself.

"Since finding Wilic Ellington is on the top of our to-do list, you would not happen to have any bit of information you could provide to us to help our search for him. Or maybe." He grinned, "Do you happen to know where his Handbook may be?"

Oceana thought back on the letter, thought back on looking for Bellus Timidus, finding the connection between all of those. She also thought about the handbook which was currently sitting inside her coat pocket. Why did Hildith want the handbook? What was so important about it? It was just notes. Was it? She looked at the ground, weighed her options for a moment, and immediately realized what she needed to do. She looked up at Hildith and said, "No."

"No?" Hildith repeated.

"Yeah. No. No information I could provide about my grandpa's whereabouts." she gave a shrug.

"He did not provide you a letter or anything about where he could be," Hildith asked, narrowing his eyebrow at her.

"Like you said, sir." Oceana gave him a slight grin. "My family has a habit of just disappearing."

Hildith stared at her; he clearly had not enjoyed the answer she had given him. "Okay, Pirate," He almost spat. "But if I find out that you are keeping anything, so much as a bread crumb of information that could participate in the hunt for Wilic, or the search of his handbook, there will be consequences to pay, and I will make sure that you will be thrown in jail. And-" but before Hildith could carry on listing off the ways she would be punished, another KEEPIN officer in blue showed up, his badge listed to be fourth ranked.

"Hildith!" He interrupted, his voice was clearly inpatient. "We need you at the-" He stopped when he looked at Oceana

"Oh! Oceana Sanford! Just who we were looking for." He said.

"If you are here to tell me the news about my grandpa being wanted, Hildith just told me."

"We did want to inform you of that, but there is something you must check out. I am unsure how else to tell you. Follow me." He began guiding them to a motor vehicle. It had a seat placed in the back of the truck, which allowed passengers to sit in the open air, which was perfect for TOAD. However, he might be slightly too tall to be placed in the back. Oceana moved towards the vehicle. She looked around and noticed the other Blue division guards were watching her from a distance. She looked over at Hildith before he gave a smirk right before entering the truck's passenger seat next to the officer who designated them to this specific vehicle.

Oceana grabbed onto the handle and hopped on the back. She did so and waited for Jamlson, Headworth, and TOAD to do the same. Once they all sat comfortably in the seats, the vehicle moved forward to a destination none of them could know.

"My grandpa is a traitor to Cor'Meum?" Oceana whispered to the two boys that sat next to her.

"That is weird." Jamlson admitted, "Considering I remember how much of a by-the-books type of guy he was." Jamlson said. "He never struck me as a guy that would go off the grid, especially like this." He said.

"Yeah; this is all weird how close the time is between my grandpa going missing and my mother going missing. Which will mark ten full years the day after tomorrow since my mom vanished." Oceana said

"How do you know?" Jamlson question.

"Because my eighteenth birthday is the day after tomorrow." She remembered waking up expecting birthday wishes but instead was told by her mother, who seemed like she was packing like there was no tomorrow, to pack her things. It was an eventful day. It took all morning for her to pack her things. She remembered how her mom hurriedly rushed them out of the castle, ignoring the goodbyes from her fellow co-workers. "He-" Oceana began to admit. "He also wanted my grandfather's hand-book to magic."

"Well, they would have to find your grandfather first." Jamlson crossed his arms.

"Um, about that-" Oceana said,

"You-" Jamlson stopped, moved closer to Oceana and whispered. "You have it?"

"It's been in my jacket this whole time." She said,

"Perhaps it would be best if we didn't say anything." Headworth commented. Oceana and Jamlson both nodded their heads.

The ride had come to a short end when the vehicle made a complete stop, allowing the travelers to exit safely. Oceana hopped out of the KEEPIN truck and brushed off the dirt that had attached itself to her pants. A gust of wind cruised by, which made her shiver in response. She held onto herself in her red coat. The officer and Hildith stepped out from the driver and passenger sides of the truck.

"We are here." The officer said. Oceana nodded at him and moved her way past him, she moved her hand inside her coat pocket to feel the presence of the book. She had to keep her mouth shut about the where-abouts of it. She then stopped, in front of her were stairs that led down, their destination a large area that held microscopic rocks that almost felt smooth when you picked them up. The water that touched the tiny rocks scattered everywhere would have been a beautiful sight if it weren't for the number of trucks scattered around in a place they had no belonging.

Oceana made her way down the stairs to enter the bay area of the site. She had no idea that Fovero was so incredibly close to the Ocean. This place was beautiful, so what prevented many residents from traveling here?

Once reaching the sand, no longer standing on any solid ground, Oceana looked around the place and was able to get a better look at what had brought so many KEEPIN soldiers to search this land. Broken plywood, leftovers of a brutal war between boat and sea left their history all over the sand of this beach. Oceana did not quite understand why they had brought her here. What was so important about this plywood? When she moved around the area, passing officers looking through items inside a chest only to find wet clothes, she stopped when she reached the biggest memory of this attack. The front half of a ship, fully intact but missing the third quarter, was resting on the sand instead of floating in the water.

"I am sorry to inform you Ms. Sanford but these-"

"Ol'Sarah." He nodded in response. Oceana didn't need anyone to identify the home that she had lived in for almost a decade. She knew this ship just like the back of her hand.

"Yes." The officer said. Oceana hadn't broken her vision from the broken boat that rested in front of her. After some long passing silence, the officer moved away to give Oceana space to process the scene. It seemed so unreal. Two homes of hers were destroyed in the same week. There was something just not right about this. How could this have happened?

"Are you doing alright?" Oceana looked over at Jamlson's concerned facial expression when talking to her. No. She wasn't; half of her home was staring right in front of her, and she did not know if the people she had grown up with were alive or...no. After a couple of beats from the ocean water, Oceana peeled her eyes away from the tragedy that stood in front of her.

"Who- I can't think of anything that would create such damage like this." She said, looking at Jamlson.

"Perhaps it was just the weather; KEEPIN loses at least three water-bound ships a year." Headworth chipped in after standing next to Jamlson in silence. TOAD began to wander around the area, seemingly bored of the conversation that was happening, to explore the scenery around them.

"No," Oceana said. "We always knew when storms were coming. My grandpa was always paranoid about them. He would never let his men go out to sea, even if the chances of a storm were low." Then, she looked back at the ship, "This was an attack."

"Well, if it is." Jamlson said, "By who?"

"I don't know," Oceana said. She looked over at the other KEEPIN officers who were not too

far from them. They were all whispering and staring. "But I am determined to find out who." Oceana looked away from the officers and at the two. "This is another reason we should find Bellus," Oceana said. "We need to know if Sage Magnus is alive and what my grandpa has to do with it." TOAD had then run up to them, holding a bottle in his hand

"A bottle of lemon fizz?" Jamlson questioned. He then took it from TOAD's hand and opened the bottle. He gave a quick look inside. "Hey guys, look at this," Jamlson said, turning over the bottle with a note falling out.

"An SOS?" Headworth questioned. Oceana and Headworth made their way behind Jamlson while he had begun to open the inside letter.

"It looks like it's for your Grandpa," Jamlson said.

"What? Let me see!" When Jamlson was going to hand the letter back to Oceana a KEEPIN officer had moved up to the four of them.

"Ms. Sanford, we couldn't help but notice that your mechanical friend had picked up an object from the crime scene. I understand that this is hard for you, but you cannot take any potential information that could hinder our search for Wilic Ellington. So I would have to ask you to give the bottle to me and the note that comes with it to me." Oceana blinked at the officer.

"What- that is so-"

"I have it right here, sir," Jamlson said, holding up the letter. He carefully rolled the letter back up and stuffed it in the lemon fizz bottle. "We didn't mean to cause any harm. Hopefully, you will find it in your deepest heart to forgive us. But, we want to make sure that KEEPIN is satisfied with our loyalty. We don't want to break that." Jamlson handed the bottle to the officer.

"Right." The officer said. "Well, keep up the good work at providing your loyalty to Cor'Meum." He nodded and walked away.

"Will do! Thank you!" Jamlson said with a salute. Once the officers were gone he turned to Oceana and Headworth and gave the widest eye roll that Oceana had ever seen.

"I apologize for stepping out of line, but Jamlson are you okay?" Headworth asked with a raised eyebrow.

"Jamlson, that letter was probably important," Oceana said.

"Oh boy, sometimes I feel like you forget who I am," Jamlson said, opening his inner jacket pocket and pulling out his lemon fuzz bottle. He opened the cap and tilted the bottle to reveal the hidden note. "The card swiping trick works on bottles too." He grinned.

"You are a genius Jammy!" Oceana stated right before hugging him.

"Pft Jammy?" Headworth laughed.

"I am bigger than you Headworth." Jamlson's comment immediately killed Headworths laughter.

"Let's head back to Fovero, before they notice that the letter is missing," Oceana said, making eye contact with Hildth from a couple of miles away from the beach. They eventually all started making their way up the stairs to where their ride was waiting for them.

After they made it up the stairs, no longer being in his sight, Hildith moved back to the landed aircraft ship. He walked into the room that was declared to be his office. His name plastered in silver, mocking him of the one star he hadn't acquired. He sat down at his desk and let the air leave his lips. The phone suddenly rang. He picked it up with his human hand and brought it to the only ear that worked.

"Lieutenant Hildith speaking." He grumbled.

"Hildith!" A squeaky voice said on the other end of the phone. Hildith's eye widened, and immediately he put down the phone on the desk, not hanging it up. Instead, he stood up and moved to his office door, peered around, and shut the door. door. He walked back to his seat, grabbed the phone off his desk, and hissed into the speaker.

"You little dirty idiotic measle, I told you not to call me at my office!"

"You told me to send you a letter, I know, I am sorry, but this is very important!" The voice cried out in a hushed whisper.

"It better be. You know what they would do to me if they found I was talking to people like you?" Hildith hissed. "You are putting my life in danger."

"I am sorry!" The voice squeaked, "Please forgive me! But I needed to tell you that we finally got the information we needed from Bovark. Apparently, the Magnus family is cursed."

"Cursed? Cursed with what? What kind of curse, Pitlick?" Hildith whispered into the speaker drumming his fingers along the desk with his mechanical hand.

"We don't know, but he insists that it will prevent The Boss from getting the golden apple. Just like the boss predicted!"

"Is there a way to break it?"

"He said he doesn't know if the curse could be broken, sir! But he said everyone with Magnus blood has this curse."

"The liar! Drill Bovark for more information then!" Hildith snapped his fingers.

"We are doing that right as we speak!" The squeak came.

Hildith rubbed the bridge of his nose with his human hand. "I got a letter that indicates Wilic was captured? Surely, Mr. Pitlick this means you have the pirate's handbook? Maybe there's something in there that can tell us how to break this curse."

"Um-"

"Um?"

"He didn't have it with him- and not only that but, he escaped."

"What? How could this happen? When did this happen?" He questioned.

"Just only hours ago, We also think he knows about our plans- what we are doing on the last day of the celebration!" Pitlick whispered. "What do we do sir? Do we tell the boss? Should we cancel the plans?" Hildiths office door began to open, Hildith looked up and watched the fourth-ranked Captain walk in.

"That will not be necessary, just stick to the plan. Bless the castle." Hildith said, hanging up the phone before Pitlick could get another word in.

"Interrupting anything important?" The captain asked.

"No, nothing important at all," Hildith said with a forced toothy grin.

CHAPTER 12:

The Underground Market

WHEN Oceana and their friends returned to the area where they were initially picked up, they all mutually declined the officer's proposal to drive them home. Oceana had been relieved that she was not questioned about what she was doing, with their grandpa now missing. When the KEEPIN vehicle had moved away, Oceana's body suddenly felt less tense, a feeling she had not known she was carrying before. Why was her body reacting feverishly to the army of her country? Though it was almost as if she were very anxious right now, she decided that it would be in her best interest to shake it off and pretend that those feelings were not around, at least in the army's presence. She had felt all their eyes peering at them the whole way over here, preventing her a moment of peace to read the letter they found on the beach. They needed to find a quiet place far from here, but they first needed a ride.

The four of them left, leaving the area that was plastered with KEEPIN vehicles. The townspeople's eyes followed the four with disapproval. Oceana felt a shiver run down her back. The idea that the people associated her with KEEPIN, made her heart give out.

"We should leave this place as soon as possible," Jamlson whispered to Oceana, who could not have agreed more. The four of them moved to a passenger stop, where an auto vehicle picked up parties of ten or less to help transport them to the next town over. At the stop, Oceana felt more eyes looking at her. Their hatred for KEEPIN must have been stronger than their curiosity about the giant mechanical next to them.

After some time had passed, an auto vehicle stopped next to the sign, the other people who had waited began climbing inside, getting ready for the long ride. Oceana moved forward to place herself in the auto vehicle amongst the other passengers.

"Hey!" One of the passengers snapped, "No KEEPIN allies allowed." He spat.

"Yeah, we don't want you here!" Another one of the passengers yelled.

Oceana put her hands up in defense. "Look, I am not looking for trouble. I just need to get on so I can-"

"What? Oppresses people? Abuse power!"

"What?" Oceana stated, "No!" Oceana felt her face turn red.

"Uh-huh. Sure."

"Look!" Jamlson said, stepping in between the passengers and Oceana. "All we want is a ride. Is that too much to ask for?"

"All we want is peace!" Another passenger stepped into the conversation.

" I am not even part of KEEPIN!" Oceana said, moving next to Jamlson while waving her hands in the sky.

"Then why are you wearing a Red division coat?" Someone pointed at Oceana's bright red jacket, an official Red division KEEPIN jacket.

Oceana looked at her jacket and back at them. "This isn't mine- this used to be my grandpa's." She stated. "I am too young to be an official KEEPIN soldier! I'm seventeen!"

"Anyone can lie, especially Pirate scum!" The man spat.

"Fine!" Oceana threw her hands up again. "Whatever! I didn't even want to get on your smelly auto vehicle anyways!"

In highsight, Oceana should not have said that. Almost immediately after, everyone in the vehicle began to boo and throw their trash at her. She moved back, putting distance between herself and the motor vehicle before it took off. Oceana sighed and rolled her eyes, "Frogs on a stick!" She cursed with her hands up. "What are we supposed to do now?" She asked.

Headoworth snapped his fingers. "You could wear something that doesn't make you stick out so much."

Oceana looked down at her outfit, undoubtedly a stereotypical Pirate uniform.

"Yeah, but any clothing place she enters will just kick her out," Jamlson commented.

"Unless." Oceana smiled. "We check out that underground marketplace, the place where everyone there is sketchy."

"Are you talking about a black market?" Jamlson asked.

"No, a market that is underground!"

"Yeah," Jamlson narrowed his eyes at her, "a black market. Full of illegal activities."

"Oh whatever," Oceana said with an eye roll. "It's not like we have much of a choice."

"Black Market, hmm. They might have stuff I need to make TOAD's battery last longer." Headworth said to himself.

"C'mon! They might have something that will power TOAD longer!" Oceana said, "Come on Jamlson, think about TOAD!"

Jamlson made a face at Oceana, then looked up at TOAD, who tilted his head and blinked. Jamlson pressed his hand to his face, taking his time to slide it down. "Alright. I guess we don't have a choice, do we?"

"Yes!" Oceana stated, "I think I might know where this place is!" She grinned.

Despite the market being underground, there was still a metal ceiling. This was to keep the ground on top from falling on anyone. There were also a couple of ropes and chains that draped from the ceiling itself. Some held lights, while others were just remains of the ones that used to carry some sort of light source. There were many more people traveling the halls of the underground market than Oceana had expected.

Going down the market hall, each booth carried something unique about it. Oceana walked up to one of them that held a sign that said "Beasts: Stange and unseen." She moved up to one of them and found a long animal curled up in the cage. It appeared to be sleeping. When she moved her face closer to the cage, the animal jumped up and hissed, revealing its sharp pointy teeth and beaming red eyes. Oceana jumped back and moved along the path with Jamlson and Headworth, putting her concentration back on the mission.

"Hey, you want a fork?" A hunched man said, opening his jacket to reveal the variety of forks he possessed. "I promise I didn't lick any of them!"

"Doubt it," Jamlson said to himself.

They all continued to move down the long dark hall filled with various booths that held different sorts of items. There was one booth that had blinking color lights, TOAD went up to it and reached his claw out to touch one of the lights.

"Hey!" The man who owned the booth shouted, "No touchy!" He glared at TOAD, who only tilted his head and began to reach for the blinking light again. Headworth grabbed him by the arm and pulled him back, moving him to continue their hike down the long hall.

As they walked down the hall of the market, there was a whisper that caught Oceana's ears. She turned around and found two people who were talking amongst themselves, next to one of the book booths that sold books that were not Cor'Meum approved.

"Yeah I heard that too." The man with the hood said. "I heard Sage Magnus isn't dead. That the Knight and Magician lied. Or didn't check to see if he was really dead."

"I wouldn't be surprised." The other person said, they began to light a match. "I heard that Sage Magnus had been recovering from the battle, but when he comes back he'll be more powerful than ever."

"How old would he be?"

"Old as dirt." The other responded, "But I heard a rumor- that because the Magnus's can use all three tones, this means they could make their bodies stronger." They sighed.

"Do you believe Sage Magnus is back?"

"Honestly, yeah." The other said.

Oceana had then felt their arm tugged at, they looked over at Jamlson who gave her a look of concern. Oceana looked up at him, smiled and shook her head. They continued to walk from there. Until Oceana pointed at a modern-day clothes booth, "Perfect!" she said. She moved to the booth and found a woman there. She seemed distracted with the pipe in her mouth. She nearly choked when she noticed that Oceana was standing by her booth.

"Well, I'll be damned." She forced a laugh with her voice sounding as if it was about to give out, "If it isn't Oceana Sanford at my booth." She grinned.

"You know who I am?" Oceana raised an eyebrow.

"Who doesn't? Isn't that the real question?" She said with another forced laugh, "Let me guess, you came here to make yourself look less like, well, you?"

Oceana nodded with hesitation.

"I bet. Wearing that pirate uniform makes you stick out like a sore thumb. But you came to the right place!" She opened her arms up. "Come with me, and we will find the perfect, blend-in type outfit for you." She began to move Oceana forward behind the curtain of her booth. Jamlson and Headworth moved forward only to be stopped by her hand "No boys." She winked, clicked her heels, and moved with Oceana behind the curtains.

Behind the curtains held statues that wore the clothing that was on sale, Oceana looked around at each of the outfits that were displayed. For example, one outfit carried a black corset with a white-collar shirt that held a design of folds that were sewed on each side down the middle of the shirt. In addition, it had a long fluffy purple skirt that hung open on the side in the same design.

"My guess is, you don't want a skirt." The woman said.

Oceana shook their head. "Not really my thing."

"Are you sure all the young people are doing it?" She smiled,

"No thanks." Oceana waved her hand slightly.

"Oh well." The woman said,

Oceana continued her browsing, not knowing which one she would like amongst the displayed ones.

The woman snapped her fingers, "I know which one you would like." she said, "But before I get them," She pulled out a long thick string and moved it around Oceana's hips, grabbed another line to tie around the other end of the rope that had met with Oceana's hips. She stood up and wrapped another sting around Oceana's chest, to which Oceana had yelped in response. Much like she did before, she tied a tiny piece of string at its end. The woman moved back with the measurements she had taken, sized Oceana up, and nodded to herself, now having a good idea of what she had that could fit the girl. She disappeared amongst the other curtains that were all around the room. It was not even a second before she held a pile of clothes with pride and handed them to Oceana. "Try this on!" She insisted. Her face was close to Oceana's, to the point that she could smell the pipe remains from her breath. "I guarantee you will like this."

Oceana took the pile of clothes out of her hands and looked down at them, then she moved her attention back to the woman, who only gave her a thumbs up. Oceana sighed and moved behind one of the curtains that had appeared to be see through.

Inside, she began unclipping her belt to start changing into the new outfit she had been given. Throughout the process of changing, she felt how much tighter the new pants were. The top of it wrapped nicely and wasn't loose compared to how her previous pants had fit her. The jeans that Oceana was given were a darker brown than the boots she was wearing. She then began to button the collared shirt. The collar shirt was gray, which matched the brown corset that Oceana had difficulty putting on until the woman came inside the changing room; due to Oceana's bitter words.

Oceana looked in the mirror and smiled briefly before placing her plaid cap on top of her head, sticking the strands of hair inside the cap with clips.

"Mwa!" The woman said, throwing her hand up, "You look wonderful! You no longer look like an army pirate!"

"Did you make this yourself?" Oceana questioned, turning to the mirror to look at her reflection. The outfit was definitely in her taste if she had to pick one that did not spark public attention. She could tell that the threading done on this was with care, including the hat she wore. She noticed the word 'KEEPIN' was not sewed on. Oceana couldn't help but feel lost without wearing the word. However she decided to not pay attention to that. Perhaps she would have felt weird wearing the word too, after today. It's been confusing. Though that hat seemed to be a bit bulky, it was placed nicely on her head while managing to cover her white strands.

"Yes!" The woman said proudly.

"This is incredible!" Oceana responded, looking at her, though she did take a moment to pause. "You have such an amazing talent for this. Why not bring your company up from underground and make a real living off of this?"

"I would love to!" The woman gave a half-smile. However, it didn't take long for the smile to be pulled down by the heavyweight of reality. "Though Sanford, not everyone in Cor'Meum has it easy; as an old Vibrius citizen, it truly is a struggle to maintain a business on the ground."

"What do you mean?" Oceana asked.

"When you are born from a place no one seems to care about, they start to not care so much about you. My shop above ground was attacked by KEEPIN officers more times than I can count."

"KEEPIN officers?" Oceana asked, wondering if she had misheard the information. The woman nodded,

"But here in the underground market, everyone has a place to sell what they love, to reach their passions. Some may come off as questionable, but no one here discourages Vibrius or not."

Oceana gave a small smile to the woman. She reached into the coat pocket of her Red jacket and handed the woman a handful of the Prelacies she had stuffed in there. "Thank you." Oceana said, "Thank you for not turning away."

"In the underground market, all are welcomed." The woman replied.

Oceana nodded and turned to the curtains. She began to walk out to meet with Headworth and Jamlson again. Much like she predicted, they were both shocked to see her in such a normal style of clothes. Though

Oceana's fashion was aligned with military clothing, seeing the girl in the usual manner in itself was unusual.

"You actually look like you are ready to blend in amongst the masses," Jamlson said, giving a thumbs up.

"Yeah." Headworth laughed. Oceana held up her old clothing,

"TOAD, can hold onto that!" Headworth took her clothes, turned around and opened TOAD's backpack, he then stuffed the clothing inside of it. Headworth, stopped "Your jacket is a bit heavy." "It must be the handbook." Oceana waved. Headworth finished stuffing the jacket in the backpack TOAD carried, he took a step back next to TOAD and smiled at Oceana.

"What do you think TOAD? Of Oceana's new outfit?" Headworth asked.

TOAD blinked in response, his yellow eyes giving a small flash,

"I think he likes it," Jamlson said, making Oceana and Headworth laugh.

Oceana could feel herself, despite being in an underground black market, feel completely comfortable with herself and the two boys she had grown to know more of on their travels. Despite having a weird connection with Headworth and not knowing how to talk to him almost eighty percent of the time. She had grown to understand his mindset, and the way he sees the world. She had forgiven him for anything that he may have inflicted on her life in the past. She couldn't tell anyone why she no longer felt mad, but it had disappeared. Maybe there were just more things that were on her mind. Perhaps she thought she couldn't entirely fault him for doing something that reckless. But it seemed like he understood what was wrong and was trying to grow from it.

Jamlson, they could not have remembered the last time she spent so much time with him. He had been by her side throughout this entire journey. He was still the coolest person she had known in her book, even cooler than the Magician, whoever he was. They were excited to continue this path with him by their side. To find out the truth of what had happened to her grandpa. Nothing could have ruined this moment between the three friends, now including TOAD, which she supposedly made four. While everything was chaotic and out of control, it seemed this moment of peace could just last forever. Nothing too big or too small could put this perfect chapter to a halt. However, Oceana could not have been so much more wrong; in that same minute of absolute, while the world seemed about ready to be at peace, a gunshot went off.

CHAPTER 13:

A simple song

THE ground began to shake, caused by the fearful screams amongst the crowd of people. Everyone forced themselves in the opposite direction of where the shot had come from. Oceana felt herself be pushed by a wave of people, her legs moving backward as hard bodies bumped into hers. Sounds of shattering glass came from all directions. No one had any mercy on the booths that were displayed. They were trampled on and destroyed within seconds of the gunshot. The screams of people did not die down. A howler of a man that pleaded to the crowd for help was buried amongst the other shouts. The once panicked crowd that feared for their lives and wanted nothing but to escape the underground market had turned against one another, ready to loot any vulnerable victim.

Oceana moved in circles and noticed that Headworth and Jamlson weren't by her side. They had disappeared in the bustling bodies of people. She moved in small circles, hauled more air than her lungs could carry, and shouted.

"Headworth! Jamlson!" It only felt when she shouted. Her voice expired immediately in the cluster of human bodies. It was not too long before she felt herself being shoved by the flock again, the bodies moving at such a fast pace larger than her own. There was another shove from one of the panicked members in the crowd running towards the exit. When Oceana was hit by the impact, they fell to the floor.

She hurriedly tried to get to her feet, but before she realized the mistake she had made by pressing her hands on the ground, she immediately felt her fingers become crushed by the stampede. When she found her footing to stand up, she felt someone tug on her belt. She turned around and found a man covered in his own sweat, trying to unhook the scabbard from her belt. Despite the fact that her dominant hand had been crushed moments ago, she raised her left hand and flung it forward, directed toward the man's face. The guy must have been starving. With one punch from what Oceana would consider one of her weaker throws, he was out like a light. She moved her attention towards her falling scabbard and began clipping it back to her belt. With her failed attempt of clicking the two pieces of it with one of her hands, she had to face the fact that this process required two. She looked at her hand, which had been screaming at her in pain. Each fingertip already had turned to the color of purple, bending in ways Oceana knew were not natural. She took her broken hand, used all her strength to gently hold onto the leather ends, and snapped the belt together once again.

Another sound of glass shattered. This was followed by the sound of fire. Oceana did not feel too comfortable being where she was; she began fighting her way through the crowd. She used all her might to bump into people before they could bump into her. It only took a few minutes for Oceana to face the truth. If she were to continue to force her way into the crowd, she would be trampled on again. She looked around at what she could find, anything to climb on, to keep herself separate from the violent shoppers around her. In the flood of screams and heavy movement, Oceana managed to find a bench to stand on to get a better view. Something she could use to physically separate herself from the crowd completely.

Once on the bench, Oceana looked around. She could see from a couple of feet surrounding her the riot unfolding. She watched two people not too far from one another throw fists at one another for who knows what. A woman crying, broken, holding pieces of what was left of her own shop. Over to the very far right of the small underground facility. Then close to that she found Headworth who sat on the shoulders of TOAD, who maneuvered carefully around the crowd.

Oceana knew standing on this bench would not provide safekeeping for too much longer. She already had people jump on it to only jump off immediately after. She needed to find a permanent spot where Headworth and TOAD could save her from. She scanned the area around her and couldn't find anything beneficial. In frustration, she leaned her head back, vocalizing her anger with a loud grunt, only to find the solution right in front of her. She did not like this idea, but it was the only one she had.

She moved her hand up and grabbed onto the rope that hung ever so innocently on the metal ceiling above. She gripped onto the rope with all her strength with the hand that was fine, but she still needed to move up, which required her other hand.

Oceana closed their eyes. The pain from her hand alone was unbearable to her. Their hand was screaming for medical help, but at this moment, she did not have the luxury of someone to heal her. She closed her eyes, brought up her weak hand, and wrapped it around the rope. She sucked in her pain, biting her inner cheeks in response to her hand putting effort in while broken. With her arm connected to her broken hand, she began pulling her body up. When the opportunity came, for her to switch hands, she changed them immediately. Her legs were dangling in the air. She looked down at the scene below her to only find the bench, which was her temporary place of heaven, now completely and utterly destroyed. It was too late to give up unless she wanted to fall into the hungry sharks of people.

She took a shaky breath in and took a breath out. She felt the nervousness in her stomach weigh her down to what could be her ends meet if she had failed to bring herself up this rope. She swung on her now broken hand to replace her more suited hand to maneuver her way up the rope. She gasped in pain. Tears began forcing their way away from her eyes. Her heart pumped faster. She felt sweat build-up from underneath the cap she was wearing. The pain that was striking her body was unspeakable. She moved her elbow up and replaced her weak hand with her strong hand to hold herself in place. She had decided that she did not need to climb any higher. Finally, she was at a spot on the rope to rest her feet on the giant knot below it. She had successfully separated herself from the mob of people, which looked like it was starting to get less aggressive. Still, Oceana remained on her rope, not wanting to risk the confrontation with the crowd.

She held onto the rope with the help of her legs and feet with one hand, finally allowing her injured hand to rest for a while. Although Oceana was too scared to look at her fingers right now, she was confident it didn't look good.

While making company on the rope, she looked around the area to see if she could spot Headworth on his mechanical again. It did not take much scanning. She found them again immediately, TOAD was walking around the crowd, probably avoiding any chance of thieves that would attempt to steal any of his body parts. Oceana waved her hand high in the air, hoping this action would draw attention to her.

"Headworth!" she shouted "Headworth over here!" Headworth looked around to find the source of the noise calling for his name. Not noticing that Oceana was dangling from a rope a couple of feet behind him. Oceana could feel herself get frustrated at Headworth's lack of sense of surroundings. She knew that if she and Headworth had switched places moments ago, Headworth would have been toast, not due to his tiny self being trampled by the crowd of people. Well, maybe that, but it also contributed to the fact that he put minimal effort in thinking outside the box, compared to herself.

Jamlson was also incredible at figuring out his surroundings when placed in a dangerous situation. Jamlson! Oceana immediately began to worry about him. She still hadn't seen him since the gunshot was fired. Why was there a gunshot fired? Did someone get hurt? Oceana shook her head; she had no time to ponder these questions now; she had to get Headworth's attention.

"Headworth!" She shouted once more.

Headworth had finally turned around, with the help of TOAD being his legs. He looked at Oceana. She could tell he had not immediately recognized her at first, almost forgetting that she was wearing a disguise.

"Oceana! Glad I found you!" He said, TOAD moved towards her.

"Yeah, same." Oceana said, "Uh can you help me?" She asked in a hurried tone of voice,

"Sure, just let go, TOAD will catch you." Oceana looked down at TOAD, who had his arms out. Then she looked over at Headworth, and closed her eyes for a brief moment.

"You know, I think I like my chances up here. I can live here forever. Build a new life on this rope." she said.

"Oceana, TOAD will catch you!"

"Are you sure he will catch me?" She questioned. She had a good view of his skinny arms, which were not good at convincing her he could carry anything above fifty pounds.

"Yes."

"Fine, alright!" She opened her eyes to look at TOAD once more. She took a wide breath in, and let go of her rope, allowing her body to fall. She was caught in TOAD's arms perfectly. They gave a small smile at TOAD before they shouted, "Headworth! We gotta look for Jamlson!"

Thankfully, TOAD was a bit taller than the average human, well above two hundred centimeters, allowing him to maneuver around the crowd. Oceana looked around to see if she could spot that conspicuous purple scarf anywhere. After running in circles, at least what Oceana had felt like they were doing, Oceana saw Jamlson sitting on the floor a couple of feet away from the rest of them.

She moved out of TOAD's arms and ran towards him, hoping he was okay. In the motion of running, she noticed that he had blood on his hands, she had not thought it was possible, but she moved faster, her heart feeling like it was going to explode out of her chest. When she was close enough, she noticed the pile of blood that surrounded him, but it was not his own. In front of him lay a man who was bleeding out.

"I wish I could help you." Jamlson said, holding the man's hand, the man only gave him a nod back at him.

The man in front of him looked drained. All the blood in his body was spilling out onto the floor. There was nothing that any of them could do to help this man. Oceana sat next to him and looked at the man. She moved close to him and bit her lip before she asked

"Do you know who did this to you?"

The man who had been too weak to respond lifted his arm and pointed at the sky. Could that mean anything? Was there something up there? Oceana looked up but only found the metal ceiling of the underground market. Maybe he had lost too much blood to think clearly. It was apparent he was becoming delusional. How could a ceiling contribute to the reason he was shot? A possibility of someone from the ceiling shooting him came to mind. However Oceana looked at his wound; that was not possible either, it had to be someone shooting him directly in front of him. Oceana sighed and looked at the man, she wished she could say anything comforting, but there was nothing she could really project to make this situation better.

Apparently, Jamlson had the same thoughts. He turned to Oceaana and looked at them with an idea. "Oceana," He said, "You should sing to him."

"What?"

"Yeah! Sing him one of those pirate songs." He said.

"Uh." she said awkwardly, "I don't know."

"Just sing a song, any one that you know."

"Fine," Oceana coughed. She thought for a second, scrambling her head for a song she might know really well. She closed her eyes and gave a heavy sigh. "Alright, this song is from my childhood. My grandpa sang this every night before I went to bed." She closed her eyes and projected her melody

""When I was a baby, I was taught to be good. I was a child when I found out the world was cruel. Empty stomachs stuffed with fears of tomorrow.

I was an adult when I found out the world won't change for good.

My mother- she swore, that they will give us our fruit, if we played the music to their tune.

Filled our appetite with sugar, bread, and lies. Can't make anything until we die.

We sit on our knees and give thanks to the ones we don't see, but behind closed doors, we know their true worth.

A fire sparks from a circle of charts, and the shadows that keep us up are merely just a show, and the water clean came all from me, this is the fate we get when we place our bets.

The charts, stolen maps from the stars, are where we sit. Oh darling lift this curse from me. We sang through the night.

Oh la la la, Oh la la la,

How lucky we are to eat

Oh la la la, Oh la la la,

This is the cycle that the beasts want to keep.

Oh la la la, Oh la la la, I was a child when I found out the world was cruel. Empty stomachs stuffed with fears of tomorrow."

Oceana finished the last beat of the song when she opened her eyes. It seemed like that man had drifted off to sleep, much similar to when she did as a child to the song. But, Oceana knew what had really happened to the man, why he had his eyes closed, and why he looked so peaceful. Oceana felt tears build up in her eyes, she had not known what this man's name was, and she felt her eyes burn for him. The tears in her eyes were too powerful against her strength to resist crying. She felt the salty water run down her face, her nose tightening itself, not allowing herself to breathe through there. What had happened here was awful. She wished she had known what had happened to him and why he was shot? Who did this horrible thing?

Now was not the time to sit and mourn. Instead, a collective of loud footsteps were heard, all marching down the thin hallway to enter the wide area of the underground market. KEEPIN soldiers. It was them. She could tell by the way that they marched.

Jamlson stood up along with Headworth and TOAD.

"We should get out of here before they arrest us," Jamlson stated.

He was right. They were in an illegal underground market, they were probably called, and this place was now exposed to them due to the chaos that had happened here today. No doubt about it, they were going to arrest anyone who had any relation to the place. Oceana stood up along with them, ready to leave. The marching was getting louder, each heavy footstep echoing throughout the area. The three of them had decided that it was best to leave. To escape being arrested. Oceana had no idea how to feel about running from KEEPIN soldiers. Her whole life, she had been on the side of KEEPIN soldiers, and was proud to associate her family and her name with them and their cause.

Then all in one afternoon, she had gone to an underground market to disguise herself to separate herself from them. Now she was running from them like a criminal because she was scared of them. Has the world gone mad? Or was it her who had gone mad?

She continued to run away from the army of KEEPIN soldiers with Jamlson, Headworth, and TOAD. It did come to her to be quite a shock that TOAD could run. They moved down one of the many narrow hallways that allowed an exit for customers. They continued to hear the marching of the soldiers. Their chosen hallway was thin and narrow but wide enough for them to all go through it. They could all hear KEEPIN soldiers yelling at one another that they caught people, their voices echoing fear in Oceana's body.

The hallway began to get dimmer, the lights that had surrounded it became more scattered, Oceana could hear the KEEPIN soldiers start moving in the hallway that they had chosen to go through. She moved faster down until they ran into a dead end. A long ladder, their savior, led up into the darkness. She had no idea if it would guide them to a ceiling or safe space, but it was too late to change their minds as to which exit they wanted to take.

Jamlson began climbing up the ladder, the first to move into the dark. Oceana had insisted that Headworth go second, to which he had no argument. It was now time for TOAD to climb the ladder. The mechanical blinked at the metal railing and looked at Oceana. Oceana pointed at the ladder, and TOAD gave another blink

"Oh so you're telling me, you know how to shoot bullets but you don't know how to climb a ladder!" Oceana yelled under one breath.

TOAD blinked again, and Oceana could feel herself losing her mind. She grabbed the mechanicals hand and forced it on one of the metal poles, she then grabbed one of TOAD's feet and pressed it on the metal pole.

"Look!" She insisted. "That is how you do it!"

TOAD looked at his hand and moved it up the other metal pole,

"Yes! Like that!" Oceana snapped, "But do that again with your other metal hand!" She said she could hear the soldiers' footsteps echo louder.

TOAD moved his other hand onto the other metal pole and looked around. He then moved his feet from one metal pole to the other.

"Yes! Keep doing that, but faster, please, they are coming!" Oceana insisted.

TOAD began moving faster up the ladder and then disappeared in the darkness along with everyone else. Oceana grabbed onto the metal pole but was instantly shot with pain in her hand. She had forgotten entirely that her fingers were broken. She closed her eyes and took a breath in once more, like she had done with the rope, and began climbing up the ladder, ignoring the horrible pain coursing through her body. When she felt the darkness surrounding her as she made her way up the ladder, she heard KEEPIN soldiers talk amongst themselves on the bottom, where she once was just seconds ago.

"Hm, don't see anyone here. Check the ladder, though." The voices echoed.

Oceana could feel her heart race, her body wanting to take a break due to her fingers' pain. She now understood where everyone had gone. There was a hole. She could see the sky. It was gray and gloomy, which explained why no light had crept in. She continued to move up, hearing not too far behind her the voices and beats of KEEPIN soldiers. When she made it to the top of the hole, she sprung out onto the wet grassy land.

She sat up and turned to Jamlson. "They are coming up the ladder!" She said despite feeling like her whole body would disintegrate if she did anything else.

Jamlson nodded and moved the hatch back down its rightful place, and sat up, the hole being sealed away from the world. Next, Jamlson moved the large circle on the top of the cap, which made loud clicking sounds. The clicking sounds stopped when Jamlson did not have the ability to turn the circle more. There were a couple of bangs from inside the tube, officers demanding that the tube be reopened, but after the failed attempts they stopped. The soldiers had realized that their efforts were useless.

CHAPTER 14:

BattleShip

O CEANA sat in the field, her heart beating faster than normal. She had not believed what she had just been through. Jamlson looked over at Oceana and made a face.

"Your fingers." He pointed out

"Yeah I know." She said,

"Oh! I think I have a program here that allows TOAD to fix your fingers." Headworth said, patting TOAD's back; the mechanical moved close to her. She jumped back.

"Get away from me!" She yelled.

"Oceana, are you okay?" Jamlson asked with hesitation.

"Oh, yeah, I am terrific!" She said with an eye roll, "Today I found out that my childhood ship was destroyed along with the people I grew up with, my grandfather is now a wanted man, and on top of that, I just ran away from KEEPIN soldiers! People who are my allies!" She said, "So yeah, today is fantastic! Thank you for asking!"

"Okay, well, you didn't need to have that tone," Jamlson replied.

"Oh really, let me make you comfortable and try to calm down! Only for you, Jamlson," Oceana said, throwing their hands up before deciding she had better just keep them crossed.

"Alright, I didn't mean that." He insisted. He tried to move forward, but Oceana had only taken a step back, keeping their distance.

"Then how did you mean it?" They spat. Jamlson looked around, then looked at Headworth, who only gave him a shrug. He turned back to Oceana, bit his lips, and moved his hands out.

"Can we just, uh," He stopped and tried to think of the right words, "pause a second?"

"Oh yeah! Let's pause!" She said, "You do that here, and I will let's see, do that over there," She pointed at a hill a couple feet away.

"Oceana...."

"Just, please leave me alone." Oceana insisted.

She moved into the open grasslands, far away enough to hardly hear both Headworth and Jamlson. She began to sit on the grass, and for a small moment, she debated whether or not she wanted to lay down on the wetland. Her tired body had instantly won the argument, and she laid on the open field. She kept her eyes on the gray sky, and the clouds who danced around the heavens. The resitial brought in a cold, gentle breeze,

Oceana closed her eyes for a moment, and the sound of a bell beating against the ocean caused her to open her eyes again.

"Hey, be careful with those boxes!" A man dressed in red shouted with the label KEEPIN printed on the back of his coat. He had called at the two. The smaller, skinnier men lifted the heavy box onto the boat. They seemed annoyed that the man was telling them what to do, but they continued their mission nonetheless. The sound of a seagull screeched its song in motivation for the two men who had a hard time carrying the boxes.

Oceana looked over at them. She wondered what was inside the box and what made it so heavy. Was it food? Or was it something secretive? Her answer was revealed when the two men moved on board with the box, with a giant label that stated food.

"Take it to the pantry!" The man in red who had been shouting at them said.

Oceana watched the two men groan, making their way to the pantry with the fresh food supply. She had only hoped deep inside that there was bread in there.

"Hey!" Another voice snapped. Oceana looked over to find her Grandpa. His eyebrows were narrow, which obviously meant he was not too happy with her. "Stop losing your attention and focus." He said sternly. He then moved his sword back up and pointed it at the wooden dummy that rested in front of him. "Now watch me demonstrate how you thrust a sword properly, blocking any potentiality of an attack." He moved his sword up, then back down. He moved so slowly Oceana could guarantee that if she left the boat and walked to the other side of town and back, her Grandpa would still be on the first thrusting movement.

"See!" He said proudly. "Now, you try."

Oceana put low effort into moving the dull wooden sword much like her Grandpa. She moved the sword upon one shoulder, then moved it to the other shoulder. She looked over at her Grandpa with a bored expression. He only flashed a smile back at her.

"Great!" he said, then moved his attention back to the wooden dummy, "Now, if you do this." He went back to demonstrating another swordsmanship technique. Laughter was heard outside the premise of the boat. Oceana looked over and found children her age, about eleven or so, standing by the pier giggling at each other.

"Alright, you're it!" One of the boys shouted, and the kids ran away from the child they designated to be "it."

Oceana watched from the boat and smiled at the children playing below. She completely forgot where she was until she heard the booming sound of her Grandpa's voice.

"Oceana!" He snapped at her. "You are not paying attention to this sword technique!" he stated. "Watch." He was about to rehearse the movements but was interrupted by an outside sound.

"Ugh!" She groaned, "This is boring!"

"How is this boring?" Wilic asked, "We are learning the skills of swordsmanship from hundreds of years! This is Cor'Meum's most honorable skill. A master at this is a guarantee high ranking in KEEPIN!" Wilic smiled.

"I'm not having fun." Oceana plainly stated.

"This is not supposed to be fun. This is supposed to teach you how to defend yourself and others when the time comes."

"I would rather learn magic!" Oceana said, smiling at the idea of producing magical ability.

"We tried that." Wilic threw his hand at his face, grooming his beard. "But you got bored with the books I gave you."

Oceana rolled their eyes. "The books you gave me are boring," She yelled, "Why can't you just show me how to use magic the same way you are showing me how to do this useless sword stuff."

"I told you Oceana, I can't do magic."

"Then why do you have a handbook on magic?"

"This handbook helps me understand magic better for the purpose of KEEPIN missions. To understand the strengths, weaknesses and limitations of the people who do use magic, and who use it against us." He said, "They trust me with this part of the job, because I can't perform it."

"Why can't you do magic?"

"Some people are born magicless Oceana." Wilic said. "But if you do want to learn magic- '' Wilic coughed. "Read the books I gave you!" Oceana responded by giving him a pout. Wilic laughed in response, "Also, this isn't useless sword stuff. You are learning combat skills! You'll become Cor'Meum's finest with this skill! It's an honorary skill to learn!"

"It is a boring skill! Training for a million hours a day is boring! Also, I always wake up with my body hurting!"

"It's not millions. It's ten hours a day." Wilic corrected. "Being sore just means you are growing stronger!" He smiled.

"Can I please quit?"

"No- you are going to learn this." Wilic said

"But-"

"Oceana- I told you the answer is no!"

"Hope I am not interrupting anything." A heavy voice announced, pushing its way into the conversation. Hildith walked on board, wearing his Blue division uniform with pride, keeping a mocking smile directed at Wilic.

"Hildith, a pleasure," Wilic responded with a tone of dry sarcasm. "What's the occasion for coming on board a pirate ship?"

"Can I get a word with you?" Hildith asked with a confident grin spread across his face.

"Of course." Wilic then turned to Oceana "Continue the thrust technique while I have a talk with Hildith." Oceana watched as Wilic walked away from her to move toward Hildith.

Oceana began moving the sword upon one shoulder of the dummy to the other, the hushed voice of Hildith stopped her from moving her wooden sword. She looked over at the two adults, looked back at the dummy, tilting her head a bit hoping to get a better ear to what they were saying.

"I noticed that you brought your entire army," Wilic commented, keeping an eye out for the men in blue uniforms below.

"Ah, yes." Hildith said, "If I had brought all of my men, you wouldn't be having that cocky smile on your face Ellington."

Wilic looked at him. "What brought you here on my ship today, if you don't mind me asking ,Hildith?"

Hilditih gave a coiled grin and moved in circles around Wilic like a shark, keeping an eye on him with the human side of his face. "I have noticed you haven't made progress on your deal." His words came out much like a snake. "I felt I should remind you in person what will happen if you fail to keep your end of the bargain."

Wilic looked around at his crew, who kept attending to their duties, but all giving little glances at the two ever so often. Wilic moved to Hildith. He smoothed his own red vest, then groomed his beard. He kept his eyes away from him and gave a moment to collect himself. Obviously, Hildith was eager to provoke an angry response out of Wilic. "Well, the terms you placed for our deal are very high demanding." Wilic said

"Maybe," Hildith hissed. "If you give me your handbook, I can complete your side of the deal myself." "You have no grounds to take my handbook." Wilic said, "If you want, you can make an executive claim to confiscate it from me." Wilic moved his hand to his coat pocket and pulled out the brown book. "However, that would mean it would go straight into the hands of a fourth ranked officer, and you aren't there yet." He smiled and moved his fingers along the pages.

Hildith gritted his teeth and if a glare could kill, then Wilic would have been striked down. "Since you want to play games with me, Wilic, I'll show you what fun games I can play." Hildith snapped his fingers, and two of his men in blue began marching onto the docked boat. They moved towards one of the Red division crew members and grabbed him by his long hair dragging him towards the other end of the boat before violently throwing him overboard.

Everyone in Red turned to Hildith, cracking their knuckles, getting ready to fight him and everyone in his Blue division army. Wilic held out his hand and turned to his men, once he did he moved the handbook back into his coat.

"Stop." He simply said, "Go check on him." He pointed at one of the crew members, "And get him a towel when he visits Ol'Sarah again." Wilic pointed at the other, who immediately ran off.

Hildith grinned. "You wouldn't want something drastic like that to happen to someone precious, would you?" He asked, Oceana watched his eyes move towards her, however Wilic moved in between his vision and where Oceana stood.

Wilic ran his fingers through his silver hair, looked at Hildith, and straightened his collar, "Thank you for the demonstration. But I fully intend on keeping my end of the deal. There's no need to take my book." Wilic simply replied.

"Very well, Wilic, I should be on my way, I have important Blue division tasks to get to. I know you and your Red division wouldn't understand what an important task means, but I don't have time to give you a lesson on it." He grinned widely and gave a wave before he and his army made their way to leave the boat.

Everyone remained silent, and watched Hildith leave, Wilic turned around and watched his crew stare at him, "The shows over!" Wilic shouted, "Get back to work before I throw all of you overboard!" The crew immediately began to work again.

Oceana stood up straight and began to go back to what she would call her own pointless task. She listened to the crew loudly chat about getting ready to take off soon. Rain droplets fell onto her skin. She looked up at the sky, who's grey only grew to a darker shade. Oceana closed her eyes, not wanting the rain to get in them.

"Alright! The sky is as blue as ever! Time to take off!" A crew member shouted.

Oceana then opened her eyes. She was lying on the wet grass in the open field where she must have drifted off to sleep. She sat up immediately and decided to take a look at her fingers. They were not pleasant to stare at. She sighed and looked around the field. There was no sign of Jamlson and Headworth. She ought to start looking for them before she becomes soaked, she thought. She stood up carefully and headed back to where she had last seen them.

When she moved over the hill and walked around the area looking for her fellow travelers, the rain was striking harder onto the grass, and the atmosphere had an intense shift. It all felt like a cold hand was pressing itself on her back, tickling its fingernails down her spine. She moved her hands under her arms and began trotting through the wet mud. Gloom surrounded her; her memory's directions were useless, and she could not grasp where she was.

Two lights were seen in the darkness. She heard heavy thuds that gave squishing sounds when hitting the wet dirt underneath. She stopped in her tracks, watching the two lights approach her. She squinted her eyes, trying to see what the lights were. Finally, they began to emerge from the fog. In front of her was TOAD. She looked up at him.

"Sorry for freaking out on you earlier." She paused. "Right when I became more comfortable with you, I messed it up. I guess I'm good at doing that. Messing things up."

The mechanical stared at her, tilted his head, and blinked his yellow eyes. TOAD straightened up and held out his hand, or rather claw, Oceana could not tell the difference.

"You want me to come with you?" Oceana asked the mechanical.

TOAD nodded his head in response to Oceana's question, Oceana admittedly found it weird that TOAD understood her like that but remembered that Headworth had mentioned TOAD's understanding of things was much similar to a human five year old.

"I don't know." She said, "Not because of you." She corrected, then paused again and added, "Just- I don't know how to return. I am so confused. I don't understand any of my thoughts. I am getting these weird-" She pressed her hand to her chest and then shook her head. Heartaches? Around KEEPIN soldiers? "Would it be wrong to go back now?" Oceana asked.

TOAD just stared at her, keeping his claw out. Oceana looked at the claw and back at TOAD. She sighed and gave a small smile. "Perhaps you are right though, I am being silly." She grabbed his claw; the two began to set foot on the small journey back to Headworth and Jamlson.

The two reached their destination, Oceana looked at the tiny cabin in front of her, she could not believe that they managed to find some sort of shelter for the night. She looked up at TOAD who just stared at the small cabin.

"Shall we?" She asked. She moved forward and opened the door slightly. The room was small and full of junk that probably someone had owned in a house nearby. A single light was lit above the two boys who were having a conversation.

"I really don't understand why he took off." Headworth said, "He knows he isn't allowed to be out of my sight!"

"You told him to never be out of your sight?"

"He is programmed to know!" Headworth insisted.

"Well, I am sure he is fine." Jamlson rolled his eyes. "I think we should focus on- Oceana!"

"Didn't we agree to focus on how we are going to get to the Westside Mountains?" Headworth titled his head

"No, shush- Oceana!" Jamlson pointed.

Oceana gave a slight smile when seeing how excited the two were when they saw her. She hadn't expected such a surprise like this. She now felt a little ridiculous for being so nervous about coming back to them. It seemed that they weren't upset with her.

"We were wondering when you would come back!" Jamlson said.

"Perhaps admittedly, I can say that your presence here is quite important," Headworth said, looking away while pushing his glasses up.

"Yeah!" Jamlson said, "While you were gone, we were both talking about- ah!" Jamlson was cut off when Oceana threw her arms around them, pulling them in a tight squeeze.

"I am so sorry for being so upset!" She said, "It won't happen again!"

"Look, it's fine. You've well- been through more than a lot." Jamlson said.

"Yes, a lot much like this choking is," Headworth added.

"Also you are now making all of us wet!" Jamlson said, "I don't want rain all over me!" He said, hoping that would be enough for her to stop hugging.

Oceana gave one last squeeze before she released the two boys from their trap. She took a step back and flashed a small smile. "I think I interrupted you Jamlson."

"Right." Jamlson moved. "By the way, Oceana, I read the letter. You might want to read this." Jamlson held out to Oceana the rolled-up letter that he had managed to keep safe since finding it earlier this evening. Oceana kept her eyes on the letter that Jamlson held. She reached her hand forward and grabbed it out of his hand. After a second of unrolling the parchment, she allowed her eyes to roll on the words. Each letter seemed to be messier than the last. The form of this writing obviously had been done in a rush.

Captain willie! This is the last time I will be able to write. you were right we shouldn't have gone. I don't have time but mermaids...I hear them whispering, they speak of hate for you. They want you dead! But I figured that the reason why Hildith has been blackmailing you to find the location of these creatures is because of the map they possess. The golden apple, they have the information, though I can not determine if they will give that up so easily! They are coming into the room, this is goodbye! It was an honor serving you. Be aware of the seas!

After reading this letter, Oceana knew it had to be Ridge who wrote it, a man she believed would never fall victim to ghost stories or rumors of any sort. He is, or perhaps was, though she hoped using such a past tense word for the man was unnecessary; one of the strongest people she had ever met.

"This is just what Bovark was talking about." Oceana said, looking at Jamlson, "The golden apple, what is it?" She questioned.

"I don't know." He said. He paused and looked at Oceana's hand. He reached over to it and lifted it on his own. "First, we should fix this."

Oceana looked at Jamlson, and then she nodded.

"Yeah." Oceana and Jamlson sat on the wooden floor, Jamlson had only a bit of the clothed wraps he used on his own hand for his bow. While he moved the cloth around her fingers, he would follow up with a small apology for the sloppy work.

Though Oceana admitted she was simply impressed that he was able to teach himself this skill in his time in the woods. When he finished, he moved his hands away from hers. Oceana moved her hand up and looked at the bandages that were wrapped around her fingers.

"Thank you," Oceana said, her eyes on the clothed bandage, covered in various knots, under a certainly not new cloth. However, she thought it was perfect.

"I wish I had more training, and I think Headworth is lying when he says TOAD can fix your hand." Jamlson said.

"I said I think he can, he might be able to fix their fingers." Headworth said from the other side of the cabin. Jamlson and Oceana laughed in response.

"I think we should head to bed now if we want to get up early in the morning," Jamlson said.

Oceana could not have agreed more. She was ready to sleep. The idea of tomorrow being the day she will meet Bellus Timidus was exciting. She had always wanted to meet him. She had so many questions for him. She also hoped that she wouldn't freak out in front of him. She was excited yet nervous and fearful. There were only mixed emotions going through her right now, but there was one thing to consider above all of that. Would the Knight find it strange that she figured out where he lived? That his personal privacy was violated? She could not say. Well, she wouldn't have invaded it if it were not an absolute emergency, which it was.

"Agreed." Oceana finally managed to say after snapping back into the real world.

The night stretched longer than anyone could recall, Oceana knew she was the last one to fall asleep with the loud snorings of both Jamlson and Headworth coming from different directions of the shed. She wished whoever owned this place had at least a blanket at hand to keep warm at night if one had wanted to sleep in their shed. But there was nothing but dusty pillows, which Jamlson reminded them was the best they could hope for. So she patted the old thing and closed her eyes, getting ready to drift off into dreamland. The last thing she heard before falling asleep was the gentle rain hitting the roof from outside.

CHAPTER 15:

Cor'Meum Today

"COR'MEUM! A place of magic! Happiness! Every citizen feels they belong! One way or another, everyone is filled with joy! Each person here lives a simple life. Everyone is well-fed, has time to enjoy the things they love, and one way or another their dreams and aspirations do come true! Sound like paradise? Sign up to be a Cor'Meum citizen today! You will love it here!" The recording shouted. "Now we present to you Cor'Meum Today! With our new host Ellvanora Green!" The sound of an audience clapping filled the room.

A young woman, around the middle of her twenties, with long brown hair, sealed together in a braid, wore a bright green suit. The green suit had a white button up. She pulled on her cardigan, which flashed a bright golden 'KEEPIN' pin. She smiled at the camera then at the audience.

"Good morning, Cor'Meum." She said, "How are you doing on this beautiful fall day?" She laughed. "Deepest apologies. I was late today, spent last night celebrating the Calamitous War." She laughed.

The crowd burst in laughter. There were some cheers that came from the audience. Ellvanora smiled and pulled some cards from her cardigan.

"Today we have a great show for you, first we will have a live band performance, later we'll have Cor'Meum's favorite Purple division guard talk about his incredible experience with Cor'Meum! Then as a treat, we will have Cor'Meum's special historian come on the show." She smiled. "Who I will be having a conversation with." She smiled, her red lipstick gave the crowd a wink. "Now let's give it up for 'Steampowered Blue Boats!'"

The audience clapped and Ellvanora moved off stage, which made room for the band to prepare a performance for the crowd. The woman moved backstage. There she moved around staring at those who had backstage passes, all engaging in exciting conversation. Her eyes found exactly who she had been looking for. A man in a Purple division KEEPIN uniform, he held all four stars under his badge.

"Oh, Vinnian!" The young woman said. "I had been dying to meet you," She walked up to him and held her hand out. The Purple division guard took her hand with his own. "When I was told you were coming, all the way from the other side of the castle. I had to meet you! At least before the show." She smiled. "Talking about your experiences with Cor'Meum? Is this a PR stunt?" She questioned.

"Be careful with your words, Ellvanora." Vinnian warned.

"You know what I mean. My heart is with the castel." Ms. Green said. "So you really are here to talk to the people?"

"Well actually, Ms. Green, I am also here to talk to you, personally."

"About what?" She raised her eyebrow.

"Follow me," He said. Ellvanora looked back at the stage, where the band was, shrugged her shoulders and moved with the guard.

Out of the recording room, the woman found herself in the hallway of the castle. Though if she were to rename the place it would be called something else. The palace was too modern, especially with the remodeling, to be called such a thing.

"Ms. Green, you know what your purpose is. Now that you are our new face for Cor'Meum Today." He said, "To be the peoples' comfort. Their guide, someone they can rely on to tell them all the good news. When I go into town all I hear is people talk about the rise of Sage Magnus."

"Oh yes I heard." She said, "I saw someone selling papers about his rise."

"Information that was not Cor'Meum approved. My men arrested him and anyone involved with the paper last night, however I feel this misinformation has already plagued the minds of many Cor'Meum citizens." He sighed. "We need to crush any talk of that- it's gotten out of hand. It has also made our King upset." He moved down the hallway with her, "Inform the people why they shouldn't be scared, get them excited about Cor'Meum! We like the set up you have today, but keep at it, go bigger." Ellanore looked around, and moved over next to the guard.

"Where are we going?" She asked.

"Your first meeting with the Royal Allegiance. Think of this as your uh-" He paused, "Your welcome to the team." He smiled. "Don't get used to them, this will probably be the only time you will speak to them, they are under a tight schedule." Ellvanora nodded, the Royal Allegiance wasn't talked about too much in Cor'Meum, but they were heavily involved in back round things. They approved of the content that flowed through the country, and the laws that were passed.

She stopped. Something caught her attention. There was a thin hallway that she could have easily missed. Inside there was a giant door, it had mysterious carvings on it, and the top of it had a golden plate. She moved up to the door and put her hands on the doorknob.

"What's this?" She questioned. When she turned the handle, a hard click came out, the click informed her that the door was locked.

"That's my office," Vinnian said. "I always keep the door locked." He pressed his hand on her shoulder, "Let's keep moving." Ellvanora looked at the door one more time and moved down the rest of the castle with Vinnian.

The two stopped in front of an entrance, Ellvanora looked around while she waited for Vinnian to unlock the door. She wondered what was in Vinnian's office, something about it had attracted her. Perhaps it was- When Vinnian pushed open the door there was a long table, filled with those that were older than the two of them combined. Each one wore an outfit that Ellvanora believed to cost more than her own apartment. They were lavish to stay the least, and all a bright shade of purple. It would bring attention in any given situation.

"Glad you are here." An old woman who wore a long collar dress, sitting at the end of the table. "Welcome Ellvanora, we are the Royal Allegiance. We are the faces that make the laws of our land. We carry the stamps of approval." Ellvanora pulled a chair and sat down at the table, Vinnian stood closely behind her. "You have proven to us, you're undying loyalty to Cor'Meum." She gave a yellowy toothy smile. "So we wanted to meet you face to face."

"I'll do anything for the castle." Ellvanora said sternly. "I am honored I have been selected for this position." She placed her hand over her heart.

"Yes," The woman said. "You showed real loyalty these past few months to Cor'Meum. I am sure turning in your fiancé and your friend to KEEPIN officers wasn't easy." She said, "Six years of dating and a two year engagement." Ellvanora, gripped her hand onto her heart.

"When your loyalty is with the castle it comes quite easy." Ellvanora gave a gentle smile, she brushed the loose strands of her brown hair behind her ear. "I would give anything for this country."

The old woman smiled. Satisfied with her answer. "And we wanted to show you exactly what you are fighting for. Fighting to protect our people, and our land." The woman walked over to the television screen, pressed her finger against a button, and the cable flickered on. "First we will show you this footage we have, then explain. Understood?"

Ellvanora, looked up at the woman and nodded. Just a year ago she was an intern, now she was in a meeting with the Royal Allegiance. Everything had happened fast. The screen caught her attention.

'There's a lot going on here.' A man said, he stood in front of the camera. Behind him a building was on fire, people with gas masks came out, and some of them waved a flag. Ellvanora didn't need to see the colors to recognize that it was the Vibrius flag, the same flag that was banned on Cor'Meum grounds. There were three circles on the flag, with a star in the middle of each circle. To represent a simple idea of what a magical sphere looked like. Behind the three circles, there were thirteen stripes behind them. She was unsure what the stripes had meant. 'It looks like people with gas masks-they are-' The man began to cough. 'They are coming this way.' A couple of the gas mask people came up behind the man and grabbed him. One moved up to the camera.

'People of Cor'Meum, this is only the start.' The woman said through the dark and white screen. 'We are Vibrius people- this is a revolution! We will fight for our freedom.' The old lady paused the screen. She looked at the new girl and smiled.

"We are trusting you, Ms. Green," She said with an itch, "To inform the people that these are simply cult leaders, get them excited about the future of Cor'Meum." She said, shaking her fist in the air. "Perhaps have a segment tomorrow on Cor'Meum pride."

"Oh well, that's a great idea!" Bellowed a man from one of the tables. "Ms. Green, do a segment on that," He clapped his hands. The rest of the six Royal Allegiances nodded their heads. "We should also inform-" "Sorry to interrupt." A Third ranked KEEPIN guard came into the room. Behind her were two other Purple division KEEPIN guards. They held a tight grip on a man who looked beaten. Ellvanora couldn't say from what but she had her guesses. "We have an act five."

"An act five?" One of the Royal Allegiance council members whispered. "He should be sentenced to jail."

"Hold on dear." The old woman who had spoken before. "Test him. See if he's at least eighty percent Cor'Meum, then we should simply fix him." She looked over at the other council members." They all looked at one another, a violent silence filled the room. Each of them nodded their heads. Ellvanora, watched the KEEPIN guards remove the man out of the room. He kept his head down, there were no tears, there was no sign of regret for his actions.

"An Act five," Vinnian whispered, "Is going against the castel." He said, "It can come in different forms."

"What do they mean by fixing him?" Ellvanora said. She must have spoken a bit too loudly, as one of the council members spoke up.

"When we fix someone, we change the way their brain works. We decided recently to bring the fixing back." The old woman coughed. "Our success rate is almost one hundred."

"Almost?" Ellvanora asked.

"We've had our mishaps, like Project Snowbird." The old lady said. "He committed an Act 5,

but he was the first one to test our-" She stopped. "It- it didn't go too well for the man. Project Snowbird is in the past." She said, "And we like to move on from the past. We believe in forgiveness." She smiled. "We would never want to force anyone into imprisonment if we could avoid it."

"I've never heard of fixing before." Ellvanora said.

"This is precisely why we have called you here today Ms. Green! We have tried to keep it to ourselves, until recently," The old woman said. "We love the citizens of Cor'Meum and we want them to trust that we can take care of them. It is now time to go public with the fixing- with the rise of fear amongst our people. We want to give them something to." She moved her boney fingers to her chest. "To hope for." She looked over at Ellvanora, "King Erebus has placed his trust on us, which means he is putting his trust, in you." She pointed. "The gold standard of a true Cor'Meum loyalist. We want you to announce to the world in the next few months about the fixing. We need you to tell our people they no longer need to fear never seeing the doubters again. We will fix them and reunite them." She said. "Now isn't that just beautiful? No longer will people fear the doubters in their lives will be gone forever. Families stay united. You're fiancé." She smiled. "What do you think?"

"It's amazing." Ellvanora whispered. "I would be happy to announce it."

CHAPTER 16:

The Knight

OCEANA opened her eyes; she found cracks that leaked light into the shed. She looked over to her right, with the bit of light that she had, and found Headworth sound asleep. A fly ringed around her ear, which snapped her more into reality, and she used her good hand to defend her ears. After her quick battle with the fly had ended, she looked over to her left and noticed that Jamlson was not there. She closed her eyes, stretched her arms, and got ready to move her body up and out of the cabin. Standing up was less than ideal, but it was not too painful. After sleeping on broken wood all night, she imagined it would do a number on her back. Maybe it already had, but she hadn't paid attention to it. She walked over to the door and pushed it open in slow motion, hoping the creaks that came with the door would not wake Headworth up.

When she was outside, which looked quite charming without the rain, she searched for her friend Jamlson. The field by the cabin was open. The grass abided itself to be a lovely bright green. Each flower around the field had its own charm and gave off a variant of colors, blue, purple, red, and pink. It felt as though this field was isolated from the rest of the world, undisturbed and untouched by any harmers. After a short hike down the hill, Oceana was able to find Jamlson; he was standing by a long road that reached out beyond Oceana's sight. He had his hands on his hips, staring at one end of the road that appeared after curving around the mountain ahead of them.

"What are you doing?" Oceana asked while he continued to keep his eyes on the curvy road ahead of them.

"I am seeing if any drivers would give us a lift." Jamlson lifted his thumb higher. Perhaps the power of the thumb would attract more cars in their direction.

"How long have you been standing out here?"

Jamlson paused to think, then shrugged at her. "Not too long, I think." He followed up. "It's tough to catch rides, you know. Could take all day."

"Hm, how do you know?"

"I've done it before to get around." He said, "Not like I have my own vehicle to get to places. Couldn't afford one, and even if I did have my own vehicle, I wouldn't be able to drive it." He stopped. "As cool as they are." He made sure to follow up. "You should head in; this kind of stuff usually gets all boring."

"Well, if I had to stand around being bored with someone, I would rather it be my best friend!" Oceana gave him a wink and a nudge, Jamlson only responded with a groan and an eye roll. Jamlson paused and looked over at Oceana, who watched out for any cars that might make their way down.

"About last night," Jamlson said. "Are you okay?" He asked again.

"Yeah, I am fine," Oceana said.

"Are you sure?" Jamlson asked,

"Yeah, Yeah, I'm good!" Oceana waved her hand. "Never better." That weird silence between them made its appearance again. Oceana usually felt that she was the one to always break this eerie stillness between them every time it appeared, though she had no idea what to say this time around. Maybe she should say something-

"Can I tell you a story?" Jamlson asked.

"Of course! I love stories!" Oceana said with excitement.

"Alright, alright," Jamlson moved his hands up, "When I was young, I would do anything to get my father's attention. I would learn as much as I could just to get him to even glance at me. I learned how to cook, fix things, and eventually, I learned how to use arrows." He pointed with his thumb at his back which contained his bow and arrows. "I showed him how fast I could catch food. But I eventually learned that it still wasn't enough for him." He said. "He preferred his own company, surrounded by his wall of empty bottles." He sighed. "One day, he claimed that his Blue division needed him and- he hasn't been back since," Jamlson said. There was a small pause between the two. He took another breath in. "Well, when he left, I didn't feel like I had a purpose anymore." He gripped his hand in front of him. "I eventually realized that I am more than what the old man saw me as." He stopped and looked at Oceana. "Uh, you see where I am going with this, right?"

Oceana blinked for a moment. They took in all of Jamlson's words. They understood that any topic with his father was almost forbidden. They had no idea that he felt that way. She took in a deep breath in hopes the air would push his words down. "I do," Oceana said.

For the first time in her life, she felt that he was right. She looked at the mountains they stood by and took one breath in before she began to speak. "Jamlson, for the longest time, I thought that the army was good, that we are better with them. But after being open in the world for the past couple of days, I don't know. I am scared. What if my grandpa was wrong, what if I was-" She pressed her hands to her face. "I don't know who I would be without KEEPIN."

"Maybe it's time you start breaking family tradition," Jamlson said with a slight smile. Oceana removed her hands from her face, and made eye contact with Jamlson. She smiled back at him. It hadn't taken too much of their time when another car came, Jamlson gave a wave hoping the vehicle would come to a stop, but it continued its adventure forward and without them.

"What was that?" Oceana turned to ask Jamlson.

"What?"

"That." Oceana mocked him with his lazy handwave.

"Eh, I don't see the problem."

"Are you serious?" Oceana raised an eyebrow. "Okay, if you want to catch a driver's attention, you should be seen as much as possible." Oceana jumped up and down, waving her hands and legs simultaneously when she was in the air. Jamlson laughed, watching her move in such a way that felt almost childish.

"Really? They aren't going to stop for a crazy person."

"I'm not a crazy person! I am just getting their attention!"

"But you are acting like a lunatic." Jamlson chuckled.

It was not too long until another car came, Oceana began jumping up and down, waving her arms and legs in the air. Jamlson was so embarrassed he began to bury his hands in his face, hoping that would prevent the driver from seeing him when they passed by the two. But the driver had stopped right next to the two and then began to roll down the window. It was a woman who stared at both of them. She looked like she found Oceana's incredible driver-catching dance moves entertaining.

"Need a lift?" She asked.

"Yes!" Oceana said immediately.

"Well, come on in." The woman said.

"Great, but we have two more friends. I'll go get them." Jamlson said before he made a run for it to wake Headworth up.

Oceana opened the door to the front seat where the woman sat; the woman immediately turned to Oceana and smiled.

"So, where are you guys heading?"

"We are trying to go to Westside Mountains."

"What a weird time to head there, but okay."

"What do you mean?" Oceana asked, raising an eyebrow at her.

"Rumor has it that right now, the city is being taken over by a couple of jerks who wear all black. Who think-" the woman paused then threw a shrug at her, "That the evil king is coming back."

"What? Really?" Oceana asked immediately.

"Yeah, kind of crazy when you think about it." She said,

Oceana nodded with her. "Yeah weird."

"Thank you again for the ride!" Jamlson roared, opening the door to the back before him, and Headworth climbed in.

"It's not a problem- ahh!" The woman yelled when her eyes caught the attention of TOAD. He also opened the car's backseat and made his way inside. "Uh- what-"

"You shouldn't worry. He's not dangerous." Headworth insisted.

"Trust me, he's not." Oceana tried to reassure the woman, "He's an inventor, and he just likes to create things and such."

The woman nodded "Uhhh- okay, okay." Then, she said, "What is it?"

"TOAD!" Headworth chimed. "His original purpose was to open boxes for elders but- now he's here." Headworth shrugged.

"Oh- ok-" The woman said, obviously trying to redirect her concentration back to the road. "So you guys are headed to Westside Mountains; I happen to be passing there so I can drop you guys all off there."

"Wow, that would be great!" Oceana said, "Thank you!"

"Yeah, it's no problem." The woman nodded before she hit the gas and began to head towards the city for them.

The vehicle that carried the friends drove off into the day. The car drove into the field past the trees, going off into the winding road ahead. They all sat in silence. Eventually, the woman decided to turn on the radio, hoping to erupt that silence that stagnated between the people and mechanical in the car. Instead, a buzzing of static-like radio came in. Then it cut into the mix of laughter between what Oceana assumed to be two hosts. When they had finished laughing, one of them coughed and said,

"So we all know that the Calamitous War anniversary is a week-long holiday! With its final day tomorrow!" She said, "Right on the first day of winter."

"Say goodbye to fall today folks- and hello to the first day of winter tomorrow." The other woman said with a happy tone. "I sure had fun celebrating the Calamitous War victory, drinking and partying, and I know our listeners had fun too! Isn't that right Ellvanora?"

"Oh yeah, Cor'Meum sure loves their parties." The radio show host Ellvanora said. "But let's take a moment and discuss why we are celebrating the victory of this war for our young audience listeners who are perhaps still in school." She said,

"This will also go to the Cor'Meum patriots who love listening to the retelling of our favorite historical event in Cor'Meum!" The other radio host hummed.

"Right!" Ellvanora said, "The reason we are celebrating the victory of the Calamitous War, a war between Vibrius and Cor'Meum that happened now over forty years ago, is to celebrate the direction we are guiding Vibrius in!" Oceana could hear the smile behind the radio. "As we know, before the Calamitous War- there were five countries on the Tetrad Aurum; Cor'Meum, Vibrius, Amare, Fortis Tacet, and Apricius."

"Apricius is a name I haven't heard in years, Ellvanora." The other host commented.

"It can be difficult talking about a country that no longer exists," The other host said, clearing her throat. "Vibrius's King at the time, King Lucian Magnus, wanted more land. Because, remember in eighteen fifty-five, at that point, it was Vibrius that was the strongest nation. Or rather, both Cor'Meum and Vibrius were strong-" The host corrected herself quickly, "Because Vibrius was a fast-developing nation- Apricius at this point was at least a hundred years behind."

"Weren't they preaching at that point how they were the true people of the sun? I know the country Amare was annoyed at them for that." One of the hosts said.

"Yes- they believed everyone who was not of Apricius blood was a descendant of pure evil." The other host hesitantly said. "Apricius was unwilling to give Vibrius their own land- so Vibrius attacked them. proceeding to kill every single one of them. By eighteen-sixty-three, every Apricius citizen was dead." There was an itchy silence between the two. "It was-" The host continued. "It was unfortunate that no one knew of these horrendous crimes until later. Cor'Meum wanted revenge for their fellow countrymen. Once King Lucian Magnus died, Sage Magnus took over Vibrius. Cor'Meum told Vibrius they had to pay for what they did- Sage Magnus being the evil King, laughed at the face of the new Cor'Meum King, Alexsander Roseario- who had replaced his brother Odis Roseario." She threw in the fact.

Oceana knew Cor'Meum history, and from what she had read King Odis was only a King for a week before he died of unknown causes. "Sage Magnus was going to do to Cor'Meum what his father did to Apricius- so Cor'Meum had no choice but to fight the wicked King- the war had then begun in eighteen seventy-five- and after ten long years of fighting- the war finally ended with Cor'Meum on top! Thanks to our Knight and Magician!"

"Of course!" The other host cheered.

"After the war, we changed our name from the King's Knights to KEEPIN! Immediately sending our new soldiers into Vibrius territory! We still have KEEPIN soldiers in Virbus today!" Cheered by the other radio star. "As we enter the fortieth anniversary of the Calamitous War, we hope to continue teaching Virbus about peace, not violence!"

"Thank you!" Ellvanora said. "With all the week-long drinking going on, we would like to thank our two sponsors today, KEEPIN, and hang-over fruit juice Lofty! First, KEEPIN! Keeping Everlasting Extravagant Peace In the Nation! Do you have what it takes to join KEEPIN? Sign up today! Up next we will interview Vinnian! After the break" Soon after, some classic radio tunes began to play, which filled the car with volume for the remainder of the trip.

Oceana closed her eyes, her mind only focused on the new musical beats that filled the vehicle. She had no complaints about what was playing. She had much rather listen to a song's melody than two guys talking any day.

After passing the 'Welcome to Westside Mountains' sign, Oceana could now tell why Westside Mountains had been so famous. It was not for the fact that this great city held ideas of the future much like Magna East and Ferndale had. Which included motor vehicles everywhere, shops full of gadgets, and signs that stated how everything here was 'state of the art', but it seemed that this city carried another tone that Magna East hadn't. When peering out the car window, Oceana saw a group of five men on stage playing instruments to a crowd of people. In addition, they passed several song players. There was even one woman playing a quiet melody next to a statue of King Erebus.

"This is where we part ways." The woman stopped the car. When everyone had exited the vehicle, Oceana turned around and reached inside TOADS backpack to grab money from the pocket of her red coat. Once she had the small amount of cash she handed it to the driver.

"Thank you. This is really sweet of you."

"All yours." Oceana responded and the woman nodded. With that, she drove off.

"What- how much did you give her?" Jamlson asked.

"Uh, all of the money I had." Oceana threw a shrug at him, to which he facepalmed in response. "What? It's not like we need it."

"What about breakfast?" Headworth threw in.

"I didn't have enough for breakfast." Oceana responded, "Not paying her would have been wrong."

"It's fine. I have some money." Jamlson said.

"See Jamlson has our backs." Oceana grinned.

Both Headworth and Jamlson groaned at her response, but nevertheless, they began to march down the city of the Westside Mountains.

It was incredible, the city, there were music players everywhere, not only was there a lovely song in each corner of the block, but there would be the occasional painter, who would sit by and you could watch them practice art. They all eventually walked past another park that carried people on stage wearing the most bizarre costumes that Oceana had ever seen. A man wearing a rabbit mask with a bright purple suit pointed his finger up in the sky.

"Radio stars are a thing of the past! Do you want to get your name out there? Look no further! We are currently hiring actors!" Then, he shouted, "For picture shows!"

The crowd clapped in joy, excited at the new idea of picture shows; technology indeed had come a long way.

"Hey, you!" The man who talked pointed in the crowd. Oceana felt her spine shiver- did they recognize her? Was she caught? Was the outfit not slick enough? "Yes, sir, with the purple scarf!" Oceana sighed in relief, however, her attention was now gripped on what the man had to say to Jamlson. "You are a very handsome young lad. Why don't you come here and sign up to become an actor! You would be hired immediately with looks alone!" Jamlson noticed the number of eyes piercing at him. A couple of the people from the crowd exchanged words of whispers in agreement. "Come on lad- you can't waste that handsome face!" Jamlson moved his scarf up to cover his face and turned around. He moved away from the crowd faster than the rest of his group.

"Look at you!" Oceana said to him when she finally caught up to him.

"Shut up-. They try to butter up any unsuspecting travelers," Jamlson mumbled.

"New News! New News!" A woman shouted. She held up the cover of a magazine paper in her hands. "Check it out! Dangerous situation! The rise of a cult!" Oceana stopped and walked up to the woman.

"The rise of a cult?"

"Oh yes!" She stepped off her box. "Read it here." She moved the magazine close to Oceana's face. "They are coming in numbers! Very scary if you ask me!" She said with wide eyes.

"I heard-" Another woman walked up to the two, dressed similarly to the girl next to her. "That Sage Magnus is coming back."

"Oh, hush-" The other girl said. "Sage Magnus is dead. We shouldn't be questioning the Knight and Magician's work." She threw in.

"Do you think it's true?" Oceana asked. The women stopped talking.

"We keep our hearts locked in Cor'Meum's doors." The woman said.

"Do read our paper!" The other woman threw Oceana the magazine. She looked at the paper's headline.

"Big Underground Tragedy!"

'Violent Criminals underground tried to overthrow our beloved Cor'Meum. Luckily KEEPIN officers were there to stop them. They sold things such as weapons, knives, bombs, any and all things to hurt our beloved capital with." our double agents state, "All the things that were sold there were weapons. Nothing there was harmless- all the people in there were clearly dangerous. It was truly a miracle that the underground market was stopped. We thank the king. "'

This was simply not true, she thought. How could Cor'Meum publish facts that aren't based on truth? However, before Oceana could continue her thought, she felt her shirt pulled at.

"Oceana- come on." Jamlson said..

"I have to go! Bye!" Oceana handed the paper back to the woman.

"Wait, you can't just read for free!" She yelled. But Oceana was far gone."Ugh, I am so sick of these freeloaders." She mumbled.

They walked past several buildings. Headworth stopped in front of a very tall brown one that held gears in the front to count the time passing by. He looked over at Jamlson and Oceana, and nodded, Oceana then stepped in front of him and pushed the glass doors open to step inside.

Inside, an expansive room held two sofas and a coffee table in front of them. Aside from that, the place was empty, Oceana looked over to the right and found two doors. One seemed normal. One had buttons next to it.

"Uh, what story is he on?"

"The tenth."

Oceana looked at the buttons on the door and pressed them. The elevator's top buttons glowed, and the doors opened, welcoming anyone to join it. She looked over at Headworth and Jamlson and stepped inside the thing. When TOAD stepped inside the elevator, it gave a bit of a jiggle which nearly gave Oceana a heart attack. The doors then began to close, trapping the four of them inside.

It felt like it was an eternity when going up the elevator. Oceana watched the numbers glow with each story they had passed. They were almost done. Once the doors opened, Oceana was the first to step out.

"Let's find Bellus Timidus." She insisted and turned to the hallway. It was not hard to find his room number. There were only three apartments on the floor.

"Well, here it is." Headworth said, standing in front of the apartment door whose numbers read 'Thirty-four B.' Oceana felt her stomach do a backward kick, and it wasn't because of the bumpy elevator ride. They stepped forward, holding out their left fist, ready to knock on the door. They closed their eyes, sighed, and pressed their knuckles on the door. Prepared to strike, but the door just pushed itself open.

The door revealed a big room with a Chantler in its middle. There were two poles on the right side of the room, opening itself to a hallway. The room was filled with bright green sofas that looked more to be used for decoration than comfort. There was also a giant window next to the couches that gave an open view of the whole city.

Oceana pushed the remainder of the door open. The music that was playing became louder the closer she got to it. It appeared to be playing on an old phonograph. A woman was humming while she listened to the music that played next to her. She seemed to be making something in the kitchen, lost in her own world. Oceana looked over at the boys behind her, none of whom seemed willing to be the ones to snap her out of her world. Oceana looked back at the woman, a long dress moving along in the beat. Her thinning dark hair was wrapped in a bandana.

"Hello?" Oceana questioned.

The woman jumped and turned around, dropped her teacup, and held onto her chest. Now seeing her face, Oceana had caught the heavy set of makeup the woman was wearing. Dark blue eyeshadow that matched her dress. She wore a pure white 'KEEPIN' pin on the right of her dress. She also wore a rich set of red lipstick. She scrunched up her face.

"Who are you?" She yelled in a whispering voice. "Why did you open my door without knocking?"

"We did knock, but the door just opened." Jamlson insisted. Both Headworth and Oceana nodded, feeling guilty about scaring her. Although Oceana honestly wished she had just closed the door and tried knocking again, it probably wasn't a great idea just walking in like that.

"Oh! That darn repairman was supposed to come by hours ago to fix the door. I warned him that intruders could come in. But he only laughed and said it wasn't possible. Now he knows that when I die, my blood is on his hands! Good luck living the rest of your days knowing you sent a sweet old woman to her death!" She then began to curse at the man. Oceana felt it was an excellent time to step in, attempting to explain why they were here.

"Oh no! We promise we aren't trying to rob you!" Oceana put her hands out and looked back at Headworth and Jamlson who nodded along.

"Oh yeah?" The old woman raised her eyebrow, leaving her hands on her hips.

"Yeah! We are only here to talk to Bellus Timidus." She said,

The old woman took off her headband, ran her fingers through her short curly hair, and gave a long sigh before shooting them a look of distrust.

"Now, what would you want to say to a delusional man?" She asked coldly.

"What?" Oceana raised an eyebrow. "What's wrong? Is he okay?"

"Bellus Timidus is sick." She replied. "He hasn't been well in quite some time. He just- he just isn't right." She moved to her kitchen counter, picked up a cigarette, and took a lighter. She began fumbling with it before she got a flame. Finally, she moved the small flame to her cigarette that rested in her mouth; once on fire, she put down the lighter and blew out a big puff of gray smoke. "Not in his head." She muttered.

"Well, umm-" Oceana paused for a moment. She felt uncertain if it was appropriate to ask, but she came all this way, and he was the key to helping her find her grandpa. There was no room for giving up, so she decided to muster up the courage to look at Mrs. Timidus. "Is it- or rather, would it be alright if I could speak to him?"

Mrs. Timidus took in the cigarette, giving in a long inhale before blowing out some smoke. "It'll be a waste of time."

"I came all this way here to speak to him," Oceana said. Mrs. Timidus raised an eyebrow at her. "Please." Oceana threw in. She kept her eyes locked on Mrs. Timidus.

Mrs. Timidus sighed and moved to the significant archways that led into a hallway. They all looked at each other. Gave one another a shrug and began to follow her down the hallway. She led them to a giant golden door. She looked at all of them and pointed.

"This is his nursery. He spends every waking second there. Every other hour the maids come in to take care of him. Besides that, that's all he does all day. Oceana looked at Jamlson and Headworth, who exchanged looks of unsettling circumstances. Oceana opened the door to just what she had expected, an old man lying in bed. He looked very sick and so skinny that the bones in his arms were practically showing. He kept his eyes on the ceiling, managing a steady pace of breath.

Oceana took a step forward. She did come all this way here. It wouldn't hurt to attempt a conversation with him.

"Hello, Bellus."

He ignored her, or maybe he didn't know she was in the room. He kept his eyes on the ceiling, not blinking them once. She couldn't tell if there was a rational process of thoughts going on in his head, or perhaps he had lost touch with the world around him. She proceeded to step closer to him. She wanted to see if her words could get through to him. Eventually, when she was near him, she grabbed a chair and sat on it in the slowest of motion, afraid that the small gust of wind would break him. She could tell that this chair was probably made by the top company in the world, meant to serve a purpose of complete comfort. She didn't feel that way right now.

She sat at the edge of the chair and kept her eyes on Bellus Timidus, who continued to keep his focus on the ceiling above him. She didn't notice how blue his eyes were until now, since she sat so close to him. He and his wife appeared to have bright blue eyes, however his eyes were very similar to her own, perhaps exact. They were blue with a gray color that rested in the middle. After years of staring at her eyes, almost wishing they were a natural purple like her mother's, she began picking up small details about her own eye color. How the gray in her eyes almost dominated the blue. It was its own brand of uniqueness, she supposed. She hadn't seen anyone else with this color, not until today.

Besides their very similar eye color, she had always hoped she would get the chance to be a legend like him. "Well." she coughed in her hand, "Since I was a little kid, I've always wanted to be like you. Someone brave that fights crime and represents the coolest army in the world! I even have a sword too! Though admittedly, since I could first remember, I had always wanted to do magic. I would still say that's my biggest goal in life!" She paused. "But since I am having a less than ideal time practicing magic, I settled for the art of the sword." She sighed, pressed her hands to her face, and then brought her attention back to him. "Well, you recently wrote a letter to my grandpa, and I wondered if you knew where he was. He's gone missing." She sighed. "It's important that I find him, I am scared he is going into something alone, and I can help him! I am strong enough! But in order for me to find him, you have to tell me where he is or what was in that letter you wrote him that set him off."

Bellus moved his eyes to look at her, but it hadn't seemed he did so to acknowledge her existence, but just the mere fact that he could. Bellus

Timidus really had no idea that she was there. He was in a whole other world beyond her and anyone in the room.

"Just give me a sign." Oceana whispered as she moved closer and picked up his hand with her own, "Anything." She paused, but Bellus kept breathing heavily, staring at her, almost as if he was staring right past her. There was only silence between the two, she stared at him, but nothing came from it. She began to feel that sense of powerlessness again. Powerless when her mother had disappeared, powerless when her home was reduced to nothing but ash. That same hopelessness overwhelmed her, that she tried to ignore since the start of this journey. She felt tears build-up, so she closed her eyes and breathed in.

She felt that it was enough. There wasn't a point to continue interviewing him. He clearly wasn't going to respond to her. She decided to stand up so he could go back to whatever he was doing inside his head. She had come all this way, hoping she would understand what had happened to her grandpa. Why she was clearly left in the dark about his disappearance. She truly hoped that she would understand at least something at this point in her journey, but it almost seemed she was even more lost and confused than before. How frustrating. Though she knew she couldn't get upset with Bellus, he was sick. While this whole trip was coming to a conclusion to be pointless, at least she got to meet one of her heroes, even if he wasn't in his right mind frame.

"Well," Oceana said. "It was a pleasure meeting you." She gave a slight smile. She then took off her hat. She felt removing it would present as more humble. Once she had done this, she and every other person in the room could not have predicted what would happen next. It was an immediate shock when the sincere silence was broken by a scream.

A blood-thinning scream came out of Bellus' mouth. It filled the whole room, actually perhaps the entire building. He trashed his body up high in the air, almost as if an invisible giant was shaking him. Then, he wailed out another scratchy scream hurting the eardrums of anyone close to him, which unfortunately was Oceana at that moment.

"Not me! Not me!" He cried. "No more!" He shouted, "I don't want to fight! Please- please!"

A couple of Bellus's personal nurses rushed into the room and grabbed hold of him. She watched them open a box and pull out a syringe and some bottles filled with mysterious clear liquids.

"Please! No more! No more! I'm sorry!" Bellus sobbed. The scene was shocking. Oceana did not notice how long she was staring until one of the nurses turned to her and pointed at the door. The nurse insisted that Oceana should leave. Before Oceana could exit the room, she felt a cold hand wrap around her wrist. She turned her attention to Bellus! His eyes shot her with fear! His blood-curdling screams continued!

"Back! Back!" He wailed. "Magnus is back! Magnus!" He cried. "Magnus is back! I- don't hurt me!" Oceana tried to pull their hand away, but his grip tightened. He yanked her towards him. "The devil is real, child," He shouted under his breath, his voice dipped deeper. "And it's inside you too. He's there- I see your evil. You can't hide it from me. I see it. I know who you are. Who you really are! Get ready for the rise of the Magnus! Because-" Oceana didn't know what more he had to say. His grip softened, and his eyes closed. Oceana moved her attention to the nurse who had the needle inside his other arm. Another nurse grabbed Oceana and guided her out of the room. They all carried a look of disapproval.

Once Oceana was out of the room, she placed her hat back on her head. She looked down at her wrist, which was slightly pink from moments before.

Jamlson closed the door leaving the nurses to attend to their patient.

"What a weirdo- what did he say to you?" Jamlson question. Oceana shook her head.

"Just uh- nonsense-" She lied. "I only hope he's okay," Oceana said; a heavy feeling in her heart came about. So Magnus was coming back- was it Sage Magnus?

"I'm sure he's fine," Jamlson said insistently. "He seems like he's under good care." The screaming from inside the room stopped. Whatever the nurses were doing, they were successfully calming him down.

"Well, did you get anything out of my unstable husband?" Mrs. Timidus asked with her arms crossed,

"No." Oceana admitted.

"Figures." Mrs. Timidus said. "Since you kids came all the way here, do you want any tea?" The three of them all looked at one another and nodded.

The radio had been turned off. Usually, when living next to such a busy city like the Westside Mountains the melody of vehicles would play all day long. The room itself was covered in various portraits of either beautiful men or women in tasteful outfits. The shelves that surrounded them carried small glass artifacts that felt like if one would breathe on it, the artifact would cease to exist. They all sat around the couch awkwardly, in silence, and they all agreed to wait for the maid to bring their tea to them.

TOAD had not understood the definition of standstill, Mrs. Timidus had denied permission for the mechanical to sit on the couch, afraid that he would break it. TOAD wandered around the room, and stared at all the decorations, he reached his claw to touch one of the small glass statues that rested above the fireplace, only to be interrupted by Headworth who shouted at him to not touch anything. With his quiet defeat, he went back to exploring the rest of the room, remaining in the eye of everyone.

"Where did you guys come from?" Mrs. Timidus asked. The three kids all shared a couch.

"Magna East. All of us are from there." Oceana said.

"A long way." Mrs. Timidus said. The maid finally presented all of them with their tea, placing it on the coffee table. Oceana grabbed hers in such a quick motion that she had forgotten to not use her right hand, which sent a surprise shock of pain that invoked her to drop her cup, shattering it on the ground.

"I am so sorry!" Oceana apologized immediately.

Mrs. Timidus shook her head and clapped her hands, "Mindy!" She shouted, and in one fast motion, one of the housekeepers came with a white rag and began to clean the mess Oceana had created. "It's fine. Mindy is really good at making this place look spotless." Mrs. Timidus said proudly. Almost if she herself was taking credit for the work, her maids were doing. She looked over at Oceana's hand, "What is that gross bandage? It's so dirty, you will not be touching my silverware with that." She said, not giving Oceana room to respond. "We have a nurse here who could properly wrap that up for you." This comment made Oceana want to hide her fingers, but she probably should get them treated. Mrs. Timidus called over one of her personal nurses, who immediately began to work on Oceana's hand. The nurse removed the original cloth Jamlson had wrapped.

"Mrs. Timidus, I have the cake as requested." Another one of the maids placed a small cake in front of them, already sliced up and ready to grab.

"Thank you." Mrs. Timidus smiled and grabbed a slice. She looked up at them and noticed the three of them weren't taking any pieces. "What are you allergic to good pastries?" She questioned. "Grab one!"

The nurse that worked on Oceana's hand stepped back once she had finished, This allowed Oceana to begin eating the cake at Mrs. Timidus' request. Oceana looked at her hand, which was wrapped in a white bandage. It felt like her fingers were being forced to move back in place. Oceana leaned in and grabbed the slice of cake. Mrs. Timidus was definitely intense, it seemed that not eating this cake would be insulting to her.

Oceana stabbed the vanilla cake with her fork and took a small bite out of it. The cake was pretty good, she could not remember when she last had a pastry, and her stomach was on the empty side. On the other hand, it felt weird taking the cake from a woman whose place she just busted through. She couldn't help but wonder how often Mrs. Timidus had company over, if ever at all.

"This is really good," Oceana said, maneuvering her fork to snatch another piece of the sweetness.

"Of course it is. I only have the best cake to offer! If your husband made money-saving this country from chaos, you would only have the best cake there is." She said,

"With that reputation, we might not be the first intruders you had offered cake too." Jamlson joked, but it only made the room fall flat. Mrs.

Timidus did not look too pleased with the comment, this made Jamlson stick more cake in his mouth.

"Why in the Westside Mountains?" Oceana asked. "Don't retired army men move to Annularity?"

"Annularity is too crowded for us. Kind of like how East Magna would have been too." She pointed her fork at all of them.

"But isn't the Westside Mountains also big?" Oceana asked.

"It isn't huge, I suppose." She said, taking in her drink. "Living in a big city is a hassle but in a small town." She shuddered. "We would never live near those. They usually have some folks who live by the ways of magic." She said coldly.

"Is that a bad thing?" Oceana asked right away. She didn't mean to appear so hostile in the question she had just asked, but she had no idea what Mrs. Timidus was referring to.

"Of course, magic prevents invitations from happening. It's also the main source of what those Vibriusians use; trash. You know they are the reason why we were thinking about moving out of here."

"What do you mean?" Oceana asked immediately, she felt her heart racing. It took everything in her not to shout. Her husband was the Knight, how could she be saying this? Her husband was the face of peace between Vibrius and Cor'Meum, and she was talking down on them. Her husband was inadvertently a part of KEEPIN. Yet he also had these views? How many other KEEPIN offers felt this way? Oceana felt a shiver run down her back and the thought of associating herself with that. "When you say trash? Virbius people or magic?" Oceana asked; her heart pounding with anger, the grip on her silverware tightened.

"Magic users! Maybe some of them are dirty Virbus people, but the magic. They make these streets scary to walk on these days. Like those revolutionaries." Oceana was about to stand up from the way she had talked about Virbus people, but the mention of the revolution stopped her. Was this what the gas mask people were a part of? Suddenly she remembered some talks about a revolution on her grandfather's ship! This was a few weeks before he disappeared. She hadn't thought anything of it at the time, but maybe her grandfather was a part of this somehow..

"A-a revolution?" Oceana asked.

"The revolution! I am surprised you haven't heard of it. Maybe the media here is trying to cover it up to grab more fools into living here. Under these dangerous times."

Headworth decided he didn't want to eat more of the cake from the woman who was speaking like this, served him. So he delicately put the plate down and turned to Oceana.

"I am grabbing TOAD, not because I feel uncomfortable." He said and stood up, leaving the room to find his buddy. Oceana turned back to Mrs. Timidus, who was now looking out the huge window behind her couch, which allowed her a full view of the park across the street.

"Look at them." She whispered under her breath. "The fools, all of them."

"What's this revolution?" Oceana asked. "What is it about? I heard about it a few weeks ago, and I don't know what it means."

"It means something bad is happening. I see them at night. At midnight they meet there." She pressed her finger on the window. "The magic users conspire. They are after my husband and me. They want us. They think he lied, that there is a hidden truth."

"Why would they think that?" Oceana asked. Her heart skipped a beat. She thought back on what the women in the street told her. What Bellus had told her.

"I don't know." Finally, she snapped. She was still facing the window. "I don't really know. magic users just hate us."

"Why?" Oceana asked, "Who are they? What do they think he lied about?"

Mrs. Timidus turned around, ran her fingers through her dark hair, and looked at the two who remained on the couch. "They think my husband lied about killing Sage Magnus, they-" She paused and then glared at the two, "think he is coming back."

Oceana felt her stomach drop. Had this been the confirmation she was looking for? The men who kidnapped Bovark at the bar, the strange people that Headworth had been sending information to, the weird letter that Mr. Williams had sent to her grandpa. Even Bellus said so himself. Was this the tie? Was this what brought everything together, the fact that there was a possibility that Sage Magnus was coming back from the dead. Perhaps that is why the Magician, wherever he was, decided to remain in hiding because when the truth came out, he didn't want to face the consequences.

"Do you believe that this is true?" Oceana asked with hesitation.

"No! Of course not!" Mrs. Bellus threw her hand up. "If you ask me, they are all crazy! All of them!"

"Right." Jamlson whispered, "They're crazy."

"I know my husband killed that jack's man!" Mrs. Timidus yelled. "Anyone who doubts him should be ashamed, ashamed of themselves.

He worked so hard." She said, thoroughly brushing off the fact that he worked with one of the most powerful Magicians in history other than the Magnes', the only family that could use three tones of magic.

"What happened to your husband?" Jamlson asked.

"What?"

"I saw some bruises on his arm. Like someone had been physically attacking him." Jamlson pointed out, "It seems it's covered with the skin blush powder." He pointed at his own arm for an example, "I could tell because my mom uses that powder for her face to make her skin look clear."

"That's enough tea and cake for you! You all better be on your way!" She clapped her hands, and the maid came back and began collecting all of their dishes. "Out, go on out with you!" She pointed at the door.

Both Oceana and Jamlson stood up, gearing themselves to the exit of the large apartment. They managed to grab Headworth and TOAD before they had left the premises, leaving the Timidus residence. After the door had shut, Mrs. Timidus stood in the company of the radio's sounds.

"That was the end of the song 'She's driving me crazy!' by Harvey Hill! Before getting into our next playlist, we want to thank today's sponsor! KEEPIN! That is right, Keepin! Keeping Everlasting Extravagant Peace-" Though it was predictable what the following lines had followed, Mrs. Timidus did not want to hear the rest. She had taken her talk box and threw it on the ground before proceeding to stomp on it.

"Madam!" The maid explained, running out of the room where her husband was being taken care of. "Are you okay?"

"Does it look like I am okay?" She snipped at the other woman, who was standing behind the hall with a frightened look on her face.

"You didn't tell them what happened, did you? Or that you sent a letter to Wilic."

"Are you asking so you could report me you wrench?" Mrs. Timidus asked,

"Of course not! I would never do that!" The maid Mindy explained that she had then dared to leave her hallway wall of protection. "Madam, you look sicker and sicker every day. Maybe you should have confined that kid to what has happened. I think she was-"

"I know who they are! She and her family are why my husband is there, fighting for his sanity and life!" She pointed at the room where her husband was being confined. There was silence now. The maid had once again felt brave enough to raise her voice.

"Madam what happened, really?" She asked, "Why did KEEPIN officers come in here and torture your husband? What did they want from him?"

Mrs. Timidus moved in circles, and she pressed her fingers to her lips. "He kept a secret. A dangerously foolish one from our King." Mrs. Timidus moved to look out the open window and kept her eyes on the people below who walked across the street without a care in the world. The cars drove by in an orderly fashion as they were supposed to. The children played on the swings and slides while their parents' lurking eyes pierced them from a nearby bench.

"That Marlyn Sanford was adopted."

The Cor'Meum flag with the diamond-encrusted eye waved proudly on the flagpole that rested outside the home of Timidus. A flag that shared the colors of that of the army of KEEPIN. A flag whose eyes have become symbolized, always being watched, taking care of all Cor'Meum citizens.

CHAPTER 17:

The rise of a Dead King

THE group of friends that stood next to this pole had their own thoughts on what they had just witnessed. However, Jamlson decided to be the first to say a thought they all had in common.

"What a bunch of weirdos." He looked back at the building and stared at the large tinted window that belonged to them. "I am sorry, Oceana, that this whole trip has been a complete waste of time," he added.

Oceana pressed her hand on her chin, indicating that she had something on her mind. "Maybe, but not really." She said, "I think we got a lot from that meeting." she said.

"How could you find anything useful from that crazy woman?" Headworth asked. "She is completely out of her head!" He threw his arms up. "She scared, TOAD! TOAD!"

"Yes, I agree, but she talked about a revolution," Oceana said.

"What do you mean?" Jamlson asked, scared of where this was going.

"Well, I mean, if we, you know, say we tried to sneak into one of these revolutionary meetings, we could perhaps,"

"No," Jamlson said.

"Maybe get in."

"No." Jamlson said again. "This seems like it is too dangerous and something that is beyond our control. So let's just have the KEEPIN soldiers or whatever take care of it."

"I don't know if KEEPIN soldiers even know about this. It all seems like it's very hushed up." Oceana said, "Plus, they are looking for my grandpa. He's a wanted man."

"If something this out in the open is known by town members, I am sure KEEPIN soldiers know about it," Jamlson said.

"Maybe," Oceana said, "Or maybe they don't, or if they do, they think it's a waste of time."

"They're right to think that," Headworth stated. "That woman was insane. It is unbelievable you two are discussing the possibility of this being real." Headworth said. "Lunacy." He finished his sentence.

"You're right, Headworth. We shouldn't talk about this." Oceana stated, "We should have a stakeout and catch these people red-handed!" She snapped her fingers with her left hand.

"What?" Jamlson asked, "This mission is risky."

"You are right. It is risky, but you are also right that we came so far." She said, "What are we supposed to do? Give up?" She said, "We are so close. This might be the answer we are looking for. This could be the missing puzzle piece to how we find my grandpa." They said with a slight smile. "Please."

Jamlson kept his eyes on her. It felt like they were staring at one another for hours when it probably was only just a minute or so. A sweat began to break on Jamlson's head. The awkwardness was too much for him, he threw his head back with a slightly annoyed groan before he said, "Fine, I am in."

"Speak for yourself," Headworth said.

"Excuse me?" Jamlson raised an eyebrow. "May I remind you who risked her life grabbing your mechanical when no one else did? Who forgave you for almost burning them alive? Who also paid for every meal you've had in the past few days?"

Headworth groaned. "Before you continue your persistence for a minute longer, I believe I get the point," Headworth said sharply, "You are trying to make. So I feel that my vote is revoked for sure." Headworth almost whispered, then looked over at TOAD, who gave a couple of blinks at him. "TOAD would also like to participate."

Oceana smiled widely. "Great!" She turned to Jamlson. "I truly believe this is the answer we have been looking for!" She said,

"If you feel like this is the right thing to do, I am behind you to ensure you don't get yourself blown up," Jamlson said with a grin and eye roll. "Kind of my only friend."

Oceana smiled. "Yes!" She said, "This is great! We should come back tonight! See what this whole meeting thing is about."

The group moved down the street, to explore what the rest of the town had to offer before their big mission that night. Oceana stopped in front of a glass wall, behind it there were examples of the latest televisions. "New and improved," the bright red stickers told those who stopped by. Oceana looked at the screen to view what was playing. It was interesting to her that screenings were becoming more popular than the projections.

Trapped in black and white, was an image of King Erebus himself, in front of him was a girl like no other, Aster. She had a bored expression on her face, while her father flashed a smile at the camera. He wore a suit, his long hair that was normally frizzy was held together by the world's strongest rubber band. His beard also looked like it was groomed today.

"Aster just won first place in the Cor'Meum 'Art of Swords' regionals!" The interviewer announced. "You really crushed that other girl! How do you feel? Are you confident that you'll win nationals." Aster moved her mouth to open it, but it appeared that King Erebus must have believed the question was directed for him.

"Aster of course is number one!" He said with a smile. "She only gets first place and would never settle for a second place prize. She's our perfect star. Did you know Aster graduated from her private school at the top of her class?" King Erebus grinned and rested a hand on the girl's shoulder. Aster remained where she stood.

"I have heard about Aster's accomplishments and ongoing winning streak!" The interviewer said. "You must be proud!"

"Oh we are beyond proud. I know if her mother were here, she would be too." King Erebus smiled. "She is showing the country how strong and capable she is! She can overcome any sort of challenge. She is quite literally the best at everything."

"Oh we know! She sure is talented! What an honor to interview her! Oh- it also looks like we are out of time!" The interviewer nodded his head. "That concludes our interview with Princess Aster! We can't wait to interview you again next week!"

"She'll be ready." King Erebus chimed. Oceana watched Aster look away from the camera with the same bored expression, before it was quickly turned to another station. Oceana was impressed with all the achievements Aster had been winning the past several years! Life must be so exciting for her. "Oceana!" She heard Jamlson shout. "What are you doing? Come here!"

"Yeah!" Headworth said. "This man is tricking the public that he is made of metal by painting himself in silver!" Headworth said and almost sounded offended by the man's acts.

The Westside Mountains began to shut its eyes to the hardworking locals that lived in the beautiful town. Public Gadgets began to close once the sun started to set, and the people remained inside their homes to either begin to sleep or to finish up their dinners. Everything in the town seemed almost still. Not even the dogs barked their furious cries at the moon. Behind a building nearby, Oceana, Jamlson, Headworth, and TOAD stood. They waited in silence for anything to happen in front of the park. As Mrs. Timidus stated, it happens every night. Oceana heard the gentle swinging of the swings that were near. Swinging with the help of the light winds that had been trotting on since the afternoon. She watched the street lights loom the dark streets to a brighter presence, though not helping the atmosphere of the stakeout.

"Do you really think they are coming?" Headworth asked, "The lady is crazy."

"We just gotta wait," Oceana replied.

"Fine."

Another hour had passed since the conversation. Nothing had happened. Everything remained the same. The streets were untouched. The swing had managed to stop swaying after the wind had given up its journey tonight. Maybe it will pick it back up tomorrow. There was nothing that indicated a live presence on the street. Everyone was home and asleep, which was something Oceana had desperately wanted to do herself. But she needed to wait. Her grandpa taught her that patience was the key to success. If a man licked the leak, there would be no more water for him. But if he waited and let the water accumulate in a cup, he would be able to drink. This meant that she needed to stay. She shouldn't dry the leak yet, which she rationalized this stakeout to be. Another hour had passed without a word exchanged amongst those who could talk. Oceana could feel their eyes drop. The heaviness of this steakout was getting to her.

"Oceana." Jamlson said after breaking the very long silence, "I think we should go. Maybe Headworth was right. The old woman was a bit crazy."

"Give it like one more minute." Oceana held their hand out.

"Oceana."

"Wait! Shh! I think I just heard something!" Oceana hushed.

After a long heavy silence, there was a clank. Everyone held their breaths, wondering what it could be. The street light flickered back on, detecting some motions. This was what they all had been waiting for. Another clank was heard, and a tumble came after. Within the next second, a trash can that rested not too far from the park fell down, and a heavy wailing of a cat cried out in the dark. The cat bolted next to them, giving one last cry before taking off in the night. Once the cat had disappeared, there was nothing but silence again. This left them in the same position they had been in for the past few hours.

"Oceana, maybe we should-" But Jamlson was interrupted by someone

"Ah, crab cakes on a stick!" A man shouted, moving into the light with another man. "That cat nearly gave me a damn heart attack!"

"You are fine." The other man said. "Anyways, where is Maddalin with the new recruits?"

"I don't know! If it were me grabbing them, I would have been here hours ago."

"Whatever The Boss wants new people to try out leadership, waste of time if you ask me."

Both the men were wearing identical black suits and black gas masks with the green-lit up eyes that matched the people at Bo's bar. Also, who was this boss guy she keeps hearing about? Maybe if they followed them, she might be able to meet 'The Boss'. She just had to wait for the right time.

The four of them waited in silence with the two masked individuals. Another half-hour had passed before they exchanged more conversations with one another.

"Never will Maddalin be put in charge again." The taller of the two said.

But before the other one could speak, another masked individual came out of the darkness, following behind him around fifteen other people who weren't wearing masks like the other three. Finally, the third masked man leading the group of people put his hands up, and jogged ahead of the crowd.

"Sorry, sorry, sorry I'm late." He said, "You said we are leaving this location after tonight, and I wanted to gather as many supporters as possible."

The two masked men that were waiting looked at one another, then at the crowd of people,

"Yeah, this will do." The taller one said, "Good job Maddalin." He moved in front of him to face the crowd. "People of the new resistance, come with me! The truth will shine a light on all of you soon." He turned around and began to lead the crowd away.

"Let's sneak in," Oceana said, pulling her hat forward.

"What about TOAD?" Headworth asked.

"Uhh, just have him bend or something." Oceana shrugged.

"Right; right bend or something. Because you know the frameworks of the mechanical that I have created in just the span of a day." Headworth crossed his arms. Headworth looked over at TOAD and moved his finger in circles, to which TOAD bent his legs in response.

The four of them ran across the street, hidden in the cloak of the night. They managed to make their way organically into the crowd of people. Oceana looked around and got on her toes to see the back of the heads of the masked men. They continued to walk amongst the crowd, Oceana was too far to hear the conversation that was happening amongst the masked individuals. She decided she needed a better ear.

Oceana moved inside the crowd, lightly pushing herself amongst the people inside, climbing her way to the front. Once she had achieved that, she moved amongst the show to silently listen to what the masked men would say or the purpose of this gathering. Maybe she'll find Bo through them.

"I really hope they waited for us. That would be really annoying if we missed the ceremony." The short one said amongst the three of them.

"They wouldn't start unless they had everyone here. We aren't Cor'Meum scum. We believe every human is worth the wait." The taller one said, "Are you positive that no KEEPIN soldiers followed us."

"Yeah, I checked the perimeter," Maddalin said; Oceana could tell it was him for Maddalin's accent was a lot thicker than the two next to him. They all moved forward in the night. They didn't pick up their conversation again for the remainder of the journey. Oceana couldn't help but think what ceremony this 'boss' was going to be at? Who was he? She wondered if 'The Boss' was Sage Magnus. After all, he was a powerful man. He and his family were the only ones that could control three tones of magic. She wouldn't be surprised if he managed to escape with his life all those years ago with that amount of power. They all stopped moving.

Oceana looked around and realized that they were in the city's center. How long was she thinking? She hadn't even realized they walked that much or for how long. She looked around to see exactly where they were in the city. All she knew was that they were away from the park. She moved her eyes to look in front of them. They were all standing in front of a huge building. It stood just like the others with all the lights off. The building held up a sign that said "Workman's Toyshop, " which surprised her. That's a kids' toyshop. This was being used to hold these secret meetings. The tall masked man knocked on the door in a strange rhythmic beat, indicating to whoever was inside that it was safe to open it.

When the door opened Oceana was not surprised that there was another masked individual on the other side,

"You're late." The door opener said with no hesitation.

"Yeah, we're sorry. But, hopefully, the crowd will make up for it."

The one behind the door took a peek outside. They looked at the large group of people waiting outside the toyshop. Then, the person turned their attention to the tall, similarly masked individual. "It will do." They said, taking a step back to let all the other people in.

When Oceana stepped inside the grey room, she barely saw where she was going until the tall masked man opened the door behind the check-out area, letting light seep in from the existing light next door. When the room brightened, the door that guided them was immediately shut.

"A mechanical?" The door opener's voice stabbed the attention of everyone in the room.

Oceana turned around, seeing Headworth sweat. He took his glasses off and tried to hide that he was shaking. "Ah yes, I was hoping to present my machine of war to The Boss. So he could perhaps use the ideological code to modify perfect copies that could be similar to the one presented in front of us." He smiled and finished cleaning his glasses to press them back on his face.

"Maddalin," The masked door opener boomed, "You brought an inventor on our team?"

Maddalin looked around at the other two masked men standing next to him. He then nodded at the door opener.

"Yes!" He said

"Well, good job." The door opener replied and locked the door before throwing two fingers at the taller masked individual. He moved away from the door, letting people come into the brighter room. Chattering began to start up. Oceana tried to make her way back to Jamlson and Headworth, but the crowd pushed her towards the room. Before she went in, she looked at the taller masked individual in the eyes through their dark green goggles. She moved the cap of her hat back in front of her face before a shiver ran down her back. She didn't have a good feeling about this meeting, but she couldn't back out of it now. She had to know what this was about. When entering the room, the light became a bit more blinding for half of a second. She opened her eyes to find a large room already filled with other revolution members.

Some chairs were neatly ordered. There were four large sections across the room, each carried about, maybe if Oceana had to guess without counting, fifty to forty chairs each. She had underestimated how large this group was.

"Take a seat in an empty chair, and the ceremony will begin." The tall masked man said.

Oceana walked down the stairs in front of her. Then moved her way down the aisle of one of the sections. She took a seat next to an older woman who was about to burst with excitement. Oceana wished she could feel a sense of excitement, but she only felt her stomach turn and burn similarly to an uncertain campfire. She pressed her hand on her tummy, hoping it would do the trick of calming her down. Footsteps interrupted her thoughts. When she looked up at the stage, she saw a man grin widely at the crowd.

"What a turnout!" He said, throwing his hands up, which encouraged the crowd to cheer with a heavy breeze of excitement. Oceana clapped with the group so as not to appear conspicuous. "Wow! When I first joined the revolution," the man said, "We hadn't thought we would be where we are now! But look at us!" He said. He took a breath in to admire the crowd.

"We grow more and more members every day, thanks to you guys!" He pointed at the crowd, which cheered back; Oceana looked around at the excited members of the group. "Now, I know many of you expected to find The Boss here today, but unfortunately, there was a situation." The man sighed. "So I will apologize on behalf of 'The Boss.'" He then gave a wide grin. "But we do have a special guest," He pointed to the side of the stage. "Give a warm welcome to The Boss's right-hand man or rather lady," He gave a wink at the crowd, to which they laughed in response. "Pakimet Ignis!"

Oceana felt her heart drop. She collided in her chair and pulled the cap of her hat closer to her face. She watched the familiar woman with long curly dark hair move along finely on the stage. Her bright red shoes gave a click with each step she took. She moved in front of the microphone, and the man took a step back to give her room to talk. She cleared her throat before her brown eyes averted her attention to the crowd present in front of her.

"Thank you so much for the introduction. It is a pleasure standing before all of you today." She grinned. Her heavy accent filled the room. "I was a Vibrius citizen, growing up on farmland. Eating nothing but scratches that my father provided. Unable to use magic due to Cor'Meum's strike policy, banning us from practicing our own culture!" She said, to which the crowd booed. She put her hands up, which stuck everyone in silence. "My parents had a hard time feeding three children. It would kill them to see us starve. It killed them so much that my mother starved to death so my siblings and I could eat!" She shouted. "Want to know who is to blame for that? KEEPIN!" She said firmly as the crowd began to boo at the name "Why are Vibrius citizens suffering for a war that most of us weren't alive to participate in? Why does Cor'Meum think they have the right to have their own soldiers surveil us like we are monsters- take food from us? Food that would have given my mother the strength to be here today!" She yelled. The crowd was quick to shout in response and mutter in anger. "Why must we be punished for merely existing as people?" She asked. The crowd nodded in agreement.

When the crowd began to quiet down, she began to talk again, "When my mother died, my family was never the same. It is all thanks to KEEPIN soldiers stealing our hard-earned food from us! They hover over us, watching us, ensuring our magic doesn't get too out of hand." She held her hand up and snapped her fingers. An orange sphere appeared, it was soon surrounded by a dust of red. Pakiment moved her finger in a circular motion. This turned the red fog into flames.

"They try to convince you that magic is farmers' work, that it is nothing more than old tradition." She said, "But I know some of you in this crowd can perform magic! Risking your lives to learn the way of our people, to live another day. We must use it to defend ourselves against them! High tone, fire and air, middle tone, water and earth, and low tone, light and darkness. Elements that can destroy their machines any day." She paused and looked up at the crowd. "Which I know isn't the way of our ancestors, but haven't our people had enough of being pushed around? They put restrictions on our use of it. Do you want to know why?" She paused before taking one breath in. "Because they are scared! They know how powerful we are! We will rise up together! We will unite as Vibrius people! No more will we be shunned out of existence, and we will take our country back! We will find the Golden Apple before Cor'Meum does, and use it to fight them!" The crowd began to shout in excitement.

"But before we reach the apple, we will start small. By destroying the same tower that Bellus Timidus lives in tonight at midnight!" She shouted. Everyone stood up and cheered in response. "We can easily take down the glorified war criminal!" She emphasizes the word criminal. "He and everyone that lives in that building are KEEPIN soldiers- all with a history of brutalizing- attacking our people!" She shouted. "Of course, in Cor'Meum- its KEEPIN officers live in beautiful lavish buildings while we all starve on the streets.

Oceana only felt drenched in her own sweat, much like Headworth earlier. Golden Apple again? Explode the tower? She had to warn KEEPIN soldiers. But would they believe her? Her grandpa is a wanted man, after all. How could she warn people about this awful tragedy that would take place? Everyone was cheering, and Oceana did not understand why.

"By the way." Pakimet cleared her throat. "The Boss wanted me to tell you that we will not be using the name 'The Boss' anymore. We shall now be referring to The Boss as Sage Magnus! Do not be afraid to say his name!" She shouted.

"Sage Magnus!" A person from the audience shouted, "Sage Magnus! Sage Magnus!" Someone stood up chanting, and soon another person from the crowd stood up and shouted the same name. This brought on the excitement from the rest of the crowd. In just a short time, the rest of the crowd began to stand up, chanting the name Sage Magnus together at the same time, working together to be one unit of power.

"Thank you, everyone!" Pakimet kissed the crowd. She moved away from the stage, the masked people escorting her to the back. The crowd continued their cheer. They shouted his name freely and openly. Oceana felt it was now time to go. She stood up and turned around but couldn't find Jamlson or Headworth anywhere. Everyone was standing and cheering at this point. She began making her way down the hall to find them. It was incredibly frustrating because TOAD was a tall mechanical, one would think he was an easy eyesore to spot, but Headworth must have hid him when Pakimet came onto the stage.

She felt her head spin and felt the world around her would bend. The idea that everything she had been saying was all true- scared her. Though she knew that this outcome was the most reliable, she was not prepared for it to be the most honest. Oceana bit her lip, trying to remain calm, which she was not alone in trying to do.

"Alright, everyone, let's get back and settle in our seats, we sure do love our Pakimet, but this meeting isn't over yet! We have-" But Oceana couldn't say what his following words were going to be, the door was kicked down, and people in blue uniforms came. Excitement turned into an immediate panic.

Oceana was reminded of her time in the underground market and was pushed back by a flood of people. She watched KEEPIN soldiers attack members of the audience, some attempting to throw their own magic at them. Oceana turned around and found that KEEPIN Soldiers were wearing similarly structured masks as the revolutionary soldiers.

"Throw it!" Was the last thing Oceana heard until she heard the sound of a spark and snap. An explosion was released, and soon what came after it was a giant cloud of blue smoke; it effectively covered the room immediately. Oceana stood up but began seeing doubles of everyone,

"Wait," she said with a weak voice.

"Get the ones with masks!" She could hear, but she didn't know where.

"Stop it." She croaked out, but her legs began to give up. She tried to keep her eyes open, but it felt like a heavy weight was forcing her eyes to shut. She stumbled around before she felt her body falling, but her eyes closed before she could hit the ground.

Her eyes opened back up, and she found herself lying on a sofa in a dimly lit room. She was confused, not understanding how or when she had gotten here. She sat up from the couch and looked around to see if perhaps she could get a reasonable estimate of where she was. Unfortunately, all of her final conclusions led to a dead end. When she looked at the only window that appeared in the room, she was able to see the bright white ball in the sky, which told her not much time had passed. Aside from the sofa that she awoke from, a couch rested in front of her. In between the two couches, there was a small table. The two lamps that were parallel next to the only door that led into this small room were the only light source.

The only door to the room opened. There was an older man. His brown hair was slicked back, enough to see his widow's peak. His eyes were gray and tired. He walked with a posture so high, Oceana was nervous he would go through the ceiling. She also noticed he was wearing a Purple division uniform. He must have been sent from the castle.

He firmly placed himself on the couch in front of her, crossed his legs, and then placed a file on the table. "Oceana Liesbeth Sanford. Child of former fourth-ranked Purple division KEEPIN officer Marlyn Sarah Sanford." He simply said, "Who lived with yet another former fourth-ranked Red division officer Wilic Ellington." He pressed his fingers on his clean-shaven face and looked up at them.

Oceana looked at the man's purple uniform and saw the four golden stars displayed perfectly there. A fourth-ranked purple KEEPIN officer, Oceana began to wonder who he was.

"That is right." She said in a hurried voice. Her heart was pounding all of a sudden. But why? It probably was that sudden anxiety that seemed to swallow her lately. It came about whenever she confronted any KEEPIN officer. To which she still hadn't understood why. "But who are you? Also, where am I?" She asked almost in one breath.

The man combed his fingers through his aligned hair. It looked as if the man took at least an hour of his day to make his hair look perfect yet almost look fake. Like a mannequin. She watched him shift his position and stare at her. His chin moved down, and he removed his fingers from his chin to press them against one another. "Ms. Sanford I can't stress enough the kind of position you are in." He calmly stated, "You were found in enemy headquarters, with the added fact that your parental guardian is a wanted man."

"I have nothing to do with any of the reasons for him being wanted! I-I don't even know why he is wanted!" Oceana threw her hands up.

"We feel like your involvement is unassailable." He leaned back in his chair.

"It's not!" She snapped back.

"Why were you conspiring with the enemy?" The officer asked.

"I wasn't conspiring with the enemy!" Oceana yelled. She felt frustrated; and thought that she was already labeled a traitor without her side being recognized. "I was there to listen to what they had to say."

"Interesting. Why?" He asked, edging close to his chair to look at her.

"To know what was going on!" She felt her frustration build up higher inside her. "I promise I am not involving myself with the enemy!"

"Information?"

"Yes!"

"What information could you have possibly gotten at a cult-like that?" She moved her position on the couch, and what information did she get out of it? Was it a waste of time? What- No it wasn't- She did get information out of it.

"That there is a bomb that is going to go off tonight! In the building where the Knight lives!" Indeed this would prove her to be innocent. But the officer had no reaction. His blue eyes kept a focus on her.

"I highly doubt that any sort of bomb was placed in the Knight's home." He coughed, "We have very tight security that prevents such things from happening." He said, which had only confused Oceana. She didn't see any security when she entered the apartment today. "But I heard them-" She was cut off by the officer asking the next question.

"Why didn't you inform a KEEPIN officer before entering the facility? If they were supposedly plotting to kill the Knight?"

"Well I-" She stopped. She had no answer. Maybe she got too caught up in the moment with everything happening so fast. She didn't think about informing an authority. Or perhaps it might have to do with the ongoing fear she had directed towards KEEPIN officers. She, of course, wouldn't tell a KEEPIN officer that she had been having doubts about the military's performance lately. That she was maybe starting to question the motivations of the King's direction. She sat in silence. She didn't have an answer, but she needed to come up with one quickly. One that pointed to her underlying allyship with Cor'Meum, how she would never associate with the enemy. "I was trying to be just like my mom." She said, attempting to sound convincing. "Catching the bad guys and taking them down, you know."

"I see." The officer said, again another pause boiled between the two.

"I promise I am not the enemy." She said, "I would do anything to protect the people of Cor'Meum. I honestly do love this country."

"Anything?" The man asked, not convinced.

"Yes!" Oceana said with determination. Oceana moved towards the edge of the couch to perhaps move closer to the officer. "But I need to know, why is my grandpa wanted?" She asked in a harsh whisper, but before she could get an answer, there was a knock on the door. A man peered into the room dressed in a purple KEEPIN uniform. However, he was one star below the man in front of Oceana.

"Sir Timidus, you have a call on sector three."

"Oh!" Oceana snapped, now knowing the identity of his last name. It all clicked in her head at once. "Wait! You're Vinnian Timidus! The only son of Bellus!" She grinned, "You replaced my mom as a fourth-ranked Purple officer, didn't you?"

Vinnian gritted his teeth and looked at the man who interrupted the meeting and said between his teeth, "Tell them not now."

"But sir," The man said with a croak, "It's King Erebus." When the mention of the King himself was presented in front of him, he gave a heavy sigh before he pressed his hands on the armchairs and stood up. He looked back at Oceana, who quietly sat where she was. He pointed to her and said, "Stay here." He moved to the door and glared at the other purple officer before he shut the door behind him, leaving Oceana alone in the room.

CHAPTER 18:

The Great Escape

OCEANA sat still, much like Vinnian had told her. She really wondered how long she was out. Was it an hour? Was it longer? Why was her grandpa wanted? That had always been the question since she had found out he was requested for prison time. Maybe going to that meeting was not the most incredible idea. She shouldn't have put more pressure on her family name than there already was. She didn't even learn the reasoning behind her grandpa's disappearance, though why would she? Maybe it was in her head that the meeting had any form of connection with Grandpa.

She stopped and looked around, and a realization had hit her faster than a speeding train. The bomb, there was going to be a bombing at Bellus's building, she had to warn the people! Wait, she should tell someone- no! If a fourth-ranked officer hadn't believed her, she had to do this independently. She had no choice.

She looked around the room and wondered what she needed to do in a time that had a pending threat that required immediate action. She would usually jump right into that, but some part of her decided that she needed a plan. A plan. She had to figure out where exactly she was. She stood up from the couch and made her way towards the window, and tried to look out of it. However, the glass was dirty, and what she saw beyond the moon was nothing but foggy.

She turned around from the window and pressed her back to the wall, dedicating some minutes to trying to gamble on where she was. She knew she wasn't underground. If she was, she wouldn't be able to see the moon, especially that close. Was she in a KEEPIN facility? Was there one around here in Westside Mountains? No. She knew the locations of each KEEPIN facility in Cor'Meum, the closest one was a two-hour drive from where they were, and that one was underground. Maybe she was; an idea had struck her. She moved towards the wall and pressed her ear against it, holding her breath in. She heard a slight humming of a machine inside, which confirmed what she had predicted. Aircraft.

She moved her ear away from the wall and paced around the room, wondering what she should do next. She had no idea how high in the air she was, and she didn't know how much time she had until the bomb would go off. She looked around the room to find anything that would clue her to the current position. There wasn't anything in the room beside the furniture. Maybe the files on the desk that Viannian left. She stopped and looked over at the files that rested on the table. Viannian had forgotten to take these with him. She opened the envelope and began reading through her own files. If she could find any clue or any type of official statement about where these came from, she could possibly understand what type of aircraft she was on. This would be used to play the role of a directory for her next move. She found some printed words on the bottom right of her file. The print came from a Purple division aircraft, the seven-point five, the most modern version. She supposed that she should have figured it was a Purple division ship, based on the two Purple division KEEPIN men.

Right, now what? She paced around the room, her head full of thoughts about the next stage of her plan. She moved her hand and scratched her head. She was honestly drawing a blank. She wasn't really good at this kind of stuff. Who was really better at carefully planning was Jamlson, but she had no idea where he was. Unless. That's it. She had to find Jamlson. She couldn't do this on her own. She needed his help. How would she find him? Based on how she was treated, perhaps Jamlson, Headworth, and TOAD were all viewed as part of the conspiracy. Usually, prisoners would be dispersed in vehicles, especially many of them. Maybe because the three of them were always seen with her, they would be marked to be traitors too. She was also sure that both Jamlson and Headworth had their IDs. That proved they were Cor'Meum citizens. They had to be on this ship! There would be no protocol to place them amongst the rest of the revolutionary meeting.

It was time to move; the present was whistling away before her. If she didn't start searching for the boys, she might be too late to stop the bomb. She pressed her ear to the door, reeling in any sounds that might pass by. It was silent. She pressed her hand on the door and gave it a slow push before it began creaking open. The room Oceana was previously in had officially purged any presence of her when she moved out of the space completely.

The hallway between the room and the door was much brighter than the room itself. However, the hallway was quite thin. If Oceana stretched her hands out, her palms would touch each end of the walls next to her. There were about five doors. Each door had a little window to it. This granted both the hallway traveler and the room resident a clear visual of one another. Seeing that these windows could be a problem, Oceana ducked down and began their travels forward, avoiding any unwanted eyes in her direction.

"Yes, don't worry." A voice came from one of the rooms. Oceana recognized it to belong to Vinnian. He was on the phone. OH, he was on the phone with the King, Oceana had remembered. She needed to continue her adventure down the hall and find where the others were. Time was of the essence, and she knew she didn't have a lot of it left before midnight. But also, she wanted to know what Vinnian was saying. What were he and the King discussing? She moved her legs forward and made a small effort to ignore the both of them, but eventually her curiosity got the best of her. She pressed her back against the door and listened to the ongoing conversation. "Look, everything is under control. The Tetrad Aurum peace treaty hasn't been broken, and it never will be. Both Amare and Fortis tacet are on our side. We don't need to worry about this Sage Magnus rumor. My father killed him over forty years ago." Vinnian reassured. "They have their men in Vibrius; because our KEEPIN troops can't be the only ones keeping an eye out on them." Vinnian said with a sigh, "Do you want me to tell their men to stand back?" He asked. There was silence. Before Oceana could get another listen-in to the conversation, she heard one of the doors open, unsure what to do. Oceana ran to the other door across the hallway before shutting it behind her.

Once she had done this, she heard the door on the opposite end of the hallway completely open, and out came two KEEPIN guards who hadn't noticed Oceana shutting the other door, too busy wrapped in their conversation.

"That guy in the watchtower, you know by the castle, is getting a raise."

"What? Why?"

"Guess he caught a couple of looneys with gas masks attempting to break into the castle."

"Wow." This is all Oceana heard before they moved on to the next room inside the narrow hallway. Oceana let out a small sigh, relieved she hadn't been caught. But who knows when a KEEPIN guard would come out of hiding. She had to move fast and now. When her heart had finally calmed down from its rapid pace, she opened the door and took one last peek, there were still so many doors, and each entry led to another room covered in KEEPIN officers. How was she supposed to find the boys at this rate? She turned around and found something unbelievable. Maybe luck was on her side after all. The room she was in was a designated laundry room for all the KEEPIN officers who used this ship as living quarters. Besides the long tube full of dirty Purple division uniforms, some dry uniforms were organized neatly on a long string.

She looked around at all the uniforms and grabbed one she believed would fit her the best. She buttoned the jacket over her clothes, the same ones she had been using to make herself look less like a pirate. She took off the hat that had been doing a fine job covering her white hair and placed a KEEPIN officer hat on herself. Which was usually optional for KEEPIN soldiers to wear. There weren't any KEEPIN pants that fit her, all of them being too big. She decided to wear a pair of KEEPIN pants over her regular pants and proceeded to stuff any remainder of the pants in her boots, trying not to make it appear that the pants were eating her up.

Oceana looked over at the mirror to see how she looked in the KEEPIN uniform. She felt a pain stab right through her. The first thought that came to her head was her mom, who wore this exact outfit before her disappearance. Every day she would watch her mother put on this uniform and attach four golden stars to her left and the Cor'Meum flag to her right. Her mother, a KEEPIN soldier. Chills ran down Oceana's back; she decided she didn't want to spend more time looking at herself in the uniform through the mirror. She needed to remind herself again that there wasn't much time left to save everyone in the building, and she still needed to find the boys. She tilted the cap of the hat more towards her face before she moved back to the door once again and reunited with the unfamiliar hallway.

Down the hallway, when she heard the doors open, she had to remind herself to not immediately jump, that there were no real signs of her endangerment with the disguise that she was wearing. She moved towards each door, and when there were no KEEPIN officers' in sight, she would peek inside to see if any of her friends were there. Each time came up with nothing. On the last door of the hallway, she felt this sensation of defeat until she found a framed portrait of the ship's anatomy. She stared at the sketch of the ship and looked around, gulping the layout details. Alright, she had thought, where was she? There! She found the hallway that she was standing in. Great, now to get a good sense of where the boys were. She kept her eyes on the map locating any possibility of where the three of them were currently being held. Aside from being in literal KEEPIN clothing, Oceana decided to put herself in their shoes. If she wanted to keep captives who she was unsure were on the right side or not, where would they be?

She moved her fingers to her chin, she continued to stare at the map, and that is when she found it. OH! This next door would lead to a long hallway to a large room on the other side of the ship. Then, on the third door to the left, some stairs led down to the ship's basement. That is where her friends were. Oceana went to the last entry and began her journey down the new long hallway that directed her to the other side of the ship. The journey there wasn't pleasant. Thoughts kept invading her head. What if someone recognizes her? When Vinnian returns to the room only to discover she wasn't there, what will happen? What if Jamlson, Headworth, and TOAD weren't below the ship? What if they were taken somewhere else? She must have not noticed how nervous she was until a KEEPIN officer that passed her turned to her.

"Hey, what are you doing?" he asked sharply. Oceana stopped with her back facing him. Does he know it's her? Did she not do a good enough job hiding her hair? What would happen to her once Vinnian found out she was out of her room? Oh- frogs on a stick. She had been silent for too long. "Are you deaf?" The officer asked. He moved towards her.

Oceana began fake coughing, which stopped the man's tracks. "Sorry," Oceana said through the coughing fit she was having. "I am a bit under the weather. I am going to report to the lieutenant before I return to my post." Oceana recalled hearing something along those lines once on her grandpa's ship. She hoped that she hadn't given herself away or labeled herself a fraud. The man cleared his throat and turned around from her.

"Ah, very well. Carry on." He said before he moved down the opposite direction from her. Once the distance between the two was more than clear, Oceana sighed and felt the release on her shoulders roll off her. She took one breath in and continued her journey down the hallway.

When she had made it to the other side of the ship, the room used as a passage for the other rooms was much more comprehensive than the last one. Third door to the left, she moved her pacing faster and opened the door, which immediately revealed a wooden staircase that led down. Without a second thought, she moved down the stairs deeper into the room. The stairs were not too terrible. Reaching the bottom hadn't taken the amount of time that she had predicted it to be. However, even though her timing was off, the location's purpose wasn't. Inside the room were three large cells; one of the three was occupied. When she moved closer to the cell, it was a jackpot. All of her friends were there. They sat in silence. Two Blue division guards kept watch.

Oceana hadn't planned for this part, or her next move; she needed to get them away from the cell so she could free them. But, then, an idea came to her, a foolish idea; nevertheless, it was an idea, and there wasn't any time to come up with a better one. Oceana coughed once more in her hand. This brought the attention of the KEEPIN guards.

"What are you doing here?" Oceana asked, trying to make her voice sound deeper than it was.

"Standing post. Vinnian's orders." One of them responded.

"What are you doing here?" The other officer asked, his eyebrow raised.

"Oh, so you haven't heard?" Oceana asked, curling her lips.

"Haven't heard what?" The first Blue division officer asked.

"Maintenance check. You know- bag check."

"What? We had one just yesterday." The blue officer said, his voice full of suspicion. "Also, I don't recall seeing you before." He pointed at Oceana, who felt her sweat come in. "Who are you?" He asked sharply. Oceana began to shake. Had she been caught already? No. She came too far for this. She glared down at the man, and this time, she decided to point her finger at him.

"How dare you question a third-ranked Purple division officer! I ought to write you up for that! What is your name and badge number?" Oceana asked with confidence, the man began to look nervous, and so did his buddy.

"No need for that!" The man said. "I am sorry, I didn't mean to step out of line!" He said in a shaken tone of voice. "Is that maintenance check now?" He asked.

"Yes," Oceana said sternly, crossing her arms.

"Right, it's just we were told to watch the prisoners and-"

"Hand me the keys, officer. I will watch the prisoners." Oceana held a hand out. The Blue officer who had been doing most of the talking looked over at his quiet buddy, who looked nervous.

"Come on, just do what she asks." He said, "We can't afford to get written up again." He threw in. The officer nodded at him, unhooked the keys from his belt, handed them to Oceana, and gave a quiet salute before he and the other officer took off.

Oceana then turned to the boys who had just witnessed the most unusual scene of their lives, Jamlson moved up to the bars of the cell and gave Oceana a strange look.

"What are you doing here?" Jamlson asked.

"And where did you find that Purple division uniform?" Headworth chimed in before reciting some laws and forms of punishments Oceana could face for wrongfully wearing one, even going around and impersonating one.

"Yeah yeah." Oceana waved her hand in the sky momentarily. "I know." Of course she had, two of her family members are part of the highest possible rank you could receive in KEEPIN, or rather they were. Would they be disappointed in her for disobeying the laws of the country? Or perhaps their disappearance had to do with the unfairness that this country placed on people- she stopped. What was she thinking? She shouldn't have thoughts such as this. Respect KEEPIN, remember? That's what she had grown up to do. Just because she was having doubts, didn't mean she must abandon the army altogether and have negative things to say that were similar to Jamlson's. Unless KEEPIN wasn't good.

"The bomb, what are we going to do about it?" Jamlson asked, snapping her out of her daydream, "We have to warn the others."

"I agree, but how?" Oceana asked. "We are in a Purple division aircraft, I don't know how many miles off the ground, and when I told Vinnian- a fourth-ranked Purple division officer, he didn't believe me," she said.

"Right," Jamlson pressed his hands on his chin, "We are on a Purple division ship, you say?" He thought, "Don't they usually have sky cruisers on their deck?" He asked. "We could just-"

"Genius!" Oceana shouted at Jamlson before he could finish his sentence. "We would have to pass all the guards, though! When I walked here, it felt that there were around three or two in every corner." She said, "I don't know how I could explain to them what," she moved her fingers to put them in quotations, "'a Purple division guard is doing with three prisoners."

"Right," Jamlson said. The four of them sat in silence.

"Maybe." Headworth chimed in for a moment. "We need a perfect distraction." He said with a grin.

"Okay, we have the distraction." Jamlson said with an eye roll, "What do we do next? We still need to figure out how to get inside the sky cruisers. Better yet, drive them."

"Oh, Jamlson," Headworth pushed his glasses up. "After all this time, you doubt my talent for mechanical processing."

"You know how to drive sky cruisers?" Oceana chipped in.

"I am sure the framework of a working one would be no different from the fake ones I engineer in my fathers' study."

"Alright, so we have a plan," Oceana said. "We should act fast. We don't know how much time we have left till midnight." She said, and both boys nodded while TOAD blinked excitedly. Jamlson grabbed his bow and arrows that were confiscated from him.

When they reached the top of the stairs, Oceana decided to be the first one to take a peak, determining whether the coast was clear or not. It seemed that the hallway wasn't going to have the companionship of any KEEPIN soldiers for a while. Oceana looked back at the three and nodded. They all moved up back in the hallway that, to their convenience, remained empty.

Headworth looked at TOAD and pointed down the hallway, to which TOAD nodded and ran towards the direction that Headworth had pointed. Great, their distraction was on the move. Now it was time to go outside on the deck. Oceana already knew which way led to the deck of the aircraft; she had noticed it when reviewing the map just not too long ago. She moved along with Jamlson and Headworth. Though the door to the deck was pretty close, she hadn't seen a single KEEPIN guard. Which she was positive that they would have run into by now.

She stopped at the door that led to the deck. She moved to the door's window; again, it was quiet. There wasn't a single KEEPIN guard in sight. How peculiar. She looked over at Jamlson and Headworth, who appeared just as confused as her. She looked over and out the window one last time. Still no guards on deck. This was strange. Being an experienced pirate herself, she knew that there was always someone on deck, no matter what. That was protocol. So why wasn't there anyone standing guard? She moved away from the window and rested her back against the door.

"Something isn't right. There's no KEEPIN guards out there." She informed the other two.

"Well, we have no choice but to go out there." Jamlson said, "It's our only way to escape." Right, he was right. This was their only real way of getting out of here, and if they continued to move at this slow pace, they would be too late. They indeed were the only ones that could save everyone from the attack. She gave a confirming nod at the two and pushed open the door.

What hit her first was the heavy impact of the cold nightly wind. The icy chills ran down her back while she made her way forward onto the ship's platform. The wind pushed hard against all of them, Oceana began losing the feeling of the tip of her nose. Suppose she should be thankful that the windows that blocked such harsh winds were down. This would make it easier to escape. Eventually, the wind had pushed so violently she watched her hat fly off into the arms of the gust, she tried to reach for the runaway hat, but it was too late. The three moved towards the sky cruisers, which weren't too far from them. There were about five or seven of them that rested untouched on the large platform of the ship.

"That one!" Headworth shouted, pointing at the one that stood in front of the rest of them. Jamlson and Oceana nodded and made their way towards the gold cruiser. The sky cruisers up close looked like a golden box carried by three skinny wheels on the bottom. The wings of the sky cruisers were on the top; it reminded Oceana of those bikes at home that children use to glide in the air for a bit. She remembered reading about how wings were gaining popularity in the modern world.

Gaining a closer look at the cruisers, Oceana hadn't realized how small it was. Unlike a vehicle with a back and a front, the sky cruisers had only a front seat. When Oceana examined the sky cruiser, she noticed how the front was just one long couch, similar to the backseat of cars. A clicking sound grabbed Oceana's attention. She looked over at Headworth, who had managed to open the door.

"How did you do that?" Oceana asked. She believed Headworth would give a good explanation, or perhaps he would have merely said that the door to the sky cruiser was unlocked. But, unfortunately, this is what Oceana would never know because, at that moment, they were interrupted by a loud SNAP!

Bright white lights around them flashed on and pointed at them from every direction. Oceana squinted her eyes to prevent the white light from slipping into the back of her head, which was already in pain from the sudden flash.

"Oceana Sanford!" A voice on a megaphone boomed. "Stop what you are doing and put your hands in the air, fingers apart!" Oceana did precisely what the loud voice told her, Headworth and Jamlson decided to follow along. She managed to peek her eyes open. The two of them looked nervous. What did they see that she couldn't? The safest thing to bet was that they were surrounded by KEEPIN officers, all armed. She kept her hands in the air, complying with the KEEPIN officers' demand. KEEPIN already marked her and her friends as enemies of the state at this point. They failed their mission. They were cornered, and Bellus and his wife would be nothing but ash soon. She felt her heart sink at the idea of not just them who would be victims of this awful thing but the retired KEEPIN officers that lived there too. A soft humming sound was heard in this moment of despair and hopelessness. Was this the end? Were they going to shoot them? But the humming sound got progressively louder. It took a moment for Oceana to realize that it wasn't humming, but music.

She looked around at the KEEPIN officers who had the three surrounded, all of them were just as confused as she was. The music got louder, filling the deck with its presence despite the high winds, which attempted to drown it out; but the music was too powerful.

"Once I went home, at 2 am, I scared my partner, oh they were terrified!" The music sang, "I am a member of the evening gang!" The lights had begun to dim. After they had dimmed, they brightened again. Once the lights were bright, they grew dark once again, stuck in a pattern loop.

"Someone is in the control room!" Oceana believed she heard someone shout, "Stop them!" One KEEPIN officer from the crowd pulled out their weapon. He was more than ready to shoot, aiming at Headworth, however Jamlson reacted, unclipped his bow and pulled out an arrow. He slung his shot before a wink; his arrow stabbed into the neck of the gun, now permanently damaged. This added bonus created confusion and distraction amongst the KEEPIN officers. Now was their cue to get in the sky cruiser and take off, Oceana was glad that the boys were already one step ahead of her. A gun went off, and Jamlson was quick to sling his arrow into another with no hesitation. All of them made their way inside the sky cruiser.

Inside the sky cruiser, a single wheel rested in the middle. Bright-colored buttons on each side of the pilot's chair were in front of the passengers, her and Jamlson. Headworth, sitting in the middle, held onto the wheel carefully, and pressed a couple of buttons. Oceana could not say what each button's purpose was. She looked out the window and watched the wings give a slight giggle. She yelped and looked at Headworth.

"Are you sure you know how to drive this?" She asked nervously, now doubting Headworth's abilities. She knew he was brilliant, but did he have the actual ability to fly this thing? She looked over at Jamlson, who seemed to have a good grasp of the seat under him. He was already shaking.

"Yeah, of course, I know how to drive this," Headworth said confidently. He flipped on one more button before the sky cruiser moved forward and bounced on the small wheels below them. "I think." He mumbled.

"Wait! I think?" Oceana shouted. But by the time she could lecture or yell at Headworth to stop, and for them to come up with another plan, the sky cruiser moved forward and rolled around the ship's deck.

"Oh- there's not enough room for a proper take-off," Headworth said.

"Which means?!" Oceana asked.

"Hold on." Headworth flipped some switches, and the sky cruiser drove around on the ship's deck. KEEPIN officers had to jump out of the way to avoid being run over. Headworth flipped another switch, and the sky cruiser moved in the direction of the ledge of the ship. This is it. Oceana thought to herself, shutting her eyes closed. She felt forced off the seat. The sky cruiser made a nose dive towards the street miles below them. Both her and Jamlson were screaming, Oceana opened her eyes only to watch them seemingly plummet to their deaths. Then Headworth pressed a couple more buttons, pulled the wheel, and the sky cruiser halted the crash landing, and moved up immediately. "And you doubted my abilities," Headoworth said with a laugh. They were all soaring in the sky. Headworth had managed to learn how to make the sky cruiser fly.

Oceana sat on the edge of her seat and pressed her face to the window. She got a good scope of the whole city of Westside Mountains. She knew that this place was full of the retired, so there was overwhelming darkness to ensure that the people would get a good night's sleep. Oceana moved her head to look at the sky, dazzled with stars. She had never seen all of them so up close before. When she traveled by her grandfather's ship, she would sometimes sneak out at night to stare at them, enjoying their presence and generosity to fill the night with their show. These were the same stars that gave her comfort as a kid. She was so close. She could press her fingertips to their bright light.

"Oceana." Headworth said, which snapped her out of her gaze. She looked over at him. He kept his eyes on his view, "Can you guide me to Bellus's apartment." This wasn't a stated question. Instead, he said this with command. She looked back down at the city, it was a bit difficult to tell where they were from high up, but perhaps she could find some familiar landmarks that would help her find exactly where they needed to go. She kept her eyes down, scanning the area until she found the large park; she pointed.

"There, I know the Timidus' live right next to that place." She said; Headworth nodded and guided the sky cruiser closer to the park.

"Right, Oceana, I can't stop this thing. You and Jamlson need to jump when I get close enough."

"What?" Jamlson shouted the first thing he had said since they had taken off. His face looked like he was trying hard not to lose his lunch.

Oceana looked back at Headworth and nodded.

"Right." She said, "No problem! We got this, right Jamlson?" She smiled.

"Uhhh yeah." He replied, clutched onto his stomach, and gave a half-smile before returning to his fears. Headworth dipped the sky cruiser down and began gliding not too far from the ground, Oceana opened her door and held onto it, not allowing the wind to close it again.

"This is as close as I can go without crashing!" Headworth shouted. "You have to jump now!" Oceana looked back down at the ground. The jump wasn't too high. She just had to prepare herself to jump, ensuring to not break a bone or something. Oceana took one breath in and jumped out of the sky cruiser.

When she fell, she felt her body spin. It moved up and down before ultimately making a halt in the wet mud. Finally, she was on the ground and safe. She looked around, did Jamlson jump? The answer to her question came with a groan. She got on her feet and felt her body crack a bit. However, Oceana decided not to pay attention to it and moved towards the sound, which wasn't too far from her. What she found was a defeated Jamlson lying in a pile of wet mud.

"Come on, we don't have much time," Oceana said. She extended her hand toward him. He gave one last groan, raised his own arm, and grabbed her hand.

"Remind me to never get in a sky cruiser again." He said, followed by a couple of mumbled swears.

"There!" She pointed at the building in front of them, "We need to evacuate everyone!"

"Right, and how do we do that?" Jamlson asked with a raised eyebrow. "Do you think people are going to listen to us?" Oceana pressed her fingers on her chin. Yeah, he was right. Would anyone listen to a couple of random strangers telling them to evacuate immediately? She knew she wouldn't if she were in their circumstances. The only way she would listen is if it were someone important, perhaps.

"Well, not us." She said, "But perhaps a KEEPIN officer." Oceana began to remove the Purple division coat and unbuttoned each of the golden pins that had kept the suit intact. When she took it off, she handed it to Jamlson, "Might be tight-fitting, but wear this." She said, "Tell everyone to leave the building. I will get Timidus."

Jamlson took the coat and began putting it on. It hardly fit him. The buttons refused to pin together over his body. He looked at her and nodded. "Do you know how much time we have?" He asked.

"I don't know, but it's safe to assume not a lot." She replied, and the two began making their way towards the building just like that.

When they had gotten inside, the man who Oceana assumed was supposed to be the excellent security Vinnian mentioned; looked at the two with a raised eyebrow.

"What are you doing here at this hour? The building is closed." Jamlson stepped in and pointed his thumb to his chest, attempting to hide the fact that the uniform he wore did not fit him.

"I am a Purple division KEEPIN officer and this!" He pointed at Oceana. "This is none other than the famous Oceana Sanford next to me!" He shouted. "We have been informed that a bomb will be set off at midnight. So we have to make an emergency evacuation!"

"What?" The security guard questioned, "That's in half an hour! Where are the other KEEPIN officers?" He asked. "Also, you realize you are covered in dirt, sir!"

"Yes- but- there's no time! We can't reach them!" Jamlson yelled. "If we want everyone to leave this building safely, we have to act now!" The security guard nodded.

"I will wake the staff!" He said and ran to the other room, Jamlson looked over at Oceana and gave a confirming nod. She threw him back a determined smile and made her way to the stairs. Time to save Timidus. After running up several flights of stairs, she finally reached her point of destination. She pressed her knuckles against the apartment door of 238 several times compelling someone to open it. Finally, the door slammed open, it was Mrs. Timidus in her robes, with a look of anger mixed with tiredness.

"What?" She snapped, "Here to spur more nonsense?" She asked, raising her eyebrow.

"Mrs. Timidus, this building is going to explode!" Oceana immediately responded,

"See more nonsense." But almost as if on cue, an explosive went off. This had made the building jolt. One of the bombs must have gone off early, from what Oceana assumed. Nevertheless, it wasn't midnight yet, and the building managed to keep standing proudly. The explosion, though, was more than convincing to get Mrs. Timidus to turn around to grab her husband. Oceana followed her inside the room, where she ran down the hall and lifted him out of bed.

"You get one side." she snapped; Oceana nodded and looked over at the clock. They only had fifteen minutes to get out of there. Oceana threw

Bellus's arm around her neck, helping him onto his feet, to which it seemed he hadn't remembered how to use. But there was no time for a quick tutorial on how to move like a person with functioning legs. They made their way out of the apartment. Oceana grabbed the handle to the door that carried stairs that went endlessly down. The hallway, due to the explosion, was covered in smoke, and the sprinklers were going off. This drenched the three of them from head to toe while they tried to escape carefully.

"We have to hurry!" Oceana said to Mrs. Bellus, who looked like she couldn't agree more. It was already tricky carrying Bellus out of bed. They traded in their time for an apparent escape for Bellus to corporate. He resisted by dragging his feet. Going down the flight of stairs was brutal. It seemed that it was either going to be herself or Mrs. Timidus that would trip over one or the other on the stairs.

Oceana was surprised that by the time they had made it to the last set of stairs, the building was still intact. The bottom seemed empty. Jamlson and the guard had managed to evacuate everyone just in time. But they still had to move as far as they could away from the place that would be reduced to nothing but ash by the last hour of the night.

"Come on! We are almost there!" Oceana shouted. She pushed the front door open, and there she saw a large crowd of people miles away from where they stood. She kept pushing herself to move, she needed to, but it was complex with Bellus' refusal to move any further. She almost began to debate if she would even make it out alive with him dragging his feet. No. She couldn't leave him behind, not because he was some national celebrity, but it would be wrong. When she looked back at the amount of distance she put between them and the building, her heart plummeted. They weren't far enough. Midnight was soon. Oceana shook her head and kept her eyes ahead, but what she saw was a figure running toward them. Who was that? It didn't take too long for her to see that it was Jamlson.

"Guys, we have to hurry!"

"We are trying!" Oceana croaked, "But Bellus is refusing." Jamlson looked at them.

"Okay, put him down." He said.

"If you think we are leaving my husband-" Mrs. Timidus shouted but was cut off by Jamlson, who grabbed Bellus and lifted him bridally into his arms. Oceana admitted she had no idea that Jamlson was this strong, or really never gave his ability on strength much thought before.

"Come on." He said and began jogging to the best of his ability while carrying another person. With Jamlson's help in taking Bellus, they were able to put some distance between themselves and the building. Oceana knew that they were close to everyone. She saw lights from KEEPIN vehicles, but that was when she learned the clock had struck midnight. At that moment, a loud blast was heard.

Oceana turned around and watched the building fall. It looked much similar to the destruction of a sandcastle, like ones that she would build on beaches during her journeys when she was small. She watched the building crumble downwards; to her relief, it was not launching forward, which was an initial fear. Smoke began to accumulate, spreading rapidly throughout where the explosion had happened. Oceana hadn't realized how much of the smoke had launched towards them until Jamlson shouted,

"Down!" They turned around, their backs facing the ash while it sped past them. Oceana kept her eyes closed and brought the collar of her shirt to the front of her face. It took a good couple of minutes before Oceana noticed the smoke clear up around them.

She looked over at Jamlson, she hadn't realized this before, but he had taken the KEEPIN jacket and his own jacket off and placed them around Mrs and Mr Timidus. The shirt he wore did not protect him from the burning rocks the building threw.

Oceana looked over at the building, or what used to be the building for the retired KEEPIN officers in the Westside Mountains. There was nothing but smoke covering the surrounding area.

When Oceana took a breath in, she felt a taste in her mouth, almost metallic-like. She brought her hand to her mouth and then moved her hand to get a good look at it... blood. She was bleeding? When did this happen? She thought back long and hard but couldn't recall when she felt any sort of pain in her face. Perhaps she was too worried about making it out alive to really notice.

Oceana snapped out of her daze and turned immediately to Jamlson, who was in worse condition. "Jamlson!" She shouted and got on her knees. She put her arm around him and began shaking him, "Jamlson! Say something!" She said.

"I am alright! Oceana, it's fine!" He said with a cough. She stared at him.

"You- you idiot! You didn't have to take the hit for all of us!" She shouted

"Oceana relax."

"Don't tell me what to do!" She snapped.

"Seriously?" He laughed. "Oceana stop worrying. All of us are okay! You did it! You saved everyone." He said. Oceana could feel her face burn. How could he be thinking of the outcome of all of this instead of himself?

He was supposed to be sir grumpy, but he was actually smiling right now. She wanted to say something, but before she could open her mouth, she was surrounded by a couple of KEEPIN guards.

"Hands where we can see them." One of them demanded it. To which Oceana and Jamlson had immediately compiled.

Oceana watched the KEEPIN guards gently take Mrs. and Mr. Timidus away from the scene, Oceana heard Mrs. Timidus complain the entire time until she was out of earshot. Everything became a bit of a blur from there. Perhaps Oceana had begun to remember why her head was open. On her way out of the building, one of the sprinklers fell and cut the top of her forehead. She must have been too busy with her's and the Timidus's lives on the line to necessarily care. But now that everything started to slow down, and she knew she was safe from any explosions, she was able to process things with ease. She closed her eyes for just a moment, hoping that the world around her would stop moving in a blur.

CHAPTER 19:

Ten Years Ago

W HEN she had opened her eyes once more, she noticed she was lying in a bed. She was in a room she had never seen before. The moment she opened her eyes, she only wanted to close them again. But something stopped her, and that force of nature was Vinnian. He kept his eyes on her; she noticed that his eye color was very similar to that of his fathers, and also her own. "Ms. Sanford." He said, "How's your head?" He asked.

"Uh," She paused and placed her hand on her head, "Better." She said, fighting through the drowsiness of her body.

"I would like to humbly apologize to you. I shouldn't have ignored you." He said. "Thank you for saving my parents." He said.

"Oh well, I did break the law in the process of that," Oceana said. She felt immediately embarrassed. Why did she say that? Was she going to get in trouble now? But she supposed it wasn't a secret that she did break the law, well, several of them. Then, she heard a chuckle, and when she looked up, she was surprised to see Vinnian laughing.

"Right." He said. "Oh, your friends, by the way. They are okay. They are being taken care of. Your friend who drove the sky cruiser has amazing skills with that thing. He may be young now, but it would be an honor for him to join us." he said with a smile. Oceana couldn't think of any worse punishment for Headworth than being forced to join KEEPIN. She knew that Vinnian had phrased this to be something honorable, but Oceana only felt nauseous at the idea.

"What about Jamlson?" Oceana asked.

"Jamlson?" Vinnian raised an eyebrow but nodded, "Oh, the boy that carried my father." He said. "He is doing fine. We are examining his wounds in the other room." Oceana felt a sigh of relief, knowing that Jamlson was okay. She had already known or instead had a feeling that Headworth and TOAD were going to be alright. By now, anything remotely technological Headworth was around, he could use it to his advantage. "By the way," Vinnian said. "Word got around about your heroism." He said. "And the king himself would like to invite you to a party that he is throwing tomorrow- or rather later tonight," Vinnian said, keeping track that it was now very early in the morning.

"A party?" Oceana questioned.

"Yes! He is throwing a party to celebrate forty years of our victory in the Calamitous War! He has also invited you and your friends to stay the night, which is where we are headed."

"We are headed towards the castle?" Oceana asked with a raised eyebrow. Vinnian nodded.

"Oh," Oceana only said. She hadn't been in the castle in over ten years. Living in the castle for the year that she did was one of her strongest childhood memories with her mother. All her other memories with her mother before living in the castle came in fragments, hard to hold onto. She just remembered how life-changing it was for her to live in such a place. She began to wonder how much things had changed there in the past decade if at all. So this was it. She began to feel the heaviness of her body again. She couldn't stay awake much longer. She honestly didn't care to fight it now, knowing her friends were safe. She felt her eyelids close once more and allowed her head to rest.

Tick, tick, tick, tick.... the clock awoke the girl. The weather felt bitter. It was opposite to the mood of what the day should be about, a celebration. Sunshine! Happiness! It was the turning of a new age, another year Oceana had been on this planet. The small girl woke up in the bed she called her own. She stretched her arms and looked out the window, not too pleased with the clouds in the sky but yet not surprised. Her birthday fell on the first winter day. She moved out of bed. Her bare feet touched the glossed wooden ground. She was full of energy and excited to see what the day would be like for her. Turning eight was a big deal! She ran to the door clutching onto the night dress she wore with one hand, careful to not trip on it, a mistake she was prepared not to repeat for the hundredth time. She opened the door, careful not to wake the other children with whom she shared the room, and left to find her mother's room.

The castle and its enormous size made her home in the woods seem ever so small. Getting lost in the castle was easy and something Oceana thought she would have figured out after a year of living there. Well. Oceana had thought to herself. Practice makes perfect. Plus, the castle was perfect for hiding and seeking. A game that Oceana, unlike home, held the championship for amongst the other Purple division guards' children. Except for Aster though, who had managed to always beat her in hide and seek.

When Oceana found her mother's room, she pushed open the door, excited to see her on this beautiful cloudy, perhaps a snowy day. But, instead of birthday wishes, she found her mother in a hurried motion packing her belongings, stuffing her outfits in a suitcase that rested on her bed.

"Mom?" Oceana questioned. Her mother had probably not noticed her presence before, due to her slight jump. She turned around and looked at Oceana. She seemed slightly annoyed by the girl. "What are you doing?" the little girl questioned. She kept her eyes on the clothes that scattered around her bed. Her mother turned around and resumed packing; her back facing her child.

"We are leaving." She said,

"Leaving?" Oceana questioned.

"Yes, now go to your room and pack whatever you can fit in your bag." She said, then moved to the other side of her room, opened her closet, and began to rummage inside it. "Where is it? I thought I left it here- where is that necklace ...."

"I don't want to leave!" Oceana said. "I want to stay here! I want to celebrate-"

"Do not make me repeat myself Oceana!" Her mother snapped and turned to glare at her. Then, when Oceana had nothing to say, she turned back around, not remembering she had left the closet door open, and smacked her face into it. "OW! Frogs on a stick!"

"Are you okay?" Oceana asked hurriedly.

"Ugh, look what you did!" she yelled and moved her hand to rub her face, "Just do what you were asked." Her mother threw in. After another beat, her mother whispered. "Why do you always mess things up?" She hadn't known Oceana picked up on what she said. "Pack your things and come back here in an hour," She mumbled and went back to scavenging her closet.

"But-"

"Now." Her mother said without taking a glance at her child. Oceana nodded. She kept her head down and turned to leave the door, leaving her mother alone in her own mess. Tick, tick, tick,tick.

CHAPTER 20:

Happy Birthday

Tɪᴄᴋ, tick, tick, tick, Oceana immediately got up and moved to the window next to the large bed she had slept on. When she drew open the curtains, she found Purple Division guards talking to one another from a couple of stories down from her view. She couldn't remember where she had fallen asleep or where she was, but her thoughts were interrupted by a knock at the door that stretched across the other side of the room. The door opened before Oceana could answer or say anything really, and a woman in a long purple dress with an apron came in.

"Oh! Good! You are awake!" She hummed.

"Where am I?" Oceana asked, "Am I?"

"If you are going to say King's castle, then that is correct."

"What? We are here?" Oceana shouted and looked out the window again. She heard the woman walk closer to her, making her way towards the bed.

"You fell asleep on the aircraft, so instead of waking you up, they decided to move you to your room so you could catch the sleep you needed." The maid said.

"What?" Oceana shouted and turned around. She was now face to face with the maid. Oceana felt herself turning red "I-" she explained, "They could have woken me up! She said, "They didn't need to put me here!"

"Nonsense." The woman said with a smile, then patted the folded clothes she placed on the bed. "A boy told me these were your original clothes, and you would probably want them back."

Oceana looked at the folded clothes that the maid had placed, "Oh, thank you!" They said,

"Be sure to keep your head and fingers rested." She hummed and turned towards the door, shutting it behind her.

Oceana looked at the pile of clothes and moved their hand in front of them. She stared at the new fabric that was laced around each of her injured fingers perfectly. Instead of the pure white fabric she had before, it was now wrapped in new colors. Purple, red, and blue.

All of a sudden, her attention turned to a card placed on the desk that rested next to her bed. She leaned over and picked up the little paper stained in yellow. When she opened it there was a message left on it that stated 'Happy Birthday Oceana! Hope you have a BLAST!' She grinned at the kind message. She couldn't believe Jamlson had left her a birthday card. She would have completely forgotten it was her birthday if he hadn't sent her the thoughtful note. She decided to place it back where it belonged to look back at it later.

Oceana moved over to her pile of clothes, she lifted her coat and moved to the pocket inside, found the small red button, and popped it open. She was relieved that the handbook was still there. She closed the pocket once again to conceal the presence of it. She then began to get dressed back into her old and original pirate-like outfit. As she did so, she moved towards the large window in her room. While she was tying the bow on her neck, she looked down through the window. She noticed she wasn't that high, second floor maybe. But, she was close enough to the ground to see the rose garden filled with bushes, each holding a different shape.

She noticed two Purple division guards were still engaged in conversation. They both soon made eye contact with her. Oceana gave a smile and began waving at the two. Only for them to respond by moving toward each other, exchanging some last words, and then shuffling away from the window. Strange.

Once she was done tying the small lace bow, and after clipping the red gem on top, she looked at herself in the mirror. She gave a smile, before she played with her bangs one last time. Then something caught her eye, she looked at the desk that stood close to the mirror. On top of the desk rested a golden pin with the words 'KEEPIN.' on it. She felt a cold stillness run through her body. She looked at the pin, and then looked at herself in the mirror. There was no need to add anymore accessories to her vest, the red gem was enough. She moved away from both the mirror and the pin.

Since Oceana was dressed, she was ready to face the new day; an extraordinary day nonetheless. She moved towards the door, opened it, and made her way down the kingdom hallway. The area brought back old memories from before she lived with her grandpa.

She hadn't remembered having a negative experience living in the palace. She felt, in fact, much like royalty when she lived here. But in hindsight, when she lived on the boat and traveled from place to place, it was more suited to her needs than residing in a castle forever. She couldn't imagine why anyone would willingly want to stay put in one place forever.

On her way down the castle hallway, she couldn't help but stop at the long wall full of trophies, ribbons and medals. They were all placed in a display that would best please the eyes. Oceana moved closer to the medals. All of them were marked first place, with the name Aster Roseario. She was impressed. There were probably a hundred first-place medals on the wall. She couldn't find anything that was less. Could one girl really be the best at everything?

When she decided to turn around, she felt a heavy impact hit her immediately. She fell to the floor. She rubbed her bottom before she made her way back up on her feet.

"I am so sorry!" Oceana said.

"Yeah, watch where you are going." The reply was cold. The other girl then looked up at Oceana and narrowed her eyes. "Oh, it's you." She groaned. Oceana's eyes widened, and she clapped her hands together.

"Oh! Ash! It's been forever since I have seen you! Of course, I have seen you in magazines- the screens- billboards- but not in person!" Oceana grinned. "How are you? How is sword fighting going?" Aster looked the same as ever from what Oceana could see. She still had her short brown curly hair. Her eyelashes were still very long, and her eyes were just as golden as she remembered them. The only thing that Oceana noticed that was different about Aster was that she had three or four piercings on her ears, which looked really cool. She wondered if she could get that too.

"You are asking me about hobbies I did when I was eight." The girl responded. "And don't call me Ash, like we are best friends forever, make little friendship bracelets, and talk about boys or whatnot." She mocked, "It's Princess Aster to you."

"So you're not doing sword fighting anymore?" Oceana asked, tilting her head. She could have sworn she just watched her win one of the biggest competitions in the state.

Aster rolled her eyes. "I am," Aster then continued down the hallway; Oceana decided to follow her.

"I saw you on the screen! You are really incredible!"

"Oh, look, now she's following me," Aster said under her breath, but Oceana had decided to ignore her.

"You know, when we were kids, I always thought that your sword fighting practices were so- well- incredible! I wanted to do that too, but I was way more into magic, you know, I mean- you don't because Roseario's don't really do magic, but since I can't really do magic, I mean I am practicing or trying to do it all the time! So I can do magic, eventually."

"Does this story have a point?"

"Right, well! I can also sword fight!"

Aster stopped in her tracks and looked back up at Oceana, only to laugh at her face. She covered her hand with her mouth while doing so, to which Oceana raised an eyebrow. Aster pressed her hand to her mouth to contain her smile before she glanced at Oceana,

"You can sword fight?"

"Yes, I am actually quite good at it."

"Okay, well, maybe you are 'okay,' but I highly doubt you are- good," Aster said.

"Well, I am!" Oceana insisted.

"Right, as good as one can get by training with an old man on a water-bound pirate ship." Aster shrugged. "I was trained by the palace's finest." She pointed at herself. "I also began my training when I was eight." She said, "So longer than you, better trainers than you, better than you." She grinned.

"I began practicing at age ten, so it's not that big of a difference, only two years after you."

"Well, you-" If Oceana had to guess what the princess's next words were going to be, it would probably be something hurtful.

"Oh shush," A voice came. Oceana saw a boy in a similarly fashioned royal purple uniform, much like the girl. But instead, his was designed to be more masculine presenting. "Do you have to be a jerk to everyone?"

Aster only crossed her arms and rolled her eyes, which almost became complete gold when the light had decided to touch them.

"You know Oceana saved the people in the Westside Mountains from an explosion." He said, "Show respect to them. She is our honorary guest."

"They did so out of pure luck! No skill was required! Anyone could have done what they did!" Aster yelled.

The boy stared at her and gave a smirk. This only angered the girl more.

"You know I don't have time for this." She walked ahead of them

"Well, ain't she just a doll. Thought she would be at least a bit different." Oceana turned to the boy, realizing who she was talking to, she remembered him hardly. She knew he was Aster's older brother, Crocus, famous in the Kingdom of Cor'Meum. She had bits and pieces of personal memories with him during her time in the castle. She remembered his arrival for a special event before he had left again. He was constantly being trained to be King. "I mean, no disrespect to the princess."

"By all means, say whatever you want about her. It's not like it hasn't been said." Crocus said, "She acts like she is above everyone constantly. But she is just covering herself up," He said with a laugh.

"From what?" Oceana asked with a raised eyebrow.

"It doesn't matter-" He then snapped his fingers, "Oh! My father had requested to see you for breakfast." He pointed.

Oceana's heart almost sank. She didn't believe she'd ever had a conversation with the King before, let alone breakfast. That was usually her mom who did. Had the King forgotten who she was? She wasn't anything special, just the grandchild of a pirate, or rather of a Red division soldier. Maybe she shouldn't start giving into the stereotype of calling Red division officers pirates. The term was used to put down their role of importance. But she thought it was a cool name and wanted to own it, but again probably would not be a correct term to use in front of the King himself. She gulped the big lump in her throat and closed her eyes, and nodded.

"Yeah, oh right, okay." She said, "Makes logical sense to me." She said to the Prince in front of her. "Uh, I shall be right there," She began to move forward down the hall.

"Where are you going?" Crocus raised an eyebrow

"What?"

"The breakfast table is down this way." He pointed in the opposite direction that she had been going.

"Oh, ha- right." She laughed. "Right, uh, I knew that!" She said along with fake confidence, then began moving towards the opposite way which she was going.

While walking down the halls, she noticed that the castle hadn't really changed since her last visit. The walls all had the same old stone decoration, a call back to reminisce on previous Kings and Queens of the past. Oceana noticed that the painting she had seen during her last visit was still there. The one that caught her eye was a painting of King Erebus and his second wife, who was holding her new child, while the child of the last woman, a tiny boy who, much like his father, had long dirty blond hair and bright blue eyes.

Oceana remembered hearing the news about her untimely death a few years ago and only thought of Aster that whole week. It was her mother, after all, and poor Crocus, though the Queen was his stepmom, it must have been hard on him too. Not everyone could lose two mothers in one lifetime.

It seemed that this portrait's purpose was not a reflection of what the Kingdom is currently but a reflection of a simple past. She smiled at baby Aster, she looked less angry, but from the portrait alone, one could tell she would grow big hair, now seeing the little curls that the baby held.

She realized she couldn't stare at a portrait of baby Aster all day. She needed to have breakfast with the King. She couldn't believe she was even thinking about it as part of her plan. So she kept marching down the long gray stoned hallway of the castle. She found some Purple division guards talking and quickly asked them where the King was eating breakfast, they pointed in the direction, and she followed.

It almost seemed hopeless, and she was just going to roam around the castle forever, that is until she found a large archway that stretched to the height of a second story. It held two golden poles on each side, alluring any visitor to come in. She noticed a conversation going on inside, with the echoes of muttering. She moved into the room to find Purple division guards standing on either side of the pole, waiting in silence. She looked over to the actual interior of the giant room, which held three chandeliers that she could promise were more prominent than the size of her body. She looked over to find tall windows that had beautiful pieces of glass light sweeping through the room. Essentially telling the room, through its prideful usage of bringing the vision in, that the morning was closing. She found a long table that was primarily empty, to which it only held two people, whom she assumed to be the two voices that she heard having a conversation earlier. One person held the position of the last person she would ever want to see, which was Hildith, who still carried that same look of disgust. He was indeed an older man who looked like he would not hesitate to beat up a baby to gain what he wanted. Aside from his half metal face, something about the man was strange.

The person Hilidth was having a conversation with was none other than the King himself, he sat there with a purple uniform that held a fluffy blue cape, and he had red garments, earrings, rings, and belts. The King's long hair was draped down. Oceana walked over to him with caution. She didn't want to interrupt the conversation he was having with Hildith.

"I say we should bring troops to the north," Hilith said. "With much due respect, sir."

"No, that is my final word. "We are staying on the right course. We don't need to expand further yet. KEEPIN soldiers are at their finest as of now." The King stopped and looked over at Oceana. He immediately stopped grooming the ruffles on his face and gave a wide grin

"Ah! The famous Oceana Sanford! I am very excited to have you here! Please sit down! Have you eaten yet?"

"Uh- Not yet sir." Oceana stammered.

"Well, sit down and eat! Won't you?" King Erebus turned to Hildith. His blue eyes glared at Hildiths pale green one. "We will continue our conversation later. But, first, let me enjoy having a nice breakfast with Ms. Sanford."

"Yes, sir," Hilidth said. Although Oceana could tell he wasn't too happy with his tone of voice, it was apparent that King hadn't cared that Hildith was annoyed either.

"So what would you like to eat? We have eggs, we have toast, we have bagels, we have pie, we have fruits and vegetables! You name it!"

"Oh well, that is a lot!" Oceana said. "They all sound perfect!"

"Waiter!" The King shouted, and a man came running to him, panting as if he had just run from across the castle's other side.

"Yes, sir?" He asked.

"Tell the chef she will have one of everything!" The King said,

The waiter nodded and ran off. Oceana blinked. She really could not tell anyone what had just happened. Did he say one of everything?

"So Ms. Sanford." The King almost shouted, interrupting her thoughts, "Heard that you helped save our beloved hero 'The Knight.'"

"Oh well, I-"

"Oh, don't humble yourself! You can say whatever you want to me!" He said, "It's not like I could kill you. I mean, I can." He paused, "But I would never use my power in such a way!" He laughed. "Unless I did!" He paused, then laughed. "Kidding, of course!"

Oceana couldn't help but laugh, too, she didn't find the joke too amusing, but it was funny enough to where she felt that her heart might just die on the spot.

"So, Ms. Sanford, besides being part of the Red division, is there anything else I should know about you?" He asked with a grin.

"Nothing else, really." She said,

"Nothing? Well, that's impossible! I have tried doing nothing once for an entire hour! It was dreadful. I can still feel traces of boredom in me today!" The King said.

"Well, I am trying to practice magic," Oceana said with hesitance.

"magic?" The King almost laughed but immediately contained his laughter back under his throat. "That is very different from kids in Cor'Meum, especially at your age!"

"I know, but I like it! I don't know why- but I feel like it speaks to me." Oceana said, looking at her hands.

"Oh! Well, what tone of magic are you doing?" The King asked.

"Uh, well."

"Well?"

"Well, I am not currently practicing any tones," she admitted with a bit of guilt. She always had felt a bit ridiculous explaining that she was studying magic but couldn't perform it quite yet.

"Not really practicing magic? Or not doing it right? What are we talking about?" The King asked while moving his hands in circles.

"I haven't got any of the tones down. I am still learning the basics!"

"Basics!" The King snapped. "Better than nothing! Oh, and will you look at that? Food is here!" He said with joy and a clap.

Three different men came out with plates full of food. All made their way to the two that currently had nothing to dine on in front of them. They placed the plates down to reveal food Oceana had never seen before. The smell of hot eggs and spices hit her directly in the face. She honestly had never smelled food that was this good before. Although she really felt like it was a special treat for her, she smiled and grabbed a fork and knife, and began eating the meal laid out in front of her.

"Ah yes, we have the finest chef in the kingdom!" King Erebus said proudly.

Oceana began eating her plate. It felt that her stomach was happy with her incredible decision to fill it with food once again. She hadn't realized how hungry she was until she shoved most of her plate down her mouth, sucking it till it vanished.

"So, what do you think about returning here to the castle?" The King asked.

"Oh, so you remember me?" Oceana asked him, almost jumping up in the process. The King nodded.

"Of course, I remember you! You are Marlyn's kid! Plus, with that white hair, how could one ever forget you? Even if they tried!" He said, "You are iconic!"

"Oh well, thank you." Oceana smiled, "So, um, speaking of my family." She said "If you don't mind me asking," she paused- debating whether she should ask, only to conclude that she did have the right to know. "Why is my grandpa a wanted man?" She asked with her eyebrow raised.

"So you really don't know?" The King asked.

"Yeah," Oceana said awkwardly, "He never really told me anything."

"The reason your grandpa is wanted is- well- how do I say this?" The King looked away from Oceana, turning his entire body in the process, "Well, because-" He started up again, "he was conspiring with the cult trying to kill me! I mean! Me-" He turned around to face Oceana again. "The king!" He said, knocking on his crown almost as if it was not a constant reminder of his power. "It isn't personal. I mean, it is. But not to you." He said.

"Right." Oceana forced a smile. "They called themselves revolutionaries, though."

"No, they are a cult," The King said, keeping a smile on his face. He had already taken his fork and began stabbing his egg. "Nothing but a messy little cult," He turned his fork, grinding the silverware into the yolk as it began to bleed its yellow jell all over the plate. "Who has no real power in this world." There was this pause, the King stared at his plate in disgust, but when he looked at Oceana his smile appeared as if it had only taken a short vacation in the world of hatred. "While also the palace papers do say they are a cult! Are you really going to argue with the papers? Cor'Meum's papers?"

"Uh, well, I suppose if you put it that way," Oceana said. She did not understand why the King insisted they be called such a different name.

But she made sure to keep a mental reminder to not refer to the group as revolutionists. It was strange how much the King wanted to deny the word. So also, her grandpa was involved? Why did she have a tough time believing that? She almost felt as if she was accusing the King of lying right now in her mind.

"If it makes you feel better, you will be the first to talk to him when we get him, and I will use my power to reason things out with him. I can guarantee you the sentence will not be harsh." He winked.

"You'll seriously let me talk to him?" Oceana asked immediately.

"Of course! I try to make sure all my citizens are taken care of!" He grinned.

"Oh- wow! Thank you!"

"Well, of course!"

Oceana continued to eat the rest of her breakfast. Their conversation carried on about what the King was doing to prepare for such an extravagant event. He was inviting all the celebrities in the city of Annularity. Which was the city that the Kingdom stood proudly next to. It carried a melting pot of culture and people. Everyone wanted to live in Annularity. It was also known for caring for thousands of light bugs at night, which made the place very exciting.

"King Erebus." Oceana said, thinking out loud. She paused. "Sir,"

"Yes, Ms. Sanford?"

"Have you heard of the golden apple?" She asked. When she had asked this question, the King dropped his fork on his plate. He began to whip his napkin with his face.

"Oceana, why are you asking me this?" His voice shifted, no longer being at its upbeat high energetic tone.

"I have been hearing things about it," Oceana responded, feeling instant regret that she had brought it up. Perhaps asking about weird obscure legends she did not quite understand was not the most excellent idea to bring up with the King. There was silence between the two for a long moment. Oceana had never felt so nervous in her whole life. That nervousness was not just storming in her own head. The palace guards and royal servants all stood in silence. None of them dared to even draw a breath. Finally, the King closed his eyes and took a breath before giving Oceana a wide smile.

"The golden apple isn't real!" He picked up his fork. "Just a story that some wacko came up with! Probably because they wanted to desperately believe in the existence of magical creatures!" The King laughed. "You know what is real? Technology and the innovation of robotic use! We are so close to perfecting each large town in Cor'Meum with Ferndale's same technological resources!" The King said. Though it was clear that the King no longer had the desire to continue the conversation regarding the golden apple. Oceana decided to comply and listen to the rest of what the King had to say in silence.

The conversation came to a close when a Palace guard moved up to the King. He was informed that there was a mishap in one of his plans. Oceana assumed it was the party. The King stood up from the table and smiled at Oceana.

"It was a pleasure talking to you, I have a feeling you will be just as amazing as your mother was!" Oceana was very confused at what the statement had meant, but she only threw the King a polite smile to not be rude.

"Thank you." She said, Then the King went off. Oceana looked at her plate. She tried tracing back the King's statement and what it had meant. She closed her eyes and decided that she would move on forward from the silly thing the King said and continue to eat her delicious breakfast.

Once she was done, the maids insisted that they take her dishes and clean them up for her. It felt peculiar having others clean a mess initiated by herself, though she did not complain. Once she got up and saw how many leftovers there were, the sinking feeling of disappointment hit. She had not understood why the King had ordered so much food if there was no intention of completion. She gave one last painful look before she exited the dining room.

Oceana moved down the halls of the castle. She wondered how she was going to get to her room. She had no idea where everything was located. It seemed that this palace was much like a labyrinth. She could have sworn that she had seen the same portrait now three times when she turned the corner. It was one of the previous kings with the most unusual mustache. It looked almost as if the King wanted to start a trend in mustache shapes only to fail and realize it would not be appealing for that time, nor would it be for any other times in the future. With such an unusual portrait, it was hard to consider the possibility that Oceana was taking steps in the right direction or any progressive steps at all. Oceana moved around once more, only this time deciding to take another sharp left instead of all the rights she had been going for. She was introduced to a new hallway, one that had seemed mysterious to her. The hallway stretched for a good couple of feet until there was a door at its end.

Oceana looked around the area. Some part of her knew she was most likely prohibited from opening the door. However, there was no one in sight to stop her. So she decided to investigate the mysterious golden door in front of her. After she carried her feet down the dark gray hall and placed herself just a couple of inches in front of the door, which now seeing up close, had strange symbols on a golden crested plate hanging above it. One of the symbols looked like a moon with an eye inside it. Next to the moon was a sun with an eye in it. She tilted her head and tried to determine what the gold symbols meant. After a solid minute, she gave up and moved on.

She reached out to the doorknob and pressed on the round handle that would grant her permission to enter the room hidden behind. When she went to move her hand forward, a voice beamed out. This stopped her from taking any more action.

"What are you doing?" Oceana turned to find Aster's annoyed face staring right at hers. She felt her eyes piercing into her soul. She had no idea what she was doing, actually...

"I was uh,"

"You were uhh- what?" Aster asked sharply, "You know you are not allowed here."

"I actually didn't know that. I honestly got lost."

"So being lost is a good excuse to snoop around parts of the castle you don't belong in?"

"I honestly can't find my room." Oceana had taken her hand off the doorknob and moved both her hands up in defense.

"Temporary room." Aster smacked in. Oceana gave a big huff before she pressed her hands on her hips, and she narrowed her eyes down at Aster.

"Let me tell you, Aster, you have been nothing but mean to me! We used to be friends- and now-" She paused. "Why are you acting like this?"

"Actually, Pirate, let me tell you this. You think you are all that because your mother was some quick snap big-shot, well let me tell you're not! Now she's a nobody- just like you. You are nothing. Learn your place." She said coldly.

"I-" Oceana paused, "I'm not a nobody!"

"What does a pirate like you have, hmm? I am obviously far beyond everything that you can even comprehend!" Aster smirked, and looked up at her. "Face it- I am better than you."

"Better than me at everything? Well, then I challenge you!" Oceana pointed at Aster with her bandaged hand. "I challenge you to a duel." She said, projecting more confidence than she actually had. "If you are so much better at sword fighting, I challenge you to fight me. If you beat me, then I will admit that you were right. I am a loser. But if I win, you have to be nicer to me. Oh- and wish me a happy birthday." Oceana added.

"Oh- Kill me!" Aster complained.

"But if you are so good at everything, you don't have to worry about that happening!" Oceana sniped in. Aster glared at her before she rolled her eyes.

"Fine- Sure- Let's duel in the garden this afternoon."

"Then it is a deal," Oceana said and gave Aster a very long and intense stare.

CHAPTER 21:

Pirate vs Princess

O CEANA stood in the expansive grass field. She held her sword with an iron grip, ignoring the slight pain in her fingers. She decided to take her jacket off for the battle that was about to come. She waited for Aster, in the green field. She hadn't realized that Aster had announced their contest until several servants and guards gathered around the halls above the garden to watch the scene. It must be exciting for them. To view the battle from their point of view, a princess battling the grandchild of a pirate. She waited patiently in the green grassy field, waiting for Aster to make her appearance. She was late for her own duel, Oceana decided to look up at the audience to see if she could find Jamlson hiding in the crowd somewhere. Perhaps he caught a word of what was going to happen this afternoon. But his face remained absent, much like it had all day.

"Looks like the princess is a no-show." Oceana chuckled. Her laughter was cut short once Aster made her presence known. She carried a grin on her face, and she was wearing lighter clothes, short bottoms, and a sleeveless shirt, which all kept the colors purple, red, and blue. Oceana's face had suddenly heated up, and her stomach moved in circles. What was this? Oceana told herself it must be duel nerves, though she never usually gets nervous before duels. She got into her stance, ready for the battle.

"It's not too late to back out now." She said, drawing her sword. Clouds were slowly seeping in, it made the battle arena appear dark and gloomy. Aster's sword was different compared to Oceana's. Her's was brightly colored, and had a style of that of an old knight, not similar to one of a pirate. In all fairness, Oceana only brought her sword to show what it had looked like, to perhaps get a wooden one that was similar to her own taste. But it appeared that Aster wanted to use their real swords. Some part of Oceana thought that she should mention that they shouldn't use real weapons for a harmless battle, but another and stronger part of her did not want to show Aster a glimpse of fear.

"Not a chance," Oceana said with a smile on her face.

Aster grinned and moved forward, making the first swing at Oceana, marking the start of the battle. The two swords clashed, and their harmony echoed throughout the garden. With Aster's quick draw, Oceana almost missed when it came to defending herself. Aster withdrew her sword, and they began to circle around one another, holding their swords out in front of them. Oceana waited for Aster's next attack hoping she could figure out what Aster's tactics were.

Aster then moved in to attack, too much to Oceana's predictions. She moved her sword up to defend herself from the blow, each time the blades clanked Oceana felt her fingers scream for a rest. Aster then swung her sword back to her, and they went back to moving in circles. Who was going to throw the next attack? This question was quickly answered when Oceana used all her strength to throw her own sword attack on Aster herself.

Aster moved her sword up in a hasty response, not letting Oceana get the best of her. Her sword launched towards Oceana, sliding next to her sword. Oceana moved out of the sword's reach. If Oceana hadn't dodged, she would have been impaled in the face. Frogs on a stick! Was Aster trying to kill her? Oceana felt her temper rising, and she turned around and had already planned her own attack on Aster. If it wasn't for Aster's quick thinking, perhaps there would have been a public beheading. Aster moved her sword up, and Oceana did the same thing too, their swords clashing against one another. Oceana slid her sword up and Aster did the same thing. The two of them then moved in to attack one another. This happened more times than anyone in the ring could count. Aster swung, almost stabbing Oceana, for now, the second time in this battle.

Though the stakes were initially supposed to be low, winning this match meant everything between the two trained sword fighters. They continued to keep their pacing around one another. It was an intense scene. The palace guards and the palace servants cheered and shouted for the battle to continue. Both girls had their eyes locked on one another. Perhaps they had both forgotten that they shouldn't actually attempt to stab the other swordsman. Oceana decided to go for a low throw. That was when Aster spun her body and moved her own arms down to block her attack, Oceana wasted no more time but to strike again.

Aster blocked Oceana's next quick attack, ducked before she could throw in another attack, rolled on the ground, and threw her own attack. Oceana would have hated to admit that she almost missed the opportunity to block, which would have led to her loss. But Oceana was not the type to give up so easily. She would not lose this fight against Aster out of all people. Oceana was determined to claim this victory, Oceana moved in for an attack, but Aster only blocked her. She carried a lot of skill, Oceana had already known that before going into the battle. The two continued to bump swords for what felt like a solid minute, to the pain in Oceana's hand forever. This all had happened before Oceana was pushed back by a heavy push on Aster's side.

Aster grinned and moved diligently through the air. Almost as if she allowed the wind to guide her to the path of victory. Aster moved her sword up. This was her mistake, Oceana saw an opening and moved her sword up with all her might. Aster fell back and had almost hit the ground, Oceana knew this was her chance. She had to get her while she was down. Oceana moved in for one fast motion and began to attack while she was down, Aster managed to defend herself in the middle of recovering from Oceana's swing but hadn't recovered fast enough for Oceana's next hit. This was it, it seemed that victory had belonged to Oceana, but before she knew it, Oceana could have sworn she heard Aster snapping her fingers. Then from the corner of her eyes, she found clouds of red, beaming inside an orange light that ripped itself in half. Once the sphere had split there was a heavy wind.

The rush of a heavy hot wind hit her face. Oceana moved off balance and fell to the ground, the crowd began to go crazy, her sword out of her hand, but before she could go and reach it, Aster had her own sword pointed at her. Oceana looked up from her position on the grass, Aster had a wide grin on her face, with the tip of her sword pointed just a feel inches away from her face.

"Looks like I am better than you at this." She managed to say between breaths. "Admit it! Admit that I am better!"

"How did you do that?" Oceana asked.

"Do what?" Aster asked, squinting her eyes at her.

"Magic!" Oceana said. "You used magic!" Oceana said.

"I have no idea what you are talking about." Aster sharply responded.

"You are using a high tone too! That's the same one I am training for!" Oceana said between breaths herself, "It was amazing. You have to teach me!" But before Aster could open her mouth to say anything that could be remotely negative towards the girl, Vinnian came running down and got in between the two.

"Stop! Stop this madness!" He shouted, "Honestly," He said, "What were you two thinking?" He turned and looked up at the large gathering, many of the castle's staff members stood there. "Are you all getting paid to stand here and watch?" He asked, "Get out of here!" He shouted, and with his words, everyone began to dispatch. He turned back to the two teenage girls in front of him. He pressed his fingers to his nose and looked over at Aster,

"Go; your father is waiting for you." He said. Aster nodded and looked at Oceana before she disappeared into the garden. Vinnian looked at Oceana, who was still on the ground. "Get up. What were you doing?"

"Sorry, I was-"

"Sorry doesn't cut it, battling the Kings' daughter? Really? Have you lost your mind?"

"Look, she was challenging me and-"

"I don't care who was challenging who. You should know better, Ms. Sanford." He said, "The King invites you to his home and to his party, and this is how you thank him by roughhousing with his kid?"

Oceana stopped. He was right; she shouldn't be battling Aster, even if she had turned into this mean spirited person, or more of one since they were kids. Instead, she should start becoming a bigger person. Especially when it comes to petty arguments. Even if Aster got under her skin, it ultimately hadn't mattered, Aster was still the princess, and she was not. "Sorry, I will do better next time," Oceana mumbled to Vinnian.

"Be better next time. Come on, let's go to your room." He said.

"Alright," Oceana mumbled. Vinnian and her began to walk inside the castle, Vinnian looked over at her and let out a breath.

"Don't worry, you're not in trouble with anyone-" Then smiled at her. "I get it- she can be" He lost his words; however it hadn't taken Oceana too much time to find them.

"Annoying?" Oceana raised an eyebrow. Vinnian stopped and sighed, then gave a smile.

"Well- as the King's right-hand man, I do not encourage such negative words to be thrown at his daughter like that." He then quickly looked around before he gave a single nod. Oceana smiled. Inside the castle, Oceana let her eyes wander around the paintings that were hung up, the long walls, and the chandeliers that dangled miles above her.

"This place, I always forget how huge it is."

"It is a castle."

"I still remember living here when I was eight years old." She said, "I can't believe it's already been ten years."

"I remember you."

"You do?" Oceana was shocked.

"You were the little girl that was always getting into trouble."
He laughed.

"Exploring is fun! How else are you supposed to find your way
around here?" She questioned. Then paused. "If you were here, you must
have known my mother!"

"Not entirely," Vinnian said. "I only spoke to her once."

"Once?"

"I met her once at this party called the Bell Harbor Celebration. We
were the only purple tier guests there." He said. "Only talked to her that
night and a bit after the next day." Vinnian then laughed. "Your mother
is charming! Wonderful woman." He stopped, then smiled "Cor'Meum's
true hero." He added quickly.

Oceana laughed, then stopped and remembered the battle and how
it ended. Maybe if she told Vinnian what had happened, he would know
what she was talking about, being the King's right-hand man. "I think
Aster knows how to do magic." There was silence before Oceana decided
it was her cue to elaborate on what that had meant. "When I was battling
Aster, she was able to use magic on me. No one else noticed, but I did.
That's how she won. Aster is a magic user!" She explained.

"Aster does not know how to use magic because Rosearios don't use
magic. It's family tradition, its-"

"I know, I know, it's been like that forever. They are forward think-
ers, yeah, yeah." Oceana waved her hand. "But I know what I saw, or rather
what I had felt." She said, "Aster knows how to use magic." She said,

"Why would Aster risk her whole family's reputation over such a petty sword game like the one she participated in. Also, why would Aster destroy the family tradition as a whole? Just to learn magic?" Vinnian said.

"I don't know," Oceana said. "I honestly felt that she did use magic."

"Ms. Sanford, I would advise not making these accusations in such a projecting tone." Vinnian coughed.

Oceana decided it was time to drop the idea. Maybe she was mistaken about Aster being able to control magic. Rosearios don't use magic. That was the family's one rule, and it has been part of their family for many generations. Why would Aster break that rule? Not to mention that Aster was the type of girl who would only stay within the rules given to her. She had never seemed like the girl that would break them. She was always a go-by-the-book type.

CHAPTER 22:

Big news

THE two had made their way down the castle. Oceana was happy that Vinnian knew the way back to her room. He then explained how she could find her way back here if she was ever lost, but Oceana became too embarrassed to ask again after a few attempts. She snapped her fingers with her good hand and nodded her head.

"Thank you! I get it now!" She lied.

"Great!" Vinnian said with a smile. "I expect to see you at the dance tonight." He said. Oceana nodded her head in response. She had then managed to close the door. Once she did, she pressed her back on it and slid down. Today had been a day so far, and it was not even nightfall yet. She couldn't tell if today was so strange because it was her birthday. Or perhaps she went from running from KEEPIN guards just the other day to being protected by them. No less in the castle that rested next to the beautiful city of Annularity.

She pressed her hands to her face, it was strange that no one had mentioned to her or had given her a happy birthday, but she couldn't expect everyone to know. The only person that it had mattered to her who remembered was Jamlson. It was nice that he left her a happy birthday note next to her bed for her to wake to. She would have to thank him for that later. Hopefully, she would be able to see him at some point today. His absence had been quite noticeable. Where was he when she wanted to tell a silly joke, only for him to roll his eyes at her and ask her to stop forever? She began to chuckle to herself at the idea of Jamlson. Spending the rest of the day on her bedroom floor was not ideal. She then got up. After being on her two feet, the wooden surface told her someone was on the other side of her door.

Oceana turned around, wondering who was there, perhaps it was the maids coming in to drop more things off, but she could not recall what more she would need to have dropped off in the room she was staying. So she turned around and opened the door to find Headworth and TOAD. TOAD gave a wave at Oceana, who smiled back at the mechanic and shared her own friendly wave.

"I hope you have a minute of your time to engage in a conversation," Headworth said.

"Of course, what's up?" Oceana asked him.

"I had remembered that it was an important date to you, so did Jamlson, so Jamlson and I." TOAD looked at Headworth and began to blink his eyes, the lights going on and off. "Fine and TOAD too." Headworth sighed and looked at the mechanical "Worked together to find you a birthday gift." He said, "I think I pointed out you aren't very materialistic, but you are sentimental about things." Headworth coughed.

"Aw, you guys- that's so sweet."

"Don't interrupt," Headworth said.

"Oh sorry," Oceana said. "Please continue."

"Well." Headworth said, "It took all morning, but we had to jump through hoops to retrieve this." Headworth held out what looked to be a diamond necklace. It wasn't just any sort of diamond. Her mother wore the same chain in all her portraits and paintings. Her mother was so devastated when she had to leave the castle without being able to find it. The purple rock in the necklace always stole Oceana's attention. It wasn't just a beautiful color, but inside the rock, there was a white flicker. "You said your mother worked here. She apparently left this here before she separated herself from this place. Palace guards believed she misplaced it." Headworth looked around.

Oceana took the purple necklace in her hands and stared at its beauty; in all her memories, her mother would wear this necklace. She believed that her mother hadn't loved anything more in this world than this necklace. She looked over at Headworth and hugged him, "Thank you so much!" She opened her eyes to watch TOAD stare. She brought her arm out and made TOAD join the hug. Headworth eventually pushed himself away from Oceana's tight grip.

"Okay, okay, that will do." He said, then coughed once more before he pushed his glasses back up. "I apologize for taking so long. I had no idea where you were staying. I looked all afternoon." Headworth said, but then TOAD blinked at him. "Okay fine, we looked all afternoon." He said.

"Why didn't you take Jamlson with you?" Oceana asked.

"He said he was busy. I think he is having difficulty putting on his outfit for tonight's gathering." Headworth said, "Which I should be doing myself." Headworth admitted, "Would be embarrassing if I came underdressed." He looked at Oceana and nodded. "Happy birthday." he said before he made his way down the hall. TOAD gave Oceana one more wave before he followed Headworth down the hall.

Oceana closed the door and gave one long sigh, Headworth acting almost like an average person had to be a sign that today was different. Yet who knew? What is the true definition of normal? Could Oceana call herself a normal person. Not in the sense of her white hair but her personality or how she acted. Well, none of that mattered. She was an adult now! Today was her birthday. Today was the day she would start acting like her age. The sword duel with Aster did not count, of course. Before she could continue her interior monologue, another knock was heard at her door. She honestly wondered if it was Headworth forgetting to say something. Or maybe it could be Vinnian? The list was unknown until she opened the door. About three or four of the palace maids were standing there when Oceana opened the door.

"What? What is going on?" Oceana asked.

"There has been a request to get you dressed up for the dance."

"Help? I don't need help!" Oceana almost insisted. The maids all looked at one another and raised eyebrows. Then, the one before pressed her hand onto her own face and pointed at Oceana.

"What were you planning on wearing?" The same girl asked.

"Uh, I guess this." Oceana pointed at her outfit, and the maids all laughed amongst one another, "What?" Oceana could feel her face going red. "What's so funny?"

"Look, you are going to the biggest formal," the maid emphasized 'the' and 'formal,' "event of the year, and your fashion choice is the definition of a stereotypical Red division pirate." Then, the clear leader of the maids said as he threw his hand up, "That is not going to happen. Also, the press is going to be here. You wouldn't want to look well- that."

"I suppose not?" Oceana said with her eyebrows up.

"Great! People get her all cleaned up! I will choose what she will wear."

Oceana didn't know what all cleaning up meant, but she could feel the other maids push her into the bathroom that came with the room. Before Oceana knew it, the two girls were scrubbing them and trying to get them to be cleaner than ever. Then, from what they had heard, the male maids left the bathroom together to prepare makeup. They promised that she hated every minute of it.

When they were done, she could feel one of the maids do her hair, there was not much to work with when it came to hair that rested above someone's shoulders, but this woman somehow managed to find a way to make it stylish. The two other maids were playing with her face.

"Tell me, Oceana, have you ever worn makeup before?" One of them asked.

"Uhhh, no?" Oceana responded.

"Oh! Well, you should wear it more often. You would look marvelous." The other guy said. Oceana could not tell if the man was insulting her physical appearance or not, Oceana remembered being called scruffy looking. But who had time to care about what one looked like? She never had that time. So she supposed she was okay with her appearance. It was being compared to her beautiful mother that threw her off sometimes. Whoever her father was, she probably took whatever he looked like.

"Okay, almost done. Try not to move so much." The maid insisted. "Be still." Oceana held her breath. It seemed that the maids would get frustrated with her with any of the slightest breathing. Then yell at her to sit still. But once the maid was done. Oceana was not allowed to look in the mirror to see what she looked like. She was dragged outside the bathroom. In front of her, there was the leader again. He had a grin on his face.

"I was able to find the best outfit for you. Now put it on." He threw it at her. Oceana caught the dress and a coat that came with it and placed it over herself. She felt the dress flow down while it began to place itself on her. The guy walked behind her and pulled up the zipper that rested behind it.

The dress suddenly became tighter, and she felt it fit perfectly on her. "Turn around!" He said. Oceana turned around, the bottom half of the dress looked like a red wave. The front of it showed her legs, while the back was like a cape. It was a beautiful dress. The maid then said, "Untie the ties you have all over your hair." Oceana grabbed all the bands that were in her hair. She could feel her hair flow down. She grabbed the next red fluffy fabric and placed her arms through the sleeves.

"Wow, you look amazing!" One of the maids said.

"Yeah, you look pretty!" The other maid said.

"Here, wear this," The other maid handed Oceana a pair of golden slippers. "I figured if I gave you high heels, you would probably fall on your face."

"Yeah," Oceana said, laughing. She slipped the shoes on and turned around, and found a tall mirror that waited patiently to be used.

When Oceana looked at the person in the mirror, they almost seemed unrecognizable. Her white hair looked neatly curly, different from her usual tangled mess. She hadn't noticed that they put long orange earrings on her. She looked at her makeup too, which made her look fancy. She could tell the maids hadn't put too much on her, but it was enough to notice. However, they did put enough on to hide the new scar on her forehead. She had also noticed she was wearing pink lipstick, which she had never seen herself wear before. It was nice. Her eyes wandered over to the dress itself, a floral red. It had a fluorescent pattern on it. The dress covered the bottom of her neck, to her elbows, to just a bit below the knees. The only tight part of her dress was around her chest, but she figured that was just part of the design. She also had fallen in love with the giant red fur coat she was wearing. It looked as if flames were eating her, and she loved it. The only thing that wasn't red about the dress was her purple necklace placed neatly above her heart.

"So, how is it?" He asked

"I am not usually a fan of dresses, but it is nice." Oceana admitted, "Thank you!" The maid nodded.

"You can always trust me to find an outfit that will best match a person's personality and complexion." He said with a grin, "You do look like a princess tonight."

"Aha, really?" Oceana asked.

"Honestly!" He responded,

"Thank you!"

Again, there was a knock on the door, "I'll get it." Oceana said. She moved over to the door and opened it. At first, she believed that her eyes were deceiving her, but when she found it true, she found Jamlson, in a suit out of all things. He wasn't even wearing his purple scarf, which she had never seen him not wear before.

"Ugh, they made me wear this outfit." He complained, looking at his sleeves. "They said if I wanted to attend this ridiculous event, I had to dress up." He rolled his eyes.

"How's your back?" Oceana asked, ignoring his protests of complaints.

"It's better. I have a bandage around it, but they said it's supposed to heal next week or something." Jamlson stopped when he looked at Oceana for the first time. "Wow." He said.

"What?" Oceana raised an eyebrow.

"Well, you look, well," He paused. It seemed like he was trying to find the right words. "Well, you know, you look different."

"Different?" Oceana raised her own eyebrow. "What's that supposed to mean?"

"It doesn't mean anything!" Jamlson defended.

"So it means nothing?"

"Right!"

"So you're saying I look like; nothing?" Oceana rephrased her eyebrow had moved up.

"Yes!" Jamlson snapped his fingers in excitement, then stopped "I- I mean no!" Jamlson said, "I meant-" But before Jamlson could continue, the maid stepped in and whispered to Oceana

"The King needs you to be at the attendance hall."

"Right." Oceana stated. She looked over at Jamlson, "I have to go."

"Of course. I will see you at the event?" Jamlson said.

"Yes!" She had then turned around, but before she completely took off, she realized something and turned around to face Jamlson. "By the way, thank you for the birthday letter!" She snapped. Jamlson's eyebrow raised.

"Birthday letter? I didn't send you a birthday letter." Oceana was confused by this statement, but the maids had begun to push her forward, separating the two. Jamlson didn't write her the letter? If he didn't, who did? She wanted to ponder over this and start making a checklist of people who could have possibly written her the letter, but she was interrupted by one of the maids.

"Do you know which way you are going Ms. Sanford?" He questioned. Oceana stopped. No, she had no idea where she was going and admitted it so, embarrassingly to him. To which he nodded, and led them down a very long hallway. It took several minutes before they stopped behind two huge doors. Oceana could hear a muffle of a crowd outside. She took a breath and looked at the man who helped her not wander around the castle forever.

"Thank you," Oceana said, nodding and walking off. Oceana turned to the door before she pushed it open. When she did, she was quickly introduced to the flashing lights that came with clicking sounds, all of which blinded her. She closed her eyes, rubbed them, and moved forward, closing the door behind her. Once she regained her eyesight, she found herself on the castle's top stairs, behind King Erebus, talking with a podium in front of him. Next to him were Vinnian, Aster, Crocus, and an older man she had never seen before.

"I promise you." King Erebus said, "We will not be hearing about these cults soon enough. We have it all taken care of." He reassured the crowd of people who were holding cameras.

"But aren't these cults you speak of really a revolution?" In the crowd, one of the men said, "Aren't you scared that they are trying to take over?"

"There is no revolution, trust me. These are a small group of people that are trying to represent the entirety of one country. Nothing is happening under our watch. So I am not scared." The King stated calmly.

"What about the explosion that happened in the Westside Mountains?"

"Fortunately, there were no casualties. We arrested the members involved. We have a team that's investigating any remaining members. Soon we will not be hearing of them." King Erebus assured the crowd. He looked over at Oceana. "I do, however, have an announcement to make." He said. "We are very fortunate to have a brilliant young person on our team. Without their help, we wouldn't have stopped these cult members. Therefore, I would like to publicly announce that Oceana Sanford will be a new member of the Purple division and under the guidance of my own right-hand man, Vinnian Timidus." He said and moved back to allow Oceana to stand behind the podium.

Oceana hadn't expected this to be what the King had in mind. She was completely thrown off. It seemed like she might have no choice but to accept this position. She knew that many people would kill to be where she was. This was incredible, especially having it be announced by the King himself. Now that she could recall, she was probably the youngest person to have this position of power. She just turned eighteen. She walked over to the podium. She noticed there were tiny stairs she could use to stand.

She moved up the small spaces, happy that she wasn't wearing heels. Once she reached the top step, she was already blinded by the flashes of cameras.

"Ms. Sanford! Where is your mother? Are you trying to become the next Marlyn Sanford?" A reporter asked.

"Oceana! Over here! Do you believe that these cults are part of a bigger scheme?"

"Why are your grandpa and mother missing?"

"Oceana, do you know if there is anything more to what we know?"

"Ms. Sanford! What are your statements."

"Why are you wearing red? Is it to support your grandpa?"

"Is it true you were a pirate?"

"Do you know what happened to your grandpa's boat?"

The crowd only grew louder, and Oceana could feel her stomach turn while the crowd got louder, with more aggressive flashing. She closed her eyes and took in a deep sigh before she opened them again, seeing the wave of people whose eyes flashed on her. She felt herself get a bit shaky, but she would not let that get in the way of talking to the people in front of her. She took in one more breath before she allowed herself to speak.

"To answer the question I have been hearing the most, I don't know where my grandfather is." When Oceana stated that more people began talking all at once, she decided she would point at an individual, allowing that person to ask a question. She pointed to a random cameraman in the crowd. He understood he was allowed to ask her a question.

"Do you know why your grandpa is missing or why he is wanted right now?" He asked. "There have been rumors that he has been conspiring with the cult. That he is the reason that his boat was destroyed!"

"Are we really going to throw our judgments at people with mere rumors?" Oceana asked, avoiding the question on purpose. She understood that King Erebus told her that he did betray the kingdom, but there was some part of her that believed it was a big misunderstanding. Maybe the King himself was not giving her the whole story.

"My grandpa loved the men that were on the boat as a family! Hopefully, we will be able to find them soon!"

"You don't believe the men on the boat are dead?"

"No. Next Question."

"Is it true that there will be a war with the revolutionists and Cor'Meum?"

"I-" Oceana felt baffled. "No. Much like what King Erebus said, there isn't going to be a war." She reassured the crowd. "I am excited to work with the King and Vinnian to shape Cor'Meum and stop these people from hurting our country. But I can promise there isn't going to be a war." She said,

"Will you be replacing your mother?"

"I don't believe I will be," Oceana said sheepishly.

"Thank you, Ms. Sanford!" King Erebus said, which Oceana figured was her cue to get off the podium. She made her way next to Vinnian and stood quietly next to him. She thought it would be weird if she walked back inside or got off the platform. Instead, she watched King Erebus grin widely at the crowd.

"So I know what you are all thinking! Who is this gentleman that is standing next to me?" He laughed. "Many of you might already know who he is from your favorite programs! He is part of my celebrity invite! But in more ways than one!" King Erebus said, "Get ready for your mind to be blown when I tell you that this fantastic gentleman Pséftis, the man behind talk-boxes, is actually the wonderful Magician who defeated Sage Magnus Forty years ago!"

Oceana's heart dropped, and she watched Pséftis take the stage. He had messy long hair in all the photos she had seen of him. With an event such as this. He decided to tie all the gray mess up, leaving it in a neat bun. His bright green eyes fell upon the people who waited in anticipation. She had listened to his talk-box shows before and had always thought they were corny; she hadn't realized that he was the Magician. Why did he wait forty years to tell the world who he was? What made it so urgent for him to come up like this? She watched him take the podium. He smiled at the crowd. He looked like a natural.

"Thank you King Erebus, for the introduction. That is right, I am the Magician!" He said, he rested his hand on top of his bright purple 'KEEPIN' pin. "After I had defeated Sage Magnus all those years ago, I wanted a fresh new life! To live my dream to bring entertainment to the public!" He said, "I am very proud that I, the great Pséftis, was able to bring joy into all of your lives in more ways than one!" He coughed in his hand. "It has been a great honor to be the public's hero of comedy and war. It does pain me to see my old partner Bellus Timidus in his state of mind, so I decided to come out as the Magician, to represent the face that gives hope. To assure you that I did kill the evil Sage Magnus many years ago, and that any rumor said otherwise is only trying to bring fear to all of you!"

Oceana watched Pséftis begin to take the crowd's questions. She had always wanted to meet the Magician, and she was this close to him.

Though she was starting to feel bad that she and her grandpa made fun of him when he would come on the talk-box, whenever they went and ate somewhere at a pitstop. They hadn't found any of his jokes funny. They both felt they always landed flat, that he was an awful comedian. Maybe it was best that he was going back to magic. She watched him take questions; she felt she was standing there forever, while her heart felt like it was cycling through mini-explosions. This lasted until the King stepped in and cleared his throat.

"Thank you, Pséftis, and before we conclude our meeting today, we wanted to take the opportunity to thank KEEPIN for their hard work and their dedication to keeping this and other countries at peace. We also want to thank one KEEPIN officer in particular, Sir Avular Gonder,"

Oceana raised an eyebrow and watched a man in a blue KEEPIN uniform step onto the stage. The King himself moved forward and began to shake his hand. He moved back to the crowd while he rested his hand on the officer's shoulder.

"Avular, with dedication and skills, managed to find an underground black market that was used to plot attacks on our precious military in Fovero. We thank him for his bravery, how he stepped in when the time was right, even taking down one of those terrible people! For that, I will be awarding Sir Avular with a golden medal of bravery."

Oceana could feel her legs go stiff in fear. So that's what the man had meant when he pointed at the sky, the sky was the kingdom, and the kingdom was KEEPIN. They shot an innocent man, and now they were celebrating it by awarding his murderer a golden medal? What was KEEPIN? Was this indeed her country? Was it always like this, and she just never saw it? At that exact moment, Oceana became repulsed at the idea of her new position.

CHAPTER 23:

A booming party

T HE blue sky had finally decided to turn in for the night. The room where Oceana and King Erebus had breakfast in the morning was now full of people in such fantastic clothing. Oceana couldn't even begin to talk about how beautiful all the women and men were. There was a stage filled with people playing instruments, and there was a woman in the front singing. Oceana could listen to her voice all day. She noticed that around the room, there were talk boxes. They must have just placed them there for the party. She wandered around the room, listening to the live music that filled the room. When she reached one of the corners of the room, she found a long table, wrapped in a cloth decorated in the colors that represented Cor'Meum. The food that was displayed showed how fancy this party truly was.

On top of one of the tables were several small purple robots that marched up and down the table, carrying plates of food that probably cost more than the dress Oceana was wearing. There was also food that moved around from giant hands that must have been recently installed into the wall. The arms would reach towards the plate, and move it around, rearranging the order of food, to show guests the variety that the castle had to offer. Oceana noticed there were some plates being carried by small flying machines for the guests that desired food but didn't want to walk to it, they also collected plates from those who had finished their meals as well.

Oceana looked around the table, she couldn't decide which one she wanted, all the options looked amazing. She knew that if she didn't make a decision now, the mechanicals would present her with more options which would make the task of finding food much harder.

"You know the food is only for the real guests." Oceana turned around and looked at Aster, who wore a long tight purple dress. Aster must have also worn high heels, because she was now the same height as Oceana. She was also wearing make-up which, in Oceana's opinion, looked beautiful. Well of course Aster looked beautiful, she was the most beautiful girl in Cor'Meum, Oceana didn't need a magazine cover to tell her that. Oceana felt her stomach let up, and her face burned up.

"Oh, well, that would be me," Oceana said, ignoring the fact her heart decided to fly. She moved her hand to grab one of the dishes that the giant hand offered as a choice to her. She did not break eye contact with Aster, who had her face scrunched up.

"Oh well," Aster mocked. "You may think that you are so great, but guess what? You're not." She said,

"I don't know." Oceana sang, "My new position says otherwise," She said with a grin and gave her food a poke with her fork. Aster scrunched her eyes and gave Oceana, one more glare.

"Don't get a big head pirate." She said before she walked away. Oceana rolled her eyes,

"Pirate." she mumbled, "She says it like it's an insult." Oceana began to actually eat the food she forced off the table, which was some sort of bird she wouldn't recognize the name of. She walked around the room some more. She wondered if she could find any other big celebrities at this party. Though she had no idea what other celebrities there were. She never had the chance to listen to talk-boxes or watch motion pictures too much; she filled her time either training or reading. Oceana now began to wonder if she ever met any celebrity that she hadn't known was one; because of her lack of knowledge in modern culture. She started to feel out of touch with her time and for the first time felt old. Old perhaps because it was her birthday, and that's what birthdays do to people. Birthday's make people feel like an old person for the next several weeks before they decide to get over it.

She continued to move around the room, she then noticed her plate was empty, and a flying robot was right there next to her ready to collect her empty plate. She placed her plate on the golden box with wings, small claws from the opposite end of where the wings were placed, and grabbed the plate. After it had a firm grasp on the plate, the box flew away. She watched as her empty plate flew into the distance. When she looked back down onto the dance floor, that is when she found Pséftis. Finding him was not a huge accomplishment. He was the only guest wearing a bright yellow and white suit at the party. It wasn't the most fashionable suit in the ballroom, but it was the most attention-grabbing.

He had been leading a conversation to a crowd of people. It seemed like he was saying something important, so Oceana decided to listen to what he had to share amongst the characters in the crowd.

"So that's when I decided to be a talk-box star!" He said. "The war, it became too much for me to think about. Am I proud of killing that wretched king?" He shouted. "Of course I am! If my poor partner Bellus were here, he would tell you all about how I heroically saved the world. Sadly he has gone a bit crazy. But I am very proud of this generation of upcoming heroes." He stopped and noticed that Oceana was in the crowd. He managed to grab her and pull her next to him "Like Ms. Sanford here. They're going to be a great hero like me one day. I mean, not as great as me." He said to the crowd, who laughed. "But good enough!" He grinned. "Right?"

"Oh uh, right?" She said with a slight smile.

"So tell me Oceana, wait- smile." He looked at the camera that was right ahead of them, Oceana hadn't noticed but tried to throw in a smile before the camera flashed. She rubbed her eyes, Pséftis continued to speak, "Are you planning on becoming a magic user such as myself?- oh smile!" Oceana was in the middle of giving a smile, but then the camera went off.

"Yeah!" She said while rubbing her eyes again. "I want to be an amazing Magician too!" She said, "I had always wanted to be just like you for as long as I could remember!" They said, "Being able to use magic has always been my dream! Some part of me feels like I was born to be the greatest Magician of all time! Magic is a big part of who I am. Kind of embarrassing, but it's true. I mean- did you always feel like you were meant for greater things- before you became a famous Magician?" She asked, but when she turned to look at Pséftis he was already getting ready to smile at the next set of cameras, when he realized she was done talking, he grinned.

"Oh yeah, uh huh, I know I am amazing." He turned to sign a paperback someone held out for him. "So you said you didn't want to use magic, hmmm maybe you can become a swordsman-woman or something, oh hey! Let's take another photo together. The crowd loves seeing the two of us together!" He said.

He wrapped his arm around Oceana, and another camera flashed, Pséftis began waving at the crowd. At this point, Oceana had decided that now was her chance to sneak out, which she did easily.

Navigating her way down the hall, she realized she missed the company of Jamlson and Headworth, and would rather be with them, than surrounded by all these cameras and strangers. She walked around the big room.

Eventually, she got tired and decided to step outside on the oversized patio that held grounds for the people who would rather sit, eat, and be able to have a conversation without music blasting in their ears. Oceana leaned on the railing. She looked up at the sky. There was not a single star to be seen. When she looked down to view the city of Annularity. It looked as though all the stars in the sky had fallen into the hands of the city's people. She stared at the golden twinkles the city of Annularity gave. She sighed and smiled at the people below. She wondered what life you have to live to be able to live in such close proximity to the kingdom itself. Each person must have a luxurious life to tell.

"Room for one more?" Oceana looked over to find Jamlson. She nodded and watched him stand next to her, while he leaned on the rail.

"Uh, sorry about my comment earlier."

"Oh, it's fine. I was shocked when I saw myself in this thing too." She said with a laugh. Jamlson chuckled back.

"Yeah?" He said. The two both watched the inside of the ballroom from where they had stood. They could both see Headworth awkwardly dancing with TOAD.

"Wow, I had no idea that it was possible for him to loosen up." Jamlson chuckled, and took a sip from his drink.

Oceana laughed "I know, right!" They explained.

"You know he has gone a whole hour without telling me a fact!"

"Are you serious?" Oceana asked.

"It's a record," Jamlson grinned.

"A world-breaking record!" Oceana threw her arms up. Jamlson laughed in response, which only made her laugh along with him. After the fit of laughter, they didn't exchange words between them. What had prevented the two from standing in complete silence was the music from the party inside. Jamslon decided he would be the first to break the silence, at least that's what Oceana interpreted when he took a big breath and moved in front of her.

"Do you- do you want to dance?" He asked with a sly smile. He extended his hand forward. This caught Oceana by surprise. This day had been full of well- unique turns of events. So perhaps this didn't stretch too far away from the weirdness that was going on. Not that dancing with Jamlson was weird or anything. She just had never pictured it. But she supposed a dance wouldn't be too bad, she would be dancing with one of the coolest guys she knew!

She nodded and took his hand. She looked up at him and gave him a smile back. "Should be fun!" She said, her voice giving a small happy hum. They both moved to the dance floor.

Multiple horns blared into the room, giving the room's listeners upbeat energy to follow. Oceana felt her feet dance on their own. Jamlson spun around and pointed his fingers at her. She hadn't a single idea of what he was doing, but she loved it. The smile on her face wouldn't leave while she watched the boy in front of her attempt more dance moves.

"You're in a good mood!" She said with a grin.

"As opposed to?"

"Well, you know." She turned her face into a pout and crossed her arms.

"Oceana Liesbeth Sanford!" Jamlson smirked, "Are you suggesting that I am always- grumpy?" Jamlson then attempted to give her a personal acting performance by providing a fake gasping sound.

"You did not have to say my full name like that-" She hit him.

"What? Is that not your name? Oceana Liesbeth Sanford."

"Stop it!" She grinned.

"I can even say it backwards-"

"No!"

"Sanford Liesbeth Oceana." He was amusing himself.

"You are so annoying! You jerk!"

"Yeah- I am a jerk- The same jerk who traveled the country with you out of the kindness of his heart."

"Kind people don't point out how kind they are, jerk."

"This one does." He pointed at himself with his thumb. The two laughed until the music tone shifted, and everyone's movements became that of something slower. Oceana watched the way everyone else moved. She looked over at Jamlson, who clearly had not planned for this to happen. He moved his hand to his mouth with a clenched fist. Oceana looked up at him. When they made eye contact, he cleared his throat.

"Uh-" He said. He opened his mouth but closed it again. The two stood in the middle of the ballroom; maybe they should leave and wait until the music picked up the pace again. "Oceana-" he said. "Uh- would you want- I mean-Would you like to-"

"May I have this dance?" A foreign voice had cut in between the two. Oceana looked over to find Crocus. He wore a charming smile, his blonde hair pinned back with what looked like gems. His eyes sparkled. "If you don't mind?" He accompanied this question with a small smile. "You also wouldn't mind if I borrowed the young officer for a moment, would you, sir?" He asked Jamlson whose face turned pink.

Whether it was from being called a sir. Or if it was the Prince asking him permission for something. Even if he had already decided he would have the dance. The illusion of giving Jamlson a choice was considered a gentle kindness. Jamlson, who immediately put his hands up, gave an attempt to speak, however his brain temporarily forgot how to articulate words.

"Oh- uh- go ahead- we were just done dancing- I will be- over there." Jamlson pointed back outside where the balcony was. "I will see you- later." He moved his hand in perhaps the shortest wave Oceana had seen, then left the two alone.

"What a kind man you got there."

"Friend," Oceana corrected, "He's my best friend." She smiled at Prince Crocus. He gave her a small smile back and held out his hand.

"So, will you join this dance with me?" Oceana felt her blood crawl up her face. The Prince was asking her to dance? Oceana gave a slight nod and moved her hand into his. Prince Crocus wasted no time pulling her close to him, hand on hip, and led her onto the dance. Oceana looked over his shoulder, and noticed the King's smile, along with everyone else's in the room. She looked over at Aster. She couldn't tell what her expression was previously, but when she noticed they've made eye contact, she rolled her own, and walked away. "I feel pretty honored dancing with KEEPIN's newest Purple division guard." Her heart dropped. He was honored to dance with her? She was honored by dancing with the Prince himself. She had no idea how to respond. Was she giddy? Excited?

On the one hand, she was currently in the arms of the two-time year prettiest boy in Cor'Meum. Oceana remembered secretly buying the magazines that were published that day. If you had asked her about it, she would only say that she merely supported her country. Also, the manufacturer that printed the magazine of the Prince sold the copies with a thick line of paper, and Oceana simply liked the feeling of the clean sheet under her fingertips. If Oceana knew more women, she would claim that every girl bought it, and she wouldn't be wrong.

Reality crept up her neck and struck her in the head; that was right. She was a KEEPIN officer now. She began to feel sick again. She wondered if there was a bathroom near. Perhaps she could use it to get rid of the dancing circus in her stomach. It must have been obvious she wasn't feeling good. Even the Prince gave her a puzzled look.

"What's wrong, Oceana?" Prince Crocus gently asked. Oceana looked up at him, and when she found his blue eyes, she couldn't help but look away.

"Uh-" She said quickly. "It's-nothing." She said, and it wasn't convincing.

"You know it's a crime for a KEEPIN officer to lie to a prince?" Crocus grinned.

"Oh- No- I!" Oceana stammered.

"Oceana, relax. I am only joking." Oceana looked up at him, and she was there to witness the smile on his face. She looked away again, her face felt warm. "I would love to know what is on your mind?"

"Uh."

"Hm?"

"I was thinking about the new position of being a Purple division guard." She said,

"Isn't it great?" Crocus asked with excitement.

"Yay." She said weakly. She should have emphasized her reaction. Now Prince Crocus gave her a stare.

"Oceana, can you tell me what's wrong?" That was a heavily loaded question. What was wrong? She got what she always wanted. She was now taking a job that her mother and grandpa would be proud of her taking. She was a KEEPIN soldier. It was an honor. More than that, perhaps. But after what she saw, what KEEPIN stood for, Jamlson was right. They weren't good guys. She saw something a KEEPIN officer was willing to do in the open. What were they like behind closed doors? Her stomach crawled up to her throat, but she swallowed her insides back down.

"KEEPIN." She responded. "Keeping Everlasting Extravagant Peace In the Nation." She whispered. What was she going to say? She was scared. Her heart was ready to jump, but she had to confront this. How could she expect to do her duties as an officer with this feeling on her shoulders? "I have seen things that KEEPIN has done. They hurt people. How can we call them soldiers of peace if we allow such corruption? As a citizen of Cor'Meum- I have always looked up to them- but now I know the truth, they attack people! People who never provoked any sort of violence! How could we let this happen?" Oceana asked. She kept her eyes on the Prince. "If we allow them to continue hurting people, whether they are country-men or not, how is that something to be proud of? If this is what's going on; then Cor'Meum is a cowardice country." Oceana suddenly stopped. She looked at Prince Crocus's surprised face.

Oh no! What did she do? Why did she say that? She could be executed for saying something like that to royalty. Was she insane? She needed to get her head checked before the country demanded that it should leave her body. She was going to die! This was the end! She was going to be killed on her eighteenth birthday. Her heart gave another jump when she heard a small and gentle laugh. She blinked. She had entirely forgotten she was staring at the Prince still. Her face was burning. It had to be the same shade as her dress.

Prince Crocus continued to laugh. Did he find what she had said funny? It was not. She was serious. So why was he laughing? Perhaps this was some royal tradition to do before executing someone in the middle of the dance floor.

"I admire your bravery Oceana." Prince Crocus finally said. "I agree with you." He smiled. "Cor'Meum has become corrupted in recent years. When I become king, I promise to fix that." He said. Oceana blinked at him.

"You'll fix it?"

"I will. I will ensure that everyone will continue to feel safe in this country. Whether they are countrymen or rule-following co-countrymen." He said.

"What about Vibrius? They feel that we are taking over! That they need to be their own country!" Oceana dared herself into saying.

"I will see if they are ready to become their own country. If they are, I will move a quarter of the Red division out and begin to pull them back here." He smiled. "They will rule themselves once more. With a steady eye." This was a better response than Oceana had hoped for. She couldn't believe she had doubts about KEEPIN. They were great, and so was the Prince. Oceana could feel herself smiling. She knew she should have kept her faith in Cor'Meum. The song began coming to a close, and a voice of a Purple division guard was what broke them apart.

"Prince Crocus. Your father wants to see you in the study in five minutes." The officer said.

"That's on the other side of the castle." Prince Crocus groaned. "Why does he need me?" The officer gave a slight shrug, and Prince Crocus sighed. "It was a pleasure dancing with you, officer. I look forward to our next meeting." He gave a bow, then clicked his shoes, and made his way out of the ballroom. Oceana stood there in the middle of the ballroom. She should probably make her way back to Jamlson.

It was an easy task finding Jamlson, he had been leaning on the balcony gates that were overlooking the city. His eyes kept on the colorful light show that popped and sizzled in the cold winter air. She moved next to him with her arms crossed. She gave a small sigh that grabbed Jamlson's attention. He turned around and moved his focus on her. He crossed his arms along with her.

"Are you okay?" He asked.

"Oh! Yeah! I am fine, just excited." They shifted their position. "You know?" They gave a slight smile.

"What?" Jamlson seemed more confused.

"For the future and everything!" She leaned on the balcony again. Jamlson moved next to her and moved his body close to the edge with her. Jamlson looked down at the city with her. There was this silence between them. The only thing that stood between them was the background noise of the party, and cracking of the light show in front of them.

"So Purple division guard now? Or whatever?" He said.

"Yeah." Oceana said, "I mean whatever helps me find my grandpa." She shrugged. "Being part of KEEPIN might just- help me."

"Right," Jamlson said. "KEEPIN." He took a sip from his drink.

"You're using that tone again when you talk about the military," Oceana mumbled. Jamlson almost spat out a laugh.

"I mean, is this what you want, Oceana? Do you really want to become a Purple division guard?" He raised an eyebrow. "Is this your dream? Didn't you say you wanted to branch out yesterday? What happened to that?"

"Wh-what, of course, it is!" Oceana felt her cheeks flush. "I want to be a Purple division guard! This is what I've always wanted! I was just confused. Now I know what I need to do."

"Yeah, sure," Jamlson said.

"But it is. Crocus told me that good things will change in the military!" She said with determination and a smile. "This is why I want this!"

"Where did he get that phrase from, his dad or his grandpa?" Jamlson asked.

"He said things were going to be different!" She hissed. "That I was going to help make those changes with him! I will help change Cor'Meum Jamlson, so you can be proud of this country like you're supposed to." Jamlson laughed.

"What changes did he say he was going to make? I am curious."

"W-well, he said that he would pull the Red division out of Vibrius once he sees some good changes for himself."

"Oh yeah." Jamlson laughed. "Just like his grandpa, King Alexsander Roseario, who said in the year Eighteen-eighty eight, that Cor'Meum was only going to invade Vibrius for five years. Then when he kicked the bucket in nineteen o'four, King Erebus said that he would pull the Red division out that same year." Jamlson rolled his eyes.

"He's different," Oceana said.

"He's not!" Jamlson said. "Cor'Meum isn't great Oceana. You need to get out of that mentality." He said. "You just want to blend into the crowd and be like everybody else in this awful country. Be your own person! Find your own dreams, forget about this Purple division soldier thing, and stop being brainwashed by this dumb country! This is not your dream!"

"Uh-" Oceana snapped; "What do you know about dreams? I don't see you telling me any goals or ambitions you have."

"Well, I know enough about being miserable, and I can tell that you aren't happy," Jamlson said with a shrug. Oceana gritted her teeth at him in response to his statement.

"I am happy."

"Are you?"

"Yes! Jamlson! Why can't you be a supportive friend and just be happy for me?" Oceana raised her voice.

"I will support you when you start doing things you love!" His tone of voice moved up along with hers.

"This is what I love!" Oceana yelled, convincing herself and him that this statement had the truth. She moved her posture up, no longer in a relaxed position on the balcony.

"Is it what you love or is it what your family would love for you to do?" He asked, now standing completely up, no longer relaxed against the balcony. Though he was taller than her, Oceana would not let that stop her from arguing with him.

"Oh, what do you mean by that?" Oceana threw her arms up.

"It means that you can't go a single second," Jamlson hissed. "thinking for yourself! You need your family to tell you what to do!"

"Oh really now?" Oceana yelled.

"Yes!" Jamlson shouted, "This is why you're doing this! You are just becoming your mom! A military person! Someone you shouldn't be looking up to! Oceana, just accept that she's gone! She left you and she's never coming back!" He shouted. Oceana stared at him and looked around, everyone was watching them.

"Yeah, Jamlson." She felt tears swell up in her eyes, "At least there's a better chance for my mother to come back; because she wasn't a drunk loser when she left." She stared at him, she felt her stomach turn and she already regretted saying that to Jamlson. There was only silence between the two. Jamlson had opened his mouth but Oceana was not going to hear what he had to say, so she turned around and stormed off. She looked behind her for a moment; Jamlson looked as though he wanted to chase her, but he was cut off by a sudden pain in his back.

CHAPTER 24:

Cor'Meum's Hero

SHE didn't know where she was going. She knew she didn't want to be close enough to hear or see the party anymore. She wanted to find a corner, crawl inside it, and just pretend she didn't have a presence in this world. Her legs moved fast for flats. She continued through a mysterious hallway. Her steps echoed miles. The sound of her footsteps was a much better music choice than listening to the blasting of the ballroom. Now that she had stopped, she looked around the area where her legs had taken her. She once again could not tell where she was. She needed to learn how to navigate the castle better. She walked around, maybe she might find one of the staff or a guard, and they could point her in the direction of her bedroom. There, she could lay in bed and pretend it was tomorrow.

The moon's natural light set its way into the castle's glass, illustrating its nightly features on those who wish to find comfort in the dark. Oceana moved towards the glass, her eyes fixed on the nightly sky, the same nightly sky that she would read books about, the same sky that she would stare at when she had trouble resting. The same sky that created the bond between her and her grandpa when they would spend hours of the night talking about magical creatures.

She looked up at the sky, pretending that the stars were there, how they had always been when she was out at sea, performing a ballet, dancing in perfect unity, that she would only hope one day she could do too. Was Jamlson right? Did she want to be a Purple division guard? Is that what she had really desired in this life? Her mother had left being a Purple division guard. But her grandpa is part of KEEPIN, and wouldn't he be proud of her for joining the military like him?

She sighed. She should really get going to find her room if she wants to get a head start on sleep. The beds here were incredibly comfortable. Once she would rest on her bed, she knew she would be out. Unfortunately, she hit her head against something heavy when she moved forward. Her first thought was that she was such a dimwit for walking right into the wall. However, once she had opened her eyes, she found TOAD standing there. She rubbed her eyes in case her vision was playing some sort of prank on her.

"TOAD? What are you doing here?" TOAD blinked in response; Oceana raised their eyebrows. "Sorry, I don't know what that means." Oceana sighed. They looked back at the moon. It rested so nicely in the sky with its unique purpose in this world. Yet Oceana had no idea what her own goal was, she was now eighteen, the start of becoming an adult, and she felt just as lost or maybe more so since she was a kid.

"I don't know what is happening TOAD. I can't figure out what I am doing. When I started this journey, if you had asked me what I had felt about-" she stopped. "I don't know." She admitted, "I just have a feeling. It's a bad feeling." She looked over at TOAD who only blinked several times. "The King says that everything is fine, but something is off." She said, "Like Bo!" She snapped her fingers. "Bo was kidnapped by the revolutionary people! I haven't heard anything about him returning!" She said, "He even wanted to say something to me before he was taken." She sighed. "I wish I knew what he was going to say." She looked over at TOAD, who gave a blink. She pressed her hands on her face, and looked back at the city through the large window. "Perhaps, maybe he escaped." She said in a hopeful tone. "It's not like there is a specific way to reach me. I am kind of all over the place." She looked back at TOAD, who stared at her. "No comment?"

TOAD then blinked, Oceana gave another sigh and looked back at the city.

"It's like," she paused. "It feels as though the whole world has suddenly turned upside down on me" She took a moment, "and I need to keep up before I fall into space." she bit her lip. TOAD only blinked at her, to which Oceana only sighed in response. "Right."

She continued to stare at the city in front of her. "Another thing too," She said, "while in Fovero, the woman, uh, what was her name?" Oceana began to snap her fingers until she remembered, then turned to TOAD and pointed, "Pakimet!" She said, "Pakimet also wanted to tell me something before you put a roof on her head!" She laughed. "But I guess she is one tough lady because she gave a speech just a few days later!" Then, she said, "I also wonder what she was going to say."

Suddenly, she heard a record scratching noise, audio that seemed unrecognizable. Oceana turned around, and for the first time, she watched TOAD's gears rush from the inside. "Oceana!" A speaker said from inside TOAD. Oceana jumped back and looked up at TOAD. She could hear crumbling sounds. She could even hear her own voice and Headworths voice in the midst of things. Oceana felt her heart race. This was insane; she all of a sudden had remembered Headworth mentioning that TOAD repeats things. She just didn't think about it. She couldn't figure out why she didn't bother remembering until now. So she stayed silent and listened to the voice.

"Oceana- I-I know where your mother is!" Her heart sank. She did not understand what had just happened. She knew where her mom was? How? She looked up at TOAD and grabbed the robot's arms.

"TOAD!" She shouted. "What? You had this information the whole time?" she said. "And not once did you tell me about it?" She questioned. TOAD only gave her a couple of blinks. "We- we have to tell Jamlson and Headworth?" She said, and grabbed TOAD's claw, and moved her legs down the hall, forcing TOAD to keep up with her pace. While running down the hall, she found human shadows reflecting on the wall, whispering to each other.

"Are you sure we have to find her? She probably just went to her room?" A voice questioned.

"Let's make sure it's just that, and she didn't escape." The other officer whispered, their heavy footsteps growing closer. She did not know who 'she' was, but Oceana had a feeling that they were talking about her. She turned around in one swift move holding onto TOAD's arm and dragging him along with her. While she ran down the hallway, she found that one narrow hallway next to the main one, with the golden door and the weird symbols that rested above it. She heard the whispering of the men grow louder.

"In here." She whispered to TOAD, while they made their way down the hallway. They pressed their hand on the door and turned the handle. It had made a click sound, indicating, to her relief, that this place was open. She pushed TOAD inside before she ran in herself and closed the golden door behind her. She did this carefully to ensure it would not make any sounds for the men passing by. She looked through the crack and found two Purple division guards walking right past the hallway. Once they were gone, everything became brighter. She turned around and watched TOAD blink at her, his hand still on the light switch that he had just turned on.

"TOAD, we gotta get out of here before-" She stopped and looked around the room, full of drawers stuffed with paper. There were maps laid out all over the area. "What is this?" she questioned.

TOAD had walked up to the radio that innocently sat on a desk and pressed the button, playing whatever was on the airwaves. Oceana opened the drawer and found paper copies of information about plans to find the golden apple. Her eyes scanned the paper, and she shuffled around the sheets. Searching for the meaning behind this apple. What was it about? At this moment, she found a sentence that summed up what she had been looking for. Why this apple had been significantly important to her grandpa and to the revolution:

'The golden apple, unknown as to its location, is an important treasure to withhold. Its magical properties can turn anyone who consumes it' She stopped. Had she read this right? Anyone who consumes this apple? She began rereading what she had in her hands, anyone who consumes it, into a God.'

Oceana raised an eyebrow. 'Being the only apple in the world created so perfectly by all four magical creatures; mermaids, fairies, dragons, and unicorns, it has powers beyond this universe. If the location of each of the three magical creatures remains complete, Cor'Meum's success will be forever engraved.'

"This- The king wants to become a God?" She began to shake. "We can't let that happen. That is insanity. We have to-" She stopped and noticed that TOAD hadn't kept their eyes off the wall. What was TOAD looking at? She moved over to get a glimpse of what TOAD had been drawn to. The wall showed a picture of her home in perfectly normal conditions, and then it showed her home in the middle of the burning. "What-" She fell to the floor. "I-I" She stumbled. There were words printed next to the burning picture of the home that said 'Eliminate Wilic: FAILED' Her eyes moved over to the next text on the wall, there was a picture taken of her grandpa from a far, the photo looked months old. 'Objective: FAILED. Handbook could not be found.' That handbook- it was her grandfathers-they were looking for it? What was in there? She should have finished reading the book- but she knew where it was and she needed to go to it. "We can't stay here." When she had got up to exit the room, what blocked her path had surprised both her and TOAD..

"I can't let you leave Sanford." The man in the purple KEEPIN uniform said, standing at the base of the door.

"Vinnian?" Oceana raised her eyebrow, "What are you doing?" She asked.

"I have direct orders from the King to ensure that you do not leave this castle." He said.

"So was naming me a Purple division guard just a trick to get me to willingly stay here?" Oceana questioned. Vinnian was silent in his response. "I'm going to not be offended by that because I know I am talented enough to be a Purple division guard." There was silence, and Oceana began to move forward. "Okay, move. I am leaving!"

"No, Sanford." Vinnian pulled out a gun from his purple coat jacket. "You'll be coming with me." Oceana gasped. But that hadn't stopped her from blurting out.

"I will not!"

"Please, if you know what is best, you would forget about this. Don't make the same mistakes your grandpa made. You don't have to be like him." Vinnian pleaded. "The King wants you here and alive, you should be grateful."

"A prisoner!" Oceana responded. "You guys lied to me! You were never going to take my grandpa in peacefully. You were going- you were-" she stared right into him, "going to end his life!"

"Oceana, this is all way bigger than you could imagine." Oceana moved backward slightly, when she had done this Vinnian had taken a step forward, still pointing the gun at her, "You don't have to be on the wrong side of history for this. We can all work together," He took another step forward. "Be part of Cor'Meum's dream. Be the future- ahh!" Vinnian hadn't seen it coming, and neither did TOAD; if TOAD could communicate that with anyone.

Oceana had ducked down and moved her leg to bring Vinnian on his back. Before he had fallen, he dropped his gun; he tried reaching for Oceana before hitting the floor, however he only snatched her necklace off. Oceana noticed that she had only a few moments to find it fast with the weapon out of his hand. It was just her luck that she immediately saw the gun and picked it up, stood up before she pointed it at Vinnian, who had still remained on the floor, hand gripping her necklace.

"You know Vinnian, for someone who just discovered that magical creatures exist, even I know what's real and a fairytale." she said, "What Cor'Meum is doing is wrong!"

"You don't know what you are doing, Sanford. You don't even know half of what's going on! You are making a mistake!"

"I feel like I do for the first time in my life." She looked over at TOAD "Tie him up," TOAD blinked before moving around the room, scavenging for something to bond him with. TOAD held up cuffs, Oceana nodded and grabbed them, then made her way behind Vinnian, chaining him to his new temporary prison, the handles of a drilled down drawer. The radio suddenly switched from the fun music it had been playing to a static noise that would win awards for creating the most obnoxious sound. Apparently, this static noise was not just a thing that was happening to Oceana's radio. Everyone at the party had suddenly fallen flat to the talk-box static. The music blasting from miles away from the castle was no more. The live concert halted their tunes, the talk-box no longer amplifying their tunes.

"Greetings Cor'Meum party people." A voice had gently said on the radio. Oceana had recognized that voice, but she could not recall from where. "Hope you are all having a fun night celebrating the ending of the Calamitous War, with fancy food, dancing to your great music, making conversation, and everything else! Hope you are enjoying your very last party." Oceana looked over at TOAD and then at Vinnian, who seemed like he was trying to connect the pieces together. "Some may refer to me as The Boss. Others might have in the past called me Sage Magnus." Oceana's heart dropped. "These names have hidden truths, but they are not my real identity." Oceana had now known where that voice had belonged to...but it couldn't be.? "But you may call me Marlyn Sanford, the true daughter of Sage Magnus!" Now Oceana knew who else would have known about her birthday, and the card at that moment made sense.

"Wait- I know what she is going to do! We have to stop her!" Oceana shouted. Her body moved toward the door, she had to leave this room, go warn everyone! She turned the handle and opened the door. But it felt slow compared to the events that began to happen.

"Each one of you in this room is guilty of the destruction and poverty that Vibrius has been facing. A storm of death on your front door, yet you do nothing! Tonight all of you will pay for that. The revolution is here, and we will not stand for it anymore!" Marlyn said, "This next gift is for King Erebus and the lovely guests at his party, all from your neighboring country." In that moment, before Oceana could step into the hallway, it was being consumed by the rapid fiery beast.

Oceana felt the force of the heat that screamed from the flames pushed her on her back, her head hitting the solid ground with a thud. Her eyes began to close, the heat of the fire close to her skin. A minute or so must have passed before the strong presence of the beast was gone. With much strength Oceana pulled herself up onto her feet; she stepped into the hallway with its new high temperature.

"She's here," Vinnian mumbled. Oceana looked over at him, from where she stood.. "She has come to get her revenge." He forced out a laugh to himself. "She made a mistake. She shouldn't have attacked the capital, out of all places."

"TOAD." Oceana said. "Keep an eye on him. Don't let him escape from where he sits." She pointed,

"Oceana." Vinnian said. "You aren't going to be happy with what you find." Oceana gave him one last look before she closed the door that stood between her and them.

The air was poisoned by small clouds of gray that moved away from its original red. While making her way down the hallway, Oceana decided to throw off her red jacket, for it was merely holding her down rather than keeping her warm in the strapless dress. From what Oceana would assume, the building gave a slight rumble coming out of its shock from the sudden explosion.

She moved in what she guessed was the right direction of where her room was, she just needed her sword, and her jacket that contained the handbook that Cor'Meum was looking for. Once she got that, she could look for her friends and find out what was happening. It was still a lot for her to process that her mom was the one behind all the attacks. She was the one that conducted the attack on Cor'Meum. It was her that was Sage Magnus- no, the daughter of Sage Magnus- what did that make Oceana? Was she related to the evilest man? There was no way her mother would have made such a large claim if it were not perhaps true- the sword. She had to focus on the sword and the book- nothing else mattered until she got them in her possession.

After she turned into a hallway that she believed she had seen before, she found the familiar door frame that she knew was the space she had occupied once before. She opened the door and was relieved to find the room where she had left the book. On her bed, there was her sword and her jacket! She opened the jacket, and looked inside the pocket. There it was! Her grandfather's handbook! If they had checked her jacket they may have missed it, the pocket was easy to miss and the rest of the jacket was padded. Oceana put her jacket on and clipped her sword on her hips. Now it was time to find her friends- she hoped they weren't caught up in the explosion. But, if they were she would- She heard a creak from behind her and turned around to find a person in a gas mask. They raised their knife at her and plunged their way down towards her.

Oceana moved her sword up to defend herself from the stranger's sudden attack. The person moved back, Oceana moved into a fighting position, utilizing the position to feel less exposed to the sudden endangerment due to her lack of proper clothing. It also took this distance to realize that one of them was here in the castle. How did they get in here? Did they use the explosion as a distraction?

"You know it's against the law to suddenly attack a fourth-ranked Purple division guard." Oceana half-joked. The masked individual shook their head.

"Cor'Meum laws are not applicable towards my moral compass." She responded. Oceana kept her stance. The woman in the gas mask took another step closer to her.

"I don't want to fight you," Oceana said. She felt the grip on her sword tighten. "I am not your enemy. I want to help you guys-" The masked individual moved closer to her.

"I don't believe you." She moved her knife up. Oceana, with her sword, was able to swipe away from her attack. The next one was soon followed by a couple more after that. Oceana could feel the sweat roll down her face, taking away the makeup. Was this person going to kill her? Or was she- before Oceana could think of the next thought, the woman came in for another attack, aiming toward Oceana's stomach. It was a combination of both luck and skill that Oceana was able to evade the attack, heading towards the floor and moving her legs to attempt to make the attacker fall. However, she jumped away from her.

Oceana moved to her feet immediately with the sword still in hand. Was she getting rusty? After just only a few days away from training? The woman got in another fighting stance, Oceana reflected. Now footsteps were coming from the right of Oceana. She turned to see more of the woman's allies show up. It was five against one, and if they were tough fighters like the woman in front of Oceana; she had no chance of taking them all down. This hadn't stopped her from raising her sword, pretending that she had the ability and confidence to take them all down in a fight.

At that second, she heard a high pitch, not giving Oceana a chance to even blink an eye. Then in the same melody, she heard a spark and an explosion from behind. What- She turned around and noticed large red clouds from behind the window, turn into flames. The flames ripped apart the glass window in front of it. Oceana moved her arms in front of her; to provide her best work to protect herself against both the heat and the shards. All came at the speed of light in her direction.

The pieces of the window and the heat from the flames gave her arms an overwhelming sense of pain, the jacket barely protected her from the heat. The explosion died out at the same span as it had arrived. Before Oceana could look at her new cuts and burns by counting the holes on the jacket, she turned around to find one of the masked soldiers attempting to slash her with their knife.

She moved her sword and blocked the attack before the sharp knife could impale her. She moved her foot up and kicked the person off of her. The attacker began to fall backward, Oceana heard another snap and looked to her right to find a dust of green smoke inside a glowing blue ball. The ball expanded, while the green smoke faded and shot out water. Oceana, whose face was covered with water, moved her hand to remove the droplets and her wet hair from in front of her face. She heard a shuffle from behind. Oceana turned around to use her sword to block what she guessed was the woman's knife from before. She moved her sword up which pushed the knife away, and moved backwards, away from the other body. She moved her arm to quickly wipe her eyes and when she gained her eyesight once more she found herself surrounded and cornered by the gasmask people. Oceana hadn't realized she had been out of breath until the sound of her desperate need for air filled the room with melody.

"Oceana Sanford."

"You know who I am." Then, Oceana asked in between breaths, "Why are you attacking me?"

"Your mother requested that you be purged from living in this world," The woman said so casually, "Think of it as an act of kindness."

"Why would a mother want to kill her own kid?"

"A mother can recognize when her child has a terminal illness. Your love for Cor'Meum is deadly. Having you alive will damage our movement, and your mother understands that it's better to kill you now to spare future pain."

"I don't believe you." Oceana raised her sword closer to her chest. The woman smiled and began to sing.

"Cor'Meum, your eyes that shine through the seas, always watching over me!" Oceana glared at her while she continued, "We sing your melody, you are the bravest we have ever seen. Skies light up when your name becomes a tune, you are here for me and you!" The woman moved closer to Oceana.

She took a step back in return. "How joyus! How Lovely! It is to be; in this country oh lucky me! A Nation of our own! A Place to call home. Oh Knights, we honor you!" She smiled, Oceana gripped onto her sword as hard as she could. "Cor'Meum, Cor'Meum, we will forever plead our allegiance to you.." She suddenly stopped.

Oceana looked to her right and noticed the flickering of an orange sphere. How did she not see that there before? The sphere flickered, its lights glaring down at Oceana menacingly- it only gave a couple of pops and crunches. The next thing Oceana knew, a hot gust of wind pushed her back, knocking her off her feet. She kept her good hand on her sword- ignoring the painful impact of the ground. She began to roll, and the wind wasn't stopping! She moved her eyes to the tall, broken window by her bed- she was going to fall!

The wind was successful at shoving her out the window! The ledge! All Oceana had to do was reach it to save herself! She moved her free hand out. She could grab it! She just needed to be a bit closer to it, and- her fingertips brushed the edge of the ledge and- she had missed. Now she was falling. The night's dry air allowed her body to fall.

CHAPTER 25:

First day of Winter

I N her whole heart, Oceana believed that when she had landed on the ground beneath her, she wouldn't be around to talk about how painful the impact was. But, to her surprise, when she opened her eyes she found herself on a bush full of flowers. The night had not gone away. In fact, she had concluded that the hour had not even passed. When she sat up from the flower bed, she immediately noticed its color had smeared her face and exposed legs. At least she was alive.

She looked around the area that surrounded her, it hadn't been the ballroom that was attacked. It looked as though the whole city was on fire from where she sat. What was going on? Where are the KEEPIN soldiers? Could KEEPIN soldiers help stop this madness? Isn't it because of them that this is happening? She needed answers, but first, she needed to get out of this bush.

She had already felt tired, her arms were in pain, her weak fingers were shaking and she must have hit her head a bit in the fall because things came at her in doubles. She wanted to close her eyes and rest for a few minutes.

What stopped her were the sounds of a shuffle. She turned around and used her bit of strength to lift her sword up. She got into a fight position, ready to head forward into her next battle. Her heartbeat was racing- wondering if she honestly had the strength to engage in a real battle with her opponent.

"Oceana?" She heard a familiar voice call out to her. She moved her sword closer to her, cautious that this voice belonged to an enemy. The figure stood just a couple of feet away from her, the light from behind them blocking their face. "Oceana, you can put your sword down. It's just me." The person stepped out of the shadow. The light that masked their identity and crept into a spot where the person's face could be revealed. Prince Crocus gave Oceana a quick warm smile but remembered her situation.

"What- what are you doing out here?" Oceana asked, keeping her sword pointed.

"Only to talk to the intruders." He said and moved both his hands up. Oceana glared at him and kept her sword pointed.

"What's going on Oceana? Why are you pointing that at me?" He asked. Oceana kept the sword at him. Was Crocus aware of his father's plans? The golden apple? The attacks on her home and her family? He had to be! She looked over at his face, covered in confusion or perhaps pretending to be. She couldn't let her guard down- everyone was attacking her- she was declared an enemy on both sides. She held her sword in front of him. "Oceana, you are bleeding- you're burned-" He said. "What happened to-"

"Not a step closer!" Oceana yelled and moved her sword up, "Take a step closer to me, and I will have no choice-" Oceana cried.

"But Oceana, I am unarmed-" Prince Crocus moved his hand towards himself.

"Stop!" Oceana yelled at him. "Stop moving!" Prince Crocus ignored her wish and promptly began to remove his jacket. It slid off him and landed on the ground behind him. He moved his hands to his front pocket. Oceana felt her heart race while he did this. It was to her surprise that he had only moved the cloth up.

"See unarmed-"

"Your fingers!" Oceana said, holding out the sword. "You can still use magic."

"Oceana, you know just as well as I do that my family refuses to use magic-"

"I don't know what to believe-" She kept the sword pointed at him.

"Oceana, come on." He took another step closer to her.

"Stop it!" They demanded, their sword held out. Their hands were shaking. However, he hadn't listened to her pleas. He only kept moving forward. He moved close enough to her that the tip of her sword was pointing at his chest. Oceana stared at him. What could she do? She couldn't fight him. Even if she had any shred of strength left. She couldn't fight him. She lowered the sword, and when she had done this, he moved to her in a flash. She closed her eyes immediately. But when she opened them, she found that she was being held. Prince Crocus moved back from her and gave a gentle smile before it fell when he looked closer at her.

"Your hurt-" He said; Oceana looked at him, and she bit her lip. He honestly had no idea then. He was unaware of his fathers' plans, the inappropriate use of magic, the people he was hurting, and the evils behind the castle. She wanted to tell him. She had to tell him. It was his right to know, right? But however, she could only just nod at the situation. She felt weak. She felt she truly had no strength to move. "Hey- don't close your eyes- come on, look at me-" Oceana looked up at him. She just noticed that there were two of him. "Come on, put your arm around me- we are going to get out of here-"

The injured person did what she was told and swung her arm around the prince. The two of them moved down the dark grass. It was dark, but they were both pushing through. Was it perhaps an hour? A few minutes? How long were they walking for?

"Where are we going?" Oceana asked.

"We are going to find you a hospital, then once we do that, I will find more survivors

and see if they need medical help. Maybe I can try to find those who are active nurses too." He mumbled.

"But you're in dan-" Oceana coughed. She moved her hand to her mouth. "You're in-"

"Please- save your breath, soldier." Prince Crocus said, which momentarily gave Oceana a feeling in her body again. "I will be fine, I will talk to Marlyn." He said

"T-talk?" Oceana questioned. "What-"

"I am going to remind her that Cor'Meum will do everything in its power to make things right with Vibrius. Keeping our allegiance and our system of peace is important." He said. Oceana went to open her mouth; she couldn't find her voice, or at least that bubble in her belly that could give her a sound that belonged to her. It didn't matter. The marching that plunged itself into the night liquid soil grasped her and Crocus's attention. They both stood there in the silence of the cold night. The large group in front of them moved up the mountain. They all shared the gas-masked uniform. In front of them, they marched in solitude with the face of something that belonged in the past.

"Mom," Oceana said under her breath. She looked almost the same. She had kept her long white hair. Her eyes were still a bright purple. She wore a black corset and black clothing that protected her shoulders and arms. Behind her was a thin gray cape that flew with grace in the wind. This made Oceana's stomach curl. Despite all these layers, she looked thinner than she last remembered her.

"Marlyn Magnus-" Prince Crocus coughed. "I would love to talk." He said, gently putting Oceana down on the grass and moved to shuffle his way closer to her.

'Don't go' Was all she could think of. Her strength had died again, and if it weren't for her heart beating, she would have given in to the cries of tiredness and the desperate want for sleep her body yearned for.

"We have never formally met- I am Prince Crocus." He said, standing in front of Oceana. He hadn't taken a step yet; her silence was piercing, though this did not make him stop. "I would love to chat with you- you see as Cor'Meum's next successor, it will be my goal to create peace in the nation, including the happiness of the Cor'Meum people and the happiness of Vibrius people. If we all worked together, we could create a strong and thriving community." He smiled and moved his hair back behind his ear. "What do you say-" He stopped.

A rock- no, a blade- this was so sudden- Oceana never heard the snapping spark of magic in front of them. The quick impaling of the rock came out of nowhere. Was that magic? Did her mother do that? Her mother can do magic? When could- how-

Prince Crocus took a step back, small sparks of green electricity surrounded him, what was left of the magic. He didn't have the strength to keep himself standing, for he fell in front of them.

Oceana moved on the ground towards the fallen prince. Her arms moved around him in an unfashionable way. This isn't real- he isn't. Prince Crocus- there was no way that- she moved her head over his heart. Come on, there had to be something, anything. She moved her hands next to his neck under his jaw, painting this part of his body in his own colors. A pulse? Was she doing this right? She had to be searching in the wrong part of his neck because she couldn't feel anything. There was nothing. But that wasn't right. There had to be something.

Her eyes burned from the drowning of her tears. The clumps of soil in front of her splashed. She looked up, and those eyes were those big purple eyes. In her attempt to swallow, she felt her own throat burn.

"You, you killed him." Oceana whispered, "You took his life- he's dead." She felt her stomach turn, but her arms around him tightened in a pathetic attempt to convince herself that he was alive.

"Oh, my precious little imbecile." Marlyn moved herself to reach eye level with them. "He was already dead- there was no saving him from the lies Cor'Meum spoon-fed him since he was born." The gates that had kept her tears from pouring, had broken. Oceana leaned her head down and felt herself openly sob. The body she held onto continued to smear what was left of the pool inside him all over her. It made her cold- though this was not enough to let go.

"Please look at me," Marlyn asked politely. Her voice showed no signs of care for their state. When they continued to sob quietly, her mother cleared her throat, "I know your ears work very well. Now, look at me." The sobbing stopped.

She gave the corpse that rested in front of her one more clutch before she looked up at the woman, who only gave a gentle smile. "Disgusting, you are covered in blood and snot." She said and moved her hands to her pocket. She had pulled out a handkerchief. "Do you feel no embarrassment when you look like this?" She questioned and pulled their face towards her, moved the handkerchief on their face, and whipped away the mixed liquids. After a few moments of this, Marlyn pulled away, took a deep breath, and smiled. "There, now have you calmed down yet?"

Oceana blinked at her, she gripped her hands on the retired prince. Her mother stared into her eyes, not a single tear or care about the situation in front of her. Her heart must have forgotten how to beat. It was curling in on itself. Another wet liquid trickled down Oceana's skin. Marlyn furrowed her eyebrows at the smaller woman.

"Now, now, you are not truly upset that the boy is dead? Are you?" Marlyn sat up, hovering her body above them below. The stench of smoke crumbled between the two, and it was almost insensitive how normal Marlyn smacked her lips together, giving a 'tsk' sound. "Very well." She said, "There is no reason for you to be upset over such silly things-" Marlyn moved her hair behind her ear. "He was going to grow up like his father- a ruthless dictator with no sense of morals or care for the people around them."

"How could you say that?" Oceana asked.

"My child, if you had ever taken a look around you- you can see that this." She moved her arms up. "Should not be normal- we should have never had to fight in this battle. Cor'Meum has to pay, and I am willing to give you, my dear, a second chance." Marlyn said.

"A-A second chance?" Oceana looked up at Marlyn.

"A second chance- I thought for a moment that it was too late, the best thing I could do for you as the queen- or as your mother," She smiled, "was to kill you. Cor'Meum propaganda is a fatal condition. But you- perhaps we can save you. Join my army- then maybe you could climb the ranks from the bottom up- show how tough you are- then you might gain your title as royalty."

"Royalty?"

"Well, you are my-" She coughed, "My child." She said through what looked like a forced smile. "You are my child." She repeated. "But first, Oceana, you have to tell me." She paused. "Do you know where Wilic's handbook is?"

"H-handbook?" Oceana questioned.

"Yes; do you know where it is?" Oceana looked into Marlyn's eyes. Her body was shaking from head to toe. She swallowed the lump in her throat.

"I think so," Oceana said,

"Then come with me, show me where the Handbook is," Oceana moved her eyes to look back at the deceased boy she cradled in her arms. She had then gently put him down. He was on the grass now, he looked so at peace with the world, and he was. He was at ease. His face looked as though he were just merely asleep. Her heart skipped another beat, and the turning inside her stomach played a game of jumping jacks. There wasn't a need to kill- this was wrong- suddenly, the only person in her mind was the man that died in the market. What about him? Would Marlyn be upset if it were him that had been taken from this world before her eyes? Why did some people deserve to die but not others? Pain could not truly be the cure for pain.

Her arm had lifted. It was so easy, though, to go with her. She didn't have a sense of belonging here. What did she have? By the end of this night, everyone will know that she was Vibrius blood, and not just Vibrius but that of royalty. They would hate her, and she would be killed for her crimes of being birthed into this world.

She had no one here in Cor'Meum. There wasn't really anything for her unless she enjoyed the idea of solitary confinement for a long while. She had no choice in this matter. She should probably go with Marlyn- her hands were so close to her own.

"Oceana!" The voice cried, halted them from moving an inch more. What- who? So recognizable. They turned, and there he was, the small boy with his slick back hair and in his fancy suit that he managed to not ruin this entire time. "Oceana!" He shouted again.

"Headworth-"

"Oceana-" He said again, his voice cracked; his swagger of confidence that he usually had carried with him was gone, his breath was out. Oceana could hear that loss of breath from only a couple of feet away from him. He clearly had just left the castle premises. "Jamlson and I have been looking all over for you- we were worried."

"Oceana, ignore him and take my hand." Marlyn said flatly, "Get up now. We have a schedule, we must get the book!"

"Hey-" Headworth had boldly shouted. "Oceana, what are you doing? Jamlson is worried about you- and quite frankly, I am too." He raised his eyebrow, commenting on the extra red.

"Stop paying attention to him." Marlyn snapped.

"Oceana, don't take her hand!" Headworth shouted. "I don't care- if she is your mother or whatever- or" He thought for a moment. "If you think my opinion about you would change over something as meaningless as blood-" He said, "That would just be illogical!" Headworth held out his own hand "Jamlson needs you-" He paused. "I need you-"

"Oceana, don't be an idiot!" Marlyn said. "Come with me- you'll have a chance to actually have meaning in my life by showing me where that book is!"

"Oceana-" Headworth mumbled. She closed her eyes and gave it a thought- pretending to give a debate to the choices that were laid out in front of her. But she already knew what she had to do. She looked up at her mother and held out her own hand to hers.

"I knew you would make the right choice-" Marlyn pulled them up from the grass and onto their feet. Oceana's fingers tightened, and her arm grew heavy once she had stood up. It took her strength, maybe all of what was left- it wasn't easy. Perhaps if she had much of that muscle energy left, it would have been cleaner. The long sword, in her hand that was not being occupied by her mother, moved up; to sever the hand from the elbow. At least it had done so up until half the bone.

Marlyn immediately let go of Oceana's hand and took several steps away from her; her scream filled the night air. New patches of red covered the grass. "You stupid witch!" She said, "How dare you- How dare you-" Oceana had never heard someone whisper and yell at the same time. Truly she felt awful for what she had done- but she couldn't risk her using her dominant magic hand on Headworth- if she were to assume that she was right-handed like she was. Oceana moved her feet and allowed herself to be carried towards Headworth.

"I'll kill you," Marlyn said. "One of these days-" She cried out in pain. Several of the officers surrounding her moved towards her, giving their attention. Oceana heard something about 'being able to save it'. She felt bad. She did.

She moved towards Headworth, and when she had tripped over her own feet, he caught her. He still carried a look of concern on his face with a mix of fear; he was obviously concerned about the masked Vibrius soldiers. He wasn't a fighter, and Oceana was out of commission currently. They were not free from the soldiers' claws.

The beating of a ship grabbed everyone's attention. It was a Purple division KEEPIN airship. It made its way over to the army in front of them. It wasn't just them that made their appearance. A few individuals ran from the other side of the castle's corner, passing the two from a few feet away with cameras. They stopped and began to take photos of the woman in front of them and her army. They stopped, and one pointed out the lying body in front of the woman.

"Is that Prince Crocus?" They whispered to each other. Marlyn took a step back. She had to leave. If she wanted to escape, it was clear that KEEPIN had surrounded her. The flashing of the light from the skyship shined down on her, almost in an angelic way.

"Marlyn Sanf- Magnus, surrender yourself to the state." She squinted at the airship, still holding on to her bleeding wrist. She looked over at the cameras, then moved her eyes to Oceana. She gave a smile. The ground around her was violently pushed up. It appeared one of her soldiers had created the magic. When the dust settled, everyone was gone. They must have moved underground, Oceana really could not think of anywhere else they could have moved to.

"Tell me it's not true!" A voice shouted. King Erebus ran across the field and dropped to his knees, in front of the deceased boy that lay on the ground. "My son!" He cried. "They killed my son!" he shouted. "They will pay!"

"We should go," Headworth whispered harshly to Oceana, who couldn't help but have their eyes glued on the situation before them. "Now." Headworth helped pull Oceana away from the scene. They should move in the dark while they can. It seemed no one had noticed them. Their attention was stuck on the king and the dead prince. They made their way against the wall, hiding in between bushes. Each time they heard the sounds of footsteps, they held their breaths. Was this how she was going to live now? Hiding from KEEPIN soldiers?

"Let's move there," Headworth whispered, directing his gaze into the long hallway that was placed in between the castle's two long towers. The hallway was known by those who occupied residency as the fairies' dancing quarters, due to all the lights that would usually glow up at night. However, the explosion must have taken away tonight's display.

Oceana moved forward down the hall, hoping a KEEPIN soldier wouldn't run into the two of them. She felt dizzy, her head was pounding, and there was no way she would survive the night. Was this what dying felt like? She realized that she couldn't remember how long they had been walking down this hallway. She wanted to close her eyes, and her fingers, all of them, grew weak. Her sword clanked on the ground. She needed to use her hands to grip the wall next to her.

"Oceana!" Headworth shouted. He turned around. His face was crushed up, his eyebrows moved closer to one another, and his eyelids opened. He picked up her sword and gripped onto the metal. "You look awful. I have never seen you behave in such a way before; are you sure the blood on you is just Crocuses and not yours?" He asked. "Perhaps you are bleeding too, and if you are, we need to rest. Or rather, you need to rest."

"I am fine Headworth, I just need to-" Oceana pressed her forehead against the wall with her eyes closed. There was no time to rest now. The two of them needed to get out of there now. It was really their only chance, while everyone was distracted by the sudden intrusion. They had to protect the book, it carried information that the King and Marlyn wanted. It was dangerous for the book to be here. Oceana had to move forward no matter what her memory did, how fuzzy her vision was, and no matter how much her head began to pound, she had to march forward. Finally, she pushed herself off the wall to conduct her walking journey out of the hallway.

Her march was cut short when she immediately crashed into a barrier that wasn't quite there before. This pushed her off her feet, and she almost fell down. Though the mystery barrier prevented that from happening, grabbing both her arms. Oceana wanted to see what had been the object of her demise, not knowing her heart would also need repairing when she found those familiar soft brown eyes. It was instant that she wrapped her arms around the man in front of her before she broke down into a sob.

"Jamlson, I thought- I am so sorry- I am sorry!"

"It's okay." Jamlson said, and wrapped his arms around her, "I am okay."

"The explosions- and what I said-"

"Oceana, I am fine, really-" Jamlson pulled her away from him, and he was okay. He hadn't been there when it happened. He was here and alive. His jaw dropped when he saw Oceana. She looked down at herself

"I'm okay too." She moved the back of her hands to her cheeks, careful not to stain her face with her painted hands. "This isn't- I- I'm okay." She said,

"Did you find TOAD?" Headworth asked immediately.

"No, I didn't," Jamlson said. "I'm sorry." He said. "I went where your tracker told me to, but TOAD wasn't there. It was completely empty," Did something happen to TOAD after Oceana left? If the room was empty, did Vinnian manage to escape. "I did, however-" Jamlson noted, "find someone else who should be here soon." He paused. "I told him where we were going to meet Headworth."

"Who?" Oceana asked. Footsteps came forward, the noise interrupting the conversation between the three. Oceana moved in front of Jamlson, her fists tightened, knowing that if it were a KEEPIN officer, she would have to get ready for a fight.

"Oceana, wait- it's okay-" Jamlson said. "It's-" The footsteps finally revealed the person it had belonged to. Oceana dropped her hands. There was no way- it couldn't be, it was. How? And when? Why now?

"Grandpa?"